The Sewing Room Girl

SUSANNA BAVIN

Allison & Busby Limited
11 Wardour Mews
London W1F 8AN
allisonandbusby.com

First published in Great Britain by Allison & Busby in 2018.
This paperback edition published by Allison & Busby in 2019.

A CIP catalogue record for this book is available from
the British Library.

10 9 8 7 6 5 4 3 2 1

ISBN 978-0-7490-2363-8

Typeset in 10.5/15.5 pt Adobe Garamond Pro by
Allison & Busby Ltd.

The paper used for this Allison & Busby publication
has been produced from trees that have been legally sourced
from well-managed and credibly certified forests.

Printed and bound by
CPI Group (UK) Ltd, Croydon, CR0 4YY

The Sewing Room Girl

To Mary Hyde, friend, colleague and lunch partner;
and to the memory of dear Molly Turner,
who made us laugh so much

Chapter One

Clough, Lancashire, 1892

Why did Mother have to be dramatic? Everyone was shocked and sorry on her behalf. Why couldn't that be enough? It was Pop who should be the focus of all thoughts today, but, oh no, Mother had to be the one in the middle, with her showy, quivering gesture.

Juliet's flesh prickled as the compassion that had swelled among the mourners when Mr Dancy proffered the small wooden box of soil turned to a flutter of disapproval and impatience as Mother, ignoring the box, held out the white rose she had clutched all through the service and let it drop onto Pop's coffin. Agnes Harper, being different: that was what everyone was thinking. Juliet knew it as surely as if it had been bellowed in chorus.

What sort of daughter was she to criticise her mother at a moment like this? If it gave Mother comfort to use a rose from the climber that Pop had planted by their cottage door, where was the harm? Mrs Grove nudged her: Mr Dancy was offering the soil. It was crumbly and moist, the rich earth that characterised his lordship's land. She stepped forward and dropped it into the grave, not looking at the coffin.

A few more minutes, more handfuls of earth, some closing words, and it was over. There was some shuffling of feet. Were they waiting for Mother? Or should Mr Nugent make the first move, since he represented no less a person than his lordship? It was an honour to have Mr Nugent at your funeral, but his lordship was good like that.

In his grey wool suit and black tie, with a black silk handkerchief peeping from his top pocket, Mr Nugent stood out among the simply dressed villagers and estate workers, with their black shawls and black armbands. He shook Mother's hand, murmuring condolences. The August afternoon was warm with approval, even gratitude. It was no small thing to have Mr Nugent pay his respects in public. Not only was he his lordship's agent, he was a real gentleman. Everybody knew the story. For all that he was plain 'mister', Harry Nugent came from the younger branch of a family of nobs, and if enough people died, he would come into the title and be a lord or a sir or something in his own right.

'Well, young lady, you've been brave today, a credit to your mother.' He cupped Juliet's chin in his hand, the warm leather of his glove as soft as butter against her skin. 'A pretty little thing.' He released her and glanced about, a benevolent look that encompassed everybody, before raising his bowler with its recent trimming of a black petersham band. He departed, leaving a flurry of admiring remarks behind him.

'Did you see that? He raised his hat to us, actually raised it, not just touched it.'

'Shall we make a move, Agnes?' said Mrs Grove. 'You can come back later if you feel the need, but just now, you've got to make ready for your guests.'

Typical Mrs Grove. It must be nice to be in charge. Juliet seemed to have spent her entire fifteen years doing what others expected. Like now. Was she meant to arrange for old Mrs Dancy to be conveyed to their cottage? Heavens, was she supposed to shove that vast old bath chair contraption, on loan for the occasion, through the village, with old Mrs Dancy complaining bitterly every bumpy step of the way?

'Shall we walk together, chick?' Ella Dancy was beside her, smiling her upside-down smile, lips together, edges turned down. It was an unusual smile and ought not to have been pretty, but it was impossible for Ella to be anything other than beautiful. 'Don't fret yourself over Granny. The men will bring her.'

They left the churchyard and walked through the straggling village, with its mix of tiled and thatched roofs. You could always tell the tile-dwellers, because they said how lovely the thatches were: they didn't have to live with spiders the size of soup plates that scuttled from the thatch into the cottage every time the rain clouds dumped their wares on the moors.

Turning into Old Lane, with its row of thatches on one side and gentle upward slope of rough greensward on the other, Juliet breathed in the sweet aroma of grass. The cinder path crunched beneath her feet. When she was little, she used to fly along the lane, the air filling with joyful cinder crackle, to meet Pop on his way home and be swept up in an earth-scented hug.

At home, the fly nets were off and the kettle was boiling. She passed plates and cups and saucers, most of which had been borrowed from up and down the row. From outside came the sound of creaking basketwork and a barrage of crotchety orders from old Mrs Dancy as she was hoisted from the bath chair and assisted into the cottage, bringing a flutter of white petals with her as she brushed against the climbing rose.

Soon the parlour was filled with neighbours.

Someone said, 'Delicious ham, Agnes.'

'I wanted a good send-off.'

'Course you did, love.'

'He deserved it.'

'It must have set you back a bob or two,' said old Mrs Dancy.

'Granny!' Ella exclaimed.

'I speak as I find,' retorted the old woman. 'How are you off for money now?'

Juliet willed Mother not to answer. 'Ham and gossip – them's why I go to funerals,' old Mrs Dancy had told her yesterday, as she sat on her wooden pail, straining her bowels.

'Well, even though the accident was on Monday and he died on Tuesday,' Mother said, her voice catching, 'he was paid to the end of this week.'

There was the usual chorus of 'his lordship's good like that'.

'But next week—' Mother began. Her face went white and she pushed her plate away.

Ella pushed it back. 'You must keep your strength up.'

'You'll still have your sewing money,' Mrs Grove pointed out, ever practical. 'But it'll be your job from now on instead of something you do on't side.'

'I've always done all the work Mrs Naseby put my way,' said Mother.

'Have you?' Mrs Hope from next door sounded surprised, as well she might: Mother had cultivated the idea that she dabbled in needlework as a favour to others. 'I thought you picked and chose.'

'No.' Mother's face flushed.

Juliet's did too. Heat started at the back of her neck and crept round to her cheeks, frying the fragile skin beneath her eyes, already tender from the tears she had shed for Pop. 'Eh, we're reet lucky to have such a special person, me and thee, Juliet,' Pop used to say. 'She could have been summat important in Manchester, but she chose us instead. In't that grand?' And as a young child, she had believed it was, but now that she was older and she was aware of the way the other women regarded her mother, the adoration had faded. Or maybe looking after old Mrs Dancy had turned her cynical.

Presently the visitors departed, leaving Mrs Grove and Ella. Mrs Grove exclaimed from the kitchen, 'There's another plate of sandwiches out here! Blood and sand, Agnes, how many folk did you think you were feeding?'

'We can eat them for supper,' Mother said defensively.

'Not this many, you can't. There's enough ham to see you and Juliet into next week. Ella, rescue the ham and put it in the meat safe. The bread will do for bread and butter pudding. Juliet, carry the crockery into the scullery. You wash and I'll dry.'

Soon the borrowed crockery was stacked in two wicker baskets, ready to be returned.

'I'm sorry I can't stay to help,' said Ella. 'I must get home to Granny.'

'Juliet can do that,' said Mother. 'It's what you pay her for.'

Ella turned her upside-down smile on Juliet. 'Not today.'

'You get along,' said Mrs Grove. 'Juliet, you can take the crockery back. I want a word with your mother.'

With her shoulder muscles pulling under the weight of the basket on each arm, Juliet stepped outside into the golden glow of early evening. The sky, which had been the blue of hyacinths this afternoon for Pop, had deepened to royal blue. Taking back the borrowed cups and saucers was the very last piece of his funeral, and when she had handed over the last things, it should be time to hide away and come to terms with this new life without Pop in it, but there wasn't time for that when you lived in a tied cottage. No matter how good and generous his lordship was, there wasn't time for that.

Returning home, she slipped round the back, dropped the baskets on the grass beside Pop's vegetable patch and pushed hard on the water pump handle. Cold water shot out and she caught some in one cupped palm, using it to splash away the threat of tears. Gathering the baskets, she slipped inside through the scullery. The door to the parlour was ajar. She crept across the flagged floor on cat feet, holding her breath as she listened.

Mother was saying, 'I don't know where we'll go, let alone how I'll pay for it.' She wailed softly – who would have thought you could wail in a whisper?

'What about that sister o' yours?' Mrs Grove asked.

'We haven't seen one another in years. Just a few lines at Christmas.'

'You've always talked about that fancy shop she's got,' said Mrs Grove. 'She can't be short of a few bob. Does she know about the accident?'

'I wrote to her and had one by return, saying how sorry she was.'

'But not saying to go and live with her?'

'I never asked.'

'Happen you should. Mind, I notice she was conspicuous today by her absence.'

'It's a fair way from Manchester.' Mother sounded defensive, though why she was defending Auntie Clara was anybody's guess. Normally she didn't have a good word to say for her.

'That's why the railways were invented,' said Mrs Grove. 'And your mother? Does she know?'

'Clara will tell her.'

Mrs Grove snorted. 'This is no time for stubborn pride, Agnes. You and the lass need somewhere to live.'

'It isn't pride. It's . . . the way it is. Mother would never let me go back and I wouldn't want to.'

'Well, if that isn't stubborn pride, I don't know what is – on both sides. Deaths are like births. They soften folk. It's a time for making amends. Your mother has never met her own granddaughter: think of that. Happen you could help her run that factory of hers. Who else is there to help her? Not your sister: she's got her posh dressmaking place to run.'

Mother laughed, a brief, bitter sound. 'I assure you, my mother is the last person to require assistance.'

Opening the door, Juliet walked in, carrying Mrs Grove's wicker basket.

'I didn't hear you come back,' said Mother. 'I hope you weren't earwigging.'

Resentment flared. Far too often, Mother spoke to her as if she was a child. It was bad enough in the ordinary way, but in front of someone else, it was humiliating.

There was a knock at the front door. When it remained shut, Mrs Grove marched across, throwing it open. When she closed it and turned round, she had a letter in her hand.

'Oh no.' Mother pressed splayed fingers against her chest. 'They've never served notice to quit, not today of all days. Oh, Beatrice, who'd have thought?' Mrs Grove tried to give her the letter, but she batted it away. 'You open it.'

'It's from Mrs Whicker. She wants to see you tomorrow afternoon.'

'What for?' Mother whispered.

'She doesn't say why,' Mrs Grove answered drily, 'just when.'

* * *

Saturday morning, not long after six and already the dew had burnt off. The sky was the soft blue of harebells and there was a brightness in the air, though it would be hot again before long. Just like last Saturday morning – and not in the slightest bit like it, because back then, when Juliet set off for the Dancys' cottage, Pop had headed in the opposite direction to work on the drystone walls at the home farm. How could they not have known? Last Saturday, how could they not have known that by this Saturday . . . ?

She let herself into the Dancys' cottage, where Mr Dancy sat in the rocking chair, pulling his boots on. Ella popped her head round the kitchen door.

'Morning, chick.' She didn't ask impossible questions like 'How are you?' but her soft eyes and rueful upside-down smile revealed her concern. It was a shame she would never be free to marry because of looking after her father and grandmother – not that she looked after old Mrs Dancy much. That was Juliet's job and had been since the morning after she left school.

She went upstairs, the soles of her ankle boots tapping on the wooden treads. The instant she opened the bedroom door, the stench slapped her. Old Mrs Dancy might be no bigger than a corn dolly but, by crikey, she produced enough motions to fertilise the top field and still have some left for her ladyship's rose beds.

'There you are, girl.'

Some folk said 'Good morning'. Some said 'How are you today?' Old Mrs Dancy said 'There you are, girl.' Every morning for the past three years.

'Morning, Mrs Dancy.'

Holding her breath, Juliet dug out the chamber pot from under the bed. Her scalp prickled as the tang swarmed round her. She hurried downstairs – but not too fast: it would be infinitely worse if she spilt it – and out the back door to the earth closet, chucking the pungent contents through the hole in the seat. For one head-spinning moment, it seemed the contents of her stomach might follow, but she retreated into the patch of garden and her nausea settled.

Dumping the chamber pot on the grass, she returned to lug the wooden pail downstairs. The pail into which old Mrs Dancy evacuated her bowels had a worse smell, but at least today it was just stools inside. Sometimes she peed in it as well and the pee seeped through a tiny crack, then Juliet would have to mop the floor.

She rinsed the chamber pot and pail under the water pump, then carried them back in.

Ella was about to put on the straw hat she wore in summer. She was lucky because she could dress her hat with flowers without the village busybodies calling it inappropriate, because her job was with flowers. She stopped with the hat halfway to her head.

'Thank you.'

She always said thank you, unlike her grandmother, who was more likely to say 'Now rub ointment into me bunions.'

Upstairs, Juliet slid the chamber pot under the bed and positioned the pail so that old Mrs Dancy would be able to slither off the mattress and hang onto her bedside table while Juliet helped her wriggle her nightdress up her scrawny thighs, before she plonked herself down on the pail for one of her noisy bowel movements.

Hearing the door shut downstairs, Juliet went to the window to watch Ella on her way. When she had started here, she had been happy to help the beautiful Ella. Now her ribs tightened in envy of Ella's job down the hill. Ella worked for a florist and came home smelling of petals and greenery. Oh, for a proper job! But, as Mother, Mrs Grove, the vicar and Uncle Tom Cobley were fond of pointing out: 'We all help one another in Clough' – so there was no hope of it. Juliet spent long days filing toenails as thick as piano keys, removing earwax with a funnel of oil, applying pennies to warts and feeling the back of old Mrs Dancy's hairbrush across her knuckles when the old lady's wisps of hair refused to stay put in a meagre bun. Every hour, she read verses from the Bible because, as old Mrs Dancy said, 'You never know when you'll gasp your last.'

But it was Pop who had gasped his last. After his fall, he had been carried home on a door and put to bed, where he had lain motionless. The women who trooped in and out, providing cups of tea and unwanted food and much-needed company, said he looked like he was fast asleep. To start with, Juliet had taken comfort from it, then she realised that you moved in your sleep, even if it was just a little wriggle. Pop lay flat on his back, the way they had arranged him.

'I'll fetch your breakfast.'

She ran downstairs to make the thin grey gruel the old lady swore by.

'Keeps me regular. You've got to be regular when you're bedfast.'

It was the start of another interminable day, made heavier by grief and shock. Anxiety too. What was to become of them without Pop? Juliet balled her fist around the saucepan handle. It wasn't right that they should have that worry. They should be allowed to concentrate on their loss.

And on top of all that, there was the boredom. No matter how often she swore to be cheerful, the irksome routine ground her down, leaving her brain sticky with tedium and her skin caked in stale air. Thank heaven Ella came home more or less when the children were let out of school.

Often, when Ella returned and set her free, Juliet would stride off along the tops to fill her lungs with clean air, but today she went straight home. Heat bounced up from the path. Her feet were hot and tight inside her boots. Doors and windows stood open, not that there was any breeze to be caught that way.

In the cottage, Mother and Mrs Grove were huddled together looking inside the tall cupboard in the alcove beside the fireplace.

'That's heavy, so it'll need to go at the bottom,' said Mrs Grove.

'I don't need telling how to pack, Beatrice,' said Mother.

'Pack?' Fear streamed through Juliet, which was daft, because she knew the rules about tied cottages.

Mother turned round. Her face, which had been drawn all week, was brighter. 'It's good news. Mrs Whicker wanted to see me because her ladyship has heard of my reputation with a needle and wants me to be her personal seamstress.' She laughed and a couple of tears spurted from her eyes. 'It's a live-in position. Imagine that. There's never been a resident seamstress at Moorside before.'

If Mother went to Moorside . . . 'Will I have to move in with old Mrs Dancy?'

'You're coming with me. It's a sign of how much they want me that they're prepared to take you as well.'

Mrs Grove snorted. 'It's a sign of what a sensible body Mrs Whicker is, more like. Say what you like about her being a slave-driver, but she guards those housemaids more closely than their own mothers. She wouldn't dream of setting you adrift, Juliet, not at your age.'

'So I'm not going to work at Moorside?'

'No, you'll stop with old Mrs Dancy.' Mrs Grove sounded as knowledgeable as if the whole thing was her idea. She talked about everything that way. 'Nowt will change for you, except for living in a different place.'

Nowt will change? It had already changed. Pop was dead, and

she and Mother were to move out of the cottage Mother had moved into as a bride on the day Pop planted the climbing rose.

'We have to pack and give the cottage a thorough spring clean,' said Mother.

'It'll keep you busy,' said Mrs Grove, 'and that's no bad thing.'

Whether it was good or bad was beside the point. There was no choice.

Lying awake long into the night, Juliet heard Mother crying. She crept next door to comfort her, slipping into bed and cuddling up.

'It's all my fault,' wept Mother. 'I never let him forget, not once. He was a good husband and a good provider, but I never let him forget.'

'Forget what?' Juliet whispered, but she already knew. There was only one thing, and Agnes Harper never let anyone forget it.

'The life I could have had if I hadn't married him. I would have had my own salon by now. The way Clara and I were brought up, all Mother's plans for us, the way she worked us so hard . . . Goodness, if Clara can manage it . . . ! I was far more talented. And now I'm to be seamstress to the Drysdale ladies and it feels as if it's my fault. The life I could have had, the career Mother planned for me, is going to happen, in a different sort of way, of course, but it feels as if I yearned for it for so long that I've made it come true. But what a price to pay.'

Juliet caught her breath. 'What happened to Pop was an accident.'

'I wish I hadn't gone on about it so much.'

'He didn't mind. He was proud of you.'

'He thought the sun shone out of my eyes. But I wish I hadn't always said "I could have had this, I could have had that." I wish sometimes I'd said "I'm glad I've got this." But I never did.'

'You must have.'

'No, not once. I withheld it on purpose. Now I can never tell him.'

Chapter Two

Juliet had never climbed so many stairs in her life. The back staircase was enclosed and gloomy, with alcoves to step into to save you bumping into someone coming the other way. Not that they had to step aside for anyone, not following behind Mrs Whicker. She marched on her way and anyone coming down leapt aside so as not to inconvenience her. Mother and Juliet followed close behind and, frankly, struggled to keep up. The housekeeper of Moorside might be as vast as one of the boulders on the moor but she took the stairs without stopping for breath.

Mrs Whicker threw open a door and led them along a landing. They followed her into a long, low-ceilinged room. She was dressed in black, relieved only by a whisper of lace around the standing collar. Round her considerable waist she wore a belt from which dangled a series of short chains, holding keys, a timepiece and a propelling pencil.

'Light,' she declared. 'The sewing room needs as much natural light as possible. There are also several lamps. This table should be of adequate size, and all the shelves and cupboards have been washed and freshly lined. You'll find a sewing machine under that cover. Your bedchamber is through that door. Your meals will be brought upstairs and served on that table in the corner. Do you require anything else?'

'No, thank you,' said Mother. 'This looks most satisfactory.'

'I'll leave you to unpack.'

The moment Mrs Whicker sailed from the room, Mother turned to Juliet.

'What do you think?'

'It's bigger than the whole of our old downstairs.'

Mother opened the connecting door to the bedroom and dismay thumped inside Juliet's chest. The bedrooms at home – their whole cottage, for that matter – had been pretty. Mother had made her own curtains, complete with piping, lining and matching pelmets; cushion covers with frills; and the antimacassars and arm caps, tablecloths and tray cloths had been embroidered. This bedroom was plain. It contained two beds with brass bedsteads, a hanging cupboard, a set of drawers and a simple washstand with a china jug-and-basin set on its marble top.

'Mrs Whicker was going to put you in with one of the maids, but I said I had to have you near me,' said Mother, 'though I didn't expect this.'

'We'll soon cheer it up. Tray cloths on the chest of drawers, a little curtain round the washstand's legs.'

'I didn't mean that. I meant, separate rooms.'

They were in the middle of their unpacking when Mrs Whicker swept into the sewing room.

'Unpacked? Good. Come in,' she called and a maid staggered in, her arms wrapped around a massive basket. 'The household mending.'

Mrs Whicker swept out again and Mother sat down with the mending beside her.

'Are you starting it now?' Juliet asked in surprise.

'It's what I'm being paid for,' was the tart reply.

'I thought you'd be making gowns for Lady Margaret and the young ladies.'

'I will, but there's the household sewing as well.'

She hadn't mentioned it before, certainly not when Juliet had heard her telling the other village women.

'Isn't it good that Mrs Whicker knows about sewing rooms?' ventured Juliet.

Mother laughed and it wasn't a pleasant sound. 'She knows nothing beyond what I told her when she sent for me, and now she's had the nerve to parrot it back to me as if it was all her own idea.' Her face changed, anxiety replacing scorn. 'Don't tell anyone I said that. I have to stay in her good books. Get on with the unpacking.'

'Old Mrs Dancy is expecting me.'

'It won't take you five minutes to get finished. Can't you see I'm busy?'

Juliet walked into their other room, a wave of homesickness washing over her for her old bedroom with the roses nodding at the window. They would be someone else's roses soon, and the neighbours who had gathered to bid them farewell an hour ago would soon be calling round to welcome the new family. Maybe they were already.

She stowed away their clothes, all beautifully made by Mother, and set out their hairbrushes on the chest of drawers. And now she really must go. Ella had arranged to go in late to the florist's this morning, so Juliet could arrive at Moorside with her mother, instead of trailing in self-consciously after her day's work.

With a swift kiss for Mother, she darted out of the sewing room and hurried along the landing. As she opened the door to the backstairs, a hand grabbed her arm from behind and swung her round. She found herself face-to-face with a girl three or four years older than herself, dressed in a maid's uniform. Her abundant black curls that just about managed to stay pinned in place and dark, clever eyes made her look like she should be wearing a scarlet skirt and golden hoops in her ears, dancing beside a Gypsy campfire. How drab Juliet's fair hair and blue eyes felt in comparison.

The girl's hand darted out and gave her a hard shove. Juliet stepped backwards, banging into the edge of the open door.

'What was that for?'

'I know who you are.' The girl tilted her head to one side, looking Juliet up and down. 'I know what you're after an' all.'

'I don't know what you're talking about.'

'I've heard about you.' She thrust her face close. Her skin was creamy smooth, her eyes filled with challenge. 'You're the girl who wipes the shitty arse of an old biddy in the village. You hope to get the next maid's position that becomes available here, and don't pretend otherwise. My sister Hannah is next in line, so don't try getting round Mrs Whicker, because if I think you're up to something, you'll be sorry.' She stepped back. 'Stick to wiping shitty arses. It's all you're fit for. Get out of my way.'

A vigorous dig from a sharp elbow heaved Juliet aside, and the girl disappeared downstairs. Would she be lying in wait further down? But Juliet wasn't aware of any other back staircases, so she had no choice but to brave this one. Her heart pounded all the way down, but she reached the ground floor without incident. The stairs gave onto a long passage running right to left, with another passage stretching away straight ahead. She nipped into this one, passing a long line of doors. Earlier, walking along here towards the stairs, she had looked forward to learning what lay behind each door. Now all she wanted was to get out of here and flee back to where she belonged.

She hurried across the stable yard's cobbles and onto the back drive that the cart had brought them along earlier. This was hidden from the main drive by a thick wall of shrubs until it curved and joined the wider main drive near the gatekeeper's lodge. No one emerged from the lodge to challenge her and she slipped through the gates and ran back to Clough.

'I wasn't expecting you this soon, chick,' said Ella. 'Are you settled in already?'

'We didn't take much with us.'

Only clothes and personal things. Their furniture had been sold or given away. Pop would be ashamed to think that the home he had proudly built up for them had been dismantled so swiftly.

'Come upstairs and tell us about it before I go,' said Ella, leading the way.

Her interest warmed Juliet and the encounter with that girl eased out of the forefront of her mind. She described the sewing room, fitted out according to Mother's wishes.

'It's near the top of the house, at the back, and the windows overlook the stable yard. We're going to have our meals in there as well.'

'It's the sign of an upper servant, having your meals fetched up to you,' said Ella. 'That's what they do for governesses. It means the seamstress has status.'

'Aye, Agnes Harper'ull like that,' said old Mrs Dancy. 'She's always been full of herself, that one.'

'Granny,' Ella chided.

Mother, an upper servant? Juliet felt a thrill of pride. Real pride.

Not the adoration Pop – and Mother – had encouraged in her when she was little, but a proper, mature pride. It hadn't sat easily with her conscience to feel critical of Mother these past two or three years after she had realised how tiresome the neighbours found her. But now, as an upper servant in the Drysdale household, as the person chosen to be the first ever live-in seamstress, Mother was bound to be content.

Juliet felt more settled too. Instead of feeling uncomfortable about old Mrs Dancy's remark, she perked up, a feeling that lingered as, later, she made her way to her new home. Fancy! She was entitled to walk between these imposing gateposts and along the shady back drive. She had no reason to feel awkward about crossing the stable yard and entering the long corridor that led to the backstairs.

'I'm back.'

She entered the sewing room. Mother sat beside a window, head bent over a sheet, needle darting in and out. The basket of mending lurked on the floor beside her, but most of its contents were now in folded piles on the table.

'Good.' Mother didn't look up. 'I've left you the socks to darn.'

'His lordship's socks?' She picked the bundle out of the bottom of the basket. No, the quality was working men's. 'You're responsible for the servants' mending?'

'Only the men's.'

Smothering a sigh, Juliet set to work. Was this how it was to be? Days with old Mrs Dancy and evenings of menial sewing? Any pleasure she might have taken in sewing had been criticised into oblivion at an early age by Mother's fault-finding tuition, which had mostly involved unpicking and doing again . . . and again.

'It's the only way to learn,' Mother used to say. 'It's how Nana Adeline taught me and it didn't do me any harm.'

When the door opened, pushed by a young maid with her back against it because she was carrying a tray, Juliet could have kissed her. She jumped up to help.

'It goes on this table over here.'

'Tablecloth, Juliet,' said Mother.

'I'll put it down here for a minute.' The maid deposited the tray on the end of the sewing table.

'Not there,' said Mother. 'That's my sewing table.'

'Well, I've got to put it somewhere,' said the girl. 'I've just fetched it up all them stairs and my arms are dropping off.'

'I'll hold it,' Juliet offered. 'You do the tablecloth.'

'In future, you must put the cloth on the table in advance, Juliet,' said Mother. She stood up and stretched her back. 'I'll tidy myself while you two lay the table.'

'I'm Cecily.' Sandy hair showed beneath a white cap. A smattering of freckles crossed her nose.

'I'm glad it's you and not – I don't know her name. I had a spat with another maid earlier.'

'Rosie.' Cecily threw the cloth over the table and smoothed it. 'She's spitting feathers about you being here.'

'She thinks I want to be a maid and she wants her sister to have the next job that's going.'

'Charity Hannah.'

Ah. That explained it. The girls in the Home for Orphaned Daughters of the Deserving Poor in Birkfield were all known as Charity This and Charity That. It kept them in their place.

'She's fourteen, so she has two more years there.' Cecily deftly laid out the cutlery. 'If she hasn't got a respectable, permanent, live-in post by her sixteenth birthday, she'll be for the workhouse.'

Mother came back, patting her hair into position. 'I imagine

26

all the talk in the servants' hall is about us moving in.'

'Not now,' Cecily answered cheerfully. 'It was about you when Mrs Whicker first told us you were coming, but we've moved on now. Mr Durbin – he's our butler, very important – announced today that there's a new gardening family coming. Harold Price, the head gardener, needs to slow down a bit now he's knocking on in years, so his son, who left here years ago to work for her ladyship's sister, is coming back to take over. They'll work side by side for a year or two, then Harold Price will step down. The son's family is coming too, of course, and d'you want to know the best bit? They say his oldest lad is a fine-looking chap of twenty. Just the right age for me.'

When the door shut behind Cecily, Mother said, 'She sounds boy mad to me. I'm not having you being friendly with a girl like that.'

'I'm fifteen, nearly grown up. You don't have to choose my friends.' She was not, absolutely not, going to shun Cecily.

The next day, Mother changed her mind.

'I've had a word with Mrs Whicker and she assures me that her maids are closely supervised.'

'That's what Mrs Grove said.'

'Followers aren't permitted under any circumstances, so you may be friends with Cecily if you wish.'

Was Juliet meant to say thank you? Her jaw tensed in annoyance. She was tired of being under everyone's thumb – Mother's, old Mrs Dancy's, even Ella's, though hers was a kind thumb.

'I'll be out when you come home tomorrow,' said Mother. 'I have to go to Naseby's to order the sewing items I require. I'm calling on Beatrice Grove on the way back, so Mrs Whicker says you may have tea downstairs.'

Juliet thought she might forego tea, but when the time came, the sewing room door banged open and Rosie marched in as if she owned the place.

'Too important to be on time, are you? Mrs Whicker says I'm to fetch you down and no hanging about.' She bunched her fists on her hips. 'Just don't let it give you any ideas. Understand?'

'What ideas?'

Rosie's eyes flashed. 'Ideas about being a maid here, for starters. Why do you think you have to eat your meals up here? Because you're not wanted downstairs, that's why. You think you're so high and mighty, you and your mam – oh, beg pardon, your *mother*. Heaven forbid that you should have owt as common as a mam.'

Rosie flounced out, leaving Juliet feeling winded. It wasn't the first time she had been picked on for talking nicely. There were times when she wished Nana Adeline had never paid for elocution lessons for Mother and Auntie Clara, but she didn't dare let her own speech lapse or Mother would have her guts for garters.

She trailed downstairs, her cheeks flaming as she entered the hall to find everyone seated and waiting.

'You're nobody, so you sit at the bottom,' said Rosie, 'lower than the scrubbing women.'

'That's an interesting question,' said Mr Durbin from the top end. 'Does she sit at the bottom because she has no official place in the household or should she sit at this end, as belonging to her ladyship's personal seamstress? What do you think, Mrs Whicker?'

Juliet made a dive for the lowliest place possible. 'I'm fine here, thank you.'

Cook poured from a gigantic teapot, and plates of sandwiches were offered round, followed by a deliciously moist batch cake and buttery shortbread, but Juliet could swallow hardly anything, only to have all eyes turn her way when Cook remarked on her poor appetite.

'And after all the trouble you go to, Cook,' Rosie commented, making everyone look at Juliet again.

'Did you have a nice tea?' Mother asked later when they were in the sewing room. Juliet was beginning to realise what living in the sewing room meant. Even in the evenings, Mother worked.

She hesitated, but she wanted to say it. 'I heard someone say they didn't think I should be allowed to have tea with the rest of them.'

Mother sighed gustily, a sure sign she was feeling put upon. 'Living-in servants aren't meant to have children. It's a great concession, your being allowed here. If it was just me, I'd eat downstairs, but I've got you and I'm not leaving you up here on your own.'

'So you're not an upper servant after all?'

'No,' Mother said sharply, 'I'm just a widow who has to make her way in the world and provide for her child. It isn't easy and you whining on about my not being an upper servant doesn't help.'

'I wasn't—'

'Don't answer back.'

Living in the sewing room was surprisingly restrictive. Once she arrived home of an afternoon, Juliet couldn't go out again. Mrs Whicker didn't permit the maids to go flitting about outside and Juliet sensed this applied to her as well. She spent some evenings in the maids' slipper room, so called because they removed their shoes, but, as much as she enjoyed Cecily's company, she was reluctant to be in there if Rosie was around. Even when Rosie wasn't there, it wasn't entirely comfortable, because the door had been taken off its hinges and you never knew who might be listening in the passage. Mrs Whicker, Cook and Mr Durbin all looked in if they passed, not to mention the handsome footmen who called through the gaping doorway, though it was more than their lives were worth to set foot over the threshold.

'Do you find it hard, being stuck indoors all day?' she asked Mother.

'It's not what I'm used to.' Mother shrugged. 'Of course, if her ladyship should require my assistance . . .' She made it sound as if she was summoned a dozen times a day to give her opinion on the latest fashions. 'Anyway, I'm going out tomorrow morning on her ladyship's business.'

'How grand. What did her ladyship tell you about it?'

Mother glanced away. 'Mrs Whicker told me, actually. Her ladyship is a patron of the Home for Orphaned Daughters of the Deserving Poor and she was invited to visit tomorrow to see the girls' progress in needlework. Unfortunately, she won't be able to attend, so I'm to go in her stead.'

Those poor charity girls. If Mother was as critical of their efforts as she had always been of Juliet's, they wouldn't know what had hit them.

The next afternoon, Juliet hurried home, knowing Mother would be eager to tell all. *Please let her have been kind to the charity girls.* As she was toiling up the backstairs, footsteps came running up behind her. She slipped into an alcove to let whoever it was pass, only to find herself trapped in the small space, confronted by Rosie.

'You bitch,' said Rosie. 'You and your precious mother, you're a pair of bitches. I were sent on an errand to Birkfield today and I sneaked into the Home for Orphaned Daughters to see our Hannah, and she was beside herself. She told me all about how your mother made a show of her in front of the warden and the vicar's wife.'

Rosie shoved Juliet into the back of the alcove, jarring her shoulders as they struck the wall, but Juliet was determined to stand up for herself.

'Mother was asked to look at the girls' progress in their sewing.'

'Aye, to look at it and say "It's coming along nicely," and congratulate the vicar's wife, who's in charge of needlework lessons. That's what your mother were supposed to do. That's what her ladyship does: arrive, make everyone feel better and leave. But, oh no, Mrs Blabbermouth Harper had to criticise every single thing, didn't she? And do you know whose work she picked on to hold up as a bad example? Three guesses!'

'I understand why you're upset, but—'

'The two of you planned it, didn't you? Show up our Hannah, so that she has to wear the Disgraced Apron for the rest of the day, which means her name is written in the Disgraced Book, and that's one step closer to not being allowed to stay in the home. It's not just our dead parents that have to be deserving, you know. The girls have to be an' all. Do you know what happens to anyone who gets chucked out? They get sent to yon workhouse over in Ladyfield. Some already have brothers there, since no one thought of setting up a home for sons of the deserving poor. That's where my brother was sent when me and Hannah went to the Home for Orphaned Daughters. He left three years ago and he'd *kill* me if I let our Hannah end up there.'

Juliet gasped as Rosie yanked her from the alcove. She missed her footing and stumbled down a few stairs before she grabbed the handrail, nearly jolting her arm out of its socket. Rosie bounded downstairs, leaving her to gather herself and stumble to the sewing room, where she found Mother, Mrs Whicker and her ladyship's personal maid, Miss Marchant, drinking tea and looking tired but satisfied.

Miss Marchant rose. 'I must return to her ladyship's chamber.'

Mrs Whicker's chair creaked as she raised her bulk. 'I, too, must return to my duties. I'll send a girl to fetch the tea tray.'

They left. Mother bustled about, humming as she wound her tape measure into a neat coil. The door opened and Rosie entered, looking sullen.

'It's a proper sewing room now,' Mother declared. 'Her ladyship came to be measured for an alteration. She stood on that very footstool to have her hem turned up.' She gazed at the stool as if it were a holy relic. 'She's coming tomorrow afternoon to try the new length. I want you back here promptly from old Mrs Dancy's, Juliet. I'll press your Sunday best, and you can hold the pins.'

There was an angry rattle of china as Rosie marched out, hooking the door shut with her foot.

The next afternoon, Juliet arrived dry-mouthed after running through merciless sunshine.

'Your hair's a mess,' carped Mother. 'Get changed, and wash your face and hands.'

She freshened up, but when she took her Sunday dress from the cupboard, there was a stain on it. Mother took one look and boxed her ears. Juliet lifted a hand to her smarting ear, but her temper hurt more. She knew who was responsible for this.

'Put on a fresh blouse,' Mother ordered.

There was just time before Miss Marchant opened the door and her ladyship sailed in, the last word in elegance in an afternoon dress of blue velveteen. Miss Marchant unhooked its skirt and assisted her ladyship into the altered skirt of a promenade gown of green silk, ablaze with white lace round the trained hem. It had nearly killed Mother to get it finished in time. Mother positioned mirrors all round. Her ladyship asked for this mirror or that one to be moved a fraction as she scrutinised her appearance. Honestly, couldn't she just take a step to the left? Juliet stood by with the pin cushion. There was a breathless silence, then her ladyship pronounced the new length acceptable and Miss Marchant helped her back into the velveteen gown.

As her ladyship was leaving, she glanced at Juliet. 'Is this your daughter, Harper?'

'Yes, Your Ladyship.'

'Does she take after you?'

'Juliet is a competent little needlewoman, Your Ladyship.'

'Good. Come, Marchant.'

Miss Marchant beamed approvingly at Juliet, making her feel like a prize exhibit, before she opened the door for her ladyship to sweep through.

'Don't let it go to your head,' said Mother, but when Cecily came to hear all the details, Mother regaled her with the tale of how Juliet had been noticed, while Juliet groaned inwardly.

Later, it was Rosie who brought their evening meal.

'Thank you, Rosie,' said Mother.

Thank you, Rosie, Rosie mimicked silently behind her back. She unloaded the tray, then held Juliet's gaze while her mouth worked. Staring straight at Juliet, she leant over and spat a great glistening gobbet onto Juliet's plate.

'Don't let it get cold,' she said.

Chapter Three

It was simple for Juliet: she could sigh beside her father's grave, feeling nothing but sorrow. Not so for Agnes. Her sighs were complicated, packed with as much guilt as sorrow. She had never let her dear husband forget his good fortune in having lured her away from her professional path to owning her own salon. She wished she could come here more often, but she didn't have the freedom. Once a week on Sundays had to suffice.

She had never had her movements curtailed before. No, that wasn't true. Mother had kept a tight rein on her and Clara. Would Clara have informed Mother that she had been widowed? She wanted Mother to know, but was too proud to write the letter herself. After being cast aside upon her marriage, she couldn't possibly contact Mother again. Crawling back: that's what Mother would call it.

She touched Juliet's arm. It was time to join the rest of the congregation inside. Rain pattered softly on the stained-glass windows during the service and afterwards everyone emerged to the fresh scent of damp grass. Agnes never used to be a great one for hanging about after church, but now these moments with her old neighbours were precious. She had considered herself above them when they lived cheek by jowl. Now, separated from them, she realised how much she had become one of them.

'How are you getting on, Agnes?' asked Beatrice, and the group moved closer in a way that was most flattering.

She described her ladyship's visits to the sewing room and once she started, she couldn't keep her mouth shut. Out it poured, not just the successful alteration, but all about how the best kind of seamstress would grow as close to her mistress as any lady's maid. Florence Hope's mouth fell open in admiration, and Agnes held back a gratified sigh.

'Aye, but you're still a long way off that, aren't you?' Trust Beatrice to bring things down to earth.

'If you say so, Beatrice.' Agnes gave a little laugh. 'But perhaps you'd care to explain how else I came to represent her ladyship at the Home for Orphaned Daughters of the Deserving Poor.'

'You represented her ladyship?' breathed Florence. 'Oh, Agnes, what an honour.'

'What's next on the cards?' Beatrice's tone might lack the admiring quality of everyone else's but she was listening just as avidly.

'There'll be a house party in the autumn, and her ladyship and the young ladies are travelling to Manchester to choose fabrics for their ballgowns.'

'Fancy, and are you going with them?' asked Ella.

'Supplying advice is part of the seamstress's role,' she said modestly.

'Manchester?' said Beatrice. 'Happen you could drop in on that sister of yours in her fancy shop.'

Oh, how wonderful to swan into Clara's salon, or Mademoiselle Antoinette as she called herself these days, and show off her exalted position as personal seamstress to Lady Margaret Drysdale – a lady in her own right, no less. His lordship was a minor sort of lord, but her ladyship was the daughter of a marquis. That would be one in the eye for Clara. She glanced away to hide her smiles.

It was one of those glorious September days when the air glowed and the sky was as blue as cornflowers. Cecily paused for a breather as she tramped across the tops to Little Clough. Not being allowed to leave until after church was a swine, because it meant she couldn't go at a leisurely pace. She wanted to see her family, but . . . well, she didn't enjoy her visits home anything like as much as she used to.

How proud everyone had been when she got the position at Moorside. The whole village had turned out to see her off, and she had felt like the Queen of the May. Could she have known how cruelly restricted her chances would be of meeting a chap, she wouldn't have been so keen. She was eighteen now, and still without a ring on her finger. Barbara and Sally, seventeen and sixteen, were both wed. If their Miranda got hitched before she did, she would throw herself down the well.

She pushed open the door, and a pile of cutlery was thrust at her.

Mam paused long enough to bestow a swift kiss. 'Be a love and lay the table.'

Times were when everyone stopped what they were doing when she arrived. Now, she was simply the one who pitched up one Sunday a month. Was it always going to be like this? The job at Moorside that everyone had told her was so wonderful felt more like a prison sentence. Oh, the work itself was all right, and she enjoyed being with the other maids, but how was she ever to find a chap? These days, when she saw Barbara and Sally, jealousy rolled deep in her gut.

No sooner had she set the table than Mam dished up. Cecily couldn't help feeling she didn't matter as much as she used to. Mind you, the tables were turned later, after she had helped with the washing-up, when she said she must go soon.

'But you've not been here five minutes,' said Mam.

'I only get the one afternoon and—'

'She wants a bit of time to herself,' Nan put in. 'She's got herself a fella, haven't you, gal?'

'No.' A flush seeped across her cheeks.

'Bet you anything she has,' Nan crowed.

'I just felt like doing something different.' It sounded feeble, but it was true. One afternoon a month was all she got, and all she ever did with it was come here and not be made a fuss of.

'So, what something different will you be doing?' Dad asked.

'Just going for a walk.'

'Aye – with a man friend, I bet.' Nan was like a dog with a bone when she got going.

Cecily was glad to escape. She hurried down the hill to Birkfield. She had heard in the slipper room that Hal Price, grandson of Mr Harold Price, had been granted permission to spend a couple of hours on Sunday afternoons to work in the Charlesworths' garden. It was Rosie who had supplied the information. The lucky creature had already met Hal.

'It's because of his plans for the future,' Rosie had said, though she hadn't elaborated, and Cecily, though dying for more, had kept her lips tight shut. She had great hopes of Hal Price. Oh, to be able to go home one Sunday and say, 'You were right, Nan, I do have a fellow.'

In Birkfield, she made a beeline for the row of cottages where Mr Rex Charlesworth – daft name, made him sound like a dog –

and his sister lived. Mr Charlesworth was drawing master to the young ladies, so presumably that was why Hal was allowed to do a spot of work for him.

As she approached, she saw him kneeling in front of a flower bed, his fingers diving expertly here and there. She had prepared a couple of kiss curls for the occasion, fixing them with sugar water to ensure they kept their shape, and she tugged them into view before she ambled oh so casually past the cottages. She paused beside the garden wall, but he didn't look up.

'Afternoon,' she said. 'Lovely day.'

He sat back on his heels. She braced herself to feel all shivery inside. Was this the moment? He pushed his cloth cap to the back of his head, revealing light-brown eyes.

'Beautiful,' he agreed.

He stood and she rejoiced at this willingness to pass the time of day. He touched his cap to her. His sleeves were rolled up above the elbows. His arms were strong, his hands covered in soil. His waistcoat hung open, and Cecily readied herself to quell the urge to slip her hands inside it.

She didn't feel any such urge. Maybe a spot of flirting would help.

'I know who you are.'

She had read stories in which the heroine fluttered her eyelashes, but when she had tried this in the looking-glass, it had looked like she had something in her eye. She settled for tilting her head to one side.

'Oh aye?'

The corners of his mouth twitched into a smile. He had a friendly smile. Boyish. Would this be what set her all quivery inside? No. But it didn't matter, because he was so good-looking that something was bound to set her heart racing.

'You're Hal Price. Your dad's going to take over as head gardener.'

'That's right, when Grandad hangs up his trowel. Do you work at Moorside?'

'I'm Cecily. Pleased to meet you, I'm sure.'

To her unutterable delight, he reached over the wall to shake hands, but withdrew his hand with a laugh, holding up his grubby palm. 'We'll have to save the handshake for another time.'

Did that mean he wanted to see her again? Surely that should set her senses scattering. But it didn't. Never mind. She was on the brink. She had to be. Barbara and Sally were both married, and Barbara was in the family way. She was in danger of being the spinster aunt.

'How come you're gardening here?' she asked. She peered over the wall at the flower beds. She would have to learn some of the names if she was going to be a gardener's girl. 'Do you want to be a jobbing gardener in small gardens instead of working on an estate?'

'Actually, I want to be a garden designer one day.'

'I see.'

But she didn't, not really. And it didn't matter, did it, because, no matter how handsome he was, no matter how strong and capable his slim figure looked, no matter how likeable his manner or how friendly his smile, her pulses weren't jumping all over the place and her insides weren't quivering. Bugger, bugger, bugger.

Juliet crossed the stable yard and entered the house. As she paced down the long corridor, heading for the backstairs, a couple of kitchen maids coming towards her nudged one another and giggled, then dived into the pickling room, and the knife boy, racing past, yelled over his scrawny shoulder, 'I wouldn't be in your shoes for all the tea in China.'

What was going on? She gained the far end of the passage, where the other long corridor crossed it left to right. Before she could reach the stairs, a voice called from behind her.

'Hang on a mo.' One of the kitchen maids came running. 'I wanted to warn you. Rosie's out for blood. She's heard about—'

'Oh aye, I've heard all right.'

A hand grabbed Juliet from behind and swung her about. There stood Rosie, eyes flashing. Heat bubbled up inside Juliet. She was sick to death of being picked on. She shoved back and darted free. Cecily appeared from the stairs, carrying an ash pan. Juliet snatched it and dumped its load squarely over Rosie's head. Cold ashes smothered her cap and hair, plopping down to spatter her shoulders and smear her face. Juliet caught her breath in a mixture of jubilation and horror, savouring the look of astonishment on Rosie's face.

For one breathless moment, they all froze. Then Rosie released a shrill scream of shock and fury before launching herself at Juliet like an avenging demon. Juliet's stomach was almost left behind as she went hurtling backwards. Rosie clawed and pummelled, terrifying Juliet with her strength, and she was never more relieved in her life than when others waded in and dragged them apart.

'Mrs Whicker will have forty fits if she gets to know about this.' Thomasina, the most senior of the parlourmaids, appeared from nowhere. 'Cecily, help Rosie get cleaned up. Juliet, upstairs this instant.'

Juliet obeyed with wings on her feet – and in her heart. She practically danced into the sewing room.

'There you are,' said Mother.

'You sound like old Mrs Dancy. She says that every morning.'

'Don't be cheeky. You look pleased with yourself.'

'Do I?' And no wonder. She had upended an ash pan on Rosie's head. 'Can't think why.'

'Well, you'll be pleased with yourself in a minute.' Mother's face burst into a smile. 'You know that the Drysdales are hosting a house party in the autumn?'

'Yes, and you're accompanying her ladyship and the young ladies to Manchester to choose materials for their ballgowns.'

'There are other garments to be made too. It's going to be a lot of work, so I said to Mrs Whicker, "That's a mountain of work for me to get through, not forgetting my everyday sewing." Then, the next time I saw her, I mentioned how I've taught you to sew and what a help you could be to me. Lo and behold, this morning, she had the idea of taking you on in here for September.'

'In here?'

'In the sewing room. She'd never have agreed if I'd asked outright. This way, it's her idea, which is all she cares about. So, you'll be working for me for a few weeks. What do you say to that?'

What, work in the sewing room? Alongside Mother, with her carping and criticism?

'But if I'm to come here, who'll take care of old Mrs Dancy?'

'Is that all you can say, when I've just offered you this marvellous opportunity? You're to work here through September, and that maid with the sulky mouth – what's her name? – Rosie – Rosie will look after old Mrs Dancy.'

They had left her behind. The Drysdales had gone to Manchester and left her behind. The skin squeezed Agnes's bones as humiliation rippled through her, making her feel naked and on show. And after she had boasted to her old neighbours too. How was she to face them on Sunday? Wait. Next week was Auntie Juley's anniversary, so she could legitimately dash away the moment the service ended to visit Auntie Juley's grave in Birkfield.

She hated to use Auntie Juley, but it couldn't be helped, and she would have visited the grave anyway, because she had loved Auntie Juley, who had been far more of a mum to her and Clara than Mother ever had. Auntie Juley was Mother's aunt. She had kept house for them while Mother worked. Without her, there would have been no bedtime stories, no trips to the park, no one to kiss it better when they fell. It would have been nowt but work, work, work, sew, sew, sew, from the earliest age. Everybody in the vicinity of Moorside reckoned Mrs Whicker was a slave-driver with her maids, but they didn't know the meaning of the word. Adeline Tewson – now there was a real slave-driver. Relentless. Unforgiving. She was strong and ruthless, and God help any mere male who came up against her. According to Clara's Christmas letters, Mother's textiles business was flourishing.

In her later years, Auntie Juley had retired to Birkfield, the home of her childhood. When she fell ill and needed help, Agnes and Clara had expected Clara, the less talented, the more easily dispensable, to be sent, but Mother had sent Agnes.

'You've got more about you than Clara. Auntie Juley needs someone with a bit of nous and Clara's worse than useless.'

So Agnes had come here – and had never left. If Mother had sent Clara, Agnes would now be running a high-class salon, with well-to-do ladies clamouring for her advice on what suited them. A sour taste filled Agnes's mouth. Didn't her ladyship realise what an asset she would have been to the Manchester trip?

All at once it felt a trial to have Juliet working in the sewing room. Her help would be useful, of course, but manoeuvring Mrs Whicker into having the idea had been all wrapped up in Agnes's happy anticipation of her triumphant spree in Manchester. Filled with generosity, she had gone to Naseby's to buy Juliet her own sewing box, its padded lid embroidered with snowdrops, and she had taken pleasure in filling it with the tools of the trade: scissors for different purposes, sharps of various sizes, pins, threads in all the basic colours, a tin for buttons, a selection of ribbons and braids, and a darning mushroom and wool.

'Thank you, Mother,' said Juliet. 'It'll be most useful.'

That was the moment when – if she had been included in the Manchester trip, if she had felt as special and important as she was meant to feel – she would have hugged Juliet and promised, 'I know it doesn't seem like the best gift just now, because I felt the same when Mother presented me with my sewing box. Years of sewing samples and nothing ever being good enough made a sewing box the last thing I wanted. But later, all those years paid off and I came to love sewing, and then I was proud of my sewing box. One day, you will be too.'

That was what she had planned to say. But now, all she said was, 'You ought to have your own sewing box. I'm fed up of you raiding mine.'

When the fabrics arrived, Agnes snipped the string and folded back the brown paper on the first plump parcel, her own soft intake of breath echoed in Juliet's delighted gasp. Silks in cream, ivory and pale buttermilk yellow shimmered enticingly and slid like liquid between her fingers.

'Her ladyship's silk has its own sound.' Juliet's fingertips trailed wonderingly along the midnight blue shot through with silver thread.

'The best silks do have that rustle, almost a crackle.'

They started on Miss Louisa's ballgown. There was a phenomenal quantity of silk because the skirt was to be knife-pleated, precision work that called for perfect measuring. Agnes assigned to Juliet the task of making the short puffed sleeves. As well as its dozens of knife pleats, the skirt was to have an embroidered panel down the front, and this was another task given to Juliet.

'I want it to look as if the flowers are scattered all over,' said Agnes.

'With ivy winding in and out.'

Agnes pursed her lips. 'I never said anything about ivy.'

'It was only an idea.'

'It's not your place to have ideas.'

Juliet duly presented a drawing, carefully coloured, stitches listed down the side. She had spread roses and peonies down the length, and filled in the spaces with smaller blooms. At first glance, Agnes was pleased – more pleased than she had expected to be. Impressed, in fact, and her gaze flicked upwards in vexation. The junior member of staff wasn't supposed to be this good. There was another sheet of paper underneath, with the same design, but this time incorporating ivy leaves.

'This is your idea of how to carry on, is it? Defying my wishes, wasting time on a second design? You'd be sacked for that, my girl, if you worked in my salon. There!' She clouted Juliet round the ear. The palm of her hand felt hot with vindication, though honesty forced her to concede stiffly, 'The ivy brings out the colours in the flowers. You may work that design.'

But she wished she hadn't agreed to it when the embroidery started taking shape, the ivy providing a subtle counterpoint to the flowers. Chill rippled through her shoulders. Juliet had known instinctively what would look perfect and she was right. Not that Agnes had any intention of praising her. You didn't praise junior members of staff. You looked stern and said 'Hmm' when you scrutinised their efforts. It kept them on their toes. She should know. Mother had kept her and Clara on their toes for years and it hadn't done them any harm.

To her amazement, Juliet enjoyed working in the sewing room. Handling the glorious fabrics, watching the stylish gowns take shape, actually working on the gowns herself – she loved it. Having disliked sewing all her life, suddenly those years of endless practice had become worthwhile. As for designing the embroidered panel, that had been pure bliss. After her first tentative pencil strokes, the design had grown naturally, and she was proud to create it for real, using the precise shades of embroidery floss. As for her stitching, it was faultless. Even the French knots, which had been the bane of her life, were of uniform size in their dainty clusters.

How was she ever to go back to emptying old Mrs Dancy's night pail? In the three years since she left school, it had never occurred to her that work might be enjoyable. Yet here she was, lapping up every moment.

So engrossed was she that it was almost a disappointment to be despatched to Birkfield to purchase supplies from Naseby's, but once she was outside, the morning air worked its magic, and she took the back drive at a brisk pace, relishing the cool, damp feel that the thick shrubbery endowed on the surroundings and giving a cheery wave to the gatekeeper's wife as she passed the lodge.

She didn't go through the village, because their old neighbours would detain her, and Mother would be timing her to the minute, but headed straight for the main path down the steep hillside. At the top, she stopped to breathe in the scents of grass and gorse, its bright yellow blooms still flowering within bushes of needle-like leaves. Down in the valley sprawled the market town of Birkfield and further along, with two or three miles between them, the smaller town of Ladyfield. It was intriguing to think of Mother having hailed from Manchester, which might even be big enough to fill the whole valley. Imagine that! The biggest place Juliet had ever been to was Birkfield, though she had walked along the tops to look down at Annerby in the next valley. Annerby occupied the valley floor as well as climbing partway up the opposite hill.

'Look at that,' Pop had said with scorn in his voice. 'Who'd want to live their lives in that place, with its railway line and its tall chimneys, when they could live up here? Give me a fresh-air job any day. I've never been down there to Annerby and I never will.'

Juliet never had either, though sometimes she had watched the steam engine pulling its line of carriages away from the town. What was it like to travel on a train?

Plunging down the path to Birkfield, she kept her rhythm steady. A real calf-stretcher of a walk, Pop used to call it, and it was important to pace yourself, especially on the way back up. Pink stemless thistles and yellow cat's ears grew on either side of the path, and halfway down was a small offshoot with a bench, so you could have a breather. His lordship had had the bench put there. He was good like that.

At the bottom, creamy-coloured field pansies sprouted on a patch of wasteland before she entered the town. Naseby's was in one of the cobbled streets off the market square. The drapery-cum-haberdashery had never particularly interested her before, but now she was glad that a couple of customers were inside, mulling over buttons with Mrs Naseby, giving Juliet a chance to mooch around and examine the bolts of materials. Mrs Naseby stocked plain, serviceable fabrics. Juliet pictured the silks, velvets and taffeta in the sewing room and felt privileged. No wonder Mother had been so disappointed not to accompany the Drysdales on their shopping expedition. She hadn't said much, but her stony expression and bitter smiles made it clear she was crushed. Juliet felt an ache of compassion. She was going to feel crushed herself when she had to leave the sewing room.

A piece of card was propped up on a little stand on one of the counters. *Help Wanted*. Before she could read what it said underneath, the shop bell jingled as the customers departed.

'Now then, Juliet, what can I do for you?' In her pin-tucked white blouse with discreetly puffed upper sleeves, Mrs Naseby was a good advertisement for the dressmaking service she offered. 'Are you here for yourself or for the sewing room?'

'The sewing room.'

Mrs Naseby stood straighter. 'It's a pleasure to supply goods to her ladyship.'

Juliet drew Mother's list from her pocket, but instead of unfolding it, she nodded at the card. *Help Wanted*.

'Are you looking for another dressmaker to replace my mother?'

'No, I need a new assistant in the shop. Dora's leaving to get wed.'

'You could put the card in the window. More folk will see it.'

'Nay, you can't have just anyone working in an establishment like this. It has to be someone who knows about sewing.'

Someone who knows about sewing.

Someone who doesn't want to spend her days swilling out chamber pots.

'Mrs Naseby,' she said. 'Would you mind if I applied for the position?'

47

Chapter Four

Mother was in a ratty mood, so Juliet didn't mention her forthcoming interview. Mother in a good temper would be proud, but Mother with a cob on might accuse her of going behind her back. Mother was in a flap because Mrs Whicker had invited her to share a pot of tea with her that evening.

'Can't you just tell her how busy we are?' Juliet suggested. 'It's the young ladies' final fittings tomorrow.'

'You don't say no to the housekeeper, no matter how busy you are. I suppose this means I'll have to work till midnight. You'll have to work instead of going to the slipper room.'

That was no hardship. She hadn't been near the slipper room since she started in the sewing room, because the embroidered panel had taken so much time. Besides, she had no desire to cross swords with Rosie.

When Cecily brought their evening tray, Juliet said, 'Mother is having tea with Mrs Whicker later, so come and keep me company.'

'As long as you don't distract Juliet from her work,' sniffed Mother.

Cecily arrived so promptly that Mother was still there. They practically pushed her out of the door. Juliet picked up her sewing, noticing the eagerness in Cecily's face that said she was ready for a good gossip.

'Rosie tells everyone you're skulking up here to avoid her.'

'I've no desire to get my eyes scratched out.'

They grinned at one another.

'I reckon your old lady in the village will be lucky to survive the month,' said Cecily. 'Rosie is inches from committing murder. The only thing stopping her is that she finishes mid afternoon and takes her time trailing back through the grounds and accidentally on purpose running into Hal Price.'

'Really? I thought you were looking forward to meeting him.'

Cecily pulled a face. 'I was, but he's not the chap for me. Don't get me wrong, he's handsome, but he's more interested in his future career than anything else.'

'That's good, surely? It shows he means to get on.'

'Anyroad, he'll be doing it without me. I don't fancy him.'

She sounded so downcast that Juliet chuckled.

'It's all right for you,' said Cecily. 'You're only fifteen. I'm eighteen and time's running out.'

'So Hal has been bagged by Rosie.'

'If he hasn't, it's not for the want of her trying. Don't tell your mother. If Mrs Whicker gets a sniff of it, there'll be hell to pay.'

Juliet had no intention of telling tales on Rosie, but if Rosie ever started on at her again, she would threaten to without a qualm. Anyroad, if she got the job at Naseby's, that would prove she had no wish to be a Moorside maid.

All she had to do now was tell Mother she had an interview the day after tomorrow, but with Mother half-thrilled and half-angry in anticipation of the final fittings, she couldn't find the right moment. Mother's anger wasn't really anger. It was fear.

She had been angry when Pop lay unconscious following his accident.

'Don't let it upset you, Juliet,' Mrs Grove had advised, her normally matter-of-fact manner softening for once. 'Your mother's scared. With some folk, when they're frightened, it comes out as weeping or dithering. With your mother, it shows as vexation. It makes it difficult for the rest of us, but there you are.'

At last the hour arrived for the fittings. Miss Marchant opened the door and her ladyship entered, looking regal in bottle green with leg-o'-mutton sleeves, followed by the Misses Louisa, Phoebe and Vicky. Behind them came Miss Louisa's maid and the maid her sisters shared.

The young ladies twirled about, looking as if they never wanted to take off their new gowns.

'All these layers of frills around my skirt are wonderful,' said Miss Vicky.

'They will flare when you dance, Miss Vicky,' said Mother.

'The embroidery on mine is exquisite,' said Miss Louisa.

Juliet looked expectantly at Mother, but Mother merely said, 'It's all in the design, Miss Louisa,' and steadfastly kept her eyes on the young ladies. Until now, Juliet had enjoyed their delight, but now she wanted them gone. She felt betrayed.

At last they were assisted out of their ballgowns, and her ladyship's entourage departed.

'Why—?' Juliet began.

'Not now.' Mother fussed in her work basket. 'What have I told you about tidiness in the sewing room? You can see to the mirrors.'

Filled with indignant strength, Juliet lugged them about. At last Mother stopped chasing her own tail and she pounced.

'Why didn't you tell Miss Louisa I did her embroidered panel?'

'She didn't ask.'

'You made it sound like it was your work.'

'I can't have her ladyship thinking the sewing room girl can produce work like that.'

'But I did.'

'That's not the point. The point is that her ladyship should have a high opinion of her personal seamstress. Besides, if you produce good work, it's thanks to my tuition, so it amounts to the same thing. Now let that be the end of it. You'll be back with old Mrs Dancy in no time. Do you imagine Miss Louisa would wish her panel to have been designed by the chit who takes care of the village crone?'

Juliet quivered with indignation. 'I might not go back to old Mrs Dancy. There's a position going at Naseby's. I have an interview tomorrow afternoon.'

Mother's eyes narrowed. 'How dare you do this without reference to me?'

'You should be pleased. Don't you want me to have a better job?'

'Pleased? Don't tell me how to feel. Vexed is how I feel; let down is how I feel. My own daughter gadding off in search of a new job without my permission! What about poor Ella Dancy? What is she supposed to do?'

'Mrs Naseby doesn't need her new assistant until October, so if I get the position, there'll be time to find someone for old Mrs Dancy.'

'You're impossible!'

Mother's hand shot out and delivered a mighty slap across Juliet's cheek. Juliet's eyes popped open in shock. A second passed before she felt the pain. It started as a patch the size of a penny, then it leaked outwards like an ink stain, filling her cheek with hot distress.

'Now see what you made me do,' said Mother.

'I'll come to the interview with you,' Mother declared over breakfast, as if yesterday's outburst had never happened. The end of the sewing room with their dining table smelt of toast and kedgeree. Beside each place was a circular dish with a pat of butter stamped with the Drysdales' coat of arms.

'I'm fifteen, not twelve,' Juliet objected.

'Mrs Naseby will expect me to be there. She's only interested in you because you're my daughter. Have you got your samples ready?'

'Mrs Naseby wants a shop girl, not a dressmaker.'

'Get them out and I'll choose the best ones.'

Juliet had slung her samples in the back of the cupboard the day they moved in and hadn't looked at them since. Dratted things! Nana Adeline had made Mother and Auntie Clara work on samples of different types of sewing when they were growing up, and Mother had followed suit with her. Every time she waded through a sample of pin-tucking or French pleating, it had to be an improvement on the earlier sample, which was then discarded. For Mother and Auntie Clara, the idea had been to build up a body of work to show the mademoiselle of a salon, who might take them on, but for Juliet the purpose had been . . . non-existent. The cutter of old Mrs Dancy's toenails hardly needed to be an expert in blanket stitch.

Now she sifted through her samples with pride and a desire to improve. Who would have thought it? Glancing round to ensure Mother wasn't watching, she popped her embroidery design in the basket.

She categorically was not going to have Mother waltzing into

Naseby's, treating the interview as if it was for the greater glory of Agnes Harper, so she lied about the time Mrs Naseby expected her, then slipped out far earlier than she really needed to, scurrying across the stable yard and onto the back drive. She would be horrendously early, but it was better to hang about in the market square than be accompanied by Mother.

'Excuse me.'

She jumped, tiny pulses springing into action all over her body. A young man had stepped out from the shrubbery. He was unshaven and beneath his cap his hair was too long. His shirt was collarless and, instead of a tie, he wore a neckerchief.

'I didn't mean to scare you. I'm looking for one of the maids at the big house. Her name's Rosie.'

So this was Hal Price. What was all the fuss about? Cecily had called him handsome and Rosie had claimed him for herself. Well, she was welcome to him. He was nowt special. Rosie went down a notch or two in Juliet's estimation. Much as she disliked, even feared, Rosie, she had expected her to have better taste than this.

'Can you send her out to me?' he asked.

Why not? It would kill a bit of time and save her having to hang about so long in Birkfield.

'It'll take me a few minutes.'

'I'll wait in there.' He jerked one thumb at the shrubbery. 'Just tell her to walk down the back drive.'

She returned to the house. Rosie should arrive back from old Mrs Dancy's about now. Yes – there she was, entering the stable yard from the other side.

'What do you want?' Rosie demanded as she drew near.

'There's no need to take that tone. I'm doing you a favour. Hal's waiting—'

'Keep your voice down!' Rosie hissed. 'Where?'

'He said to walk down the back drive. He'll find you.'

A smile played across Rosie's full lips and her eyes sparkled beneath her finely arched eyebrows. She was a real beauty and no mistake. 'I'll freshen up first.' She walked away without another word.

'Thanks, Juliet,' Juliet murmured.

She hurried on her way, having no desire to be anywhere near when the lovebirds flew into each other's arms. It was odd to go down the back drive, knowing that somewhere in the shrubbery, Hal Price was watching her pass. Uncomfortable. It was a relief to reach the gatekeeper's lodge and strike out for the path down the hill.

When the clock in the market square chimed half past four, she opened the door and entered Naseby's, setting the shop bell jingling.

'You're prompt, I see,' said Mrs Naseby. 'That's important.' She frowned. 'But it doesn't go in your favour that you combined this interview with doing your shopping.'

Juliet placed her basket on the counter. 'It's samples of my sewing. Mother thought you'd wish to see them.'

Mrs Naseby glanced at them. 'Seams, darts . . . accordion pleating . . . Excellent workmanship, but it wasn't necessary to bring them. Wait – what's this?'

'It's my design for the embroidered panel on Miss Louisa's ballgown.'

'I like the way the ivy makes the colours stand out. Still, it won't butter no parsnips in the shop. Suppose a customer buys goods to the value of one and thruppence three farthings and pays with half a crown. What change does she require?'

They used to do a lot of this at school. 'One and tuppence farthing.'

There were more questions like that, then Mrs Naseby opened some of the shallow drawers in which her wares were kept, asking questions like 'How could this braid be used?' and 'Which of these ribbons would be best for a child's bonnet?' Juliet did her best to answer, wanting the job more with each passing minute.

'I think you'll suit,' Mrs Naseby said at last. 'Dora finishes on the last day of September, which is a Friday, so you can start on the Saturday.'

'Thank you, Mrs Naseby.' Juliet threw her arms round the shopkeeper. Later she would die of embarrassment, but right now, she didn't care.

'Eh, get on with you.' But Mrs Naseby didn't sound annoyed. 'I pay weekly and until you're sixteen, your wages will go to your mother.'

It took some of the gloss off Juliet's happiness, but that was just her being daft. Some girls didn't see a penny of their wages until they turned twenty-one.

'You look chirpy,' said the gatekeeper's wife as she entered the grounds.

Tempting as it was to share her good news, she held her tongue. Mother was going to be vexed enough, without others knowing before she did.

Juliet hummed to herself as she walked up the back drive. A violent rustling in the shrubbery brought her up short. Leaves swayed and Rosie burst through, face bruised, blood smeared across her temple. She clutched the front of her blouse to her, but there was no disguising the rent that started at the collar and worked downwards.

'Rosie . . .'

Rosie staggered towards her, limping badly. One shoe was missing, but it was more than that causing her limp. Her face was white, her clothes disarranged, shoulders caved in.

'You bitch.' Rosie's voice was quiet, filled with tears, though her eyes were dry. 'Leave me alone,' she hissed as Juliet went to her. 'Don't touch me. This is your fault. You said it were Hal. Looked like Hal, did he?'

The hairs on Juliet's arms prickled. 'I've never seen Hal.'

'You stupid, stupid bitch.'

Rosie grabbed Juliet's arm, letting go of the front of her blouse. A flap of fabric flopped down, exposing—Juliet looked away, but not before she had glimpsed a mixture of flesh and purple bruising. Rosie uttered a cry in which rage and tears spurted out as one. Flinging Juliet aside, she covered herself again.

'You're going to get me up to the attic without being seen, do you hear? And you won't say a word. I'll say I tripped on the stairs. And if anyone gets told any different, so help me, I'll slash your face open with broken glass. Understand?'

Juliet had been at Naseby's barely a week when a message came one morning to say Mrs Naseby's daughter had had her baby, and Mrs Naseby immediately set off, promising to be back before the shop shut for dinner. Juliet served a couple of customers, then the door flew open and in dashed her old teacher.

'Juliet, what a surprise. How long have you worked here?'

'I've just started. How may I help you?'

'I've torn my jacket sleeve. Can it be mended today? I have an appointment straight after school. Is Mrs Naseby here?'

'Not at the moment, but I can mend it.'

'Can you?' Miss Bradley's pretty face expressed a mixture of hope and doubt.

'I've a lot of experience of sewing.'

'Of course you have. I was forgetting. Here.' She took care removing her jacket. 'I must hurry back before playtime ends. I hope Mr Ferguson doesn't see me or I'll be fined for dressing inappropriately.'

On closer inspection, the tear was a full-blown rent. Juliet settled down to it, putting it aside each time a customer came in. If she looked too busy to serve, she could lose her job.

Mrs Naseby came bustling in with a beaming smile. 'Put the kettle on, Juliet. That's a fair old walk.'

She made tea and showed Mrs Naseby the mending. 'I hope I did the right thing in starting, only Miss Bradley needs it in a hurry.'

Mrs Naseby scrutinised it over the tops of her spectacles. 'Putting in new lining was the right thing to do. And look at it, all the stitches the same size. It's perfect.'

Juliet blinked. So accustomed was she to meagre crumbs of praise from Mother that these generous words took her breath away. 'Are you going to finish it?' she asked, expecting to have it taken off her.

'Not if you can produce work of this standard.'

More praise. Gratification warmed her. She worked on the mend in between customers and all through her dinner hour, finishing shortly before the end of school. Mrs Naseby checked her work and smiled her approval.

'Your mother has taught you well. I'll show you how to write up the bill and I'll pay you one-third of the fee. When you've been here two years, I'll pay you half.'

'Does that mean you'll put more mending my way?'

'Aye, dressmaking too, if you're up to it. Mrs Cottrell is coming over from Ladyfield to be measured for her new Sunday best. Me and thee can work on it together and I'll see how you shape. I pay a higher rate for dressmaking. Sewing money will be paid straight to you an' all, not put in with your wages.'

'Thank you. I won't let you down.'

'Dressmaking is done on the premises, but mends and alterations you take home and do in your own time.'

Juliet parcelled up the jacket and the bill, and raced round to St Chad's.

Miss Bradley was thrilled. 'Such service – and what perfect needlework.'

To have her sewing called perfect not once but twice almost made her heart jump out of her chest. She had received more praise today than she had from Mother in the whole of her life. That was how it felt, anyroad.

She couldn't wait to get home to tell Mother, though she would have to be careful how she said it. She didn't want Mother calling her big-headed.

When she reached the gatekeeper's lodge, instead of heading for the back drive, she went the other way. She wasn't keen on the back drive any more, after what had happened to Rosie. If she went the other way, through his lordship's parkland, she could weave her way round out of sight of the house and enter the stable yard from the other side.

At this distance from the house, wild flowers were allowed to grow. Yellow stars of St John's wort and wood sage's long spikes of yellowy-green above its heart-shaped leaves brightened the ground. Above, sunshine struck leaves that were on the turn, greens giving way to gold and russet. It was a warm afternoon, but a snap in the air betokened the change of season. Pop had cherished his outdoor life, and while Juliet now loved her sewing, she also loved being outside.

'Help! Help!'

Rosie flashed into her mind – Rosie, shocked and bruised after the attack. But this was a child's voice, reedy with panic. A small girl in a grubby cotton dress dashed through the trees, hair streaming behind her, hair ribbons half-undone and clinging on for dear life. Juliet had one moment in which to brace herself before the child slammed into her.

'Steady on, chick. What's wrong?'

Scared eyes and a button nose turned up to her. 'Oh, miss, it's our Sophie. She's fell down a hole, going after Mo, and they've both broke their legs. Come quick. They might *die*.'

'Show me.'

The child dragged her to a part of the park where the trees grew more densely. They burst into a grassy clearing with a low mound in the middle.

'There, miss.'

Juliet dropped the child's hand. There wasn't a hole to be seen. The girl ran ahead and fell to her knees at the base of the mound, pointing to a black gap at its base, like an oversized letter box.

The child put her mouth to the hole. 'I've brought a lady, our Sophie.'

Juliet gently pushed her aside. 'Sophie! Can you hear me?'

A muffled moan wavered through the gap.

'Are you hurt?'

'It's me foot . . . and Mo's leg is funny. He has to lie down. He's panting.'

Juliet frowned at the child beside her. 'Mo?'

'The dog. He went in first and sort of screamed, then Sophie went in and she screamed an' all.'

'It sounds like they've had a nasty fall. I want you to stop here and talk to Sophie while I fetch help from the big house.'

'Don't leave us.'

'I have to, chick.'

The thud of footsteps made her look round. A young man, corduroy jacket flapping open, pounded into the clearing, with another child bobbing behind. He strode across, the gaiters that protected him from boot tops to just below the knees of his twill trousers declaring him to be an outdoor worker. He dropped to his knees beside her; she moved so he could see the hole.

'I gather there's a girl and a dog trapped inside.' Although he spoke with urgency, there was no panic in his voice. He smelt of grass and earth and woodsmoke.

'I don't know how far they fell.'

'I've been looking over plans of the grounds recently.' His eyes were light brown – not hazel – proper brown, only not the usual dark brown. 'If I'm right, this is a hiding place built in the Civil War. It was sealed up two-hundred-odd years ago. I can't get through this gap, but you might just about be able to. Will you try?'

Her hands went clammy at the thought, but she nodded.

He looked over his shoulder. 'You two, run to the big house. Fetch help.' He turned back to Juliet. 'Don't worry. I won't let you take any risks.' A smile flashed across his face. 'We don't want to add to the heap of bodies at the bottom. You're going to lie on your front and shuffle in feet first. I'll hold you and I won't let go. Feel around with your feet. If there's nothing but wall, I'll pull you out, but there might be steps if we're near the old entrance.'

Lying down, she wriggled backwards. Her skirt bunched up, so she stopped and scooped it round her legs, then tried again, pushing herself backwards, dimly aware of the young man's murmurs of encouragement, the sound giving her confidence as she fed feet and calves through the narrow hole. As her hips wriggled through, the smallness of the gap and the emptiness behind her made her insides feel wobbly, and she almost clawed her way back out again.

'Don't panic. The ground under your tummy: is it crumbling? If it is, even the tiniest bit, I'll pull you out now.'

'It's firm.'

'If your feet are to feel about, you need to reverse until your waist is on the edge. I'll lie down in front of you and hold onto your wrists, so whatever happens, you won't fall.'

He settled into position, his hands wrapping warmly around her wrists, strong and sure, the hands of a working man. Not work-coarsened like Pop's after years of toil on the estate, but faintly, reassuringly rough.

Juliet slid further into the hole, legs swinging awkwardly. Then her waist rushed to the edge – the gap was about to swallow her whole – her heart thumped – her hands twisted – the young man's hands moved and grasped hers in his, fingers twining together.

'I've got you. You're safe.'

Her heart raced, and every muscle in her body roared with discomfort. Then her eyes met his and she was aware of nothing but strong hands, a reassuring voice and an unwavering gaze that stilled the pulses jumping madly all around her body. His steadfastness became hers. Her heart delivered an altogether different kind of thump, but that was just the emotion of the moment.

'Are you sure you can do this?'

She nodded, feeling the wall with her toes, gradually swinging one leg at a time in an arc to reach as much wall as possible.

'Anything?' he asked.

'Nothing. Wait.' She clung to his hands. 'I need to slide a bit further . . . There! A ledge . . . steps . . .'

'Made of what? Can you tell? Wood will be rotten.'

'Stone, I think.'

'If I help you through the gap, can you get onto them safely? Safely, mind.'

'Yes.'

'Once you're in there, take your time. Feel your way. It'll be dark.'

With his help, she edged deeper through the gap and onto the top step, her nostrils filling with dank air.

'Sophie,' she called. 'I'm coming.'

She started by putting one hand on the wall and feeling for each step with her toes, but with darkness all around, it felt safer to sit down and shuffle from step to step on her bottom.

Reaching the floor, she coaxed, 'Talk to me, Sophie. Help me find you,' and then crawled across packed earth towards the thin sound of the child's voice. 'There. I've got you. Let's get you out of here.'

'Take Mo first.'

'You're more important. I'll come back for Mo, I promise.'

'You won't find him in the dark. Take him – please.'

It made sense. She let Sophie guide her hands to the dog. She spoke soothingly as she touched its short coat. It was a little creature, a ratter, lying quietly but shaking, poor thing. Carefully, she wrapped it in her jacket and carried it up the steps, holding out the bundle until she was positive it was safely in the young man's hands. Then she returned for Sophie.

'If I crouch down, can you climb on and I'll give you a piggyback up the steps?'

Whimpering, Sophie obeyed. Juliet pushed herself to her feet, finding it harder than she expected. Gingerly, she made her way to the steps, leaning forwards and testing Sophie's weight each time she lifted a foot. By the time she reached the top, her shoulders were ready to unhinge themselves and fall off.

'Down you get.' Her knees were about to crack under the strain. 'Keep your bad foot clear of the step.'

'I've twisted my shirt into a rope,' the young man said through the gap. 'Put the loop over Sophie's head and under her armpits, then hand the end to me and I'll pull her through.'

The little girl had grit. Apart from a couple of sharp gasps, there wasn't a peep out of her as this was accomplished.

'Reach for my wrist,' the young man told Juliet, 'and I'll hold yours. You'll need to take a step into thin air before I can reach your other wrist, then I'll pull you out, but you have to take that step first. Do you trust me?'

She froze, but only for a moment. The hold on her wrist tightened. She stepped sideways. Her stomach swooped and her breath hitched. Then she thrust her free hand upwards – and he seized it, hauling her up through the gap onto the grass. She twisted into a sitting position and he sat beside her, drawing her into a one-armed hug. This close – and him with no shirt, though he did have his waistcoat and jacket on – she caught an eyeful of his chest and stomach, and her face was hot enough to fry an egg on. She made to wriggle free, and he released her immediately, but instead of feeling relieved, she wanted to pull his arm round her again.

She scrambled to her feet.

'We'll soon have you home.' As he spoke to Sophie, he did

up his waistcoat over his grubby, flat stomach. To Juliet, he said, 'What's your name? I want to tell everyone how brave you were.'

'Juliet Harper. My mother is seamstress to her ladyship.'

'I'm Hal Price. My dad's going to be head gardener when my grandfather retires.'

Juliet's heart delivered another of those thumps, and it wasn't just the emotion of the moment. Cecily was right: he was handsome. But Cecily wasn't attracted to him. Why ever not? He was top notch. Capable, resourceful, kind and strong. Top notch.

Chapter Five

Mrs Naseby sent Juliet to buy a bottle of ink. As she walked past the Saturday market, enjoying the stallholders' familiar cries and the earthy scents of freshly pulled vegetables, and the sweet aroma of barley sugar and toffee apples, a shower sent her scurrying for cover and she found herself sharing the awning of the second-hand-clothes stall with Miss Bradley.

'I've been looking at this coat,' said Miss Bradley. 'It's in a sad state. The lining's in tatters and the hem's coming down – but I love the colour. What do you think?'

How flattering to be consulted. 'New lining is easy, and so is the hem. The main problem is this wear on the collar.'

'Can it be repaired?'

'Personally, I'd replace it.'

Miss Bradley frowned. 'But that means finding the same fabric.'

'Use a contrast, and,' she added, suddenly seeing it inside her head, 'trim the cuffs with it too.'

'Will you do all that for me?'

'If Mrs Naseby gives me the job.'

Miss Bradley brought in the coat later that day, and Mrs Naseby helped her select a contrasting fabric. Juliet would have enjoyed doing that, but didn't push herself forward.

'Could Juliet do the alteration?' Miss Bradley asked. 'She did such a good job on my jacket.'

'Certainly. She is permitted to do mending and alterations, but she isn't doing dressmaking yet; though, between me and thee,' and Mrs Naseby didn't trouble to lower her voice, even though Juliet was standing by with her ears flapping, 'it won't be long before I start giving her dressmaking to do. She's been assisting me on a Sunday-best tweed costume and her work is of a high standard. I only wanted a shop girl when I employed her, but she's much more than that.'

Energy rushed through Juliet's veins. Later, she took Miss Bradley's coat home with her, planning as she made her way through the parkland's evening darkness how to tackle the work.

'Good evening.'

Hal! She turned instinctively towards his voice.

'I hope I didn't startle you.' He came towards her. 'I've been hoping to see you to make sure you're none the worse for our adventure.'

'I'm fine, thanks. I've been wondering about Sophie.'

'A bad sprain, nothing more. She's one of the gardeners' daughters. And Mo is on the mend too. If you're heading for the house, I'll walk part of the way with you.' He fell in step beside her. 'That's a big bundle. Shall I carry it for you?'

'It's not heavy. It's a coat.' She explained the work that needed doing, then bit her lip. You couldn't expect a man to be interested in sewing.

But Hal said, 'Do you intend to run your own shop or dressmaking service one day?'

'I – I haven't given it any thought. I've only just started at Naseby's.'

'Early days, eh? Still, it's good to plan ahead. I know what I'm going to do.'

'Be head gardener?'

He laughed. 'That's what Ma would like: follow in Dad's footsteps, but I want more than that. Don't misunderstand. I love gardening, but I want to design gardens – and not just gardens but entire grounds. I attend the Mechanics' Institute in Birkfield two nights a week, so I can better myself. I do maths, geometry and bookkeeping. Grandad says you can't do a job properly if you can't handle money.'

'I suppose not.'

'And I go to a drawing master by the name of Charlesworth.'

'To learn how to draw flowers?'

'We've done some work on individual plants, but that's for pleasure. I'm interested in sketching lifelike flower beds, as well as things like rockeries, fountains and pieces of garden architecture. I'll have to be able to do all that as well as drawing plans to scale.'

'I see.'

'It's an honour to be taught by Mr Charlesworth. He teaches the young Drysdale ladies, so I had to have permission from Mr Nugent before I could go to him. If we'd still been living in our old place, I'd never have been taught by Lady Arabella's children's tutor, but fortunately for me, that isn't the case at Moorside.'

'His lordship's good like that.'

'So everybody says. Mr Nugent admires ambition as long as it's not misplaced and he says he'll keep an eye out for an opening for me.'

But not too soon – please, not too soon. 'It sounds . . .' She was going to say 'interesting', but anyone could say that. She wanted

67

him to know she had caught his enthusiasm. '. . . challenging.'

He stopped, and she turned to him eagerly.

'I go that way now.' He indicated with a tilt of his head. 'Will you be all right seeing yourself home from here?'

'Of course. I use this route every day now.'

'G'night, then.'

He strode into the darkness. She had to remind herself to continue on her way, thoughts of Hal keeping her warm all the way to the house, but she had to fix her mind firmly on Miss Bradley's coat when she reached the sewing room.

'Show me when you've finished,' Mother ordered. 'I'm not having second-rate work going out of my sewing room.'

'Mother! I don't do second-rate work.'

'Well, see that you don't.'

Juliet worked hard on the alterations. The contrasting fabric being her own idea made the work feel extra special.

Mother checked the finished thing with sharp eyes and tightened lips, then thrust the coat at her with a curt, 'I've seen worse.'

But when Mrs Naseby examined it – and her scrutiny was every bit as close as Mother's – she declared it an excellent piece of sewing, and Miss Bradley, when she collected it, said, 'You've made it look like new.'

Why was Mother so set against praising her?

Miss Bradley came into the shop with a friend. Beside Miss Bradley's slender figure, her companion was plump, though light on her feet.

'I have this blouse pattern,' she told Juliet. 'Can you show me suitable trimmings?'

The moment she looked at the pattern, and at the lady holding it, Juliet had an idea. 'Have you thought of altering the collar?'

'Listen to her, Grace,' Miss Bradley advised. 'This is the girl who worked wonders on my coat.' She turned to Juliet. 'Why change it?'

For a moment, she was nonplussed. Miss Bradley's friend was a little dumpling and the stand-up collar would make her look like she was overflowing with chins, but she couldn't say that. 'A softer line might be prettier. Let me show you.' Taking a pencil and paper, she sketched the basic shape of the blouse before adding a gently rounded collar.

'I don't know,' the friend said. 'It's so different – and she's very young.'

'Juliet has an excellent eye,' said Miss Bradley. 'Try this collar. Tack it on and see how you look in it. Juliet will make a paper pattern for you – won't you, Juliet?'

Juliet thought the friend was about to refuse, but instead she dimpled and said, 'No harm in trying.' She handed over the pattern. 'You'll need this for the measurements.'

'I'll have it ready for you tomorrow.'

Miss Bradley's friend duly collected the pattern, and a day or two later, Miss Bradley appeared, all smiles. The collar was a success.

'I've made arrangements to extend your education, Juliet,' she said.

Hal sprang to mind. 'At the Mechanics' Institute?'

'No, that's for men and boys. When you're explaining how a garment will look, wouldn't you like to draw it properly? That picture you did of my friend's blouse was rather childish, if I may say so, and therefore I've arranged drawing lessons. My friend is Miss Charlesworth and her brother is an artist. He'll teach you for an hour once a week for six weeks in return for altering a dress that belonged to his late mother to fit Miss Charlesworth.'

Mr Charlesworth! He taught Hal. But caution prevailed.

'I'll have to ask my mother.'

Mrs Naseby joined in. 'Tell her I said it was a good idea, because it might be of use in the shop. She can't argue with that.'

Was Mrs Naseby aware of how difficult Mother could be? Would she be difficult about this? Juliet thought of the embroidered panel and it seemed entirely possible. What if she went over Mother's head? There would be hell to pay, obviously, but wouldn't that be better than being turned down flat just because Mother had got out of bed the wrong side?

That evening, heart pounding, she knocked on Mrs Whicker's sitting-room door.

'Come.'

Mrs Whicker was a mountain of a woman, but her private domain was the last word in daintiness, with chintzy armchairs, small tables and whatnots with barley-sugar-twisted legs, and more pretty china than you could shake a stick at. Mrs Whicker and Cook sat beside the crackling fire, with a cut-glass decanter on a table between them. They each held a matching glass, containing a red liquid, and judging by the hearty flush in their cheeks, it wasn't raspberry cordial they were imbibing.

Juliet bobbed a curtsey. 'Please may I have a word?'

Mrs Whicker signalled to her to speak, and she explained Miss Bradley's proposal.

'Mrs Naseby thinks it would be useful, but I know Mr Charlesworth tutors the young ladies, so . . .'

Mrs Whicker's frowning countenance suggested refusal.

'Begging your pardon,' Juliet added, 'but Mr Price's grandson, Hal, has lessons off Mr Charlesworth. Mr Nugent gave permission, because it's for his work. Please may I have permission, since it's for my work?'

'Hm.' Mrs Whicker knocked back a thoughtful slug of the hard stuff. 'Mr Nugent granted permission, did he? I'll speak to him.'

'Thank you, Mrs Whicker.'

Juliet withdrew. Was she wrong to have gone behind Mother's back? It felt like the only way.

Agnes had to admit the drawing lessons gave Juliet a confident hand at sketching garments – but she would admit it only to herself. No point in giving the girl a big head. In truth, she was startled by Juliet's swift progress.

'Don't waste time on it,' she advised. 'It isn't as though you'll need it much. You're only a shop girl. Why Mrs Naseby thought it would be a good idea I can't imagine. And as for Mrs Whicker and Mr Nugent taking an interest, well . . .'

She let the sentence trail off. It wouldn't do to say anything against two such important people.

Outside church, though, it was a different story. Here, she could be suitably proud as she announced, 'Juliet is being taught by the young ladies' drawing master,' and lapped up the gratifying murmurs.

'What is Mr Charlesworth teaching you, Juliet?' Ella asked.

'To draw garments, obviously, but also to draw people. Not in detail. It's only to get the proportions correct.'

'How will that help with your sewing?' Beatrice enquired.

'If I'm going to alter something, or make a suggestion, I'll be able to draw what it'll look like.'

'Perhaps Mr Charlesworth will let you pay for more lessons in the same way,' said Ella.

Vexation flared in Agnes. Everybody was fussing round Juliet and it wasn't right. 'Everything Juliet knows she learnt from me. There can't be many girls who have had the grounding she's had.'

'She sounds prouder of herself than she does of Juliet,' someone murmured, but although Agnes looked round quickly, she couldn't detect who it was.

Those words niggled at her all the way home. It was a cold morning, but she didn't have the energy to stride out and keep warm.

'I wonder if I might have more lessons,' said Juliet.

'Certainly not. Goodness, to hear you talk, anyone would think you were going to design garments. You've already learnt more than you'll ever need, and I'll tell Mrs Whicker so. Let that be the end of it.'

Others might mourn the passing of summer but, to Hal, autumn was nature's greatest glory. There could be no better sight than that of the sun pouring through the park's vast canopy of gold, bronze and flame. As he went about his work, raking up drifts of crunching leaves and lifting tender perennials, he enjoyed the mixture of vibrant and pastel hues in the flower beds and looked forward to the first frosts, which would engrave sparkling patterns on the gardens as autumn faded and clusters of berries glowed in the welcome brilliance of the winter sun.

Twice a week, he tramped down the hill to the Institute. His folks were baffled by his ambition. Why couldn't he be satisfied with a life of gardening, like his dad and grandad? It was an open secret that Ma had come to Moorside with high hopes that he would meet a girl and find himself halfway up the aisle before he knew it.

'I can't settle down for years yet, Ma,' he had told her many a time.

'You could, if you'd be a proper gardener. Look at the cottages his lordship provides for his gardeners. Much better than we had at our old place. And one is empty at the moment. I mentioned to Mr Nugent t'other day—'

His senses sprang to attention. 'You mentioned what?'

'I asked if, should you need it . . .'

Oh hell. Now he would have to seek out Mr Nugent and explain that Ma had it all wrong. How embarrassing. But he couldn't have Mr Nugent of all people thinking him eager to wed or he wouldn't bother looking for an opportunity for Hal to progress.

Poor Ma. He couldn't contemplate marriage for years yet.

But . . .

But if he were to consider it, he had to admit to being rather taken by Juliet. She was on the young side, admittedly, but her features were finely honed and when she smiled, her face was lit by an inner radiance that showed the beautiful woman she would become. Moreover, when he had told her of his ambition, she had appeared interested. Most girls ran a mile at that point, foreseeing an engagement that would last years.

He had met Juliet crossing the park a few times now, each time learning a bit more about her and winkling further information out of Grandad. She had got that shop job through her own efforts and, according to his sister, Caroline, word in the village was that she was skilful with her needle. A highly capable girl, was Juliet Harper, though he didn't think she realised how capable. Imagine walking out with a girl like that. She would understand and respect his plans. She would share them, and he would encourage her to develop her own.

He couldn't settle down for years yet, but even so . . . might Juliet be the girl for him?

73

Chapter Six

January brought heavy snowfall that hushed the landscape and stilled the air beneath skies that dazzled after days of sagging with the weight of the snow. Cecily took her petticoats and stockings to bed each night and didn't emerge from beneath the covers until she had wriggled into them. Frost patterned the windowpanes inside as well as out, and she needed the long run down the backstairs to warm her up.

The outdoor world might look serene but it had them all running round like blue-arsed flies. Fires needed tending, requiring numerous journeys with coal scuttles and ash pans. The front hall had to be mopped and dried every hour, regardless of whether a member of the family had walked any snow in, and the main corridor below stairs was cleaned hourly as well. There were hand-warmers, foot-warmers and hot-water pigs to be filled, and endless requests for tea and hot chocolate to be attended to.

Juliet was stranded in Birkfield.

'I hope Mrs Naseby doesn't mind,' Mrs Harper fretted.

'Not a lot she can do about it if she does,' Cecily shrugged.

When the weather released its iron hold and the thaw set in, she noticed Mrs Harper looked pale and tired, though what did she have to be weak and wan about? She led a privileged life in the sewing room. But when Cecily asked her if she felt well, Mrs Harper's snappy reply sent her stalking from the room. So much for trying to be kind.

Leaving Mrs Harper to her solitary midday meal, Cecily went downstairs, looking forward to a hearty stew and dumplings, the aroma of which had tantalised her every time she passed the kitchen.

It wasn't until the roly-poly pudding and custard was served that she noticed the empty place: Rosie. Where was she? Before she could ask, Thomasina said, 'Cecily,' in a voice that made her sound like a teacher, and Cecily subsided. What was going on?

At the end of the meal, Mr Durbin stood. 'Parlourmaids and chambermaids, remain behind. Everyone else, please leave.'

With murmurs of surprise and curious glances, the rest departed, leaving the housemaids shifting in their seats.

'Mrs Whicker and I will interview you one at a time on a serious matter in Mrs Whicker's sitting room. Thomasina, no one is to return here following her interview. After you, Mrs Whicker.'

Immediately the door shut behind them, all eyes turned on Thomasina, who held up a hand. 'You'll have to wait till you're interviewed.'

When it was Cecily's turn to enter the housekeeper's sitting room, her heart banged so hard it almost threw her curtsey off balance.

'I require a truthful answer,' said Mrs Whicker. 'Rosie has got herself into trouble and refuses to name the father. Do you know who it might be?'

Rosie – in trouble? Cecily's jaw dropped. 'No, Mrs Whicker.' She wanted to say, 'Rosie? Are you sure? *Rosie?*'

'Think carefully before you say no,' advised Mr Durbin. 'If we know the father's name, we can arrange a marriage.'

'Has she shown an interest in a young man?' Mrs Whicker asked.

'Followers aren't permitted,' said Cecily.

'Rosie clearly broke that rule. Now we need his name. It's Rosie's only hope.'

A name did spring to mind – but why had Rosie kept her mouth shut?

'Out with it, girl,' Mrs Whicker ordered. 'You clearly know something.'

'Please, Mrs Whicker. Rosie was interested in someone, but she hasn't mentioned him in a while.'

'He undoubtedly cast her aside once he had had his way with her,' said Mr Durbin. 'His name?'

'Hal Price, sir.'

Juliet toiled upstairs. Her legs felt wobbly after that hard slog up the hill. She was grateful to Mrs Naseby, who had been kindness itself to her unexpected guest and today had said she could leave early to be sure of getting home in daylight. She walked into the sewing room. Mother was sitting in the wingback chair, facing the fireplace. Juliet didn't blame her on a day like today, but she was surprised when Mother didn't jump up to greet her after her week's absence. Standing beside the chair, she saw Mother was sound asleep and tried to draw back, but Mother woke with a jump.

'Oh – it's you. Goodness, for a moment I thought Mrs Whicker had caught me napping.' She sat bolt upright in horror. 'Have I slept all afternoon?'

'No. Mrs Naseby let me leave early.'

Mother flopped back. 'I just needed forty winks. My eyes get tired doing close work in this winter light.'

Juliet crouched in front of the fire, gingerly peeling gloves from fingers tingling their way back to life. 'Give me a minute and I'll lend a hand.' But when she returned from putting away her things, Mother still looked tired, so she offered, 'Why don't I make a start while you snatch a few more minutes?'

She was taken aback when Mother immediately sighed herself to sleep. She positioned herself on the window seat to catch the best of the remaining light.

There was a tap on the door. She bounded across to find Cecily, holding a tray.

'Cook sent a hot drink for you.'

She tried to come in, but Mother mustn't be caught slumbering, so Juliet barred her way, trying to take the tray from her. They tussled for a moment, then Cecily let go.

'There's loads to tell you,' Cecily whispered. 'Come and sit in the linen cupboard.'

Bringing her hot chocolate, she followed Cecily along the landing into the cupboard. Cupboard! It was bigger than her old bedroom in the cottage. Crisply folded linen was stacked on shelves. The air smelt of fresh washing and lavender, with the dull tang of mothballs.

The hot chocolate cooled untouched as she listened to the tale of Rosie's downfall and the interrogation of the maids a couple of hours ago. Dread expanded inside her chest.

'. . . so I said Hal.'

'Hal? You blamed Hal?'

Cecily's face reddened. 'I didn't blame him, exactly, but they could see I knew summat. Mind you, I feel right rotten now. He's been hauled into the estate office. He's up before Mr Nugent.'

'Where's the estate office?'

Dumping her drink on a shelf, she dragged Cecily to the backstairs and pushed her ahead. Cecily led the way to the ground floor, stopping beside a door that gave onto the main house. She turned anxious eyes on Juliet, but Juliet gave her a shove. Cecily opened the door and crept through. It was surprisingly gloomy, then Juliet realised they had emerged beneath a vast staircase. Following her friend from its shadow, she beheld for the first time a part of the Drysdales' home. This was only their front hall, not a proper room, but it was as big as a church, with a tiled floor and ancient woodwork.

Cecily darted across to where a corridor started. 'That door down there.'

'Thanks. Get back to your duties.'

Cecily scurried away. Juliet ghosted down the corridor. Taking the doorknob in one hand, she knocked with the other and walked in without waiting. Straight across the room was a large window, framed by brocade curtains and pelmet, through which, in the twilight, humps of snow showed where plants grew in a walled garden. At right angles to window and door stood a desk, behind which sat Mr Nugent, flanked by Mr Durbin and Mrs Whicker. Hal stood in front of the desk. He held his cloth cap, but wasn't twisting it in a subservient way. Behind him were two men whose corduroy and twill spoke of their outdoor work, and whose ages suggested they must be his father and grandfather.

All eyes turned on her, and Juliet's determination almost faltered.

'How dare you?' Mrs Whicker boomed. 'Mr Nugent, I do apologise. This young person is the sewing room girl.'

'I'm aware of her identity,' Mr Nugent answered quietly. 'Let us hear what she has to say for herself.'

His voice was smooth and low, and Juliet's thumping heart slowed in response. Without raising his voice, Mr Nugent held the situation under his control. Placing his hands on the arms of his chair, he came to his feet. Was he about to have her thrown out? She tried to blot out her awareness of Hal's proximity and kept her gaze fixed on his lordship's man of business, so he would see how honest and trustworthy she was. She hid a gulp as he walked round the desk and positioned himself in front of her, holding her gaze all the time. Should she lower her eyes? But if she looked away, might she appear dishonest?

'What have you to say to me, Juliet?'

'Begging your pardon, Mr Nugent, but if Hal's here because of what's happened to Rosie, it wasn't him. It was someone else. I know because . . . I was there.'

'You were there?' demanded Mrs Whicker.

'I understand your concern, Mrs Whicker.' Mr Nugent didn't remove his gaze from Juliet's. 'Indeed, I share it. But it behoves us to allow Juliet to explain.' He nodded to her, a tiny nod, as if they were the only two in the room. 'Go ahead.'

She didn't want to look up at him any more, not while she spoke of something so disturbing, but he didn't look away, so she couldn't either. She described her encounter with the young man whom she had assumed was Hal, and how, later, Rosie had staggered from the shrubbery, bloodied and bruised. Mr Nugent watched her the whole time. Was he looking for a flicker of a lie? She felt peeled and defenceless, but wouldn't drop her gaze.

At last he lifted his gaze away. Juliet surreptitiously rolled her shoulders. She had a crick in her neck.

Mr Nugent looked beyond her to the Price men. 'Thank you for your cooperation, gentlemen. I'm sure you appreciate this matter had to be investigated.' He nodded to them in polite dismissal and they left. Mr Nugent turned to the butler and the housekeeper. 'Well, Mrs Whicker, there's your answer. I'll leave you to take whatever steps you deem necessary.'

Sourness invaded Juliet's mouth. Poor Rosie. And all because Juliet had assumed that man was Hal.

Juliet set off early the next morning. Mrs Naseby had said it wouldn't matter if she was late, but she wanted to be punctual. Grooms and gardeners alike were clearing the stable yard of snow and slush.

'I'm reet glad to see thee, young miss.' Here was Mr Harold Price beside her. 'That were a grand thing you did yesterday for our Hal.'

'I just told the truth.'

Footsteps came crunching towards her from behind. She knew, she just knew, it was Hal, and her heartbeat quickened.

'Juliet.' He smiled at her. 'Thank you. From the bottom of my heart, thank you.'

'As soon as I heard, I had to speak up for you.'

If only she could have lingered, but he had to get on with his job and she had to get to Birkfield. Her heart sang as she tramped across the park and towards the hill.

As she neared the halfway point on her way down, she was surprised to see someone sitting on the bench: a figure with a shawl bundled around a coat. She must be mad to sit there on a day like this. Drawing level, Juliet felt a new kind of coldness as the girl's head turned and Rosie stared at her, her eyes almost black in a face pinched with cold. Two carpetbags hunched by her feet.

Juliet made an instinctive move towards her, wanting to offer compassion, but Rosie's glare stopped her.

'Come to gloat, have you?' Rosie demanded.

'I always come this way.'

With a jerk of her chin, Rosie looked away, fixing her gaze across the valley.

Juliet took a step closer. 'I'm sorry about what happened to you.'

'Which part? Being attacked or getting chucked out of my job?'

'That man asked for you by name. What was I supposed to do?'

Rosie's face swung round again. 'You could have said "Are you Hal?" instead of taking it for granted. You could have used a bit of intelligence.'

'I'm sorry, Rosie.'

'Well, that makes everything right, doesn't it.'

'What will you do?'

'I'll walk down the hill and take my pick of all the jobs on offer. That's why I'm sitting here. I'm considering all the offers I've had and deciding which suits me best.'

Juliet flinched. Was this her fault? She wanted to help, but there was nothing she could do.

'Clear off, bitch. You make me sick . . . Oh no, wait, it's not you making me sick, is it? It's the brat.'

Rosie looked away again. Juliet stood there, not knowing what to do. At last, she set off down the hill, trying to concentrate on keeping her footing, but her eyes were brimming with tears.

She rushed into Naseby's, expecting to feel relieved and . . . and safe as the door shut behind her. Hard as she tried to concentrate on her work, Rosie was there in her mind, and she found herself staring at nothing in odd moments. Not that there were many of those. Now that the thaw had set in, Naseby's had a rush of customers, and when she wasn't busy serving, she was mopping the floor clean of dirty footprints.

'Take care going home,' said Mrs Naseby at the end of the day, as Juliet piled on her outdoor things.

Would she bump into Rosie? She made it to the edge of town without an encounter and started up the hill. What if Rosie was still on the bench? But that was a stupid fear. Even so, she felt a rush of relief when she passed the bench and it was unoccupied. At last, she neared Moorside.

As she was picking her way along a dug-out path beside the vegetable garden wall, she heard men's voices around the corner. The path was slippery, and she was in the middle of a delicious daydream in which she lost her footing just as Hal appeared round the corner, caught her in his arms and pulled her to him – when her feet skidded and every limb flew in a different direction before she ended up dumped on the ground. At once there were voices around her and hands picking her up. As she was set on her feet, a twang of pain speared through her foot and exploded in her ankle. She sagged and was hauled up again by Bert, a senior groom.

'There, now, got your footing? Tom, didn't I tell you to keep these paths salted?'

'Aye, and I did.' Tom grinned hugely. 'It's not the ice what did for her. She skidded on that.'

Her heart sank to see the smeared remains of a pile of dog dirt.

'Turned your ankle, lass?' asked Bert. He scooped her up and carried her into the kitchen, causing a flutter among the staff. 'Took a tumble,' he explained, depositing her on a chair.

'Went arse over tit in a pile of dog shit,' Tom declared, loud enough for the world and his wife to hear. 'Begging your pardon, Cook.'

'I should think so an' all,' said Cook. 'Language like that in my kitchen.'

But Juliet was sure she was the only one to hear the rebuke. Everyone else was too busy laughing.

Goodness! What a lucky escape. Had Juliet been helped into the sewing room just five minutes earlier, Agnes would have been discovered sound asleep. The mere thought turned her knees to mush. She injected extra brightness into her voice to show how awake and alert she was. Juliet looked pale as Bert deposited her in the wingback chair. Was it still warm from the hour Agnes had spent slumbering in it?

'A sprain,' Mrs Whicker informed her. 'She won't be able to get down the hill for a while, that's for certain.'

'She can make herself useful here. She can start immediately.'

'She's had a nasty shock. A nap would be the best thing.'

'There's no napping in my sewing room,' said Agnes. When Mrs Whicker had gone, she looked at Juliet. 'It'll be a help, having you here. And you never know, Mrs Whicker might even pay you, because Mrs Naseby certainly won't.' She handed Juliet a velvet jacket.

'I thought you'd have finished this,' Juliet said. 'Isn't Miss Phoebe due for her final fitting tomorrow?'

'I'm a bit behind, but it doesn't matter now you're here. A blessing in disguise, that sprain.'

Within hours, Juliet's foot was purple and swollen.

'You won't be going to the shop for a few days,' Agnes declared. 'Working together in the sewing room: it'll be like the old days before the house party.'

Like the old days, Mother had said, but it wasn't. Never before had Mother gone slinking off to have naps. Never before had she abdicated responsibility, dumping all the work on Juliet's shoulders. But now . . .

Mother sighed and rubbed her eyes, setting her work aside. 'Finish this seam for me. I need forty winks.'

'What if someone comes in?'

'The wing chair has its back to the door, and with my work basket on the table, it'll look like I'm tidying it. If anyone comes, you must drop something, or speak loudly – I don't know, but make sure to rouse me.'

Two minutes later she was asleep. Juliet didn't know whether to be flabbergasted or indignant. So much for no napping in the sewing room!

When the same thing had happened several times, she voiced her concern.

'It's the snow,' Mother said. 'It gives me a headache. Forty winks is the only thing that clears it.'

'It's a good job I'm here or the sewing would fall way behind.'

Even so, Juliet was anxious to return to the shop. Being confined to the sewing room was stifling. Outside, the grounds were more green than white, but it didn't make any difference to Mother's need for her forty winks.

'I'll be fine once the snow has disappeared,' she said.

The thaw continued. Juliet returned to work with her foot strapped in so many bandages she had to borrow a bigger boot. At the same time as the primroses started showing their softly coloured faces beneath the trees in the parkland, the tiny white flowers of shepherd's purse appeared on the common land outside Birkfield. The signs of spring gladdened Juliet's heart, though she felt a twinge of sorrow too. This was Pop's favourite time of year. How proud he would have been to see her working in Naseby's, but if he had been here to see it, then she would still be helping old Mrs Dancy. She cut short that train of thought. It was far too complicated and upsetting.

'Mr Nugent! Good morning, sir, and what can I do for you today?'

Juliet was as surprised as her employer when Mr Nugent entered the shop. He looked smart in his overcoat with its buttons concealed beneath a fly front and sharp creases down the fronts of his trouser legs, which was the new style for gentlemen, as Juliet knew from the fashion magazines her ladyship sent to the sewing room when she had finished with them.

He glanced at Juliet, only a glance but it was frankly appraising. Did he like what he saw? Did he remember her as honourable for speaking up for Hal?

'I'm here to enquire after your young assistant, Mrs Naseby. As a member of his lordship's household, she is my responsibility. Is she giving satisfaction?'

'Indeed, she is, sir.'

'I'm pleased to hear it. Her mother is a skilled needlewoman, so Mrs Whicker informs me, and I never had any trouble with the father.'

'Juliet is a credit to her upbringing.'

'And to his lordship,' Mr Nugent observed.

'And to his lordship,' Mrs Naseby agreed.

Two pairs of eyes turned upon her. Mrs Naseby's were kind and pleased, Mr Nugent's dark and assessing. His nose was thin, as were his lips; his face was lean. His whole bearing was aristocratic, but then it would be, wouldn't it, because he was a younger son or a distant cousin or some such, depending whose story you listened to, of a titled family.

The bell pinged, and in came two customers. They saw who was

85

in the shop and stood close to one another, as if dying to whisper.

'I won't detain you, madam.' Mr Nugent raised his bowler to Mrs Naseby, then looked at Juliet. 'How old are you now, Juliet?'

'Fifteen, sir. Sixteen in May.'

He nodded. 'Ladies.' He raised his hat to the gawping customers before he left.

Silence quivered before Mrs Naseby exclaimed, 'Well!' and fanned her face with her hand. The customers surged forward for her explanation. 'It's what comes of having an assistant from Moorside,' Mrs Naseby finished proudly.

Juliet hurried home that evening, eager to tell Mother, but it was cast from her mind when she walked in and saw the work basket on the table beside the wing chair, even though Mother was at the sewing table. She had seen the work basket there several times and each time it had made her wonder. She had to ask.

'What a nasty suspicious mind you've got,' Mother exclaimed. 'Honestly, I put it there just once while I have forty winks and now you're accusing me of sleeping on the job every afternoon.'

'I'm not. I couldn't help noticing, that's all.'

'Well, I'll make sure not to leave it there again. Have I your permission to leave it on the sewing table or will you read something into that as well?'

Chapter Seven

Mr Nugent! What an honour. He had singled her out, drawing her aside from the women outside church. Agnes drew herself up taller. His lordship's land agent and Lady Margaret's personal seamstress in private conversation: it underlined her importance. But when he mentioned calling at Naseby's, her expression froze. Juliet hadn't said anything. Wretched girl! As Mr Nugent raised his bowler to her and walked on, Agnes could feel the air crackling with interest as her former neighbours edged closer. Feeling smug, she was more than happy to be the centre of attention.

'Mr Nugent was simply passing the time of day,' she said. 'One senior member of staff to another, you know. He wanted to congratulate me on how well Juliet is doing. He called at the shop to find out.'

'You never said a word, Agnes,' Ella accused her.

She laughed. 'I didn't want to boast.'

When they separated to walk home, Agnes was all smiles as long as she was in sight of her friends, but she hissed at Juliet from the corner of her mouth, 'Why didn't you tell me Mr Nugent went to the shop? Naseby's can expect another visitor. I'm coming to stock up.'

'I can bring anything you need.'

'I'd like to come to town. I haven't been for a while.'

She went the following afternoon. As Lady Margaret's seamstress, she was served by Mrs Naseby while Juliet dealt with other customers.

'Juliet can carry everything home,' Agnes said.

'Of course,' said Mrs Naseby. 'I'll lend her a basket.'

Agnes glowed with satisfaction. She loved the way her former employer had to accommodate her.

Climbing the hill at the end of the day, Juliet was surprised to find Mother sitting on the bench halfway up.

'Goodness, is that the time?' Mother exclaimed. 'It's so agreeable to be out that I stopped to enjoy the view.'

Juliet joined her. Remembering how stifled she had felt in the sewing room when she was laid up, she couldn't blame Mother for wanting to extend her outing. Mother lifted an elbow, and Juliet scooted along the bench to link arms and snuggle close, making contact with something hard in Mother's pocket. Mother shifted it to the other pocket, but not before Juliet saw it.

'Medicine? Are you poorly?'

'Don't panic. Mrs Whicker asked me to collect it.'

'Who's it for?'

'I don't know. It's another reason I'm here so late: I had to wait at the doctor's. Come along. We should be getting back.'

Hal was waiting as Juliet left the shop. 'Grandad sent me on an errand, so I thought I'd stop by and walk you home . . . if you don't mind?'

Mind? She was breathless with pleasure.

'And who's this?' Mrs Naseby demanded from the shop doorway.

'Hal Price, ma'am,' said Hal, 'one of his lordship's gardeners.'

'We're friends,' Juliet added.

'Mm, I see. Very well, then, but don't make a habit of it. I'm not having my assistant getting herself talked about.'

Juliet went beetroot. When they set off, Hal mooched along, looking thoughtful, and she dreaded what he must be thinking after Mrs Naseby's remark.

As they started up the hill, he asked, 'Did you mean what you said back there? That we're . . . friends?'

She panicked. Was friendship too much to claim? Then, through a terrific roaring in her ears, she heard what he was saying.

'I'd like us to be more than that.'

Her feet stopped of their own accord. She stared at him.

'I'm asking you to walk out with me. I'll be honest, I have to get on in life before I can wed, but if you'll give me your support in that, I swear I'll give you a good life one day. So, Juliet Harper, will you walk out with me?'

All she could do was nod. Had she tried to speak, she might well have burst into tears. For the first time in her life, she climbed the hill without noticing the effort. She let her hand bump against Hal's, wanting him to hold it, but he waited until they were in the parkland, where he drew her behind a tree, holding her shoulders gently as he bent his face to hers. Her eyes fluttered closed as his lips brushed hers, every nerve end in her body yearning towards him. His kiss was brief and soft, and left her wanting more.

'I want to do this properly,' he murmured. 'I'll ask your mum's permission.'

She nodded breathlessly. She couldn't wait to tell Mother.

But Mother burst into a fine old fury.

'The gardener's boy!'

'Pop was only a groundsman.'

Mother slapped her. Juliet gasped, lifting her fingers to where her face was hot and stinging. Mother looked ashamed, then obstinate.

'It's your own fault. You shouldn't talk about your father like that.'

'I didn't mean any disrespect to Pop. Anyroad, Hal's going to be a garden designer one day.'

'That remains to be seen.'

To Juliet's relief, that got the snappiness out of Mother's system. She went to meet Hal's parents, which made Juliet feel both proud and horrified.

'What did you expect?' Mother demanded. 'This is what you want, isn't it? Now is the time to back out if you're not sure.'

'I'm sure.'

And she was – blissfully, deeply sure. She lived for the time she spent with Hal, hanging on his words as he described his future – only it wasn't just his future now. It was theirs. And she didn't mind waiting for him to get established. That would be her contribution to his career.

'You should offer to sew for women on the estate and in the villages, women who can't afford to have their families' clothes made at Naseby's,' said Hal. 'You could work up a good business if you put your mind to it.'

She laughed. 'I'm happy as I am.' A thought struck her. 'Do you mean I should earn money to help us along?'

'I'll be more than able to support us when the time comes. What I meant was that you'll have a few years to fill while you wait for me. Wouldn't you like to start a business of your own?'

Frankly, she was too busy revelling in the joy of her new relationship and dreaming of her long-term future. Maybe she would think about it if and when Hal went away to work alongside a garden designer.

Having walked on air for a while, she crashed to earth after Mother was sent for by Mrs Whicker. When she returned to the sewing room, she collapsed into the wingback chair.

'Mrs Whicker says you must leave Moorside. Followers aren't allowed. Out of respect for me, she'll allow six weeks for arrangements to be made. By then, you must be living elsewhere. Maybe Mrs Naseby will have you. Or Beatrice.'

Juliet's panic at being given notice was transformed from blanket distress to crystal-clear reality. She didn't fancy living with either woman. Miss Bradley popped into her head. Might Miss Bradley look kindly on her?

With permission from Mrs Naseby, she loitered outside St Chad's at the end of the school day, crossing her fingers tightly in the folds of her skirt as she explained her situation to her old teacher.

'I'm sorry,' Miss Bradley said. 'My landlady doesn't have room for another. Best do what your mother wants.' Then she added, 'When you have more freedom, perhaps you could resume your drawing lessons. You're a bright girl, Juliet.' A sigh, a shake of the head. 'You've got a young man now. You'll be spending your time with him or sewing for your bottom drawer.'

'Hal wants me to better myself. We both want to get on.'

'Well, that's something,' said Miss Bradley.

What was that supposed to mean? She had the obscure feeling she had let Miss Bradley down. Passing the doctor's on her way home, she was hailed from the window by the doctor's wife, who then came to the door.

'Here's the medicine Doctor promised your mother.'

Juliet hurried home with this new worry chewing at her heart. But when she reached the sewing room, Mother wasn't there. She came in a few minutes later, peeling off her coat.

'Oh, you're back. I was hoping for a lie-down before you got in.'

'Where have you been?' Juliet asked.

'Beatrice's. Mrs Whicker gave me the time. Beatrice says you can lodge with her. I'd rather have you in Clough than down below.' Mother sighed. 'I'll be glad to get the weight off my feet.'

'You're poorly, aren't you? The doctor sent this.' She produced the bottle.

'Oh, that. It's a tonic, nothing more. This worry about you leaving, it's keeping me awake.'

'You never said you'd been to the doctor.'

'Goodness, what a fusspot. It's only a tonic. There's just time for me to have a rest before tea. Forty winks and a glug of tonic and I'll be right as rain.'

Mother vanished into the bedroom, leaving unease flickering across the surface of Juliet's mind. It was only a day or two since Mrs Whicker had given her notice. How could Mother have got run-down so soon? She thought back to the snow-headaches and the times she had found the work basket beside the wing chair. Now this. Living her life confined to the sewing room was sapping Mother's energy.

She kept one eye on the clock, waiting for Mother to reappear, but she didn't, so Juliet went to wake her, opening the bedroom door to what sounded like a pig with a bad cold. She grinned and shook Mother's shoulder. Mother snorted and sat up, pushing herself to her feet, smiling brightly.

'See? Forty winks was all I needed.'

'Forty?' Juliet smiled back. 'Two hundred, more like.'

Mother's hand whipped out and slapped her. Juliet stared in disbelief – though why was she disbelieving? It wasn't as though it was the first time.

'You have to stop hitting me. You never used to do it when Pop was here.'

'You're meant to be on my side.' Mother glared at her, then turned with a swish and marched out.

Hurrying to meet Hal, Juliet walked briskly, then rushed a few steps in an almost run. She ought to make the most of the drifts of snowdrops, which wouldn't be here for much longer, but she was too eager to see Hal. They were permitted to meet once a week at the Prices' cottage deep in the park.

She was almost there when she saw Mr Nugent coming along the path. He stopped, so she had to as well.

'Good afternoon, Juliet. Are you going to see your young man?'

'Yes, sir.'

'I hear you're in need of a new home.'

'Mrs Grove has offered to have me.'

'Has she? Well, we'll see. I'll be back this way in an hour or so. I'll walk with you back to the house.'

'But I stay longer than that.'

Mr Nugent fixed her with a look. 'I'm simply looking after your interests.'

He dismissed her with a nod. She hurried on, hot with indignation and disappointment. She couldn't wait to tell Hal that their precious visit was being cut short.

To her surprise, he said, 'It's an honour to have Mr Nugent keeping an eye on you.'

'I can do without the honour, thank you.'

Laughing, he looped an elbow around her shoulders, hooking her close and dropping a kiss on her temple. 'He had a word with me the other day. He told me straight not to take liberties.'

'He never!'

'He did. He said you might not work for his lordship but you're still a member of the household.'

Knowing Mr Nugent was coming for her, without knowing exactly when, only that it would be far sooner than they would like, lent an awkwardness to the visit, which was a horrible waste given that they wouldn't see one another again for a whole week. Misery stretched tight across Juliet's chest and the last thing she felt like, walking back to Moorside with her grand escort, was polite conversation.

'I might have a solution to your problem,' Mr Nugent observed. 'Ah, I thought that might perk you up a bit.'

When he said nothing more, she asked, 'What solution?'

'Wait and see.' He sounded amused. Was he teasing her? Or trying to tempt her into pressing for details? She felt obscurely uncomfortable. Anyroad, she knew where she was going to live. She didn't need another solution.

Juliet came home from work to find Mother fluttery with excitement. Her eyes were bright and her hands couldn't keep still. Usually at this time of day, she was tired and fretful.

'Wait till you hear this,' Mother said importantly. 'Who do you think came to see me today? Mr Nugent himself, here in my sewing room.'

'What did he want?'

'You.' Mother laughed. 'He wants you to join his household. Think of it! His cook has a kitchen maid and a scrubbing girl, and there's a chambermaid, a parlourmaid and a boy, but the parlourmaid, Dolly, is getting on in years. Her eyes aren't what they were and her fingers aren't as nifty, but she's been with Mr Nugent a long time and he doesn't want to lose her, which shows what a good master he is. That's where you come in.'

Juliet's heart jumped inside her chest. 'You don't mean leave Naseby's?'

'If you were at Arley House all the time, there'd be no point in keeping Dolly, so you'll keep your job at the shop, then help Dolly in the evenings.'

'You mean do a day's work, then go home and do more?' But then, wasn't this what she did anyway? She had always helped a certain amount in the sewing room, but now she was helping every evening. At least she would get paid for it at Mr Nugent's.

'There'll be no heavy work. You'll be there to do the fiddly things Dolly can't manage, like cleaning the silver.'

'And sewing?'

'That's the best of it. You'll be Mr Nugent's sewing girl. I asked if that could be your title and he said yes. It'll be a tremendous feather in your cap. Customers will be queuing up to have their alterations done by Mr Nugent's sewing girl, and Mrs Naseby will have to pay you more – well, if she has any decency.'

'Mr Nugent's sewing girl,' Juliet repeated. Better or worse than Mrs Grove's lodger?

'You'll be closer to me than if you went to the village,' Mother added.

Closer to Hal too. He would be pleased. He would see it as a way of bettering herself.

After church that Sunday, Mother was full of the news. It was as if she couldn't wait for it to happen.

Mrs Naseby was distinctly less enthusiastic. 'Just so long as you don't arrive here dopey-eyed every morning,' she observed, but that was all she said, because criticising Mr Nugent's idea would be tantamount to speaking against his lordship.

'You could find yourself sharing a room with old Dolly,' warned Cecily. 'Servants always share, apart from the high-up ones.'

So when Juliet visited Arley House with Mother to meet the staff, she was worried sick, but it turned out she was to have a room all to herself on the other side of the house from the rest of the other servants.

'That shows you're no ordinary maid,' Mother whispered, and Juliet knew that the following Sunday, the whole village would know it too.

The doctor's wife waylaid Juliet, handing her a bottle for Mother.

Juliet frowned. 'I didn't think she'd need more.'

'It's none of your concern what Doctor prescribes for his patients.'

She hurried on her way. Halfway up the hill, she saw Mr Nugent sitting on the bench and felt embarrassed. It would be rude to look at him – and just as rude not to. He solved her dilemma by addressing her, making her stop.

'Good afternoon, Juliet. On your way home, I see.'

'Good afternoon, Mr Nugent.' She stood there, feeling awkward.

'Have a seat.'

She stepped backwards. 'I couldn't.'

'I think you'll find you can. You're about to enter my employ, and I expect my orders to be obeyed.'

She slid onto the bench, perching at the far end, brown paper bag on her lap clutched in both hands.

'You'd be in my employ already, if I'd had my way,' Mr Nugent remarked. 'But your mother wanted to keep you until

96

your notice is up, and who am I to thwart a mother's wishes?'

Was she meant to thank him?

'Are you looking forward to joining my household? To becoming my . . . sewing girl?'

'Yes, sir.'

'Good. So am I.'

Juliet looked at him. She had an odd feeling of chill, like walking through bushes after rain and getting slapped by a wet branch.

'For Dolly's sake,' he added.

She nodded. She thought he might dismiss her then, but he rose and stepped forward to look at the view. Should she stand too, out of politeness? Then he walked along a few paces, crossing in front of her in the narrow space, and stopped beside the path. Good: he was going.

He turned to look at her. 'Have you bought yourself something special?'

'Oh – this. Doctor Entwistle sent it for my mother.'

'Did he now?'

'It's a tonic. She's not ill.'

Mr Nugent nodded. Dismissal. 'You'd better be getting back, don't you think?'

She came to her feet, then hesitated, waiting for him to stand aside, but he didn't move, just continued to stand there, looking at her.

'Off you go,' he said softly.

Ducking her head to hide the heat in her cheeks, she obeyed, passing so close that she brushed against him, couldn't do otherwise. She could almost feel the tiny fibres of his Norfolk jacket trying to cling to her coat. Gaining the path, she walked away as swiftly as politeness permitted.

* * *

97

Two days later, coming in from work, Juliet stopped dead in the doorway when she saw Mr Nugent sitting with her mother. Surprise vanished beneath a lurch of panic at the sight of Mother looking pale and shaken, her fingers entwined in her lap.

Mr Nugent said in his smooth voice, 'Should I tell her or shall you?'

Chapter Eight

Things happened quickly, which made it easier to evade Juliet's increasingly insistent and frightened questions. The girl wanted to talk – needed to. Agnes finally admitted the snow-headaches had been pure fabrication.

'You lied,' Juliet said wonderingly.

'I was tired.' She was weary now too. 'I didn't want to worry you.'

More questions. She admitted the tonic wasn't a tonic. It was medicine – well, in a manner of speaking.

'It dulls the pain,' she said when pressed.

'But will it make you better as well?' Juliet said anxiously.

'It's for the pain,' she repeated and returned to the packing.

They were moving. She wasn't the seamstress any more and Juliet wasn't going to Arley House. They were moving into one of his lordship's cottages, which stood by itself on the edge of the park.

'Near enough for village folk to pop in while you're at work,' said Agnes. 'One of the gates in the park wall will be unlocked during the day. It's very good of his lordship.'

'It's very good of his lordship,' everyone said after church.

And it was. His lordship would be within his rights to cast her off as unfit for work, even more so because she had kept her condition secret for so long.

'It must be a relief to have it out in the open,' Beatrice said matter-of-factly.

But it wasn't. Oh, it wasn't. It was bloody terrifying.

They were gone from Moorside in a couple of days. Juliet went to work as usual and when she came home, she went to the cottage. Mrs Grove was seated on an upright chair with wooden arms – seated on it, not in it. Beatrice Grove didn't sit in chairs, however comfortable. She sat on them, bolt upright. Mother, on the other hand, was definitely sitting in a basketwork chair. It was wide and deep, and cushions bulged behind her back.

'There you are,' Mrs Grove greeted her. 'Pop the kettle on.'

Had they been waiting for her to skivvy for them? Then she saw Mother's pale face, her eyes shadowed by fatigue, and did as she was bade.

Mrs Grove followed. 'The move has worn her out,' she said quietly, 'but she wanted to be up when you came home.' More loudly she said, 'There's bubble and squeak keeping warm and the cook up yonder sent a stew that'll do for tomorrow. Kettle's boiling. Don't forget to warm the pot.'

Soon after they had drunk their tea, Mrs Grove stood up.

'The gatekeeper will lock the side gate soon. I'll come tomorrow morning and get fettling, and Florence and Ella will be along at different times in the afternoon. Don't worry about the washing, Juliet. That'll be took care of.'

No sooner had she gone than Mother went to bed. Juliet felt hungry, but it seemed callous to fall on the food the minute Mother disappeared. She looked at the sewing basket, which Mother had insisted accompany them, though Juliet knew the work would fall to her. Ah well, better get started. She was busy darning when there was a knock and the door opened.

Without looking up, she asked, 'Did you forget something? You'd best be quick or the gate will be locked.'

'Your concern is appreciated,' Mr Nugent replied gravely.

Her head snapped up. She came to her feet, knocking the pile of mending to the floor. 'I thought you were someone else.'

'So it seems. I've come to enquire after the move. Have you settled in?'

'My mother's asleep.'

'I haven't come to see your mother. I'm here to see you. May I sit down?'

She pressed her lips together. She was tired and hungry and worried sick about Mother. She wanted to say that in an estate cottage, his lordship's agent could do whatever he jolly well pleased, but all she did was nod self-consciously, then knelt to gather the mending. That was a mistake. She should have sat down when he did. Now he was sitting and she was standing, feeling awkward about taking a seat without permission.

Which was duly given. 'Sit – please. What do you think of your new home?'

'It's very nice, thank you.' She sat on the chair – on it, not in it – as poker-straight as Mrs Grove.

'You understand why you had to leave Moorside? Once I knew the extent of your mother's illness . . .' He waved one hand expansively. 'That was thanks to you, of course, with your mention of the . . . tonic.'

'That's what I thought it was.'

He smiled genially, exonerating her from blame. 'You did right to confide in me.'

She opened her mouth to say she had done no such thing, then shut it again.

'Anywhere else, your mother would have been left to fend for herself, but not here.'

'His lordship is very good.'

'His lordship is indeed very good. He is also absent from home, enjoying North Wales with her ladyship and the young ladies. I act, of course, on his behalf and all I do is done in his name, but make no mistake, Juliet, I am the one who has been good to you.'

He looked straight at her. She wanted to look away but didn't know how.

Their old neighbours kept the cottage sparkling as well as providing Mother with company. 'Taking me out of myself', she called it. The final visitor stayed until Juliet came home, then hurried away before the gate was locked. And then – and then Mr Nugent would come. Not immediately and not every day. Occasionally Mother was present, but more often she was in bed. Knowing he might drop in, she tried to stay up, but fatigue usually overwhelmed her, and Juliet would assist her to climb the stairs, biting her lip on the way back down and hoping this evening wasn't one of those evenings.

Yet why was she uncomfortable? All he did was make conversation. She felt guilty and foolish for wishing he wouldn't come. She should be grateful for his concern. It was his concern that had given them a roof over their heads.

When she finished the mending, the basket vanished before she could return it to the big house.

'Mrs Whicker called,' said Mother. 'She brought a steamed suet pudding and apple dumplings. She saw the mending was finished and sent a footman to collect it.'

Juliet waited for the basket to be returned replenished. She wasn't sorry when it didn't appear, but Mother grew agitated.

'Ask Mrs Whicker for more. I insist on pulling my weight. We don't pay rent here, you know.'

Juliet set out. The violet haze of bluebells had given way to the rosy-pink of red campion and the dainty white stars of ransoms. Being back in Moorside made her realise how much she had missed it. Cook made a fuss of her, and everyone wanted to know how Mother was.

When she asked for another basket, Mrs Whicker refused. 'Mr Nugent's orders. He says you're the one doing the work. Make sure you thank him.'

Juliet swallowed. Another thing to be grateful for. She was already grateful for the cottage and not paying rent. The thought of seeking out Mr Nugent to thank him made her feel squirmy.

But not thanking him turned out to be the wrong thing, because a day or two later, he walked into the cottage saying, 'I don't care for disobedience.' His lips set in a tight line beneath his moustache. He threw aside his hat and gloves. 'Mrs Whicker asked if you had thanked me for relieving you of your sewing duties.'

Juliet groaned silently.

'Have the courtesy to stand when I am reprimanding you.'

She came to her feet, feeling the heat in her face.

Mr Nugent came closer. 'I thought we understood each other. I thought you were . . . grateful.'

'I am, sir.' He wasn't going to throw them out, was he?

'I don't know, Juliet. Sometimes I wonder.' He spoke in a soft, sad voice. His fingers were soft too, tracing a line down her cheek, such a gentle gesture and so brief that his hand had dropped away almost before she realised.

She blinked. He clearly expected something of her and she heard herself babbling, 'I am grateful – we both are. This cottage . . . rent-free. And not even the sewing to do. Please don't throw us out.'

'I am your benefactor.' There was that sad-sounding voice again. 'How could you think that? Even for one moment, even in panic – how could you think it?'

'I'm sorry,' she whispered. 'I'm sorry.'

And all because she hadn't said thank you. She thought of Pop, vexed with himself, saying, 'I made a right pig's whisker of that,' and of Mother and her illness, and there was a spurt of tears. There was the quiet snap of cotton being flapped free and a pristine handkerchief was pressed into her hand. She moved – towards him, away from him – she could never afterwards remember which, except that it must have been towards him because – oh, she would die of shame – his hand caressed the side of her breast. Her face flamed red-hot; tears sizzled and vanished. She stared at Mr Nugent, more than stared, gawped, honest-to-goodness gawped, eyes popping, jaw slack. But his hand wasn't there any more. Had she imagined it?

'I hope you don't do that with young Price,' said Mr Nugent. 'I hope you don't press forward at a strategic moment, so that he touches you . . . like that.'

Had she done that? Humiliation washed through her.

'Well?' said Mr Nugent. 'Do you?'

She hung her head. 'No, sir.'

'Look me in the eye, Juliet, or I might think you're lying.'

She raised her eyes, but couldn't bring herself to meet his, looking instead over his shoulder. 'Never, I swear.'

'I'm pleased to hear it.'

She dropped her head, her chin almost hitting her chest. Embarrassment roared in her ears. Mr Nugent wasn't there any more, but before she could collapse in relief, something made her look towards the door. There he stood, looking back. One more second and he would be gone. Every ounce of herself, her insides, her nerve ends, every inch of her flesh, hung on for dear life. Just one more moment and then she could give way.

But Mr Nugent paused, and the pause dragged on.

'Not that it wasn't extremely pleasant,' he said.

Juliet came home to be greeted by knowing smiles from Mother, Ella and Mrs Grove. She looked at them looking at her and knew something had happened.

'What is it?' she demanded.

'Go upstairs and see,' said Ella.

She ran to her room, stopping in the doorway. A rug. A bedside cupboard. On top of her chest of drawers was a mirror on a hinged stand. In front of it was a candleholder, a deep-lipped brass saucer with a tiny brass mouse sitting at the edge and a short holder in the centre.

She had no idea where these things had come from.

Liar.

When she reappeared, the others laughed, even Mrs Grove. Pleasure shone from their faces.

'Those things were in the room you were to have at Arley House,' said Mother. 'Mr Nugent sent them here.'

'And he sent yon footstool for your mother,' Mrs Grove added.

Mother's legs were stretched out. She said, 'Much more comfortable.'

Juliet's heart tweaked. If Mother's situation was better, how could anything else matter?

Oh, it felt wonderful. Wonderful, wonderful, wonderful. But it was essential to keep her happiness hidden, because if word got back to Mrs Whicker . . . Cecily shuddered, but it wasn't a wholehearted shudder, because she wouldn't be sorry to give William a shove in the right direction. Just imagine being shown the door by Mrs Whicker, and William scooping her up to marry her and set up home in Manchester, near where he worked.

They had met one Sunday after she had visited her family. As she left the cottage, with Mam waving her off, she had glimpsed a handsome stranger along the village street. She turned to wave and watched Mam disappear indoors, then continued on her way. The stranger wasn't there any more. Then he appeared beside her, making her jump.

The attraction was immediate. He was in the vicinity on business and today was revisiting old haunts, since he was originally from Ladyfield. Their romance had to be conducted in deadly secrecy, but Cecily would burst if she didn't tell someone, so the next time Cook sent food to the Harpers' cottage, she volunteered to take the basket.

She helped Juliet unpack the food. Out came a hunk of cheese, a jar of chutney, a slab of gingerbread, a fresh loaf and a pot of leek stew, wrapped in a cloth.

'A bite to eat?' offered Juliet. 'The beekeeper sent honey.'

'Never mind food.' She caught Juliet's hands. 'I've summat to tell you. Can you keep a secret? I've got myself a chap.'

'Cecily!'

She felt like dancing them both round the room – no, she

didn't. She dropped Juliet's hands. 'I don't mean to be tactless. I mean, with your mum so poorly . . .'

'You have no idea how good it is to hear happy news. Let's sit in the parlour and you can tell me everything. I won't breathe a word.'

'I know.' Cecily grinned. 'I'm not going to get caught like you did.'

'I didn't get caught. We did everything openly.'

'Exactly.'

'Go on then, tell all. Do I know him?'

'No, but he knows you – by sight, anyway.' She chuckled at Juliet's bewilderment. 'We spotted you walking to Hal's on Sunday and he asked who you were.'

'You mean – he comes in the park?'

'Thanks to that side gate being unlocked.'

'Is he from Birkfield?'

'He used to live over Ladyfield way, but he went to Manchester. He's here on business. He's clerk to a firm of lawyers.'

'Oh, Cecily,' Juliet breathed. 'A law clerk.'

'He's looking into a matter for a client, something about putting right a wrong that were done ages ago, but William says I mustn't ask questions because it's confidential. Besides, he's more interested in hearing about my life.'

'William?'

'William Turton. I know what you're thinking.' She smiled to herself as Juliet tried to look as if she was thinking something. 'Cecily Turton. Well, you never know, do you?'

Hurrying through the park on Sunday afternoon to see Hal, Juliet pictured Cecily sneaking around and felt relieved and grateful that her understanding with him was out in the open. She helped Mrs

Price in the kitchen, then young Sophie and some of the other gardeners' children mithered her and Hal to play French cricket. In the early days, Juliet hadn't liked this sort of thing because it ate into her precious time with Hal, but then his sister had remarked that it showed what a good dad Hal was going to be, and since then she had relished it.

When they got some time alone, they strolled among the trees, but when he slid his arms round her and kissed her, instead of melting into the embrace, she froze, remembering Mr Nugent's accusation. Did she really get so carried away that she presented her body for a feel?

Hal broke off kissing her, his face close to hers. 'Are you all right?'

Her hand snaked round his neck, pulling him back into the kiss. She loved him and he loved her, and that was all that mattered.

When he had to do greenhouse duty, she walked home. The wood sorrel was out, pretty white and violet flowers above carpets of heart-shaped leaves. Coming across a patch of sweet woodruff, with its scent not unlike that of newly mown hay, she crouched to pick a handful.

A twig snapped.

'Hal!' Rising, she looked round. Was someone else doing the greenhouses for him? But he was nowhere to be seen. 'Hal?'

She set off again. She must have imagined it. But she knew she hadn't.

She hadn't gone above a dozen paces when Mr Nugent stepped out in front of her.

'Good afternoon, Juliet. Did I startle you? You've been picking flowers, I see. His lordship's flowers.'

'They grow wild, sir.'

108

'On his lordship's property.'

She shuffled. 'Sweet woodruff smells so fresh and its scent lasts ever such a long time. It's nice to put inside drawers of clothes.'

'You like your things to smell pleasant, do you, Juliet?'

'It's not for me. I thought I'd pop some between my mother's sheets. She's in and out of bed such a lot.'

'A kind thought. But you haven't answered my question. Do you like pretty scents?'

Go away and leave me alone. 'Yes, sir. Rose is my favourite.'

'We'll have to see what we can do about that.' He looked at her as if considering the matter. 'Off you go. Your mother will be waiting.'

She didn't need telling twice.

Walking down the hill, Juliet was so deep in worry about Mother that she saw the young man only just in time to avoid a collision. Suddenly he was in front of her, so near she might have touched him. She had the oddest feeling of being crowded, but that was daft because he was merely someone she had nearly bumped into. She stepped to her right and he stepped to his left. He was dark-eyed, dark-haired. She stepped left and he stepped right. His suit was tweed and his brown bowler had a shallow crown, unlike the high-crowned bowler Mr Nugent wore. She stepped right again as he stepped left.

He said solemnly, 'Once more and then I must go.'

Laughing, she relaxed. He turned sideways to wave her past. She gave him a shy half-smile and hurried on her way.

Later, when Mrs Naseby was upstairs with a customer who had come for a fitting, the shop door opened. Juliet looked up from the new ribbons she was putting away to find herself face-to-face with the young man.

'Can I help you?'

'I'm looking for a stationer's.'

'Turn right out of the shop, walk to the market square and it's on the far corner.'

'Thanks.' He opened the door, then glanced back. 'What's your name?'

'Juliet Harper.' Was she blushing?

'You've been most helpful, Juliet Harper.'

The bell pinged over the door as it closed. You didn't often see a stranger round here, and now she had had two small encounters in one morning.

And that evening, as she neared the bench halfway up the hill, there he was, seated on it. Should she acknowledge him? When he rose, she felt obliged to stop.

'You're on your way home,' he said.

'How do you know?'

'Stands to reason. You came down the hill before the shops opened and you're heading back up when most of them have closed. I'll walk with you, if I may.'

'I'm spoken for,' she blurted out.

'I only asked to walk with you.'

He fell in step beside her. The path was wide enough for two to walk abreast. Even so, she buried her hands in her pockets so her fingers couldn't accidentally brush his.

'I'm sure it's much more respectable if you know my name,' he said. 'I'm William Turton.'

She stopped in surprise and, after another pace or two, so did he. Standing lower on the path, she found herself gazing up into his face as a mixture of relief and confidence rushed through her.

'You're Cecily's William.'

'Is that how she describes me?'

'No, of course not. I didn't mean to suggest anything.' She resumed walking, hoping she hadn't scuppered Cecily's chances. Then she realised something. 'You asked my name this morning, but you already knew it, because Cecily told you when you saw me in the park.'

'My, she does have a loose tongue, doesn't she? What else has she said?'

'Nothing. Only that you're here on business.'

'And I assume from what you said that you've got a bloke of your own. What does he do?'

'He's one of his lordship's gardeners.'

'How come you work in a shop when you live on the estate?'

'We've always lived on the estate. My parents both worked for his lordship at different times.'

'So why aren't you a maid? Your mother being seamstress, she was ideally placed to get you taken on at the big house.'

'How do you know she was seamstress?'

'Cecily told me. So why didn't you become a maid?'

She suppressed a huff of annoyance. 'Why all these questions?'

'Just making conversation. I bet most of the girls hereabouts would give their eye teeth for a maiding post up yonder.'

'Maybe, but I'm happy at Naseby's.' She slowed her pace. 'We're near the village. I – I'd rather not . . .'

'Rather not be seen keeping company?'

'We're not keeping company.'

'Then what's the problem?' He laughed. 'I'll go a different way.' He raised his bowler. 'Perhaps we'll bump into one another again.'

The next morning, she took a different path down the hill.

* * *

111

Leaving Mother settled for the night, Juliet went into her bedroom, catching a faint scent, something sweet and elusive alongside the usual smell of beeswax: rose. A fresh candle stood in the candleholder with the little brass mouse. Her white candle was gone, replaced by one of creamy-white with pieces of rose petal inside. Mrs Whicker must have brought it when she called today. According to Mrs Grove, Mrs High-and-Mighty Whicker had run her fingers over various surfaces, though not a speck of dust had she found. Juliet had felt indignant on behalf of the loyal friends who cared for the cottage, but she softened now as she breathed in the candle's aroma. Its full scent would be released only when it burnt, so she would prepare for bed by candlelight and fall asleep surrounded by the smell of roses.

She picked up her nightgown. Was that a sound? Just the cottage settling for the night. She had herself turned the key in the front door.

She slipped her nightgown over her head and when her head emerged, there was Mr Nugent.

'Cover yourself, Juliet,' he said softly. 'Standing there like that, showing your privates like any common slut.'

She dragged down the nightie, fastening the buttons on the yoke with shaking fingers.

'Well,' he said, 'I've come. I saw the candle's glow against your curtain.'

'Mrs Whicker left it for me.'

'Did she? Think again, Juliet. Who has your best interests at heart? Did Mrs Whicker put a roof over the head of your ailing mother? Did she provide this furniture? I'm disappointed in you. After everything I've done, after all your protestations of gratitude, it doesn't occur to you that this gift is from me, even though you made a point of telling me your favourite scent.'

'I never meant you to give me anything.'

'Of course you did. And all I ask in return is gratitude. I've come for some gratitude now.'

Her heart raced. She wanted to hide.

'Brush your hair for me,' he said. 'Stand in front of the looking-glass I provided and brush your hair.'

Her feet were glued to the floor. Then she stepped across to the chest of drawers. How stupid of her to have imagined the candle came from Mrs Whicker. She began to brush her hair. Mr Nugent stood behind her. She fixed her eyes on her white-faced reflection, determined not to meet his gaze in the mirror.

'Your hands are trembling.' Gently he took the brush from her and began to draw it through her hair, using his other hand to stroke her hair smooth. 'There.' Reaching over her shoulder, he replaced the brush, settling his hands lightly on her shoulders. 'Look at me.'

She dragged her eyes up to his in the mirror. Her eyes were blank with fear; his, as dark as a thunderstorm.

'Unfasten your buttons.' His fingers tightened on her shoulders, squeezing her collarbones.

Her tummy turned over, then went still and cold. Her hands raised – how they were doing it she didn't know, because it didn't seem anything to do with her – and her fingers found the tiny buttons Mother had sewn on. They had always been fiddly, but today of all days, just when she needed them to be impossible to undo, they slid straight through the buttonholes. Mr Nugent slipped one hand inside the yoke of her nightie. Her flesh went cold under the soft rasp of his fingertips. Her hands flew to grab at his through the fabric, to stop its progress, to shove it away.

'Don't be foolish,' he murmured. 'It's time to be grateful.

Think of everything I could take away if you're not grateful.'

She didn't want to remove her hands because that was like letting him. But she had to let him. For Mother's sake, she had to. Sick with reluctance, she dropped her hands, closing her eyes against whatever was going to happen next. His hand moved to cover her breast, cupping it, gently squeezing. She felt sick and cold and stupid, stupid, stupid. He uttered a soft groan, which made her think his eyes must be closed, and she opened her own, only to find his boring into them through the mirror.

Gently he withdrew his hand. 'A little gratitude, that's all I wanted.' And he left.

Chapter Nine

With a suddenness that Agnes saw reflected in the silent shock in everyone's eyes, her condition worsened. Fear rolled in her stomach, bulky and sour, but she never actually threw up. Her bones would shatter if she did. And the pain . . . She needed yet more of the medicine to dull it. God, what a wretched way to go.

Doctor Entwistle appeared at the bedside.

'I wasn't expecting you,' she said.

'Mrs Grove sent for me.'

Bloody Beatrice, throwing her weight around, but she was too exhausted to drum up resentment. Even before Doctor Entwistle left, she began to drift off. Oh, the indignity! With a massive effort, she hauled herself back to consciousness. The doctor was speaking to Beatrice.

'More medicine is the only answer. It will control the pain, up to a point anyway, and make her sleep more, but she'd be doing that in any case. It's one of the symptoms.' In a lower voice, he added, 'It's spreading through her body.' He didn't say what 'it' was. No one ever did.

She drifted off. When she woke, Juliet was there, smiling, but her eyes were scared.

She laid her hand on Juliet's. 'Good day at the shop?'

'Never mind me. How are you?'

'No worse than usual. Having Doctor Entwistle wasn't my idea.'

'Shouldn't we write to Auntie Clara?'

Agnes jerked her hand away. 'I'm not having her see me like this, thank you very much. Clara – here? Not on your life – or not on mine.'

'Mother . . .'

'If you've got nothing useful to say, leave me alone.'

As Juliet crossed the market square, William Turton appeared.

He tipped his bowler. 'Have you been avoiding me, Juliet Harper?'

'Of course not.'

'Then why have you changed your route up and down the hill?'

'I just felt like it.' Drat: here came Mrs Cobbley, a regular customer. 'I must go.'

She hurried on, smiling at Mrs Cobbley to show she wasn't ashamed of being seen talking to this young man. How did William know she was using a different path? It was a question she didn't want to answer.

Before the shop had been open half an hour, Mr Nugent walked in. The hair lifted on Juliet's arms, but he barely gave her a glance.

'Good morning, Mrs Naseby, and how are you this fine morning? A word in private, if I may. Good morning, Juliet.'

He followed Mrs Naseby through to the back, leaving Juliet to cope with a string of customers, the last of whom departed just before Mr Nugent and Mrs Naseby reappeared.

'I trust that will be satisfactory,' Mr Nugent said.

'Yes, sir,' Mrs Naseby replied, but Juliet could see it wasn't.

Mr Nugent came to the counter. 'Doctor Entwistle has informed me your mother's condition is deteriorating. She needs someone with her at all times. Therefore I've arranged with Mrs Naseby that you'll finish here at the end of the week to be at home with her.'

Juliet stared from one to the other, wanting Mrs Naseby to object, but knowing she wouldn't – couldn't.

'Your place is there now,' said Mr Nugent.

When he left, she and Mrs Naseby looked at one another.

'Well, that's that,' Mrs Naseby said.

'Will you . . . ?' She had to know. 'Will you keep my job for me?'

Mrs Naseby sighed. 'I can't manage on my own, and there's no knowing how long your poor mother will last. There, that's blunt speaking, but it has to be said. I doubt I'll find another girl as good as you, if it's any consolation.'

Juliet felt hollowed out with shock. When she got home, she didn't say a word, not in front of Mrs Grove and Ella, nor to Mother after they left. Mother would be as hurt as she was to know the job was ending.

Except that she wasn't hurt at all. Well, she was, but only by Juliet's failure to tell her.

'Why didn't you say anything?' she demanded the following evening. 'I had to hear it from Mrs Whicker.'

'I thought you'd be disappointed.'

'Disappointed? To have you here with me? I'll feel easier knowing I'm never alone. Why would that upset me?'

Put like that, why indeed? Juliet hated herself for caring about her job when it was clear where her duty lay, but she couldn't help feeling upset, not least because everybody else thought it a grand

117

idea. Even Mrs Naseby was triumphant because Miss Bradley had produced a capable girl, and Mr Nugent, in his lordship's name, prevailed upon Mr Ferguson to release her before the end of term.

On Friday evening, the night before Juliet's last day at Naseby's, Mother said, 'Mr Nugent came today. He says that . . . afterwards . . . you'll go into his household like you were going to before, only it'll be a full-time position. So that's something I needn't worry about.'

For one wild moment, she wanted to shout from the rooftops what Mr Nugent was like. But no one would believe it and, anyroad, she was too ashamed. The impulse died, sucked down in the quagmire of memory of the bedroom she had been shown in Arley House, all on its own on the other side of the building.

Walking in the demure crocodile behind Mrs Whicker and Cook, Cecily saw Juliet arrive alone at church and her heart swelled in compassion. A couple of villagers headed towards Juliet, that bossy one with the purposeful air and the pretty one with the kind eyes. The crocodile processed into church, and Cecily didn't see her again until after the service.

'Has Mrs Whicker spoken to you yet?' Cecily asked.

'What about?'

'Becoming seamstress, of course. Close your mouth, love, or you'll catch a fly. That's what's being said in the servants' hall. Not official, like, but it would make sense, wouldn't it?'

'Mr Nugent has already said I'm to go to him.'

'Not if Lady Margaret says otherwise. Goodness!' Cecily exclaimed. 'What have I said?'

Juliet smeared away a tear. 'Nothing. It's such a relief to know I'm coming back to Moorside.' She smiled. 'I met your

William Turton. He knew about Mother being seamstress.'

'Did he?'

'He said you told him.'

'Then I must have. He's so interested in hearing about everything that I forget what I've said.'

'I bumped into him earlier this week and he knew I'd been going up and down the hill a different way recently. I wondered how he knew.'

What a daft thing to care about. 'I'll ask.'

'No, don't.'

'No harm in asking.'

But the next time she sneaked away to meet William, he had more enticing things on his mind than answering daft questions, and Cecily didn't mind in the slightest.

Taking her face in his hands, William breathed kisses over it and flicked his tongue against her ear, making Cecily gasp out a desperate sigh as she arched her neck for more. Was that a chuckle she heard as he began to kiss his way down the line of her throat? His hands left her face, one snaking behind her, pulling her closer so that she couldn't have wriggled free even had she wanted to. William's mouth covered hers, and she willingly parted her lips to receive the prolonged kiss that left her yearning for more. Now she knew. Now she understood. She had been shocked when Barbara got herself in the family way while she was courting, but now she understood.

'What was it you wanted to ask?' William murmured.

She could scarcely remember. 'Juliet wondered how you knew she was using a different route, that's all.'

William nuzzled her hair. 'I've told you before. I can't . . .' Kiss. '. . . discuss . . .' Kiss. '. . . my work.'

119

Another kiss, a longer one. Cecily felt a sharp tug of desire, but even as she yearned towards him, William put her from him.

'Time for you to get back.'

She groaned, but he laughed. She tidied her hair and straightened her appearance. Would anyone notice that her lips were swollen from the potency of his kisses? After a lingering farewell, she raced away to resume her duties. She had been so certain no one would notice her carefully orchestrated absence that her heart lurched when Mrs Whicker swooped on her.

'Cecily! I wish to speak to you. Make yourself available at four o'clock precisely.'

Juliet had thought there wouldn't be much to do at home, but looking after Mother – making pots of tea, providing meals, dashing upstairs to tidy the bed when Mother dragged herself downstairs, sitting with her after she dropped off and never quite knowing whether she could move without disturbing her – was strangely time-consuming. She had to pull her weight with the housework as well. Or perhaps time-consuming wasn't the right word. It was more that the world outside the cottage seemed far away and it was only what happened inside that mattered.

Cecily came to the cottage, bringing a baked custard. 'Invalid food, Cook says. How are you? Missing the shop?'

'I'm busy here now.'

'I told William you've left Naseby's.'

Juliet rooted around for a fly net for the baked custard to avoid answering.

'I mentioned what you said about your route on the hill. He couldn't say much. It's about this case he's working on, so he has to be discreet. I s'pose he was watching someone involved in that and happened to see you at the same time. Coincidence.'

'When did you see him?'

'Yesterday. I sneaked out. There's a place where we meet.'

'Oh, Cecily, be careful.'

'Well, I shan't see him for a while, so you can stop fretting. Lady Margaret and the girls are off to London and, guess what, I'm going too, as a try-out for Miss Phoebe having her own maid instead of sharing with Miss Vicky.'

'Really? Congratulations. Mrs Whicker must be pleased with you, Miss Marchant too.'

'Aye, I've worked hard enough, though I was scared half to death when Mrs Whicker sent for me. I thought she'd found out about me and William, but it was about this.'

'It's a wonderful opportunity.'

'It'd be a lot more wonderful if Miss Phoebe was staying put and I could carry on seeing William.'

'Don't throw away this chance for his benefit.'

'That's rich coming from you,' Cecily snorted. 'You got slung out on your ear because of Hal.'

'That's different. We have an understanding.'

'So do we . . . sort of. Look, he gave me this.'

Cecily delved in her pocket. There was such a glow about her that Juliet expected a piece of jewellery, perhaps even a ring, but all Cecily produced was a piece of card.

'His business card,' she said and, give her her due, she couldn't have sounded prouder had it been a ruby surrounded by diamonds.

Juliet had a quick look. There was *William Turton* in the top corner and *Junior Clerk* underneath, and a glimpse of an address, then the card vanished into Cecily's pocket.

'I know he likes me. He goes out of his way to meet up and he wouldn't do that, would he, if he didn't like me? And let's just say he shows me how much.' Cecily giggled, starry-eyed and flushed.

'Have you let him . . . you know?'

'He hasn't tried. Mind you, if he did try, I don't think I'd be able to say no. He's so handsome and when he kisses me . . .' She shivered.

'*Cecily.*'

'Anyroad, he doesn't earn enough yet. That's why this job he's on is important. It could lead to promotion and then . . .'

'A wife?'

Cecily grinned. 'Wouldn't that be grand? Me, wed to a professional gentleman.'

'Will you write to him while you're away?'

'He's given me the address where he lodges in Manchester, but he won't be able to write back, because you have to be a senior servant before your letters get to you unopened.' Cecily heaved a sigh. 'Shall I tell you the worst thing about being Miss Phoebe's maid? They don't choose personal maids from those they think will marry. This is as good as a public announcement that I'm on the shelf.'

Juliet hugged her. 'Shall I tell you the best thing about being Miss Phoebe's maid? It's a better position than chambermaid. "My wife used to be a lady's maid" has a much better ring than "I married a chambermaid".'

'I hadn't thought of that.'

'Think of it now, Mrs Turton.'

'I will, Mrs Price.'

There were moments, like now, standing at one end of the laburnum walk, when Hal felt the tug of dedicating himself to a single estate. It was something he never voiced, because Ma would have pounced, but he understood the connection between Grandad and Moorside that was expressed both in the perceptive application of shape and colour that created flower beds of apparently casual abundance, belying the knowledge and skill that had gone into them, and in the dramatic pieces such as the laburnum walk, where two lines of laburnums had been trained to arch together to create a shimmering golden tunnel. Imagine making your mark on one place over the years. Only a fool wouldn't be tempted, but in his heart, Hal knew it wasn't for him.

It was Juliet's birthday, and he had spent hours perfecting a painting of the laburnum walk. Ma had taken it to Birkfield to be framed. To Hal, it seemed the perfect gift: a piece of his own work that showed his grandfather's craft and celebrated Moorside, the place where he and Juliet had met.

He trundled his wheelbarrow of weeds away from the flower gardens. Spying his cousin, Saul, he called, 'Finish this for me, will you? Mr Nugent wants to see me.'

'Right you are,' said Saul.

He jogged home to spruce himself up, removing his gaiters and putting on a tie and a tweed jacket. The last time he had been summoned to the big house, there had been snow on the ground. Now the front of the house was curtained in wisteria. That other time, he had been accused of fathering Rosie's baby. This time – was it foolish, presumptuous, to feel a flutter of hope? Might the summons spring from Mr Nugent's interest in him?

Tucking his cap in his pocket, he hovered outside the estate room, waiting for the grandfather clock in the hall to strike the hour. The moment it did, he knocked.

'Come,' called Mr Nugent. 'Ah, Price, come in. Thank you,

Farmer Grey. I'll be out to see the new ditches next week.'

Hal stood aside to let Farmer Grey depart and closed the door behind him, before placing himself squarely in front of Mr Nugent's desk.

'You wanted to see me, sir?'

'How are your studies coming along?'

Hal described his progress at the Institute and how he was filling notebooks with details of his grandfather's planting schemes. 'And through a fellow at the Institute, I got an introduction to a builder in Annerby, who allows me to spend my weekly afternoon off learning the basics on his construction site.'

'You do that in preference to spending your free afternoons with your young lady?'

'She understands, sir. I see her every Sunday. She comes to us for dinner and stays afterwards until I start greenhouse duty.'

'It's fortunate she is so accommodating.'

His posture was tall and proud. 'Juliet knows what I have to do.'

'Then let's hope she'll be equally agreeable about this.' Mr Nugent glanced at a letter in front of him. 'I've found a situation for you with a garden designer named Clayton, who is at present working in London. He's prepared to take you on for the remainder of his current project. If you impress him . . . who knows?'

'That's wonderful. Thank you, sir. It's precisely what I hoped for, though I never imagined it would happen so soon.'

'You'll take it?' asked Mr Nugent.

'I'd like to, obviously, but – you must know how things stand with Juliet's mother.'

'Mrs Harper, I regret to say, does not have long to live. A few weeks at best, according to her doctor.'

Hal felt torn straight down the middle. How could he leave

Juliet to face inevitable bereavement alone? His heart swelled with protective love.

'Might Mr Clayton wait until . . . ?'

'Until Mrs Harper has departed this life? Certainly not. I realise this places you in a difficult position, Price, but I require an answer directly. Either you want this opportunity or you don't, and if you don't, I shall be deeply displeased, as Clayton has offered it as a personal favour to me. You said yourself that Juliet understands what is required. I'm going to reply to Clayton's letter today. What should I tell him?'

It felt uncomfortable having a birthday under the circumstances. Inappropriate. Juliet leafed through the pages of the old cloth-bound book of embroidery stitches that had belonged to Mother for as long as she could remember. Now it belonged to her. Inside, a bold hand – Mrs Grove's? – had written *For my dear daughter on her sixteenth birthday, with best regards from* and then a weaker hand had scrawled *Mother* in writing that must have made poor Mother weep with shame, because it was so spidery and unlike her usual firm hand. Had Mother chosen the sentiment or was 'best regards' Mrs Grove's idea of a suitable inscription to a daughter? Juliet hadn't asked, because she badly wanted the message to have come from Mother's lips, if not from her hand, even though it wasn't the more loving message she would have preferred.

It was a warm afternoon and she had the windows open. Mother had tried to stay awake but had been overtaken by sleep, and Juliet had carried her chair over to the window to enjoy the fresh air, insofar as anything was enjoyable these days. Mother had shed an appalling amount of weight: her cheeks were sunken, her arms as thin as twigs. Juliet didn't want her to suffer, but she didn't want her to die either. She couldn't bear to lose her. Was that selfish? She had heard the words 'merciful release' being murmured among the village women and she wanted to bang their heads together. How dare they make it sound so simple?

Hal appeared from among the trees, carrying a huge bouquet of pinks, and her facial muscles fluttered as a smile formed. She waved to him before creeping out of Mother's room, running downstairs and meeting him halfway up the path, flying straight into the shelter of his free arm to snuggle close, and never mind that she practically got a faceful of pinks, their heavenly scent enfolding her along with his embrace. Slipping her arm about his waist, she drew him indoors.

The pinks were in a jug. Her bones melted. Trust Hal. He had provided a vase so that she wouldn't have to root around for one, a seemingly small gesture but, oh, such a meaningful and important one when her nerves were stretched to breaking point with worry, and even the tiniest additional task could pile on the tension.

'Happy birthday,' said Hal, presenting the pinks.

'Thank you. They're lovely.'

'There's this as well.' He took a flat parcel from under his arm. 'I hope you like it.'

She unwrapped it to reveal a framed watercolour of the laburnum walk. 'Did you do it? This will have pride of place on our parlour wall one day.'

She drew him to the window seat, where they could sit close together.

'I spent the walk here wondering whether it was appropriate to wish you a happy birthday,' Hal said.

'Wondering whether it's safe to say "happy" under the circumstances?' She huffed a breath. How to explain? 'Something I've learnt from Mother's illness is that it's now that matters. How

126

she feels can change so much so quickly. It isn't "How are you today, Mother?" or even "How are you this morning?" She could feel wretched from her toes to her back teeth now, then perk up in an hour or two's time. So what matters is now, this minute. And here, now, being with you, I'm happy.'

Happy. And safe. Hal's embrace was her safe place.

He pressed a kiss into her hair before drawing his face away to look at her. His light-brown eyes, though warm, were troubled, and a knot of unease appeared in Juliet's stomach. Her safe place wasn't quite so safe any more.

'I hope you'll still be happy when you hear my news,' he said. 'Mr Nugent has found me a position with a garden designer currently working in London.'

'London!'

'I know. It's a long way.'

The hairs lifted on the back of her neck. Her one safe place was going to be wrenched away.

'I'm more sorry than I can say.' Hal leant his forehead against hers. 'But if I don't accept this chance, Mr Nugent isn't going to put himself out for me a second time.'

She squared her shoulders. 'You must go. Of course you must. This is what you've been working towards all this time. It's a marvellous opportunity.'

'It is, and it's happened much earlier than I thought it would.'

'You deserve it and don't let anybody tell you otherwise.'

'Leaving you, with your mother so poorly, feels like I'm abandoning you.'

'No, you aren't. We always knew this opportunity would come. I'd rather it hadn't happened just now, but . . .' She forced a smile. 'When?'

'Soon. Mr Clayton's work is already in progress.'

She clenched her hands in her lap so as not to grab hold of him for support. 'How long will you be gone?'

'I can't say. I'm sorry, love. Nothing is decided at present.'

'Then we must make the most of the time we have.' How calm she sounded – not cheerful, precisely, but pleased. As if this were a good thing – which, of course, it was. It could be the beginning of Hal's career. She had promised to support him in everything he did. She just hadn't realised how hard it would be. For better or worse – wasn't that the marriage vow? This was both, and it was up to her to make it as easy as possible for him. 'You're not to feel bad about leaving me. Afterwards . . . I'll be going back to the big house as seamstress, so I'll be fine.'

'I'm proud of you for that.'

'You never know, maybe you'll be back before I go.'

But the look on his face told her he wouldn't. She knew it too, really. She just couldn't bear to face it. She wanted Mother to hang on and on.

Chapter Ten

There was a knock at the cottage door and in walked Alf Mulgrew. 'I'm here to remove the bolts. Mr Nugent says if there's an emergency in the night and you've bolted the doors, it could cause problems.'

Juliet stared. She had been bolting the doors, back and front, since the incident in her bedroom. Had Mr Nugent attempted to come in at night since then? She watched helplessly as Alf set about his task. Locking herself in would be no good, as there were sets of keys to all the cottages in the estate room.

She fretted all evening, but Mr Nugent didn't come. Neither did he appear the following evening. She wished he would come so she could get it over with – no, she didn't.

She went to bed, exhausted and wretched, sighing herself to sleep at long last. When she woke the next morning, she lay for a while, her head stuffed with worries. As she threw back the covers and swung her legs out, she caught a whiff of – yes, rose. Her gaze flew to the candle. She hadn't touched it since that occasion with Mr Nugent. Her heart beat faster. Had Mr Nugent—? No.

But the candle was shorter than it had been, and there was no denying the fragrance in the air.

That night, she started to heave the chest of drawers across the door, but the noise brought Mother stumbling out of bed. She sagged against the door frame, heavy-eyed and bone-thin.

'What are you playing at?'

'I dropped something down the back.'

'Leave it. I can't sleep with that racket.'

So that was the end of that. She got into bed and sat curled up with her arms locked round her knees, her back pressed against the wall. She stayed like that until she was stiff with cold and her body was screaming at her to snuggle down, but she wouldn't give in, not even when she felt herself nodding off.

She jerked her head up, breathing in sharply – and there it was, the scent of roses. Mr Nugent stood in the candlelight, one side of his face bathed in its soft glow, the other deep in shadow.

'Did you fall asleep waiting for me? How eager that makes you look. How needy. I like that. I enjoyed watching you sleep, but I prefer you awake.'

A shudder pounded through her, jarring every bone. She pressed deeper into the corner, willing the wall to crack open and suck her inside. The muscles in her neck burnt, and she moved her shoulders, trying to ease them.

'Does your neck hurt?' Mr Nugent enquired softly.

The mattress dipped as he sat. She seemed about to roll onto his lap and she squirmed away, except that there was nowhere to squirm to, because she was already flattened against the wall. Mr Nugent patted the bed beside him. Heart beating fiercely, she shook her head.

'No? Are you saying no to me?' He laughed quietly, indulgently.

'It was a simple offer of help. Your neck is painful: I can ease it. If you don't want my help, all you need say is "No, thank you, sir" and that's all there is to it.'

She swallowed. 'No, thank you, sir.'

'And then I say "Don't be foolish. I know better than you" and help you anyway.'

He lifted her towards him, turning her so her back was to him. His hands rested on her shoulders, thumbs pressing in slow circular movements, fingers kneading and manipulating. Her hardened muscles relaxed and she felt stupid, stupid, stupid.

Mr Nugent tutted softly. 'I come to collect some gratitude and end up helping you . . . again. You know I'll never refuse you. And,' he added, 'you mustn't refuse me either. Unfasten your buttons.'

She didn't move. She remembered what happened last time and she didn't move.

'You're right,' Mr Nugent murmured. 'You dear girl, you're right,' and her relief was so huge that it hurt more than the dread, until he continued, 'It has to be more each time, just a little more. Here, allow me.'

He slipped to his knees in front of her and set to work on the buttons himself. When the last of them surrendered, he pushed aside the edges of the yoke. Mother had worked hard on it, all those tiny pleats and the ribbon-work. Mr Nugent leant in and rested his cheek against her chest. He stayed like that, and she began to think it wasn't so bad, then he moved his face and slid his fingers inside each edge of the yoke, pulling them so that the gap shifted away from her chest and instead it was her breast that was exposed, only to be covered by his face, his mouth and an odd murmuring that might have been words, might have been kisses, and dear heaven above, was he sucking her? Her lips peeled back from her teeth. It hurt too, his moustache rasping across her soft flesh.

At last, with one final flick of the tongue, he withdrew. His eyelids looked heavy and he breathed deeply. He rose and looked down on her. With the candlelight at his back, his face was all shadows and darkness.

'You can't help yourself, can you?' he remarked. 'Look at you, begging for more. Cover yourself, girl.'

Snuffing out the candle between his fingers, he left the room. Desperate to wash his slobberings away, she fumbled with the lamp and poured water into her bowl, sloshing it over her breast and soaping it again and again. And again.

Juliet sat beside the window, chin in hand, elbow on the sill. Hal would be leaving soon, and it was all she could do to hang onto her heart and stop it scattering in pieces. How was she to manage without him? She had thought over and over about telling him about Mr Nugent, but shame kept her quiet. Guilt too. In her head she knew it wasn't her fault, but in her heart and her stomach, she feared it was. Besides, what would happen to Mother if she kicked up a stink? She felt frightened and dirty and stupid, stupid, stupid.

It was a fine day, all blue skies and sunshine. And trees. That was how it was here. Either rain and trees or sunshine and trees. There was nothing else – just trees. She felt hemmed in. Or maybe that was nothing to do with the trees.

She looked over her shoulder. Mother slept. She spent more time asleep than awake these days. The village women had stopped coming in the afternoons. It had become Juliet's job to sit with her then. And sit was all she did. She ought to be sewing or reading, but these were beyond her. Sometimes she tried, but it wasn't long before her mind was pulled inexorably to other matters.

'Juliet? Come here.'

She took Mother's hand. 'Do you need more medicine?'

'Want to . . . talk to you. Have to tell you something. Beatrice said there's talk going round about you.'

Cold poured through her. Surely not about her and Mr Nugent—?

'Folk are saying you'll go to Moorside as seamstress.'

Relief made her limbs tingle. 'I've heard that too. Isn't it good?'

'But you're to join Mr Nugent's household.'

'Not if Lady Margaret wants me.'

Mother's eyes sparkled with tears. 'She won't. She won't.'

'Everyone at Moorside says so. And why wouldn't she? She liked having her own seamstress.'

'But not you.'

Fear fluttered inside her. 'Why not?'

Mother lifted her hand from the bed, taking Juliet's with it, then dropped them both. 'If I'd known what was going to happen . . . If I'd known I'd be this ill, I'd have praised you to high heaven, but I couldn't know, could I? So I did you down. I told her ladyship that you're . . . capable enough under supervision but you've no flair in your own right. I told her that was why I sent you to work in Naseby's . . . because you weren't good enough for her sewing room.'

'You didn't! Why would you do that?'

'I know, I know, I shouldn't have, but I couldn't help it. You were so good at everything and I couldn't bear it. It . . . it wasn't fair, after I'd worked so hard. It's not just that you're a good needlewoman. You can design too; you've a real eye for it. I knew that when you designed the embroidered panel. It was . . . breathtaking.' Mother's face puckered as if she were about to cry. 'So I let Lady Margaret think it was my design.'

'I know.'

'The very idea of a young chit having that kind of ability!'

'But it was my work.'

'And that was our secret – until you blabbed to Mrs Naseby. It was why I stopped you having drawing lessons too, because I saw what was happening. You were so busy concentrating on getting the proportions right on the figures that you didn't notice, but I did. You dressed them. You created costumes for them out of your head. I've never done that. Give me a pattern and I can work wonders, but creating a costume from scratch, designing it . . . well, I didn't want you doing that.'

'Why not?'

An obstinate look came over Mother's face. 'I was better than Clara. Mother always said so. She was hard on Clara because of it, but she was hard on me too, because she expected more of me. Honestly, there was no pleasing her. I wanted to get my salon before Clara did, and Mother used to laugh at Clara and say she could go and work for me. That made Clara cry, which was why Mother said it, of course, and I had to comfort Clara, but really I was thinking how wonderful it would be if I had the success and she was one of my workers. Only I ended up married and she's the one with the salon.'

'But you'd rather have had Pop than a salon, wouldn't you?'

'But I haven't got him any more, have I?'

'You've got me,' Juliet whispered.

'And don't I know it! A daughter with more talent than I've got. Who wants that?'

'Aren't mothers supposed to want the best for their children?'

'You can want the best without wanting to be outshone. My mother would never have let Clara and me outshine her. That's why I was glad you got yourself hitched so young. I thought: that'll keep her busy.' Mother uttered a sound that was part splutter, part laugh. 'Hark at me, jealous of my own daughter.' Another splutter followed, this time of tears and snot. 'And if that makes me some sort of monster, so be it.' She smeared her face with the back of her hand before Juliet could pass her a hanky.

'You're not a monster.'

'I've made good and sure you'll never get that job with Lady Margaret.' Mother reached for her hand, and Juliet pretended to think she wanted the hanky. 'Still, you've got the job with Mr Nugent. You'll be all right.'

Dear God. Mr Nugent's sewing girl.

Juliet trudged home from the gardeners' cottages, a lump in her throat and hot pressure behind her eyes. Hal would be leaving for Annerby shortly to catch the train. She couldn't go to the station with him, because she couldn't leave Mother for that long. As it was, she had spent most of the morning and half the afternoon with the Prices. She was enormously proud of Hal, but, oh, she didn't want him to leave.

Hal's mum had tried to engineer her into pleading with him to stay. 'Juliet will miss you dreadfully, won't you, dear? And you with your poor mother to cope with an' all.'

'Of course I'll miss him,' said Juliet, 'but he knows how much I want him to achieve his ambition.'

'Well said, young Juliet,' chimed in Harold Price. 'Leave the lass alone, Marian. 'Tisn't fair to try to make her stand in Hal's way.'

Hal had squeezed her hand and dropped a kiss close by her ear as he murmured, 'Thank you.'

She turned her gaze towards him, wanting him to see the love shining in her eyes, even though her heart was trembling with the knowledge of how she would miss him.

Now she was on her way home. Her heart was full – and so was

135

her mind. After Mother . . . well, afterwards, what if she found a way to join Hal in London? Might she be allowed to join the Drysdales' London household as a maid? If she asked Mrs Whicker, would she have to refer the matter to Mr Nugent? Surely not for a maid. Would she simply offer Juliet's services to the London housekeeper?

'Well, well, look who it is.' William Turton stood in front of her, looking like he owned the place, feet apart, hands on hips. 'I've been waiting for you.'

She felt a spark of annoyance. The last thing she needed was company. 'Not now.'

'That's not very friendly when I've been waiting for you.' His sorrowful voice mocked her.

She stepped aside, but he blocked her path.

William's voice hardened. 'I waited here once before, only old Nugent came along and saved the day, you might say. Saved your day, at any rate. Still, it gave me the opportunity to meet you officially, as it were, on the hill and in the shop. You thought I fancied you. Why else make such a point of saying you had a bloke? That's where you've been today, isn't it, to see your gardener's boy?'

She turned to retrace her steps, but William grabbed her arm, twisting her round to face him.

'Leaving so soon? Don't you want to say goodbye? I'll be on my way after this. I've just got my business to finish up. Know about my business, do you, from Cecily? A wrong that needs righting. So – let's get it set to rights, shall we?'

'What are you talking about?'

'With your cooperation, of course. Or better yet, without it.'

His mouth set in a cruel line. She was baffled, then fear washed away her confusion. She tried to run, but he grabbed her, and she felt a fresh thrill of shock as she realised the strength of his hands and arms. She opened her mouth to yell, but William clouted her across the side of her head hard enough to make it spin, leaving her feeling stunned and sick. He fastened one arm around her waist, his other hand clamped over her mouth, as he half dragged, half carried her from the path. She struggled to pull free, but she was no match for him, staggering along beside his ground-eating stride.

William tossed her down. She threw out her hands to save herself going face first into the undergrowth. She staggered to her feet, only to be knocked down again. This time William followed her down, seizing her wrists and planting them either side of her head. Juliet started to struggle, but froze when his face appeared close above hers.

'Ever done it with the gardener's boy?'

Fresh panic coursed through her. She bucked hard, but William threw one leg across her body and straddled her. His face broke into a grin. He snapped her wrists together so he could hold them in one hand, then used his free hand to shove his way through the front of her jacket and wrench open her blouse, dragging the thin cotton of her chemise this way and that. Terrified, Juliet hauled in a breath and let out a scream, amazed at how reedy it was when it was meant to be a huge sound to bring rescue pounding this way. The sound cut off sharply when he slapped her across her face.

'Much as your cries would add to the moment, I'm afraid I can't allow them. Excuse the snot.' He stuffed a balled-up handkerchief into her mouth.

Her eyes bulged as her air supply was blocked, then she managed to sniff in a few thin breaths. William regarded her, his eyes steady. She gazed pleadingly at him, hoping against hope . . . and when he raised himself from her waist, she felt a flash of relief, but it turned to horror as he kneed her legs apart, her thighs almost cracking into pieces from the effort to resist.

She seemed to split in two. Part of her was fighting and struggling while the other part was somewhere else, somewhere distant. Only when William rammed himself into her did the two parts rush back together, and she let loose a high-pitched humming sound that was the closest she could get to a scream. His thrusts grew quicker until he pushed himself in so deep that it seemed he must be jammed there for ever. His body shuddered violently and he slumped, dropping his full weight on her, making what little breath she had left come oozing out.

She managed to pull an arm free. It felt hot and bruised and numb all at the same time. With useless fingers, she plucked at the handkerchief in her mouth. The weight on top of her eased as William raised himself on his elbows. When his hand came up, she tried to flinch away, but he simply took a pinch of the fabric and yanked the hanky out so swiftly she gagged.

If there had been even one drop of juice inside her mouth, she would have spat in his face, but the handkerchief had left her mouth parched and raw.

'Get off,' she rasped.

'My guess is I beat the gardener's boy to it.'

'Get *off*.'

'In a minute. Haven't quite finished yet. If it were up to me, I'd gladly walk away right now, leaving you lying here wondering what the bloody hell just happened. But I'm under orders, see, so I can't. Rosie wanted you to know this came from her.' He dropped a kiss on Juliet's nose. 'Love from Rosie.'

Chapter Eleven

Black dots clouded Juliet's vision and the sound of her heartbeats battered the insides of her ears as she stumbled home, her legs threatening to give way at any moment. She walked with them apart, as though she had wet herself. It was as if she had been punched hard between her legs and right up inside, all the way to the bowl of her stomach.

She skirted round the cottage to creep in through the back. Hearing voices in Mother's room, she tiptoed upstairs. Mother's door was open. Ella said, 'Here she comes,' but she couldn't face them, couldn't face anyone ever again.

She shut herself in her room and sat on the bed. Then she stood up. She didn't know what to do. Presently there was a gentle knock.

'I'm off now, petal,' said Ella. 'She's managed a little soup and has fallen asleep.' Her lovely eyes narrowed. 'Are you all right?' She sighed. 'I know, love, it's hard, but she's surrounded by friends and that counts for a lot.'

She made a move and Juliet, fearing a kindly hug that would cause her to shatter into a thousand brittle shards, stepped backwards.

'Ah, well,' Ella said. 'You know where I am.'

When she was gone, Juliet stood in Mother's doorway, watching her sleep. Her mind was frozen, but horror teemed beneath the ice. She swung away and headed downstairs. She needed to scrub herself clean, but when she attempted to lift the bath from its hook, it felt unaccountably heavy and she staggered backwards, feeling an inner swoop as she fell. Landing flat on her back, she lived again the terror of that moment when William Turton hurled her to the ground. With inarticulate sounds of fear and revulsion, she scrambled up, brushing herself down with wild hands. She wanted to scrub every bit of filth and degradation from her flesh, and when she had finished, she wanted to do it all over again to make sure.

What was the point, if Mr Nugent came tonight?

He didn't come. Nor the next night or the next. She heard he was away on business. She would have rejoiced at that last week. Now she didn't care. Couldn't.

Rosie had done this. Rosie.

'Love from Rosie,' William Turton had said. Oh, dear God, Rosie. Then he had rolled off her, already straightening his clothes as he came to his feet, while she lay there, stunned. She gasped in fear as he leant down, but all he did was tuck something in her pocket. 'My calling card,' he said and off he sauntered, whistling jauntily.

She found it a day or two later. His business card. She held it between her fingertips.

'Love from Rosie'. Oh, dear God, Rosie.

The first Juliet knew of Mr Nugent's return was when he came to pay his respects to Mother, who sat hunched in the basketwork chair, the footstool pulled close so she could draw up her knees. It was agony for her to manage the stairs now, but she remained determined to come down every morning.

Mr Nugent took one look at her and said, 'Daybed.'

Although Juliet was relieved for Mother's sake, she knew too that it was something else to be grateful for. Sure enough, there was a visit that night. Mother had slunk off to bed early, saying she might come down again later, but that was just pretence. There was a lot of pretending these days. Juliet sat with her hands folded in her lap. It was as if she was standing outside herself, observing how composed she looked. In another corner of her mind she imagined herself running round like a mad thing, barricading herself in. Perhaps she should. If she didn't, was it tantamount to agreeing to what Mr Nugent wanted? Except that she had to agree, because if she wasn't grateful, what would become of Mother? And, anyroad, after what William Turton had done—

Mr Nugent took her upstairs, set the rose candle burning and quietly ordered her to undress. When she reached for her nightgown, he stopped her and she had to stand there while he ran his hands over her, his fingertips whispering across her flesh. She ought to have shuddered, but her heart was too heavy to bother.

When he finished, she wrenched her nightgown over her head, slipped into bed and pulled up the covers. The bed dipped as he sat. He placed his hands either side of her shoulders, pressing down the bedclothes around her, making her feel trapped, making her feel the way William Turton had made her feel when he overpowered and defiled her.

Mr Nugent looked at her. She imagined spitting in his face. Then he got up, snuffing out the candle as he left.

Agnes clung to the wall at the foot of the stairs, feeling sick not just in her stomach but in every part of her body. Even her eyeballs felt sick. Her eyelids fluttered, desperate to close. Her suffering body was screaming for the release of unconsciousness. If she could just stagger back to the daybed. But Doctor Entwistle was coming. She felt a twinge of anger. Her hands fisted and her knuckles cracked. Bloody doctor. What good had he done? But she had more self-respect than to be anywhere other than in her own bed when he came.

Juliet came scurrying to the rescue.

'Have you changed the sheets?' Agnes demanded.

'Yes, Mother, and aired the room.'

Getting upstairs was a devil of a job. Every bone and muscle, every bit of her down to the tiniest shred of gristle, jangled. The gentlest touch chafed her sensitive flesh, yet she could barely move without assistance.

Nausea – sudden overwhelming nausea. Halfway upstairs, she sagged onto the step and sat hunched over, wrapping stick-thin arms round herself.

'Bowl,' she mumbled urgently. 'Get a bowl.'

But Juliet wasn't quick enough, and with a horrid lurch that nearly turned her inside out, Agnes vomited on the stairs. Tears of shame trickled into the shrunken hollows where her cheeks used to be.

'It's all right,' Juliet whispered. 'It's all right.'

'It's *not* all right.' Her breath was laced with fumes; her face twisted in disgust.

When she got back to bed, she lay trembling with pain. She was distantly aware of Juliet cleaning up the mess and opening the windows. *Please let the stench shift in time*. She still felt green around the gills, and not just the gills but everywhere else too. If only she could sleep . . .

She awoke she had no idea how much later. Someone knocked on the door. It reverberated through her bones.

Doctor Entwistle was accompanied by Beatrice. Agnes had had to swallow the fact that he required Beatrice's presence. She submitted to being examined and questioned, then had to submit to his disappearing downstairs to speak to Beatrice, no doubt with Juliet hovering close by, ignored by the great man. At least she had the dignity of paying her own fees. She had insisted on that. She would accept any other form of help, but when Mr Nugent had tactfully suggested that the estate would meet the doctor's fees, she put her foot down. Cooking and cleaning, food from the big house, the daybed – all counted as help, but money was charity.

She heard Doctor Entwistle leave, then Beatrice and Juliet came upstairs.

Beatrice sat beside the bed. 'Doctor says there's a decision to make. Wherever you sleep next, here or in the daybed, that's where you're stopping.'

'You mean I've to choose where to die,' Agnes stated bluntly. She was careful to fold her lips over her teeth when she finished speaking. Her flesh might be diminished, but her teeth weren't. They felt as big as gravestones.

'No,' Juliet cried, 'it's so you don't have to manage the stairs.'

Beatrice placed a steadying hand on Juliet's arm. 'Aye, that's about the sum of it, Agnes. Don't go making it worse for the lass.'

'I reckon I'll stay here, then,' she said.

Cecily felt torn in two. Training as a lady's maid knocked spots off laying fires and making beds, but she missed William badly and she was worried about Juliet and her mum. Mr Nugent had informed his lordship in one of his letters that Mrs Harper was nearing the end, and word had filtered down to Cecily. She wished she could be there to give her friend a hug. How must she be feeling, poor love?

Cecily had written a couple of letters, one to Mam and one to Juliet, but she wasn't much of a writer. She could talk like nobody's business, but put a pen in her hand and the words dried up. She had heard back from Juliet, a short letter, not saying much, but that was just as well, really, since maids' letters were opened and read by Mrs Goodwin, who was the Mrs Whicker of the London house. Even so, Cecily felt let down. She had imagined Juliet would be a fluent letter writer. And just what did she mean by *I have something important to tell you, but it can wait until you come back*, eh?

Not that Cecily had time to dwell on it. Miss Phoebe and Miss Marchant between them kept her on her toes. When she wasn't dressing her young lady or putting up her hair, she was removing stains under Miss Marchant's eagle eye or making bath salts or religiously following Miss Marchant's grandmother's recipe for hand whitener.

She worked more hours than she used to, because she was required to wait up for Miss Phoebe and see her to bed, and as the Drysdales had apparently come to London purely to go out every night, Cecily seldom sank into her own bed before midnight. Any disadvantage attached to this, however, was made up for by the delight of handling Miss Phoebe's beautiful clothes.

'You won't know yourself when you get home, miss,' Cecily ventured as she helped her young mistress into an afternoon dress of shell-pink silk trimmed with dainty ruffles. 'Moorside will seem very dull after this.'

Cecily's heart skipped a little faster. Miss Phoebe might be going home to a quiet life but Cecily wasn't. She was dying to be reunited with William.

'We're not going home,' said Miss Phoebe. 'We're going to the Isle of Wight, and after that to my aunt and uncle in Hertfordshire. We shan't be home for simply ages.'

Having Mother in bed all the time nearly made Juliet's heart crack down the middle at first, but soon it became normal. Each night, Juliet heaved herself out of bed several times to see if Mother was awake and if she needed anything, and each morning, she woke with the heavy-headed feeling of not having slept soundly. Her bones creaked under the weight of dark despair, a feeling so intense it made her nauseous.

All at once she had to fling aside the covers and make a dive for the wash bowl to be sick. Vomit raced up her gullet, hot and sour, and whooshed out of her with astonishing speed. Afterwards she dipped her face cloth into the jug and dabbed her face.

That was her one moment of weakness. Now she had to be strong. She drew in a deep breath. She wouldn't let Mother down.

It was better to concentrate on Mother than on . . . anything else. If she immersed herself in Mother's care, she could avoid thinking of . . . other things. She had written to Cecily, a letter that had taken several days to compose, because . . . well, just because. She had to warn Cecily about William Turton, but she couldn't put it in a letter. Even if Cecily's letters weren't read by the Drysdales' London housekeeper, she still couldn't have committed such a vile incident to paper, so she simply made a vague remark about having something to say when Cecily returned. Should she have blathered on about other things? Pretended her letter was an ordinary letter?

Neither could she write to Hal in any meaningful way. Remembering those long, chatty letters she had planned to send him every few days made her feel weighed down, as if her body was too heavy to move. Instead of bombarding him with bright, loving missives as she had intended, she wrote only in reply to his letters and cut her own short by saying she had to get back to Mother.

The days passed in a haze of weak soup, pain-dulling medicine and bed baths that, no matter how gentle you were, always resulted in Mother's being crotchety and tearful. Oh, and chamber pots. Poor Mother. When had she last visited the earth-closet? Now she was reduced to using chamber pots, like old Mrs Dancy. She wept from sheer humiliation at first, but then, like everything else, it became normal, or maybe she was too exhausted and pain-riddled to care. Her skin, stretched tight across her bones, turned yellow with jaundice, making her faded fair hair look dirty.

Juliet barely left the cottage. From Mother's window, she saw the wood anemones fade, replaced by the pink bells on the foxgloves' tall stems. Hal's letters were full of the private garden in a fancy London square, where he was not only being trained by Mr Clayton in matters of design but also – typical Hal – mucking in with the physical labour. His letters left her heart beating with a dull thud that turned her blood to sludge in her veins. She was no longer the girl he had left behind. William Turton had violated not only her body but every corner of her mind. He had violated her future. How was she ever to tell Hal? A tremor passed through her body. She could never tell anyone.

Was there something about her that made others feel free to mistreat her? Mr Nugent molested her and she had to let him, because she was grateful, but she didn't feel grateful – she felt dirty and degraded and stupid, stupid, stupid. Was it her own fault for letting him? Should she have said 'No', loudly and firmly, the very first time? Too late now. Then again, what was a bit of groping compared to what William Turton had done? 'Love from Rosie'. Rosie had never forgiven her for that mistake over Hal's identity. Was she to blame for the attack on Rosie?

'The poor lass is under such a lot of strain,' murmured the village women. 'You can see it in her eyes.'

And that made her feel like a cheat and a liar. They thought she was beside herself with worry over Mother, and she was, but it was degradation that was eating her alive.

The village women were at the cottage all day now. They sat beside Mother's bed, conversing in hushed voices across her body while she slept.

'It's as though Doctor Entwistle made her worse by saying she had to stay put,' Juliet whispered to Mrs Grove.

'Nay, lass. He could see it were time.'

But Juliet still thought the doctor's visit had been like having the Angel of Death under their roof.

When she threw up again the following morning, her blood turned to ice.

Not despair. Morning sickness.

'Why not go for a walk, chick?' suggested Ella. 'Fresh air would do you good.'

Juliet didn't want to, couldn't be bothered, but she couldn't be bothered to argue either, so off she went. Not through the park. The last time she had walked through the park . . . She slipped through the gate in the wall and headed for the village, but that was asking for trouble. Trouble: conversation, kind enquiries. Instead she took the long way round and ended up at the church. Should she visit Pop? She ought to, but knowing that Mr Dancy would soon open up his grave to receive Mother was too much to bear.

She trailed back the way she had come, entering through the side gate.

Ella came running along the path. 'There you are. Come quickly! She's took bad ways.'

They raced to the cottage. Faces turned as Juliet burst into Mother's room. She pushed past someone and gazed down at her mother, motionless and heartbreakingly thin. Her arms were lying on top of the bedclothes, neatly arranged by her sides. Juliet picked up one brittle hand and clutched it.

On the other side of the bed, Mrs Grove leant forward to speak to Mother. 'She's here now, love. You can go if you want.'

The hand in Juliet's went slack.

'Mr Nugent's downstairs. You're to go to Arley House. If you pack your things, he'll have them fetched.'

Juliet was aware of not hearing Ella's gentle words until several seconds after they were spoken. It took that long for them to penetrate the layers of grief and shock. She was at Mother's bedside. They had washed Mother's poor emaciated body and laid her out, then embarked upon a long but oddly comforting discussion about what to do with her hair, eventually plaiting it into a single braid drawn forwards over her shoulder.

The others had gone downstairs then, leaving Juliet. Mother looked peaceful, the lines of pain smoothed out. Juliet wanted to talk to her, but there was too much to say, and anyroad, she was gone.

She looked up into Ella's face. 'No. I'm staying here until after the funeral.'

Ella crept out, and she turned back to Mother. What in heaven's name was she going to do? You could get rid of a baby, but she had no idea how, except that it was dangerous and the mother sometimes died too. She would end up, oh, dear God, she would end up being sent to Ladyfield.

Ella's return cut across her thoughts. 'Mr Nugent will arrange the funeral for Friday. He says you're expected at Arley House at four o'clock that afternoon. We'll hold the wake at Beatrice's. It makes sense, pet,' she added when Juliet started to protest. 'It's a fair old walk here from the village and it'll make it easier to have this place ready an' all.'

Ready for Juliet to leave; ready to move into Mr Nugent's household. She couldn't do that; she couldn't walk into the trap of her own free will. Yet what alternative was there? She couldn't go to London to be with Hal – not now. She pressed her fist to her mouth to stifle a cry of anguish as she fought not to break down.

Arms came round her and for one wild wonderful, stupid, stupid moment, she thought it was Hal, but the arms didn't feel right, and when she looked, it was Ella.

'There, petal, you have a good skrike.'

And she did, though the hot tears were mixed with shame, because Ella thought she was crying for Mother. And she was, she was, but she was crying for herself, too, and Mr Nugent's relentless take, take, taking of gratitude and Rosie's revenge and the terrible fear that was rolling in her guts.

She didn't cry for long. She couldn't afford to.

'Come and have some tea,' Ella coaxed.

'Has Mr Nugent gone?'

'Aye, love.'

Mrs Grove and two or three others looked up as they appeared.

'We were just saying,' Mrs Grove observed, 'that we'll be in first thing tomorrow to get this place shipshape for handing back.'

'Thank you,' said Juliet. Not that the cottage needed special cleaning after the way these stalwart friends had cared for it, but that wouldn't stop them.

'I'll tell the Prices, and they can write to Hal,' said Mrs Grove. 'You must write to that aunt of yours. If it goes by the evening post, she'll get it in't morning. Not that she put herself out to come to your dad's funeral,' she added darkly.

Juliet's fingertips touched lips that had parted on a small breath. Now she knew what to do.

Chapter Twelve

While the others scrubbed and polished, Juliet hauled the rugs outside and gave them a furious beating, carrying on long after the dust wafted away. She was hitting William Turton – or possibly Mr Nugent. She was full of – she wasn't sure what she was full of, but it was hot and painful, and made her feel sick and resentful and desperate. Now that she had her plan, now that she wasn't doomed to go to Arley House, she ought to be light-hearted, only she couldn't be because there was still the baby. She imagined it coming loose inside her and bashed harder still, until her hands were grasped and pulled to a halt by Ella.

They might be Ella's hands, but it was Mrs Grove's voice saying, 'That's enough, thank you. Your mother's things want sorting and you need to get packed.'

They made neat piles of Mother's beautifully stitched clothes.

'It'll be fortunate women who receive these,' Mrs Grove observed.

'How will we carry it all?' Ella asked.

'Bundled in a sheet,' was the robust answer, and when Juliet winced, Mrs Grove added briskly, 'There are dishes in the kitchen that want returning to the big house.'

She was grateful to escape. She arrived at Moorside to be overwhelmed by kind words and before she knew it, she was fighting back tears and all she wanted was to get back to the cottage.

She returned to find virtually all her possessions had vanished.

'Mr Nugent sent a trunk,' Mrs Grove explained, 'so we packed it for you. It were collected ten minutes since.'

She stared in disbelief. All that remained was what she needed tonight and her black shop dress for tomorrow, plus her straw boater, its red ribbon replaced by black. But everything else was gone, including her work basket. It was all she could do not to groan aloud. She needed her work basket. Wait – Hal's painting still hung on the wall. Best not draw attention to it or someone would rush it over to Arley House.

'And I've got your mother's money tin to give to Mr Nugent.'

Not the money as well? 'I can do that,' Juliet said quickly.

'She entrusted the job to me and I take my responsibilities seriously. Mr Nugent will look after it for you.'

Juliet's nails bit into the palms of her hands. She wanted to scream at Mrs Grove and call her an interfering busybody.

'If you take the bundle of clothes to my cottage,' Mrs Grove instructed Ella, 'I'll fetch the tin round to Mr Nugent. We'll leave the work basket here while the morrow.'

It had been Ella's idea to give the village women items from Mother's basket after the funeral, and Juliet had agreed, because these good neighbours deserved useful little keepsakes and she had her own basket. Or she had until a few minutes ago. Now she had only her night things, tomorrow's funeral garb and the clothes she stood up in. She had no money – yes, she did. Mother's savings and the wages Juliet had tipped up were gone, but she still had her sewing money. It would have to do.

'Did this belong to your mother?' Ella held a brass candlestick. 'It was beside her bed. It should go in your room, Juliet, if it's to go to Arley House.'

'It belongs to the cottage.'

She took it upstairs when the others left, hesitating outside Mother's closed door before placing the candlestick on the shelf at the top of the stairs. She couldn't enter the room just to return the candlestick. It would be like pretending Mother was still alive.

It was a glowing summer evening with skies the blue of cornflowers and clouds edged with gold when Mother was brought downstairs for the final time. Her simple coffin was placed across wooden chairs that Juliet hadn't even realised had appeared, its lid propped discreetly in a corner. Juliet grasped Ella's hands until Mother was settled. Then the vigil began, the side gate being left unlocked all night for folk to come and go.

Mrs Grove sent Juliet to bed at dawn, waking her before she left. Juliet knew she ought to sit up and say thank you, but if she moved so much as an inch, she would have to bolt for the wash bowl.

The moment the door closed behind Mrs Grove, her stomach heaved. She clamped her mouth shut, praying for the sound of the front door. Vomit surged up her gullet, burning it, and poured into her mouth so fulsomely that she thought it would come trickling out of her nose and eyes. With bulging cheeks, she rolled out of bed and hung over the bowl. Afterwards she slipped her arms into her dressing gown and carried the bowl out to the earth-closet, holding her breath against the vile smell.

Clad in her black dress, she wound the laces up the hooks on her boots, then pulled Pop's old carpetbag from under the bed. She was feeling queasy again, but perhaps that was nerves. The carpetbag was roomy and, had they still been in her possession, would have held all her clothes, leaving her to carry her work basket in her other hand. Instead, what she had left took up next to no space and she stared in dismay.

She emptied the carpetbag and eased Mother's work basket inside, laying Hal's picture of the laburnum walk on top. It was a snug fit, but she slotted in her hairbrush and clothes brush down the sides before cramming in yesterday's clothes. Closing the bag, she fastened the straps and tested its weight: not heavy, just bulky.

She hurried to stash it in bushes on the outskirts of the village. Everyone would go from the church to Mrs Grove's cottage, and Juliet was meant to go later from there to Arley House, but instead she would double back, collect her bag and disappear, taking the path across the tops and down into Annerby to catch the train.

The queasiness was building as she headed back to the cottage. There was a horse and cart outside the gate. One of the estate men emerged from inside, carrying the bedside cabinet from her room, followed by another, carrying the mirror, wrapped in a cloth.

Mr Nugent stood in the middle of the parlour. 'If you've packed the last of your things, they can go on the cart.'

'I've taken my bag to Mrs Grove's.'

'Did you pack your special candle?'

'No, sir.'

'Then kindly fetch it.'

Upstairs, she stared at the brass candle holder with the little mouse perched on the edge of the saucer. She wanted to hurl it through the window. Nausea rolled and she clutched the chest of drawers, bending over and breathing deeply to steady herself.

She was going to be sick. She had to get rid of Mr Nugent.

Downstairs, one of the men was waiting. She gave him the candle holder.

'That's everything for Arley House,' Mr Nugent told him. When the cart rumbled away, he told Juliet, 'They'll be back later to fetch your mother.'

They had screwed down the coffin lid. She felt a pang at being denied a final farewell.

'I gather the procession is starting from the village,' Mr Nugent said.

'From Mrs Grove's, sir.'

She held onto the contents of her stomach while he put on his hat and twitched his gloves. She held on while he walked to the door and opened it, and while he stepped outside. The moment the door started to shut, she darted out to the earth-closet, where she heaved up everything but the soles of her shoes. She paused at the water pump to splash her face and swill cold water round her mouth.

When she returned, Mr Nugent was in the parlour, his jaw set, his eyes hard and glittering.

He knew.

'Sick in the morning? By Christ! You've been whoring around with that damned Price – and after I ordered him to keep his hands off you. He'll pay for this. And as for you, madam—'

Juliet didn't see it coming. Mr Nugent walloped her across the face. Her neck crunched as her head jerked sideways. Another blow sent her sprawling and she banged her ribs on the stairs. She scrambled up a few steps, only to find him looming over her.

'Haven't I treated you well, taken my time over you, broken

155

you in gently? I could have had you till your teeth rattled morning, noon and night. God, when I think of the trouble I've gone to, getting rid of Price to London, so I could have you to myself. And all the while – all the while—'

She dragged herself up a few more stairs, shrieking as he grabbed her ankle. She kicked out – wriggled – yanked herself free and sped upstairs with Mr Nugent on her heels. As she gained the landing, he caught her arm, spinning her round.

'You want to see what I can do to you?'

His hand was at her collar, his fingers sliding inside. Any second now he would rip her dress clean down the front. She kicked out, but he grasped her foot and tipped her over. She went down hard on her back, clouting her head against the wall. Mr Nugent stood two or three stairs from the top. He had lost his grip on her dress, but he still had her ankle and he tugged it, hauling her towards him. She felt the floor slide away beneath her, and a huge wave of fear consumed her. It was William Turton all over again. Her head went swimmy. Was she going to faint? She mustn't, she mustn't. She had to fight.

Mr Nugent pulled her closer, lifting her foot high in the air. She scrabbled, but it was impossible to get any purchase. Her dress dropped, exposing her thighs.

'I'm going to have you forwards, backwards and throatwise,' he informed her. 'That was going to be your Christmas present to me, having me in your mouth, the humble gift of a grateful employee.'

Another tug on her ankle, then he lowered himself into a kneeling position on the edge of the landing. Mustering all her strength, she bent her free leg, drawing her knee as far back as she could, and slammed her boot heel where it would hurt most. Mr Nugent moved at the same moment, so she caught him in the top of his thigh instead, but that was enough to make him drop her ankle and stagger back, grabbing at the rail to keep from falling. She scrambled up, but already he had righted himself, and in another moment he would be on the landing. She snatched the candlestick from the shelf and, wielding it in both hands, swung it back over her shoulder, then forwards with all her might, smashing it into the side of his head. The crunch travelled all the way up her arms. Mr Nugent blinked – staggered – missed his footing – toppled. As he crashed down the stairs, relief cascaded through her, followed by horror.

Had she killed him? They would hang her. Then she heard a sound between a gasp and a groan. Her legs wobbled, but she had to get moving – now.

Juliet stood at the top of the hill above Annerby, her gaze following the railway lines to the station. Did she have enough money for her ticket? She had run and walked and run again all the way here. The crown of her head was so hot, it felt as though her scalp was peeling: she was hatless. Would that make her noticeable? She headed down the hill.

She was reluctant to ask for directions, but she had no choice. Presently, she was seated on a bench on the station platform, next to a tub of lavender. She had only five minutes left to wait when a policeman appeared. Seizing her bag, she dived into the ladies' waiting room and dropped into a corner seat. The lower half of the windows was frosted for privacy, but through the upper part she could see the policeman's helmeted head and broad shoulders. He disappeared from view and presently walked back again.

The train was due. She chewed her lip, then stopped in case it looked like suspicious behaviour. Casually she stood and peered over the frosted glass, watching the policeman. He stopped to talk to the ticket collector – about the girl who had viciously attacked a fine upstanding gentleman, his lordship's agent, no less!

The train pulled in. Her eyes widened at the vastness of the handsome, gleaming engine. What to do? Skulk here waiting for the next one or try her luck? She couldn't afford to wait. Grasping her bag, she opened the door. The carriages were smartly painted in toning shades of brown. Up and down the platform, doors opened and slammed as passengers climbed in and out. She tried to open the nearest door, but the handle proved unexpectedly stiff.

A voice behind her said, 'Do you mean to get in first class, miss?' and there was the policeman. 'Thought not. Let's find you a place down yonder.'

He shepherded her towards third class. Whatever had brought him to Annerby Station, it wasn't the pursuit of a desperate hellcat.

A whistle blew. The train pulled forward with a solemn jolt that created an odd sensation in her tummy. It looked as if the platform was sliding past the window instead of the train moving along the platform. She was on her way, but there was no sense of triumph, just an overwhelming bleakness. She had missed Mother's funeral. She would never forgive Mr Nugent for that.

Juliet had gone – run away. Hal struggled to believe it. He had travelled up to Manchester on the milk train from Euston, then made a mad dash from Piccadilly Station to Victoria and flung himself aboard the train for Annerby, where Dad met him in the gardeners' cart. Anxious as he was to see his beloved Juliet, there hadn't been time to go to the cottage. He and his family went straight to church.

When the vicar had walked down the aisle to meet the coffin at the door, the congregation rose in readiness, but the funeral procession hadn't walked in. For a few moments, no one thought anything of it, then folk cast questioning looks at one another. Hal had tugged his jacket more firmly into place, trying to dismiss the unease.

The vicar slipped back inside and whispered to Denny Myers, whereupon Denny followed him out. Then the vicar started back up the aisle, followed by the coffin, with Denny now one of the pall-bearers. Behind the coffin came . . . no one. Sharp murmurs darted round the church, bright little echoes bouncing off the stained glass. Hal wanted to push his way out of the pew, to ask questions, to go looking, but you couldn't cause a rumpus at a funeral, could you?

Agnes Harper had barely been laid to rest with her husband before the talk started.

'It's a reet rum do,' Alf Mulgrew remarked. He had been a pall-bearer. 'When we arrived at the cottage with the cart, there was Mr Nugent lying groaning on the floor, and not sight nor sound of young Juliet. That's why we needed Denny, because Bert stopped to see to Mr Nugent.'

Hal's skin prickled as curious eyes turned his way. He didn't wait to hear anything else but took off at a run, not stopping until he reached the cottage. He burst in, only to find it empty – well, of course it was empty – what was he thinking? Hadn't Alf said Juliet wasn't there? There was no sign of Mr Nugent either. Bert must have helped him back to Arley House. Even so, Hal searched round the cottage. He even went out the back and checked the earth-closet.

He must get to Arley House. That was where Mr Nugent would have been taken. As he reached the garden gate, Saul came racing through the trees.

'There you are. You're wanted at Arley House.' Saul's chest heaved as he delivered the message. 'Bert came to church to find you. He and your dad are on their way here – aren't you going to wait for them?'

Saul stepped aside as Hal brushed past. He sprinted all the way, banging in through the back door, taking a breather while Dolly informed her master of his arrival. Stuffing his cap in his pocket, he waited for Dolly, then followed her along a corridor and through a door backed with green baize, into the grand part of the house.

Dolly opened a door for him. It was a study – desk, bookcases, a smart armchair by the hearth.

Mr Nugent was on his feet. His right temple was purple and swollen, and there was a livid red graze down the side of his face. He should have been sitting; he should have been bandaged.

'Thank you, Dolly,' said Mr Nugent. 'Don't waste your time walking in, Price. I'm going to take you outside and horsewhip you.'

Horsewhip? This was no time for tugging the forelock. 'What are you talking about?'

'Don't take that tone with me.'

'I'll take any tone I like when a man speaks of horsewhipping. I repeat: what d'you mean? Where's Juliet?'

'You tell me. I assumed she'd run off to join you until Bert said your father had collected you from the station – unless you attended the funeral to throw us off the scent.'

'All I know is Juliet's gone and I have no idea where. Why would she run away?'

'Because she's pregnant – with your child. Didn't I tell you to keep your hands to yourself?' Mr Nugent clenched his fists. 'You couldn't leave her alone, could you?'

'Pregnant? Juliet?' He almost laughed in sheer astonishment.

He looked at Mr Nugent's injured face. Had that blow to the temple addled his brain?

'Aye, and throwing up merrily, the way women do.'

'No.'

'Yes. And you're the father.'

'No.' Juliet with morning sickness? It couldn't be true. It was a horrible mistake. But Mr Nugent sounded so certain, and where was Juliet? 'The most I ever did was kiss her.' He spoke more to himself than to Mr Nugent. Juliet couldn't be pregnant, she couldn't. *Throwing up merrily the way women do*. 'She must be ill with distress over her mother.'

'It was morning sickness. She didn't try to deny it.'

'What about . . . ?' Hal touched his temple, nodding at Mr Nugent's.

'She clobbered me with a candlestick to make her escape.'

Juliet? Impossible. But there was the injury, for all to see.

'So,' snapped Mr Nugent, 'if you're not the father, who is?'

'You're wrong. Juliet would never—you're wrong.'

Mr Nugent's eyes darkened and he went very still. 'No, I'm not.' Those quiet words carried more force than any tirade. 'She's pregnant and she's run away – presumably with her lover. If you're not the father, you've been duped every bit as much as I have.'

'You've been duped?'

'Wasn't I going to welcome her into my household, in accordance with her mother's dying wish? She's made fools of us all – you, me, the village, everybody at Moorside.'

A knot tightened in Hal's belly.

'You'd better go,' said Mr Nugent. 'It seems there is to be no horsewhipping today.'

Hal opened the door. He couldn't breathe; his skin was cold and tingling.

'One more thing,' said Mr Nugent. 'I'll write to Clayton and tell him that if a girl turns up asking for you, he's to sack you on the spot.'

'What . . . ?'

'If you're not the father, you'll have nothing to fear on that score, will you?'

Hal staggered towards home. He crashed into a tree and sank to the ground, sobbing so hard it felt as though he would bring up his guts.

Chapter Thirteen

When the train pulled into Victoria Station, Juliet was hollowed out with hunger. Her ribs and back were sore, and there was an unpleasant stiffness about her jaw and the side of her face where she had been clouted. But all that was nothing compared to the sheer fear of arriving at a strange place. Her hands were clammy inside her gloves as she grasped the handles of her carpetbag. With the sharp tang of steam in her nostrils, she joined the stream of travellers walking down the platform. So many people! Watching what they did, she surrendered her ticket. First things first. There was a public convenience for ladies, and she surreptitiously watched what to do before committing her own penny. Afterwards she joined the row of women at the mirrors and was horrified to see the mark on her face. Her hand flew instinctively to cover it.

'Bash you one, did he? Eh, they're buggers, some of 'em.' A pause, an assessing look through the mirror. 'Starting young, aren't you?'

She fled, panic thrashing in her ears. Then she forced herself to stop. No one knew who she was; no one knew how she had come by her injury. No one was going to grab her by the shoulder, yelling, 'Here's the girl who clobbered Mr Nugent.'

She must find Auntie Clara's shop. At the station entrance, she halted, the smells of soot and manure and gutters swarming round her. How did folk stand it? Someone cannoned into her from behind.

'I'm sorry,' she said. 'That was my fault for stopping.'

'Yes, it was,' snapped a smart-looking gentleman. He brushed past and strode on his way.

'Rude fellow,' said an apple-cheeked woman in a tartan jacket with a basket on her arm. 'You look lost, love.'

'Do you know Caroline Street?' Juliet's grateful smile faltered when the woman shook her head. 'It's off St Ann's Square.'

'Oh, that's nowt but a hop and a skip from here.'

Juliet listened carefully and offered profuse thanks, looking at the woman intently rather than at the road, the buildings, the people, the horse-drawn traffic. The place was so busy – dusty – noisy. How would she ever cope? She shouldn't have come. With a sharp emptiness inside her, as if she were about to walk off a precipice, she stepped onto the pavement and set off, licking lips that had gone dry.

Soon she came to what must be the Royal Exchange. Her helper had told her to look out for a grand building, though fortunately she had mentioned the columns at the front, because as far as Juliet was concerned everything here was vast and grand, built on a scale she had never imagined. How could Moorside, the centre of so many lives, have seemed so impressive? She felt small and countrified – and all at once, her fear fell away. She was tiny – invisible. She didn't matter. She was anonymous. Safe. She had run away in such fear and turmoil, but maybe – maybe

164

– this was the right place for her. Somewhere to start again.

St Ann's Square housed handsome buildings several storeys high, all of which seemed to have a shop on the ground floor. What all those upper floors were for, she couldn't imagine. In Birkfield, shopkeepers lived above their shops, but perhaps that was something that happened only in the provinces. Hansom cabs were lined up along one side, ready for customers, and over there was St Ann's Church, in front of which was a statue of a man, but she didn't get to see his name because she came to Caroline Street.

It was a blind alley with three shops on either side and another at the end, each with a diamond-paned bow window. Above the middle window on the right-hand side was a green-and-cream-striped awning with a scalloped edge, an ornamental touch that didn't conceal the name of the shop, which was painted in elegant script above the window: *Mademoiselle Antoinette*.

In the bow window stood three pictures on small easels, each a detailed drawing of a lady in a fashionable costume. Behind was a green and cream panel, so Juliet couldn't see into the shop. She didn't want to go in if there were customers. Should she have written, after all? But she hadn't wanted to give Auntie Clara the opportunity to say no.

She peered through the glass panel in the door. A smartly dressed woman was seated at an elegant table, her head bent over something she was writing. There weren't any customers. She pushed open the door, automatically listening for the bell to tinkle overhead, but there was no sound – except for a sharp intake of breath across the room.

'Good afternoon,' she said. 'Please may I see Mademoiselle Antoinette?'

'How dare you enter this establishment?' The woman came to her feet. 'Depart this instant!'

Juliet felt panicky. The woman swept towards her.

'Please – I must see Mademoiselle Antoinette.'

'The presumption,' snorted the woman. She grasped Juliet by the arm.

Her head felt odd and swirly. 'You don't understand. Mademoiselle Antoinette – Miss Clara Tewson – I'm her niece.'

'I *beg* your pardon?'

And then—

Juliet opened her eyes and saw a ceiling. She was lying on the floor, her feet propped on a chair. 'She's awake,' said a voice. Swivelling her head, she saw a grey-haired woman, wearing what looked like a white pinafore but with sleeves, sitting at a big table. Juliet started to move, but had barely unhooked her feet before hands scooped her up by the armpits and deposited her on a wooden chair.

'You're not going to faint again, are you?'

'I fainted?'

'Either that or you chose a fine time for a nap. I expect a cup of tea would sort you out.' The woman's gaze flashed across the room somewhere behind Juliet. 'I'll leave you to it . . . Mademoiselle.'

Juliet turned – and gasped. Mother! Next moment, the resemblance was gone. Well, not entirely. Mother and Auntie Clara shared the same oval face and narrow nose, the same petulant mouth, but the colouring was different. Where Mother had been fair, Clara was dark – no, not dark. Mousy. And Mother had been slender whereas Clara carried more flesh, or perhaps that was the unflattering pinafore making her appear dumpy.

166

'I'm Juliet, Agnes's daughter. I'm sorry to arrive like this.'

'You're not the only one.'

Panic fluttered. 'The thing is – I'm sorry to tell you that my mother . . .' Her throat swelled.

'Yes, I know.'

'Oh.' How? Before she could ask, the door opened and in swept the woman from the shop.

Clara stood. 'Miss Selway.'

Miss Selway looked down her nose at Clara. 'Really! First you receive personal correspondence here, now a . . . relative arrives.' She cast a glance almost but not quite in Juliet's direction, as if something as common and unpleasant as a relative was beneath her notice. 'Mademoiselle will see you now.'

She swished out, followed by Clara looking anxious and downtrodden, leaving a dozen questions burning Juliet's tongue.

The grey-haired woman stuck her head in. 'Tea up. Leave your bag. I'm Dorothy Bowen, Mrs Bowen to you.'

Mrs Bowen took her to a room with two coat stands festooned with coats next to a shelf with an array of hats. A table stood in the middle and there were some chairs. Huddled together, as if they had just this second stopped whispering, were two girls not much older than Juliet, both wearing the sleeved pinafores.

'Come to gawp, have you?' said Mrs Bowen. 'Well, there's nowt to see. Sit yourself down,' she bade Juliet and handed her a tea. 'These two are Betty and Freda. They're apprentices and they're just about to go back to work.'

'I think she needs another, Mrs Bowen,' said Betty.

Juliet glanced away. She had meant to sip, but she had gulped the whole cup. The light-headedness was gone, replaced by a cracking headache.

'I'll fetch another,' said Freda. She and Betty retreated into a corner amid excited whispers.

Someone else came in, a rather lovely young woman with dark hair. Instead of the pinafore, she was wearing what resembled, but couldn't possibly be, a dressing gown.

'I heard about the drama. What's going on?'

'Oh, Miss Cunliffe,' chorused Betty and Freda.

'Don't encourage them, Kate,' Mrs Bowen said severely. She looked at Juliet. 'What's your name?'

'Juliet Harper.'

'You're the niece,' observed Kate Cunliffe. 'We were sorry to hear about your loss.'

'Thank you.' How did they know? Auntie Clara had known too.

'Did Miss Tewson really tell you she was Mademoiselle Antoinette?' Betty burst out.

'That'll do,' Mrs Bowen snapped. 'Back to work, you two, else you'll get fined.'

Betty and Freda's giggles floated back as they departed. Mrs Bowen cast her eyes up to heaven.

'I'd best get on too,' said Kate. 'Mrs Wells is due and, with Daisy away sick, I've no one to help me.' She looked at Juliet. 'You could lend a hand. What do you think, Mrs Bowen?'

'Nowt to do with me. I've done my bit, giving her a cup of tea.' She walked out, her pinafore billowing unflatteringly. Seeing it from behind, Juliet realised it was a complete overgarment, more like a nightgown but large enough to cover clothes.

She followed Kate through a couple of doors and into a room with three cheval mirrors grouped in the centre and racks nearby with four gowns hanging in readiness.

'Help me dress – and keep your voice down. Through that door is the showroom.' Kate shed her dressing gown – it really was a dressing gown – and stood unselfconsciously in her underwear. 'The blue first. Mrs Wells likes blue.'

Juliet held the heavy silk for her. 'Is this Daisy's job?'

'No. We both wear garments for the ladies to decide what they want to have made for them and we help one another in and out of them. Do the hooks and eyes for me. Did your aunt really pretend to be Mademoiselle?'

'Yes. No. I don't know that she ever wrote the actual words.'

'But she made out this place was hers? Help me with the evening gloves, then pass that fan, the one with the feathers.'

Trimmings and accessories sat on shelves. She handed Kate the fan.

Kate positioned herself in the centre of the mirrors, checking herself from all angles. 'Probably a good idea to hide. That door's going to open in a minute and it'll be Miss Selway.'

Juliet sprang behind the hanging garments just in time.

'Mrs Wells is ready, Katerina,' came Miss Selway's voice, not tight with anger any more but cultured and a trifle smarmy. 'May I present Miss Alexandrina's newest creation.'

Kate walked from the room with a measured tread. Juliet was dying to know what happened in the showroom, but the door shut. Presently, Kate reappeared with the same measured step, but the instant the door closed, she kicked off her shoes and started unbuttoning her gloves. Juliet hurried to assist.

'Is your name really Katerina?'

'Course not. It's my showroom name. Daisy's is Fleur.'

'Who's Miss Alexandrina?'

'Our designer. She'd normally be in here helping, but she's at a funeral. The lilac next.'

169

The lilac was a wonderful silk satin with sleeves that puffed above the elbow and fitted snugly below.

'Wait.' Juliet took mauve silk flowers from a shelf. 'Let me pin these on. A couple here at the waist . . . one at the shoulder . . . and one on a comb in your hair.'

Kate looked at her reflection. 'Mm, I like it.'

When the last gown had been displayed, Kate sent Juliet back to the sewing room. She found Clara and Mrs Bowen at one table and the two apprentices at another. They all looked up as she entered, the girls' faces alight with curiosity, Clara's tight with misery.

'Come on, you two. I want to see how well you tidied the cupboard,' Mrs Bowen said, and Betty and Freda were led inexorably from the room.

'Where have you been?' Clara demanded.

'Helping Miss Cunliffe.'

'Did you spare a thought for me, getting a dressing-down from Mademoiselle? Marching into the salon like that!'

'I'm sorry, but I thought you were Mademoiselle Antoinette. I'd never have presumed otherwise.'

Clara pressed her lips together. Juliet tried to conjure up something conciliatory to say.

The door opened, and Kate looked in. 'Mrs Wells ordered the lilac. It was the flowers that did it.'

'The lilac doesn't have flowers,' Clara said.

'It does now.' Kate grinned at Juliet. 'Clever girl!' And she was gone.

Juliet was still beaming as she turned back to Clara, only for the delight to drop from her face when she saw the pinched mouth and the anger squeezing out of the narrowed eyes.

'Thank you very much! Just like your mother! Swanning in, being marvellous, whatever it takes to make me look bad.'

'I didn't. I'm here because of what you told us. I hoped you'd give me a job and – and somewhere to stay. I've nowhere else to go.'

'You could go back. You've got work there, a live-in job.'

'How do you know? You knew about Mother too.'

'I had a letter yesterday. It came here – I got into trouble for that as well.'

'Not from Mrs Grove? She thought I was writing.'

'It was signed H. Nugent. He said he was Lord Drysdale's agent. Agnes had asked him to write after she passed on. He said she had done excellent work for her ladyship.'

Well, and wasn't that Mother all over, showing off even from the grave, wanting her sister to know how valued she had been by the mighty Drysdales.

'He said I wasn't to worry about you as you were about to enter his household,' said Clara, 'so you can go back tomorrow.'

'No.' Her strong tone made Clara lift her eyebrows. 'He's . . . he's got a roving eye.'

'Oh. Well, you can come with me tonight, anyhow.'

'I can pay my way.'

'Good. I can't afford you. You'll need a few coppers for your fare to start with.'

She dug her hand in her pocket, then in her other pocket. 'My purse – it's been stolen.' The man who had bumped into her or the woman who had given directions? What a start to her new life.

Juliet slept like a log until dawn, when she was woken by a dark twinge down the side of her face. Her cheekbone and jaw were sore and stiff. She moved her jaw experimentally, but even the tiniest jarring sent a spasm roaring through it. Still, it was a good thing she was awake first. It meant she was able to creep downstairs to the outside privy undetected when morning sickness struck, but when she vomited, it felt as if her jaw would break clean off, such was the pain of opening her mouth.

She staggered from the privy, holding her forehead. It was a moment before she could stand up straight. Mrs Duggan, whose two upstairs rooms Clara rented near Platt Fields, had her own backyard with a washing line, mangle and privy, which was a relief after the tales Juliet had heard back home of how, in towns, any number of families might share one stinking closet.

She slid back indoors and upstairs. The front room was Clara's sitting room. She opened the curtains and batted her way through snowy nets to look at the houses opposite. She had never lived opposite houses. She turned round, her eyes drawn to the braided cushions and embroidered tablecloth, which brightened an otherwise plain room. Recognition flickered. Mother had personalised their cottage in the same way. It was a far cry from the life she had imagined for Clara.

Clara appeared in the doorway, wrapped in a dressing gown. Juliet gripped the back of the armchair. If Clara had looked from the bedroom window and seen her lurching out of the privy . . .

'What happened to your face?' asked Clara.

She touched the bruising that had bloomed overnight. 'I slipped getting off the train. Auntie Clara, do you have writing paper? I need to write for jobs.'

'Have you got a character reference from the haberdashery?'

'I never thought to get one.'

'From the lord's household, then?' Clara sighed. 'You won't get far without a character.'

Whatever story Mr Nugent had attached to her disappearance, it wouldn't be to his detriment, and her absence from Mother's funeral would have left a nasty taste in everyone's mouths. Nevertheless, she would have to compose letters to Mrs Whicker and Mrs Naseby. She could apologise for disappearing, but she couldn't possibly explain it. Would they be prepared to recommend her?

When they went down for breakfast, Juliet promised Mrs Duggan she would find a job shortly.

'You're stopping here, then?' Clara's landlady was a scrawny, saggy-featured creature whose plain speaking would have been more of a worry if Juliet hadn't seen real warmth in her eyes.

'Looks like it,' said Clara, without glancing up from her porridge with dried fruit.

'Anyroad,' Mrs Duggan said, 'you'd best get suited soon. I'll be upping the rent come Sat'day. I'll ask Mrs Barber next door if she can fix you up. Well, not so much her as their Alice. Alice in't exactly blessed with the best brain, but she's a good lass and she's never been out o' work since the day she left school. Aye, and she left at nine an' all, as her dad said there were no point in her carrying on, what with her being so dim.'

'What does she do? I don't have my character references.'

'That won't matter if Alice vouches for you. Best cleaner between here and Stockport Road, she is.'

'I'll be cleaning?'

'Well, not so much cleaning – charring, more like.'

'Charring?' It was a huge step down from shop work, but she was in no position to turn her nose up.

Mrs Barber's Alice took a shine to her, and she started work the very next morning.

Her working day started at five. For two hours, she scrubbed, mopped, swept and polished in a big house opposite Platt Fields Park that was used for offices. Her final job each morning was to scrub the front steps. It was back-breaking work, but the more she scrubbed, the harder the baby clung on inside her.

Her second job was next door in a similar place, where, according to Alice, 'Ethel has done summat mortal to her leg,' so Juliet was taken on temporarily. It was here that her morning sickness struck, but the house boasted indoor sanitation, so being sick wasn't a problem, although she couldn't get used to the indoor lavatory. It didn't seem clean, people doing their business inside the house, even if they could pull a chain and swish it away. The lavatory was a great porcelain beast painted with violets and cleaning it was one of her jobs. The seat and lid were wooden, and she was never sure whether she was supposed to polish them.

She had more offices to clean in the evening and soon cleaning jobs came along during the day. She took them on with mixed feelings. Accepting extra work was as good as admitting that the lengthening silence from Mrs Whicker and Mrs Naseby would never be broken.

What with her early starts and her evening work, Juliet didn't see that much of Clara, which was a relief. The less she intruded, the less likely Clara was to get fed up of her.

'It's good of you to let me stay,' she said. She had come home from her evening work, had a strip wash and settled down to do Clara's darning. She made a point of being helpful.

Clara didn't look up from sewing the piping onto the edges of the golden brown three-tiered shoulder cape she was making. 'You may as well stay. I don't know what else to do with you.'

'I could go to Nana Adeline's.'

There was a pause so profound that the air vibrated. She looked up to find Clara staring at her.

'*Who?*' Clara asked.

'Nana Adeline.'

'That's what Agnes called her?'

'Yes.' Was she questioning the pretentious use of 'Nana' instead of 'Nan'?

'Nana Adeline.' Clara's lips twitched, then she spluttered and started roaring with laughter.

Juliet boggled. She had put her aunt down for a tight-lipped complainer, yet here she was, laughing without inhibition.

'What's so funny?' she asked when Clara stopped.

Clara dabbed her eyes, sighing as if the laughter had worn her out. 'I'd call her Grandmother, if I were you.'

'Am I coming with you to see her on Sunday?' Juliet asked hopefully.

'No. She wouldn't appreciate your turning up out of the blue.'

'Out of the blue? Haven't you told her I'm here?'

'We don't correspond.'

'So she doesn't know about Mother?'

'I wrote to tell her about that, obviously, but . . .'

'But not about me.'

'It was before you arrived.'

'Don't you think she'd want to know?'

Clara picked up her sewing. 'You can come next month – if she wants to see you.'

If she wants to see you. Could Nana Adeline – Grandmother – have fallen out with Mother so completely that she was prepared to dump the grudge on the shoulders of her unknown granddaughter? If so, did Juliet want to associate with her? But she couldn't afford not to. Adeline Tewson owned a textiles factory. If no character references appeared – and let's face it, they weren't going to now –

then her grandmother's factory could be her one hope of a position that didn't involve cleaning. Besides, she was curious to meet the woman Mother had spoken of with such awe and dislike.

Clara snipped off her thread, holding up the completed cape, scrutinising it. Juliet offered a few words of admiration, but Clara apparently wasn't in the mood for compliments.

To Juliet's surprise, she came home the next evening to find Clara bent over the table, cutting out another version of the same pattern, this time with two tiers.

'Not that it's any of your business,' Clara snapped, 'but I do ... private work.' She became flustered. 'No one at Mademoiselle's must ever know. I'd lose my position.'

'You work for private customers?'

Clara's mouth set in a stubborn line. 'If you must know, I know someone at Ingleby's. That's a big shop in town, haberdashery and drapery combined, and they have a successful dressmaking department as well as selling accessories to add the finishing touch.'

'A dressmaking service?'

'Miss Lindsay, the senior seamstress, is a wizard with paper patterns. Years ago, she trained as a pattern girl, you know, turning designs into patterns. Sometimes customers come with a picture of a garment and ask if she can make it.'

That night Juliet lay in bed, top to toe with Clara, too excited to sleep. Her mind was teeming with ideas and above all with hope. Before eventually falling asleep, she wrote the letter in her head, and the next day, while she mopped and swept and polished, she murmured the wording over and over, dying to put pen to paper.

But she was barely more than a couple of sentences into it when another idea struck and she stopped. It meant more time before she could approach Miss Lindsay, but it would be worth it.

Two interminable days crawled by before she could rush to Market Street in the city centre. Although she was used to the crowded environment now, the sight of the line of smart shops on either side of the long road was bewildering, but she soon found Ingleby's, a spacious shop spread over three floors, selling everything a needle worker could possibly want.

She examined fabrics, making notes on colour, texture, weight and width. She used a few precious coins to purchase samples of ribbon, braid, piping and lace trim. She drew a selection of buttons, then went into Ladies' Accessories to make more notes. She already had one costume pretty well complete inside her head. Before she left the shop, she bought some offcuts so she could start work on new samples.

Emerging from Ingleby's with hope fluttering inside her, she set off along Market Street before realising she was heading the wrong way. As she turned about, the road sign at the corner she was passing caught her eye. Rosemount Place. The hopeful flutters turned to cold shakiness. Rosemount Place: the address on William Turton's card.

Her mind screamed at her not to, but her feet forced her into the smart, quiet cul-de-sac. A line of front steps led up to a line of handsome front doors, complete with brass door furniture. Beside each door a brass plate gleamed, bearing the name of the firm.

Winterton, Sowerby and Jenks. Where William Turton worked.

She could march in and leave his career in tatters. Either that or be taken away by a policeman for daring to make such an accusation against a respectable legal clerk.

The thought of facing him again turned her stomach. She hurried home, trying to recapture the hopeful flutters.

Over the following days, she worked every spare minute,

rising early and staying up late. Soon she had created two designs, one copy of each for Miss Lindsay and one for herself. The first was a jacket and skirt, what the fashion magazines in the sewing room had called a 'walking costume'. Mindful of Ingleby's likely customers, she didn't incorporate the vast leg-o'-mutton sleeves favoured by Lady Margaret, but toned down the fullness, adding a blouse with a dainty froth of lace that would peep out from the jacket collar. To complete the costume, she chose toning gloves from Ladies' Accessories.

Her second design featured a flared skirt in brown lightweight wool, a serviceable fabric that would hang and settle nicely, with a cream silk blouse, high-collared as fashion dictated, and with the leg-o'-mutton shape softened by subtle draping. To finish, she added a narrow belt.

Now there was one thing left to do before she applied to Miss Lindsay. If she did this first, she could concentrate on building her future in sewing and not agonise over . . . her other problem. She went to the gates of the local orphanage. She had stood here a few times. Was this the right place?

A crocodile of children approached and she eased herself away. The children were dressed in blue, a sombre blue admittedly, but it was better than grey. The orphanage itself was a big house with a garden. The lawn had great patches without grass. Hal would have had something to say about that. Did they neglect the children the way they neglected the garden? Then, at a word from the woman leading the crocodile, the pairs of children burst apart with glad cries and started chasing one another about.

Juliet smiled. That was why the grass had worn away. Her decision was made.

How long before her condition revealed itself? It would be a race between Clara and Mrs Duggan to see who could throw her out first. But if she could find work with Ingleby's, her future would be a lot brighter, and now she knew where she would leave the child. That was as much planning as she could face.

Her letter to Miss Lindsay was word-perfect in her head. She wrote it in best, addressing the envelope for Miss Lindsay's personal attention. When the letter dropped into the pillar box, goosebumps popped up all over her.

Would Miss Lindsay be interested?

Chapter Fourteen

Getting up early was no hardship. Hal only wished he could rise even earlier, but he couldn't without disturbing Gil Tierney, whom he was bunking with and who, in spite of snoring like a drunken navvy all night, woke at the slightest thing, compelling Hal to lie there, battling with the questions that had tormented him since the day Agnes Harper was buried.

During the day, he mucked in with every physically demanding job, the more taxing the better.

'You don't have to construct that rockery single-handed,' Mr Clayton observed wryly. 'I know you've been let down by your girl. I'll have to employ only heartbroken chaps in future, if they all work like you.'

Let down by your girl. It was difficult to argue otherwise, and yet he couldn't accept what had happened. Had Juliet been stringing him along, hoping he would take on her baby, while keeping the other fellow in reserve? He couldn't believe it. He knew her too well. Or so he had thought. But there was no getting round the fact that she had run away. Aye, and it hadn't been on the spur of the moment either, because Mrs Harper's sewing box had gone missing at the same time . . . *which shows she had it planned all along*, according to Ma in a letter.

In another letter, she recounted how, when Mr Nugent's staff had gone through Juliet's belongings, various items were conspicuous by their absence, such as her hairbrush, *which just goes to show* – he screwed up the letter. Did Ma think she was helping by blackening Juliet's name?

Cecily! Why hadn't he thought of her before? If Juliet were to contact anyone, surely it would be Cecily, though it wouldn't be easy getting a message to her if the London housekeeper was anything like Mrs Whicker, but even if Juliet couldn't write, she might have confided in Cecily back at home. How long ago had Cecily come to London with Miss Phoebe?

It was worth a try.

'Well, that's something I never thought I'd see,' Gil Tierney exclaimed. 'You – smiling. Didn't think you knew how.'

Later, having dashed back to his digs to spruce himself up, Hal presented himself at the back door of the Drysdales' town house. He explained who he was and waited. Presently, a dark-clad woman appeared. She didn't introduce herself, but she must be Mrs Goodwin, the London housekeeper.

'What brings you here, young man?'

'I'd like to speak to Cecily – Miss Phoebe's maid. Please,' he added.

'She's not here. The family has left town. And if she were here, I wouldn't let her see you. I don't know what sort of slack household Eglantine Whicker runs in the country, but here in town we don't permit followers.'

'I'm not—'

The door closed in his face.

* * *

Juliet came home from an evening's charring to find Clara leafing through her drawings. After finishing her Ingleby's designs, she had done more, enjoying the work, not least because it took her mind off . . . other things. Clara acknowledged her with a glance, then carried on, which left Juliet even more taken aback.

'These are good.' Clara sounded surprised. 'You mentioned drawing lessons. And Agnes taught you to design, I suppose?'

'No, it's just something I enjoy. Mother wasn't that keen on my doing it, actually.'

'I bet she wasn't,' Clara said archly before settling down with the latest issue of *Vera's Voice*.

Juliet stared at her, willing her to comprehend the invasion of privacy. When Clara reached for her cup of tea without lifting her eyes from the page, she gave up and went into the bedroom for her daily strip wash. Charring was like that, rough, sweaty work, especially in summer.

She rested an assessing hand on her belly. It wouldn't be flat for much longer, and she knew her breasts had grown. She had secretly let out the darts on her white blouse and black dress. Clara had helped her make a new blouse, and Juliet had cut the pattern as full as she could without arousing comment.

She closed her eyes, overwhelmed by the need for Miss Lindsay to admire her work. She was going to meet her grandmother this Sunday. If she received a favourable reply from Miss Lindsay beforehand, what a splendid thing that would be to tell the great Adeline Tewson.

But Sunday arrived with no word from Ingleby's. Juliet set off with Clara. Ever since arriving in Manchester, she had tried asking about her grandmother, but Clara's replies were terse. 'You'll see,' was the standard response.

Clara took her to a tree-lined road in West Didsbury. Each villa stood in a leafy garden fronted by a wall of the distinctive red brick that Juliet saw everywhere she looked. Recognising mop-headed hydrangeas and the cone-shaped flowers of butterfly bushes nodding over the garden walls, she was assailed by a powerful memory of the future wife who had once hung on Hal's every word. Her heart squeezed. They came to a garden where elegant ballerina blooms of fuchsias spilt over the wall. Clara unlatched the gate and led the way up the path. The house had a vast bay window to either side of the roofed porch and three big windows above.

They were admitted by a middle-aged maid, who regarded Juliet curiously. Juliet offered a smile that wasn't returned, but she forgot the snub as her eyes popped out on stalks. The hall was larger than Clara's sitting room. There was wood everywhere – floor, staircase, newel post, bannisters – masses of it, dark and gleaming. She frowned at what looked like an extra skirting board three feet up the wall. Below it, the wallpaper was gold and brown, while that above was gold and green. She had a brief impression of potted palms and a colossal sideboard before Clara shoved her towards a door the maid was holding open.

She walked in, ready to be impressed all over again. The mantelpiece over the fireplace boasted not one but two mantelshelves and an ornate mirror. The chairs were upholstered in velvet – velvet! – and her trained eye recognised the exquisite petit point on the cushion covers. Glass domes covered wax fruit and flowers. What must Lady Margaret's morning room be like, if a factory owner could live like this? It was impossible to picture anything more splendid.

Wait a moment. In spite of the glorious day and the bay window, the room was gloomy, its wallpaper a mixture of dark green and dull red, the carpet maroon, the hearthrug black sheepskin. In her imagination, Juliet filled the room with light colours and heaps of flowers, real flowers, not artificial arrangements beneath glass domes. She pictured Mother in a tied cottage and Clara in her rented rooms and wasn't sure what to make of the contrast.

She glanced round, ready to meet her grandmother.

'Save it till it's needed,' said Clara.

'Pardon?'

'The smile. She'll make us wait. She always does.'

Sure enough, they stood there for ten minutes. Clara didn't sit down, so Juliet didn't either. Clara crossed to the window, as if admiring the garden. Juliet joined her.

'My mother never told me about this house.'

'She never saw it. Mother moved here – what? – thirteen, fourteen years ago. We lived in a poky two-up two-down in Levenshulme when we were small. I hardly remember it. What I do remember is the other children tying me up and making me eat mud because we were moving to an end terrace in a better road. Little did they know that Mother wanted the big front room for her sewing and we lived crammed in the kitchen. It was always work, work, work with Mother. After a year or two, she commandeered the upstairs front as well. She, Agnes and Auntie Juley squeezed into the back bedroom while I had to make do with under the stairs. To this day I can't bear confined spaces.'

'Why were two sewing rooms needed?'

'That was when Mother started taking on slave labour.'

'Slave labour?'

'She took on extra work and paid local needlewomen to do it. She made them come to the house, so she could crack the whip. Then she bought a sewing machine on hire purchase. Eventually she had four machines whirring away, and the women had to pay a fee to use them, which was deducted from their wages.'

'Don't sound so snotty about it, Clara,' said a crisp, dry voice.

Juliet whirled round. With her eyes full of sunlight, all she could make out was a tall outline in the doorway. As her eyes adjusted, the figure stalked into the room. Adeline Tewson was taller than her daughters, the swish of her panelled skirt suggesting long legs and stamina. Her features were heavy and strong, her hair iron-grey with wings of stark white at the sides. Her clothes were plain to the point of severity, but their cut was perfection itself.

She spared Juliet a glance that suggested a glance was all she needed, then fixed penetrating eyes on Clara.

'Those whirring machines marked the turning point of my fortunes. It's where your drawing lessons came from, and the elocution and deportment classes. I invested substantially in my daughters, my one poor investment. You were never going to amount to much, but Agnes could have been successful.' She looked at Juliet. 'And here's what she threw it away for.'

With that, she sat in a handsome fireside chair, waving her guests to the sofa before resting a hand on each wooden arm.

'Well, girl, what have you to say for yourself?'

'I'm pleased to meet you.'

'No doubt. Whether I am pleased to meet you remains to be seen.'

Juliet tensed. So much for meeting the orphaned granddaughter.

'And you, Clara – I trust you aren't in the habit of referring to my employees as slave labour. If you are, I shall speak to my solicitor.'

The silence that followed throbbed with humiliation.

'Well? Is legal action required?'

'No, Mother,' Clara whispered.

Anxious to break the moment, Juliet said, 'My mother told me you did all kinds of sewing when you were getting started.'

'I still do. Not personally. My workers do it, and I have a great many more than four machines these days. We're currently sewing for a new hotel in Southport – bedlinen, curtains, cushion covers, uniforms. That's where the money is, in the big orders. I always knew that. I saw my opportunity when the workhouse guardians in Withington stumped up the money for new winter capes for the females. The matron was ready to hand out the work to half a dozen seamstresses, but I said I'd do the whole order and if I didn't get it done in time, she could fine me, but she had to pay a bonus if I finished early. I took on three local women and sacked one at the end of the first day, which made the other two work harder. We worked day and night to get those capes ready.'

'And earned the bonus.'

'Always find a way to earn extra.' The wide mouth flickered, forming a grim line that wasn't a smile. 'I was never going to be able to have my own salon; I didn't have the background. I found my success elsewhere. It was my daughters who were meant to have the salons.' She flung Clara a dark look.

Juliet jumped in to spare Clara's blushes. 'What should I call you? Mother always referred to you as Nana Adeline.'

An eyebrow climbed up the broad forehead. 'The country air clearly addled her brains.'

That settled it. She would call her Grandmother if she must, because it was polite, but she wouldn't think of her as a grandmother. She didn't deserve it.

'You have a look of her about you,' said Adeline. 'Similar colouring. And you're evidently as unreliable.'

Juliet sat up straighter. 'I'm not unreliable. I work hard – and so did my mother.'

'Your mother, girl, was sent to take care of an invalid and

promptly went gallivanting. As for you, I go by the evidence before me. You walked out on a good position.'

'If you know that, I assume Auntie Clara also told you why.'

'The gentleman with the roving eye. It was, however, unutterably stupid of you not to furnish yourself with character references.'

'I left in a hurry. I never thought about references.'

'More fool you. Are you here to beg for employment?'

If only she had heard from Miss Lindsay! 'I have work, thank you.'

'Doing what?'

'I'm a char.' 'She's a daily maid.' She and Clara spoke together, then looked at one another.

'It doesn't surprise me. Your father was a labourer, after all.'

'Pop was an estate worker for a lord,' Juliet said fiercely.

'Precisely: a labourer.'

'Anyroad,' she said, unable to keep her mouth shut, 'I've done some designs and offered them to Ingleby's for their consideration.'

'Indeed?' Adeline spoke scornfully. 'What can you possibly produce that is worth anyone's consideration?'

The door opened to admit the maid. 'Tea is served,' she announced.

Adeline led the way into another room where Juliet looked at the table, its white cloth heavy with lace, and couldn't help smiling because it was the prettiest tea she had ever seen. The china was white, patterned with little sprays of roses, and had a gold line round the rim. There were plates of sandwiches with the crusts cut off and a cake stand displaying macaroons, Eccles cakes and petticoat tails, as well as a separate plate of scones, flanked by dishes of jam and cream. The cutlery shone, and there were snowy napkins. Gracing the centre was a silver rose bowl of honey-scented sweet peas.

Clara glanced at Adeline for permission and reached for the teapot.

'Are you going to be mother?' Juliet asked, desperate for normal conversation.

'No, she's going to play the servant,' said Adeline. 'That's all she's fit for.'

Bully. Was this how Adeline treated everyone? Bullying and carping and deriding until they were too ground down to resist? She felt unexpectedly protective towards Clara.

'One day I want to sew for a living. I'm already taking the first steps.'

'Charring?'

'Preparing samples.'

'And she claims not to want a job from me.'

'I don't.' Not any more, she didn't. Never again.

'Then you're a fool. How good is she, Clara?'

'Better than Agnes and I at that age.'

'Thank you.' She was surprised by the compliment.

Adeline snorted. 'If she's that good, why did Agnes put her in for shop work?'

'I did dressmaking as well,' said Juliet. 'I paid for drawing lessons by sewing.'

'If you hope to impress me by showing initiative, you won't succeed since your more recent show of so-called initiative led to your turning up on Clara's doorstep without a single reference to your name.'

'I thought Auntie Clara would' – beside her, Clara stiffened – '. . . help me find a job.' Evidently, Adeline knew nothing of the lies Clara had written year upon year to her sister.

'You backed the wrong horse there, girl,' Adeline scoffed.

'Please stop calling me that. My name is Juliet.'

'I could call you a lot worse, believe you me.'

'Mother – please,' Clara begged, and Juliet saw a look flash between them.

'Damned impertinence, naming you after Auntie Juley,' snapped Adeline. 'Well, Clara, what has happened at the salon since last month?'

And she blatantly ignored Juliet for the rest of the visit.

When it was time to leave, Clara asked humbly, 'Should I bring Juliet next month?'

Adeline disappeared, leaving them standing, and returned a few minutes later with a piece of paper. 'She may come if she has these ready for inspection.'

Clara took it. 'A list of samples.'

'Are you considering employing me?' Juliet asked in surprise.

'It's to determine whether you're worth the bother of having a granddaughter.'

A letter arrived from Miss Lindsay inviting Juliet to attend an interview. She borrowed one of Clara's hats, hoping to appear more grown-up, an effort that appeared fruitless when she saw her reflection glowing with health in a way that suggested anything but being older. The morning sickness had stopped, so maybe that was why.

At Ingleby's she was shown into an office-cum-workroom, which must be where Miss Lindsay worked her magic with paper patterns. Miss Lindsay was a thin, older woman with innate elegance. Her fingers were long and bony and clever.

'I was expecting someone older. Can you assure me the work you submitted is your own?'

'Everything in my letter was true, though I can't prove it because, as I explained, I don't have references.'

Miss Lindsay picked up a little brass bell. A woman answered the ring.

'The new silk, please.'

When the bolt was brought, Miss Lindsay indicated that it should be placed on her worktable. The woman pulled a length free before withdrawing.

Miss Lindsay waved her hand at it. 'Be my guest.'

The fabric had narrow stripes of brown and olive green, and it would support a crisp style. Juliet looked at Miss Lindsay.

'Design something,' Miss Lindsay ordered. 'Here – pencil and paper.'

She left the room. Part of Juliet told her she should be panicking, but the rest of her knew there was no need, because she had started formulating an idea the moment she saw the fabric. She committed a few lines to paper, creating the beginning of a blouse. She saw its back with vertical stripes, but wanted the front pieces cut on the bias, so the stripes met down the front to form a V-shape, with every slender brown stripe meeting another brown one and every olive stripe meeting olive. Only an experienced fabric cutter would manage it.

Miss Lindsay returned and picked up the unfinished drawing. 'Come with me.' She led her into haberdashery. 'These buttons – don't you agree?'

They were smooth and silvery. 'I'd choose something that toned, possibly self-covered.'

Miss Lindsay nodded. 'Show me the best fabric for a skirt and jacket to go with it.'

Soon Juliet had designed a complete costume, mostly in words, and she and Miss Lindsay were back in the office-cum-workshop.

'You may not have received formal training, but there's no doubt as to your ability or that the designs you submitted are your own work.' Miss Lindsay spoke formally. Then she smiled. 'Ingleby's will be pleased to purchase your designs. I'm authorised to offer a guinea for each.'

Two guineas! She tried not to beam her head off.

'You understand that once you sign them over, you may not use them again?'

'Of course. Shall you be interested in seeing more of my work?'

'If you submit four more designs, one of which should be this afternoon's costume, I'll select two, assuming they are good enough. If your designs are successful with our customers, I'll invite you to submit more, based on our winter fabrics. Now, I have paperwork for you to sign.'

Juliet sat with the agreement in front of her and Miss Lindsay's pen in her hand – and hesitated. She couldn't believe she was hesitating. *Always find a way to earn extra.* Not that she wanted to emulate her grandmother . . .

She looked up. 'I'd also like payment each time one of my designs is used to create a garment for a customer.'

'I beg your pardon?'

'Five shillings. Please,' she added.

'This is outrageous.'

Panic spurted through her. 'Half a crown, then.'

'Stay here.'

Miss Lindsay left the room, her back stiff with annoyance. She returned, accompanied by a tall, bespectacled man, who was bald on top. She didn't introduce him. Could he be Mr Ingleby? Together, he and Miss Lindsay did everything they could to browbeat her into submission, but she held firm – outwardly, at least. Inside, she felt hot and wobbly.

In the end, with theatrical regret, the man agreed to the guinea plus half a crown for each complete make or one shilling if just part of a design was ordered.

'But you may not offer other designs elsewhere for six months,' said the man. 'If we're to pay you these sums, we're not going to share your abilities. In six months, we'll know whether you're worth our while.'

'Six months is a long time. I can't agree to that.'

'If your work is as good as this,' said Miss Lindsay, her manner softening, 'I don't think you have anything to fear.'

Juliet signed, accepted her fee, signed for that as well. Soon she emerged onto busy Market Street, shaky but triumphant. Her grandmother would be proud of her. No, she wouldn't. Adeline Tewson would despise her for not sticking to the original five bob.

The work on the garden was nearing completion. My, but it was going to be hard returning to Moorside now that he had tasted independence. Hal flung himself into his work. Sometimes he felt churned up with pain, other times his heart felt frozen solid, but there was rubble to be shifted, earth to be dug over, planting and staking to do, saplings to be put in and a last-minute problem with the new fountain to be unclogged, and the physical labour answered a need in him to expend his energy in some way other than by driving himself insane with worry and regret and questions, questions, questions.

'I've a proposition for you,' Mr Clayton said. 'I'll stand you a meal tonight and tell you.'

Later, over a hearty steak-and-kidney pie with delicious onion gravy, he explained.

'After this commission, I've got another in Cumberland. How

would you like to come with me, as a sort of apprentice? I'm impressed by your hard work and ability, and I'm prepared to train you.'

'Really?' Hal could hardly believe what he was hearing.

Clayton laughed. 'Don't kid yourself it's for your benefit. When you're not out of the top drawer, but you work for those who are, the manner in which you present yourself is everything. My having a talented young fellow in tow will impress prospective clients. But I'm offering you real work, make no mistake about that. In time, I'll be able to take on more commissions, because I'll delegate tasks to you. What d'you say? If you accept, you'll come straight to Cumberland. I don't know when you'll see Moorside again.'

He pictured it. It would break Ma's heart, but she would be proud too. As for himself, let alone this was his dream come true, it would be a relief not to go home, where everything would remind him of Juliet and he would have to suffer pitying glances from all sides. Aye, and Ma's matchmaking.

'You compared it to an apprenticeship, but those are paid for.' He kept his voice neutral as he hovered on the brink of a shattering let-down.

'You have a patron. Lord Drysdale has offered to put up the funds.'

'His lordship?' *His lordship's good like that.*

'I don't suppose his lordship knows you from Adam,' Mr Clayton said. 'It's Mr Nugent who put you up for this.'

The September air was hot and thick. Juliet would have sold her soul for a blowy walk across the tops. She submitted four designs to Miss Lindsay, who was polite and cool, though there was no hiding the sparkle in her eyes when she examined them.

'We've already had an order for your walking costume,' she said, 'and another customer wants the blouse from the other design.'

She was shown to the top-floor office of Mr Owen, who turned out to be the man who had hectored her last time. He looked through a big book full of figures, then informed her she was owed three and sixpence, his tone suggesting such a paltry sum was beneath his notice.

'I'm also owed for two new designs,' she dared to say.

'Not until I've been informed in duplicate by Miss Lindsay.' Mr Owen produced a cash tin from a drawer, unlocked it and counted out her money. 'It isn't necessary to rush up here every time you earn a few shillings. I don't wish to see you again for at least a month. Your money will be safe in my keeping.'

And that was where she decided to leave it. She hadn't told Clara about her designing work. *Swanning in, being marvellous –* that was what Clara had accused her of when they met. Adeline would for ever hold it over Clara's head if Juliet outshone her. Juliet decided to hold back her good news until the time came to lump it together with her bombshell. Then she would leave before she was chucked out.

She broke into her three and six to buy Clara a bunch of Michaelmas daisies and a bar of Fry's Chocolate Cream.

'What are these for?' Clara demanded.

'To say thank you for letting me stay.'

'Oh yes, well.'

The next morning, Ethel, the one who had done summat mortal to her leg, came limping back to work, so Juliet was out of that job. Alice, however, knew someone who knew someone and the next day, Juliet left her early job at a run to catch an omnibus into town to clean offices over a jeweller's on Market Street.

That job led to more daytime work and she felt able to give up two of her evenings, though she was careful to give Alice time to replace her. She owed Alice a lot. Being home of an evening felt like an enormous treat. She dragged Clara out for walks in Platt Fields Park, though it wasn't the same as having a proper friend. She worried about Cecily and William Turton. But how could she warn her when any letter would be intercepted? Besides, Cecily might still be in London.

On the days leading to her free evenings, she worked all afternoon on Market Street and Deansgate. One afternoon she arrived at her final job to find the firm embroiled in a stocktake. Boxes were piled everywhere while their contents were checked. Anxious not to forego her wages, she did what she could, but with boxes all over, she had no floors to wash and had to finish early. Never mind. She would meet Clara and they could go home together.

She hovered at the corner of Caroline Street. A customer left Mademoiselle Antoinette's, a good-looking lady with a heart-shaped face and creamy skin, who walked into St Ann's Square, her face lighting up as two girls of around four and eight ran across to meet her, pulling a laughing gentleman along. Juliet couldn't take her eyes off her.

She was wearing a sleeveless bolero jacket, which displayed the sleeves of her blouse – sleeves that Juliet recognised instantly. Snugly fitted on the forearm, the fullness above the elbow was the softly draped alternative to the leg-o'-mutton that she had designed for Ingleby's.

Chapter Fifteen

'Well? What did you discover?' Adeline demanded. She sat behind the battered old table she had first used as a desk when she opened her earliest workshop. Occasionally since then, as her business had bounded from strength to strength, she had toyed with the notion of replacing it with a grand desk inlaid with French morocco leather, with a pillar of drawers to either side of the knee hole. That was what a man would do – which was precisely why she hadn't. A man might surround himself with magnificent office furnishings to intimidate rivals and minions alike, but she had had to be better, stronger, cleverer, more resolute than any man. And if any intimidating needed doing, she was perfectly capable of dishing it out herself.

Ivy Phelps stood in front of the table. She was standing up straight with her hands folded neatly in front, which was how all Adeline's employees stood to address her – or, far more likely, to be addressed by her. There was no chair on Phelps's side of the table. Everybody stood in Adeline's presence, the only exception being customers, for whom there was a chair by the wall, which was set before the table for the duration of the interview, then returned immediately afterwards.

'I've seen the work of the designer you referred to, madam,' said Phelps. 'I pretended to want a costume, and the assistant showed me this season's designs and there were some that stood out.'

'In what way?'

'More stylish, with something new and fresh about them. The assistant said they were by a new designer, who is working exclusively for Ingleby's.'

Adeline held her face in position, not giving away a single thought. 'Go home and change into your uniform. Come straight back.'

'Yes, madam.'

Adeline's eyes narrowed. So Miss Lindsay had found the girl good enough. How dare the chit offer her work elsewhere? She should have come to her grandmother, aye, come crawling on her belly after the way that mother of hers had behaved.

But she would be working for Adeline soon enough. She gave her mind to other matters. That was one of her strengths. She pictured the inside of her head as a series of boxes, each containing thoughts relating to different aspects of her life. She had the ability to open one box while keeping the others securely fastened.

But when she arrived home and read the letter awaiting her, a couple of lids were blown to kingdom come.

Juliet hurried home, astonished and betrayed. She checked her designs. They were all there. Presently, Clara arrived, looking hot and fed up from her journey.

'Why are you home early?' Clara asked tetchily.

'Have you used one of my designs?' Juliet demanded.

'I don't know what you mean,' Clara muttered, but her skin flushed an ugly red.

'I saw the customer you made my blouse for. She was coming out of Mademoiselle's. Had she been in to choose another of my designs?'

'I don't know what you're talking about.'

She waved the design under Clara's nose. 'I know you copied it.'

'Only a bit of it,' Clara said defensively. 'The skirt and bolero are Miss Alexandrina's patterns. I only copied the blouse.'

'Only! Well, that's all right, then!'

'Don't get clever with me. I took you in when you had nowhere to go.'

'That doesn't mean you can help yourself to my work.'

'It isn't work. It's something you do for pleasure. What difference does it make if I used one of them? You should be proud.'

'I've sold some of them to Ingleby's.'

Clara gasped. Her eyes glazed over. 'You've what?'

'Have you taken any others?'

'No.' A pause, hot and heavy. 'Possibly.'

'Did you sell them to Mademoiselle?'

'No, I'm on commission – eighteen shillings each time one is used.'

'Eighteen!' Juliet's heart gave a thud. 'I get two and six – and that's only if the whole costume is ordered.'

Clara smirked. 'It's what comes of working in a superior establishment. Ingleby's, indeed. It shows how Agnes's standards had sunk.'

'It shows nothing of the kind – and don't change the subject. Can't you see what you've done is wrong? You stole my designs.'

'That's an ugly word. Besides, how was I to know you were doing business behind my back?'

'What do I have to say to make you understand?' Her voice throbbed with frustration.

The door burst open. Adeline barged past Clara and made straight for Juliet, who stood frozen in surprise. She saw Adeline raise her arm and draw back her hand, but even though she could see what was going to happen, she didn't move, because she couldn't believe it.

'She what?' Cecily couldn't believe her ears. 'You're kidding. Juliet would never do anything like that.' But a look round the table in the servants' hall told her otherwise. Some eyes danced with amusement at her disbelief, other expressions showed complacency at having long since accepted what Cecily was struggling to comprehend. And it was a struggle. 'Juliet? Our Juliet?'

'Not ours, if you don't mind,' Cook said crisply. 'It's not just Hal she let down. There we were, feeling wretched for her with her mam dead and gone, and then the truth comes out.'

'If Mr Nugent hadn't been there,' added Thomasina, 'she'd have vanished and we'd never have known why.'

'Aye, and we'd have been fretting ourselves sick to this day, I don't doubt,' Cook added.

'Poor Hal,' Cecily said.

'He's gone an' all,' said Cook. 'Went to London and took up with a fellow what designs gardens, and off he's gone and never coming back.'

Mrs Whicker and Miss Marchant walked in, and everyone fell silent.

Mrs Whicker glanced round. 'I take it you have been discussing Juliet?' she enquired disapprovingly – as if she and Miss Marchant hadn't been gossiping their heads off about the very same thing in her sitting room. 'Now that Cecily has been informed, let us not refer to the matter again.' She eyed Cecily. 'I suggest you choose your friends more carefully in future.'

Cecily's mind was in turmoil. Juliet pregnant, and the baby not Hal's. Juliet with a secret lover. Juliet! It was impossible to believe. Cecily's nails bit her palms. They were meant to be friends, so why had Juliet never said anything? It wasn't as though Cecily had kept William secret. She felt betrayed and humiliated. Everyone knew she and Juliet were friends and now they knew Juliet had kept important secrets from her. She felt used.

Then she remembered the letter. *I have something important to tell you, but it can wait until you come back.* Juliet must have been going to reveal the details of her complicated love life. That made her feel a bit better.

And she couldn't feel wretched for long, anyroad. She was too excited. By sneaking the occasional letter to the post, she had let William know how her absence had been extended. She had told him when to expect her home an' all.

How easy it would be for him to get away from work was another matter, but she knew that if anyone could manage that, it was her William. Now all she had to do was contrive to slip out to their secret meeting place.

It was a risk, but well worth taking.

Adeline walloped Juliet. Her hand, far from stinging from the impact, felt cool and invigorated. The chit staggered, banged against the table and just managed to save herself from falling. Adeline stepped forward, following her quarry.

'You trollop! Coming here with your belly full. Do you hear that, Clara? Do you see how you've been taken in?'

'What do you mean, Mother?'

'Don't be stupid, Clara.' She glanced heavenwards in an exaggerated manner: Clara invariably roused scorn. 'She's with child. That's why she ran away. Forget the man with the roving eye. The only roving eye was hers. She had a young man – and what your sister was thinking, letting a girl this age have an understanding, I'll never know. But he wasn't enough for you, was he, madam?' She rounded on the girl. 'You had to put yourself about, didn't you?'

'That isn't what happened—'

'I know precisely what happened.' Adeline drowned her out. 'I wrote to Lord Drysdale's housekeeper to enquire about your work. She replied that, while honesty compelled her to praise your sewing, your moral turpitude has left the neighbourhood profoundly shocked.'

'What's turpitude?' Clara asked. Idiot.

'Mrs Whicker told me everything. The only thing I don't know is what became of the secret lover. Did he throw you over before or after you arrived in Manchester? No wonder you appeared at Mademoiselle Antoinette's without warning. Until the last minute, you had no notion you would need to throw yourself on Clara's mercy.'

'You must listen. I adored Hal. I never looked at anyone else—'

'Enough!' Adeline barked. It was like being thrown back in time. The fury, the disgust, the betrayal – this was how it had felt all those years ago, except that then, there had been blighted expectations as well. 'You're the same as your mother, a slut like she was. At least she debased herself with a man who was free to wed.'

'What do you mean?'

'Agnes had to get married because she was carrying you.'

'That's not true.'

'I offered her a way out, but she threw it back in my face, fool that she was. I'll offer you the same thing, the difference being you're under twenty-one and abandoned, which means you're in no position to refuse.'

'Refuse what?'

'You'll be sent away. The baby will be adopted and you,' she added with a sneer, 'can return to your life of charring.'

'You want to help me?'

'I don't give a fig about you, girl. It's myself I'm thinking of. My idiot of a daughter has taken you in and has brought you to my house. I will not have my good name tarnished by your lax behaviour.'

'Wait a minute.'

Adeline's eyebrows shot up her forehead. Did this chit have the brass neck to try to call a halt to proceedings?

'You wanted to send my mother away when she was having me?'

'She was pregnant out of wedlock. I could have dealt with it, but she chose to tie herself to her labourer.'

'You wanted to have me adopted?' The chit shook her head, a frown clouding her brow. 'I could have had a completely different life.'

'And your mother could have had the success for which I had prepared her.'

'Another name, another family, another . . . everything, without ever knowing who I really am.'

'Sentimental claptrap. You'd never have known any different. Your mother's downfall was tawdry and unpleasant in every respect. Don't romanticise it.'

'No.'

'Good. I'll make the arrangements—'

202

'I mean, no, I won't be sent away. You wanted to get rid of me before I was born and now you want to get rid of this child. It's . . . appalling.'

'It's common sense and it's a godsend for you. Be grateful, girl. I might have offered a visit to a louse-ridden backstreet drunkard with a bottle of gin and a sharp implement.'

'Is that what you offered my mother?'

Adeline drew in her breath on a sharp hiss. 'Be packed and ready the day after tomorrow.'

'I won't be ordered about by the person who wanted my mother to get rid of me.'

'You've no alternative. You can't stay here. Clara won't keep you – will you, Clara?' It was a command: Clara hung her head.

'It so happens I've a bit put by, with the possibility of more to come.'

'Ah yes, your Ingleby designs,' scoffed Adeline.

'How do you know they took me on?'

'More to the point, how dare you approach them? You should have shown me your work. You owe me that.'

'How can I owe you anything?'

'You learnt everything you know from Agnes, and where did she learn it? Any ability you possess belongs to me. I tell you this, girl. Ingleby's won't touch you with a ten-foot pole when they hear of your condition. Soon you'll beg me to send you away.'

The girl lifted her chin. 'If you tell Ingleby's, I'll make sure they know whose granddaughter I am. Word will spread like wildfire through the local sewing world.'

'I shan't need to say a word. Your figure will say everything that needs saying.'

'I'll post my work to them.'

'If you're designing for Ingleby's, you must be using their wares and that means visiting the shop. The only hope of earning your own way in the future is to disappear discreetly now. Be ready midday Saturday.'

The chit said nothing, but her face had drained of colour.

'Or else you'll come with just the clothes on your back,' Adeline said. 'But believe me, you'll come.'

Juliet lay awake. She had defended the baby. Yet a strange sort of defence it had been, protecting her baby (merciful heaven, had she just thought of it as *her* baby?) from adoption into a decent, well-to-do family when the best she had to offer was to dump it on the orphanage doorstep. She was ashamed of that now. She was as bad as Adeline, looking for a way to get rid.

Would Mother and Pop have married had Mother not fallen pregnant? All those times Mother said, 'I could have had my own salon.' Juliet went cold. But Mother had chosen to marry Pop and keep her baby. That was what she had to hold close to her heart.

She crept about, getting dressed, knowing Clara was wide awake, though they both pretended she was asleep. Making her way to work, she pondered her situation. This was the best time of day, with early sunshine and quiet streets, but it would be hellish come winter, dark and wet and freezing cold. Would she still be charring then? Or would everyone have sacked her for being pregnant?

How much income might she hope for from Ingleby's? Had she been a fool to agree not to approach other shops? Yet, if she hadn't, Mr Owen would have shown her the door. She sighed so deeply her bones throbbed. On top of everything else, she needed somewhere to live. Rushing from job to job, she snatched the odd moment to search newsagents' windows for cards with details of rooms to let, agonising over how cheap she might go without encountering rampant mould and equally rampant cockroaches.

She dashed home to freshen up before setting off with a few bob in her pocket for her first week's rent. The first three landladies shut the door on her because of her age and the next room was being sublet by a family renting the downstairs of a shabby terraced house, except it wasn't a room they were offering, just half a room curtained off. She came to the last address on her list, where the door was answered by a strapping middle-aged woman with an enormous bosom hanging almost to her waist.

'I'm here about the room.'

'Oh aye? Bit young, aren't you?'

'I have regular work.'

'You'll be out on your ear if you haven't. Have you burial insurance? I don't want you if you're not respectable.'

'I'm respectable,' she replied stoutly, vowing to get insurance on Monday.

'Good. I'm Mrs Busby. The room's up here.'

It was at the top of the stairs, big enough for a bed, hanging cupboard and a chair. A mirror hung on one wall and some shelves on another. The window overlooked a landscape of grey yards and the backs of red-brick terraces. It made her feel . . . friendless.

'There's no fireplace,' Mrs Busby said, 'but you can sit with us come the cold.'

She pretended to look round to avoid answering. Chances were she wouldn't be here by then, because Mrs Busby would have slung her out. What she was going to do between then and the birth, she didn't know.

'Three shillings for the room and extra for meals. I'm a good cook and you won't go hungry.'

'May I move in tomorrow?'

Mrs Busby extended a hand that was surprisingly slender considering the quantity of flesh she had up top. 'Six bob. A week in hand in case of breakages. Any time after ten tomorrow.'

She returned home. Why didn't she feel pleased? Her intentions were in turmoil. Learning of the threat that had been made against her own identity had unsettled her, arousing a protective instinct. Was this how Mother had felt? And if Juliet hated the thought of adoption for herself, how could she inflict it on this child? Yet what kind of parent would she make, young, unwed and pinching every penny until it squealed?

She arrived at Mrs Duggan's, feeling torn in half, too overwrought to care when Clara gave her the silent treatment.

Before they went to bed, she said, 'I'll be gone when you get in from work tomorrow.'

Something flickered in Clara's face. Uncertainty? Regret? But all she said was, 'I see.'

She didn't ask where and Juliet felt ridiculously hurt.

When Juliet knocked on Mrs Busby's door, a man answered. He was big-boned and jowly, with puffy bags under his eyes. 'The wife's out shopping. I'm Mr Busby. Pleased to meet you.' He had a surprisingly limp handshake. 'I'll take your bag. After you.'

The room was smaller than she remembered. Mr Busby came bustling in behind her.

'Say if you want more shelves. I'm pretty handy.' His eyes rested on her. 'The wife said you were young, but I never thought she meant this young.'

'I can pay my way.'

'I might be able to help with the rent . . . if you know what I mean.'

206

He licked his lips. 'I could slip you the odd couple of bob, a pretty girl like you. You know, you be nice to me and I'll be nice to you.'

She froze. She wanted to fly at him and rake the flesh from his face with her nails, but she couldn't move. It all came flooding back. Dirty girl, grateful girl, stupid, stupid, stupid. His hand reached towards her and in that second he could have touched her, fondled her, done anything and she couldn't have stopped him. Then the spell broke, ice turning to fire. She would never be touched that way again.

'Get away,' she said, then louder, 'Get away!'

'I only—'

'I know precisely what you only! You're disgusting. Stand aside.'

Snatching her bag, she hurtled downstairs and threw the door open. Behind her, Mr Busby blustered about a misunderstanding. Slamming the door, she ran – then halted. Six shillings was a lot of money. She went back and hammered on the door. It opened so abruptly she almost fell inside.

'I want my money back.'

'The wife took that money in good faith. Not her fault if you change your mind. I'll say you're stopping with your mam, and quite right too, a slip of a thing like you.'

'If you don't give me my money, I'll report you to the police.'

Mr Busby stood taller. 'Aye, you do that. Tell them you want to complain about Police Sergeant Busby and see where it gets you. Now bugger off.'

The door slammed. She stood there, seething, but there was nothing she could do. She walked away, fighting to put the experience behind her. She had to find somewhere else and it would look better, less desperate, if she weren't lugging around all her worldly possessions. She must take the bag back to Mrs Duggan's while she searched. But she had visited all the respectable possibilities, the ones where she would be thrown out once her condition became known. All that remained were places where her condition would be irrelevant: filthy, frightening places in diseased parts of town, sopping with damp and infested with vermin.

When she got home, who should be standing on the doorstep but Mr Owen? He clicked his tongue impatiently.

'There you are. You must come immediately.'

Mr Owen would answer no questions. Juliet had time only to pop her bag indoors before he hustled her to the bus stop. Ingleby's was far too important to her for her to refuse, but Mr Owen took her, not to Market Street, but to St Ann's Square and then into Caroline Street, where he turned into a discreet little passage that led to the alley at the back of the shops. Alarm rattled through her. Was Clara ill? But Mr Owen was nothing do with Mademoiselle Antoinette's.

She remembered the corridor from last time. There was no sign of anyone, but she could hear – was that sobbing? A door opened and the volume increased. Mrs Bowen appeared. Seeing Juliet, she was about to draw back, but Juliet glimpsed Clara draped over a chair, weeping and wailing. She darted inside and tried to put an arm round her, but Clara surged to her feet and paced about, clutching a sodden hanky.

'They found out. That blouse – those sleeves – they found out.' She grabbed Juliet's hand, her reddened eyes brimming with a hectic mixture of fear and hope. 'Say it was my design and you copied it. Tell them – or I'll lose my job.'

Mrs Bowen pulled Juliet away. 'Later. You can see her later.'

Bewildered, Juliet followed Mr Owen and found herself in a room that appeared part-office and part-sitting room, occupied by Miss Lindsay and Miss Selway. There was another woman too, middle-aged and plain, but so exquisitely turned out that it was a shame she lacked the beauty to go with it.

'It's Tewson's niece,' Miss Selway exclaimed. 'That explains it. Here's your thief, Miss Lindsay.'

'On the contrary,' Miss Lindsay replied, 'I have seen Miss Harper create a design, with my own eyes.'

'Ladies, please.' The other woman spoke mildly. She looked at Juliet. 'Thank you for coming.'

Good grief, was this Mademoiselle Antoinette? Juliet had pictured a timeless beauty, and here she was, as ordinary as you please.

Mademoiselle nodded to Miss Selway, who looked down her nose at Juliet as she explained, 'Several of our ladies have ordered a blouse with distinctive sleeves, a design that Tewson claimed as her own. Now a client has returned to complain that her housekeeper was wearing the same design, as made by Ingleby's.'

'The question is,' said Mr Owen, 'who designed it?'

'What does my aunt say?' Juliet asked.

'Tewson,' Miss Selway replied, 'is too hysterical to say anything worth listening to.'

'I've explained to Mademoiselle Antoinette and Miss Selway,' said Miss Lindsay, 'that I've seen you create the beginning of a design on paper and then put a costume together in words, as it were, by choosing fabrics and notions. I'm sure the design in question is your own. The reputation of Ingleby's is at stake.'

'As is that of Mademoiselle Antoinette's.' Miss Selway made a dismissive gesture. 'Look at her. She's too young to have this sort of ability.'

'Do as I did,' suggested Miss Lindsay. 'Give her a pencil and paper.'

Mademoiselle addressed Juliet. 'You've been asked a question.'

Juliet thought furiously. Tell the truth and Clara would be

sacked. Tell a lie and kiss goodbye to Ingleby's. She didn't want Clara to lose her job, but neither could she afford to throw away her own prospects or her reputation.

'It's my design,' she stated quietly.

'This is insupportable,' exclaimed Miss Selway and swept from the room.

Mademoiselle looked at Miss Lindsay and Mr Owen. 'This is deeply embarrassing for my salon. I trust you see no need to take matters further . . . ? The publicity would damage both our establishments. Are you still here?' She blinked at Juliet. 'You may go.'

Juliet hastened to find Clara, but she was too late. She caught up with her at the bus stop, finding her gulping deep breaths that came way too quickly. Juliet bundled her onto the next bus and got her home, where she slumped in the armchair, one hand plastered across her mouth.

'I'll put the kettle on,' said Juliet.

As she ran downstairs, she saw her carpetbag and picked it up. At the same moment, there was an imperious rap on the door. With her bag in one hand, she opened the door with the other.

'I see you're packed and ready,' said Adeline.

Chapter Sixteen

In the ten excruciatingly dismal days since returning to Moorside, Cecily had contrived to sneak out every day in the increasingly urgent hope of finding William in their secret trysting place. Every day she hoped afresh, and every day she fought back tears so as to return, stunned, to her duties with an unblemished face. Her heart had grown hungrier by the day during their enforced separation and now she was frantic with longing. William would find a way to return to her. He had to. She would die of desire if he didn't.

Perhaps she could write again. If she were to sneak a letter home, would one of her sisters help her?

But there was no need, because he came.

She didn't see him at first. She crept forward, heart pitter-pattering, her hopes as precious and as fragile as the finest Bohemian glass. A pair of arms came around her from behind. One snaked across her waist, pulling her firmly against a body; the other hand slid over her breast. She was so shocked, it took a moment for her to react, but as she started to struggle, she was whirled round and there was William.

He pulled her to him. She lifted her face, her lips eagerly seeking his, opening willingly beneath the pressure of his mouth. When he slid his tongue inside, longing tugged within her.

'I assume from that, that you missed me,' William said with a cocky grin.

'Maybe.' She gazed at him. 'Did you miss me?'

'Shall I show you?'

'Oh yes,' she breathed. She had to hold herself still so as not to tremble with anticipation, but instead of producing a ring, William kissed her again. There was one moment sharp with disappointment, then she was lost in his embrace. Her body cried out for him.

When he released her, she had to catch herself before she stumbled.

'Tell me everything,' said William.

'Didn't you read my letters?' she teased, but she happily launched into details of her travels and her new post.

'What about the folks you left behind?' William asked. 'The housekeeper, and that friend of yours – Juliet. How is she?' He looked at her. 'Your face changed when I said her name.'

'She's not here any more.' This wasn't news. News was pleasant. This hurt. 'She ran away. She got herself into trouble and it wasn't Hal's, so she ran away.'

'Where to?'

'No one knows. Let's talk about something else.'

'Wouldn't you rather . . .' William nibbled her ear. '. . . do this?'

She gave a gasp of pleasure and closed her eyes, her lashes feathering on her cheeks. Fantasies of her reunion with William had driven her wild all these weeks and now it was happening. Turning her head, she offered him her lips, taking his head in her hands to pull him down to receive her kiss, but any sense of her being in control vanished when William began plundering her mouth. She was close to swooning with desire. She had been brought up to be a good girl, but, honestly, in that moment, if he had . . . and, oh, how she wished he would . . .

William ended the kiss and loosened his hold just when she most wanted to be held tighter, to have more asked of her, just when she was more ripe and willing than she had ever been.

'Shouldn't you be getting back?' he asked.

She didn't want to go back – ever. 'Can you come again tomorrow?'

'I'm here just for today,' William said, and her heart plummeted into her boots. 'I'm supposedly visiting a sick relative and I'm due back in the office tomorrow.'

She stared at him. Her body ached with need. 'When . . . ?'

'Today week. I've a feeling my poor old uncle is going to pop his clogs. I'll have to attend the funeral and then stay for a day or two to sort out his affairs.'

'A day or two,' she breathed.

'Or three,' said William.

Juliet stood at the window. Beyond the garden wall was the pinewood. She had looked out on trees before, but these weren't like those in his lordship's park. Here, they were uniformly tall and slender. She was here as her side of the bargain, the adoption in return for Clara's future. When Adeline had arrived to collect her from Mrs Duggan's house, she soon got to the bottom of the upset she had walked in on and her scorn of Clara knew no bounds.

'Your sister was a slut and now you're a thief, and a singularly stupid one at that.' Adeline's lip had curled in disgust. 'Dismissed on the spot for professional theft and for bringing the salon into disrepute – you'll never work again. You'll lose your home too, such as it is. Unless, of course . . .'

That was how it had happened. If Juliet would do as Adeline demanded, Adeline would employ Clara. As simple – and as complicated – as that. Juliet didn't know if she had done the right thing. But she had been reeling with shock at Clara's predicament – guilt, too, because she had saved her own reputation at Clara's expense – and her skin still crawled from the encounter with Mr Busby, not to mention the knowledge of having used up every possibility of a respectable home. Did she have any choices left? If she did, she couldn't identify them. And all said and done, wasn't it better for the baby this way?

At any rate, here she was. She had been brought by train to Southport and then on a shorter train journey to a place along the coast called Freshfield. They were met by a pony and trap, and driven by a twisty-turny route along lanes between tall hedgerows teeming with bees and butterflies. They passed meadows where grazing horses came to look at them over the fence, then saw the beginnings of a pinewood, which made Juliet long for cool and shade. As she inhaled the green scent, a breeze carried a taste of salt on the air.

'How far are we from the sea?' she asked.

'Over the far side of the woods,' said the driver. 'Not that the wayward girls go to the beach.'

Was that what she was now? A wayward girl?

The trap went through a gateway and pulled up before a large house in a garden planted with masses of greenery, not at all her idea of a garden. Before she knew it, she was standing in a hall that seemed dark after the afternoon dazzle, being presented to

214

Mrs Maddox, a neat, bustling woman, who led her up two flights, peppering her with rules all the way. Mrs Maddox opened the door upon a pleasant, impersonal room and left her to unpack. She ran her fingers over her painting of Moorside's laburnum walk. The picture rail was empty. She slid the painting back into her carpetbag. She wasn't going to risk displaying it, only to have it confiscated. Who knew what other sort of rules applied in a place like this?

There were three other girls, Ruth, Emily and Tabitha. Tabitha was so huge and ungainly that Juliet felt a ripple of dismay at what lay in store. The others were well spoken and educated, but Mrs Maddox made a point of saying, 'You're all here for the same reason,' and Juliet's awkwardness slipped away.

One morning, Tabitha didn't appear at the breakfast table.

'Gone to the attic,' Ruth whispered to Emily. They bit their lips and touched their swelling bellies.

'The attic is where the babies are born,' Emily informed Juliet in an undertone.

She didn't see Tabitha again, except for a glimpse. One afternoon, the usual routine was interrupted for Juliet, Ruth and Emily to be taken for a walk through the woods by a maidservant called Yardley. She was a sturdy, capable woman with a calm manner, but Juliet had already realised that, though Yardley called you 'miss' and fussed over you pleasantly inside the house, there was no doubt as to who was in charge when she took you out.

'This is so the baby can be taken away,' Emily whispered. 'While we're out, the new parents will come for it.'

It. The baby was 'it' to the girls. Juliet had asked Mrs Maddox whether it was a boy or a girl and had been told to mind her own business.

Tabitha stayed in bed for ten days, though whether that bed

was her own or an attic bed, Juliet had no idea. On the day she left, the other three were confined to their rooms, though, hearing a sound, Juliet found that the done thing was to creep to the first floor to see what there was to be seen – which was disappointingly little. There was a glimpse of Tabitha being ushered into the sitting room, and some minutes later she was led out by a stony-faced man, presumably her father. There was the sound of the front door opening – a few stilted words of farewell – and even as the door closed, Emily and Ruth were scurrying back to their rooms, and Juliet wasn't slow in following.

Before the week was out, three more girls arrived: Florence, Violet and Rachel. To Juliet's eye, Rachel looked so obviously pregnant that it was amazing she had kept her secret so long.

'The magic of whalebone,' Rachel said blithely. 'I can't describe the relief of being free from corsets. I swear I haven't breathed since Midsummer's Day.'

'If you persist in making light of your situation,' Mrs Maddox said in a voice of quiet steel, 'I'll have your family remove you. This is a time for shame and reflection.'

Shame and reflection were helped along by piecework. The girls made artificial flowers to an exacting standard and were paid the going rate.

'Sixpence for a gross of violets,' Juliet had exclaimed on her first day. 'That's a pittance.'

Mrs Maddox looked round the group. 'If your families hadn't stood by you and sent you here, you could have ended up grubbing for a living doing this very thing.'

Buttercups were simplest, so Juliet stuck to those, her clever fingers soon acquiring the skills, though it was galling to earn even less than for violets. Sobering, too, to realise the pittance she could have been forced to exist on in different circumstances. Was Adeline's ruthless solution the right one?

Adeline sat in Mrs Maddox's sitting room. Mrs Maddox called it her sitting room and indeed it looked like one, with its fireside chairs and its array of ornaments, but its function was more that of an office. Or possibly a visitors' room – like in a prison. This was where Mrs Maddox conducted her business. It was where she discussed terms with parents and guardians. Presumably it was the room in which once wilful girls, now submissive after the gruelling experience of giving birth, were returned to their families. It must also be the room into which adoptive parents were shown.

Today it was the prison visiting room.

The chit came in. Adeline looked at her, ready to feel disgusted at the sight of her thickened waist, but instead she raised an eyebrow in acknowledgement of the girl's radiant complexion and shining hair.

'Samples of fabrics, trimmings and accessories,' she announced, indicating the box she had brought with her. 'You will create eight designs.'

'Eight?' If the chit was taken aback by the lack of pleasantries, it didn't show. 'Last time Miss Lindsay saw four and chose two.'

'This time you'll produce eight. I'll take care of your fee. I'm not handing it over to you to help you run away.'

'Would you ask Mr Owen to look after it for me?'

'Don't you trust me?'

'He's looked after it so far.'

Adeline gave a bark of sneering laughter. 'If you don't wish me to look after it, say so. You're as spineless as your aunt. You should always say what you mean.'

'Like you do?'

'Folk always know where they stand with me.'

'Yes – in the gutter.'

'So you've got a backbone, have you? That's more than your aunt's ever shown. You'll be excused piecework to do this.' She came to her feet. It was always satisfying to tower over others. 'Have the designs ready three weeks today.'

She didn't bother saying goodbye.

Juliet stood behind her chair at the dining table, along with the other girls. Mrs Maddox swept in, smiling, as if this were a select establishment for paying guests rather than a home for wayward girls, and took her place at the head of the table, signalling to the girls to join her. After a tasty meal of devilled kidneys followed by apple snow, she smiled round the table. She smiled a lot, but the smile could drop off her face if you didn't watch out.

'We have a seamstress in our midst.' She beamed at Juliet. 'Come with me, dear.'

Juliet was whisked upstairs and shown a pair of wardrobes. Mrs Maddox turned the keys and opened them.

'This is what the girls wear as they expand. You'll need clothes from here soon. Make some fresh garments and I'll pay you. We're particularly in need of nightwear.'

She was delighted to oblige, aware of the others' envy as they got sore fingers making the hated flowers, but when Mrs Maddox said she would pay, what she meant was she would save Juliet's wages to give to her grandmother.

The days went by, mellow days giving way to crisp evenings and chilly nights. The dark-green foliage of the shrubby garden was transformed into a blaze of crimson. Juliet's heart contracted: autumn was Hal's favourite season.

So much had happened since Mother's death that she had managed to hold thoughts of him at arm's length for the most part, as she threw herself into the relentless torrent of tasks, responsibilities and worries that her life had been reduced to, while her heart perched silent and still on the edge of a terrifying abyss. Now her heart was returning to life. Again and again, she pictured his hearing about her supposed secret lover. Surely he would know she would never betray him?

She could write and tell him the truth, though not yet, not until she was released from Mrs Maddox's house. Not that she could denounce Mr Nugent. It wouldn't be safe for Hal to put him in the position of knowing what Mr Nugent had done to her; she wasn't sure she could ever admit that to anyone. But she could assure Hal there hadn't been another man.

She worried dreadfully about Cecily too, wishing she could warn her that William wasn't to be trusted, but Mrs Whicker would read any letter first, before ceremonially tearing it to pieces before Cecily's eyes, with her never having been permitted to read it. Then Cecily would lose her position.

And that would thrust her straight into William's arms.

Some risks weren't risks at all. They were certainties. Cecily loved William with all her heart, and longed to marry him and have a home of her own. Before she went to London, when she had tried dropping hints, he had said he didn't yet earn enough. So what? She had grown up in a crowded cottage with a mother who had made their limited income stretch a long way, and Cecily was positive she could run their home on a small budget. She knew too about how not to have babies, because Barbara had explained about sponges soaked in vinegar. The thought of what you did that caused the need for those sponges made Cecily want to writhe in pleasure.

Those sponges could wait till they were married. Just now, what William needed was a push in the right direction.

The cottage where the Harpers had lived was empty. Purloining the spare key, she raced there, unlocked the door and made haste to return the key. The next afternoon, while Miss Phoebe and Miss Vicky were out with her ladyship, and Miss Marchant was lying down with a bad head, she returned with a blanket and some kindling. There were one or two pieces of furniture downstairs. She ran upstairs, hoping – yes, there was a bed. She laid a fire and covered the bed with the blanket.

Her heart clouted her ribs. Tomorrow she would bring William here. She couldn't wait.

Neither, it seemed, could William. They met in their usual place. William's wandering hands quickly realised there was nothing beneath her blouse but bare flesh, and from that moment there was no stopping him. Buttons flew everywhere as he wrenched her blouse open, and Cecily moaned as his lips roved across her flesh. She arched her back, presenting herself to him.

They tumbled to the ground, and as William's mouth took possession of hers, she could feel his hand working away at her lower clothes. She wriggled accommodatingly, as eager as he was for the layers to be pushed aside. Cold air prickled her thighs as William raised himself so he could fiddle with his own buttons. Then he lowered himself on top of her, kissing her ravenously. Intoxicated with desire, she snaked her arms round his neck, needing the kiss to be ever deeper.

His knee shoved her legs apart. She felt hot and juicy as he entered her, making her almost sob with gratitude. As he thrust into her, she lost control until suddenly her body was overwhelmed by a frenzy of animal gratification that released inside her a distant storm of longing that thrashed ever nearer until it burst upon her, setting her body twitching convulsively with a pleasure so intense she thought she would die.

Later, she crept home, trembling and stunned and elated, with a pocketful of buttons and a shawl protecting her modesty.

After that, she was crazy for more. William had two more days and she took him to the cottage, where they made good use of the bed. And the dining table. And the stairs.

Winter set in. The sky hung heavy, but snow didn't fall. Was it this time last year, or not until after Christmas, that Mother's 'snow-headaches' had started?

'Enjoy the fires, girls,' said Mrs Maddox. 'Some institutions wouldn't care if you turned blue with cold, but I run a superior establishment and stint on nothing. I'll ask Yardley for the toasting forks and you can toast crumpets. Juliet, I've heard from your grandmother. She'll visit tomorrow.'

Adeline arrived, looking magnificent in a floor-length woollen coat that flared from the waist and boasted a generous quantity of fur trimming around the deep collar and down the revers all the way to the hem. In contrast to the handsome coat, her hat was simple. With her tall stature and strong features, did she shun fuss and prettiness?

She produced a set of the next season's samples. 'Another eight designs.'

'Already? I wasn't expecting to be asked again till spring. Do you know how much I've earned?'

'You'll get your dues, girl. Have the new designs ready—'

'Three weeks today. I know.'

Three weeks. How easy it was to say the words. In three weeks, it would be almost Christmas, and then it would be January, and her baby was due in February.

Adeline rose. Had she come all this way just to request – no, demand – more designs? Evidently. Well, Juliet wasn't going to sit meekly while she marched out. She thrust herself to her feet, not without difficulty, catching the glimmer of distaste on Adeline's face at her clumsiness, and bolted for the door.

'Goodbye, Grandmother. Thank you for calling.'

She returned to the other girls, who were in the middle of one of their oft-repeated conversations about pregnancy, but while the others complained about their increasing girths and every single discomfort of their condition, Juliet held her tongue. She had expected to loathe everything about carrying William Turton's bastard, but instead her feeling of protectiveness deepened by the day, though she couldn't say so, for fear of provoking one of Mrs Maddox's sharp glances. She couldn't even whisper it to the other girls. They didn't seem to have doubts about their babies' futures – or their own. Some talked freely about getting on with their lives. Others were more sentimental – but only until they were challenged.

'Keep it, then,' Rachel said bluntly to a new girl called Lucy, who claimed she didn't know how she would part with her child. 'But if you do, how will you manage?' She stared at Lucy, forcing an answer.

'Well . . . I couldn't.'

'Exactly, so stop wallowing.'

And that was what it came down to. Even if Juliet could cobble together a sufficient wage, there was still the stigma of illegitimacy to contend with, which would blacken both their names. Adoption would give the baby respectability and material comfort with parents who longed for a child.

And she . . . she would spend the rest of her life wondering.

'If mine is a boy,' Rachel declared, 'I'm calling him Jonah, because I'm as big as a whale.'

'You won't know,' Juliet pointed out. 'We never know whether the babies are boys or girls.'

That was the last time she saw Rachel, because Rachel went to the attic that day. Juliet and Violet glanced at one another, acknowledging in silent apprehension that they would be next. But, unexpectedly, it was Evie who was next. Before the day was out, she was followed by Violet.

'So you must be good, quiet girls,' said Yardley, 'because Mrs Maddox and Mrs Fletcher' – this was the midwife, a woman Juliet had never set eyes on, though her name was known by all – 'will have their hands full.'

Florence looked at Juliet. 'You next.'

As if Florence had worked a magic spell, Juliet felt a warm gush between her thighs.

Juliet shifted uncomfortably in a bizarre half-world. Sometimes Mrs Maddox was there, sometimes Mrs Fletcher, sometimes both. They would slap her face and speak in bracing voices to haul her back to her senses. They said things her mind couldn't cling on to and, to her horror, Mrs Fletcher fiddled about inside her. Each time they left her, they said things like 'Good girl. You're doing well', their voices booming one second and fading the next. They said, 'This will help,' and a soft cloth was pressed over her nose and mouth. Her head filled with a sweet, cloying smell that sent her swirling into a strange grogginess where she couldn't tell if she was awake or asleep and the pains were part of the nightmare.

As the pains drew closer together, each more excruciating than the last, Mrs Maddox and Mrs Fletcher were there more. Yardley was there sometimes too, or maybe that was part of the dream. When the intensity of the pain made her cry out, something was thrust into her mouth, a rolled-up rag, with the sharp words, 'No screaming. Bite on that,' and suddenly she wasn't in bed any more, she was in the park, flat on her back, with William Turton's grotty handkerchief suffocating her. He was flattening her, hammering his way into her, pushing, pushing, harder and harder, until she was nearly ripped in two.

'Push! Here it comes. Push hard!'

Struggling to shove him off her, she gave an almighty heave that practically broke her back, then a sudden easing sent shock rippling through her.

'Can you manage, Yardley?' Mrs Fletcher's voice. 'I must get back to Evie.' And she was gone.

Juliet lay there, trembly and exhausted. A cry broke the quiet, and all traces of grogginess vanished. She pushed herself up.

'What – what is it?' she whispered.

Yardley wrapped the infant in a blanket.

'Please . . .'

'Never you mind. I'll be back in a minute. You're not finished yet.'

Fear and despair welled up in her. Before Yardley could take a step, Mrs Maddox appeared in the doorway, insisting, 'Come quick,' before disappearing. The unflappable Yardley looked flustered. There was a scream from somewhere, abruptly cut off, and Yardley thrust the bundle at Juliet with a brief, 'Here, hold this,' before she rushed away.

Juliet held her baby. Her baby, her own child. She tilted her head to look at the tiny face and fell irretrievably in love.

Chapter Seventeen

Adeline's garden sparkled in the sunshine following the showery morning. Juliet turned from the window. She had been here two days, though her heart wasn't here, that was certain. She had no means of knowing where it was. Constance could be anywhere. Her little girl. Constance Mary Harper. Thank heaven she had had the presence of mind to check the baby's gender in those few precious moments. So few – her heart clenched with pain. Just a few piercingly sweet moments with her daughter, and then Mrs Maddox had rushed in, wrenched the baby away and rushed out again, leaving her slack-jawed with shock.

She had tried to follow, only to crumple in a heap on the floor. Almost immediately Mrs Fletcher was there, then Yardley. They lifted her onto the bed. Yardley held her down while Mrs Fletcher manipulated her stomach. Was Constance a twin? But it was the afterbirth.

It was difficult to separate out what had happened next. She had sobbed so much that they used the sweet-smelling stuff on her. When she woke, she ached all over, and when she used the chamber pot, a smelly discharge came out. Days and nights merged in a blur of pain. They kept rousing her to drink cordial and they lay her on her left side, propped up by pillows, which had eased the cramps in her stomach.

When at last she woke feeling better, panic coursed through her. *Constance – where is Constance? Please don't let her have been taken away already.*

'Back in the land of the living, are we? That was a nasty infection.' It was Yardley, brisk and pleasant. 'Can you manage a bite to eat? You'll need to wait a while, mind. We've got visitors due any minute.'

What strength she possessed drained from her muscles. 'Visitors? Here to adopt?' Her heart delivered an almighty clout. 'My baby?'

'No. Not that it makes any odds. They'll all be gone soon.'

When Yardley left, Juliet staggered in search of the nursery, only to blunder into Mrs Maddox, who escorted her back to bed. The key turned when Mrs Maddox left.

They were cautious with her after that, slanting glances her way. Her questions went ignored. Neither did her pretence of calming down fool them.

A couple of days later Mrs Maddox came in, followed by Yardley. Mrs Maddox looked serious.

'It's for your own good,' she said.

Yardley appeared round the other side of the bed, and in that moment she knew with blinding clarity what would happen today: a cloth was clamped over her nose and mouth, that familiar, cloying smell – the hateful sensation of whirling and falling . . . falling—

She clawed her way back from the brink. The room slurred in and out of focus. She was alone. With a colossal effort, she heaved herself out of bed, staggered and tumbled, the floor whooshing

227

up to meet her. She crawled to the door. It was locked. Sleep overcame her then, right there on the floor. At some point she jerked awake, her head spinning. Fighting off waves of dizziness, she dragged herself up and stumbled to the window, crashing into the chair beside it and banging her forehead on the window bars. The room rolled around her. She clung to the bars, gasping and dry-mouthed. Then, looking down, she stopped breathing. A carriage stood outside.

She sat down so suddenly her teeth jolted. The next thing she knew, she was waking up, struggling back to consciousness. How could she have slept? The carriage had gone – and a baby inside it. Anguish washed through her, rendering her clear-headed, but only briefly. The dizziness returned, as did the sensation of mind and innards slewing about. Then Adeline was in the room, a taunting smile on her face. She woke up to find her cheek pressed against a bar, her neck so stiff that the tiniest movement sent pain twanging into the back of her head. She felt ill and heavy-limbed, and longed to lie down.

A carriage drove through the gates. She pressed against the bars to see. The driver climbed down to open the door and a man got out. He turned to offer his hand and his wife followed him. They kept hold of each other's hands for an extra moment. She saw the crowns of their hats turn as they shared a glance, and she felt the moment pass between them. The wife looked at the house, then she looked up and Juliet exclaimed aloud, except that it came out as a strangled slur.

Was it—could it be?

The next time she woke, struggling through a mass of weird dreams that vanished like smoke, she was tucked up in bed.

* * *

228

Even now Juliet didn't know whether it had happened. The lady she had seen outside Mademoiselle Antoinette's wearing her sleeve design – had she really come to Mrs Maddox's house? Or was it a dream? She had dreamt of her grandmother, and Adeline certainly hadn't been there. She would never know. She wasn't even meant to know she had had a little girl. Oh, Constance . . . Constance.

Now here she was at Adeline's house, with staff to make her bed and cook her meals.

'Do they know . . . about the baby?' she asked Adeline.

'What baby is that?'

She gasped. Adeline regarded her coldly until she had to look away. *What baby is that?*

Tomorrow was the last Sunday of the month and she found herself anticipating Clara's visit in a bothersome way. She badly needed Clara to be well and thriving so that, in some small way, the loss of Constance would have resulted in something worthwhile.

But Sunday came and went with no sign of Clara.

'Doesn't she visit any more?' Juliet asked.

'What for? I see her at work. Speaking of which, you've lolled around here long enough. You start work tomorrow.'

'Fine.' If Adeline was brusque, Juliet could be too. 'I assume I'll be sewing.'

'Assume what you like.'

Juliet stood beside her grandmother outside a vast building with TEWSON'S TEXTILES painted across the brickwork. She remembered standing on the hill above Annerby, seeing its factories, so dark and forbidding, but the windows here were sparkling. She recalled Mother quoting Adeline on the subject of good light. Even Mrs Whicker had ended up quoting Adeline Tewson.

Adeline led the way upstairs. Juliet emerged onto a landing with doors along one side, while on the other was nothing but a rail between her and a drop to the floor below. She gazed upon ranks of women working treadle sewing machines. Adeline strode ahead; she hurried to catch up. A woman in a grey jacket with red piping came towards them. She stood aside and curtseyed. Adeline swept by without so much as a nod. Mortified by her grandmother's rudeness, Juliet murmured a good morning.

Further along, Adeline waited for her. She gestured over the workroom below.

'My empire. Are you impressed? You should be. This is a magnificent achievement for a woman. I've had to work twice as hard as any man.'

It was impossible not to be impressed. All those machines, all those women. All the women looked the same, each one bending over her work, concentrating on the needle flashing in and out, expert fingers guiding the fabric. Then, with a snip of the scissors, the item was finished, folded and dropped into a basket on the floor even as the woman leant the other way to pluck the next piece from a basket on the other side. No one spoke, no one looked round. *It was always work, work, work with Mother.* Clara's words. Juliet remembered Adeline's description of taking on her first three workers and sacking one at the end of the first day. Did these women work under a similar threat?

'Do you still consider it will be, and I quote, "fine" to work here? A fancy sewing room and a second-rate shop in the middle of nowhere – you don't know what real work is.'

'I'll manage,' she replied.

Adeline was on the move again. Juliet scurried behind. A door opened onto a staircase. She thought Adeline would lead her downstairs to the workroom, but Adeline went up.

Leading her through another door, Adeline said, 'This is the next-door building. When I took it over, I had doors knocked through on each floor.'

This building didn't have a vast work floor with overlooking landing. Adeline opened a door to reveal a long sewing room with lines of women sitting at machines. How light it was. Yet the windows, though clean, weren't especially large, and the brightness was the same all over the room.

'Electricity,' said Adeline.

'Is it true the lamps turn on and off without you going near them?' Juliet whispered in awe.

Adeline indicated a switch in the centre of a small brass square mounted on the wall. 'According to the literature, flicking the switch is so easy that a lady may do it. No need to trouble the servants.'

Juliet's fingers itched. All those lamps being extinguished in one go was more than she could imagine.

Adeline opened door after door upon sewing rooms where women worked diligently. Presiding over each room was a woman in a grey jacket with red piping.

Adeline opened another door. 'My latest venture.'

Juliet stepped inside, expecting something different, but it was another sewing room with ranks of machines and a woman in a grey jacket with red piping.

Adeline said, 'There are three of these rooms.'

She opened the door on the next. It was the same, except that there were two women in grey jackets with red piping. One was at the desk at the front and the other was bending over a pile of finished pieces, scrutinising them. She straightened – and it was Clara.

'Auntie Clara!' Juliet hurried to greet her. 'You're an overseer. That's a responsible job.'

'Don't patronise me!' Clara hissed. 'Just because you've fallen on your feet doesn't mean I've forgotten you turning up out of nowhere, homeless and broke. And in a certain condition,' she added.

She stared. 'I only meant to congratulate you.'

'I'd rather be sewing, if you must know. Do you know what she's got me doing? Overseeing the quality, that's what.'

'It shows she trusts you.'

'Do you know who gets fined if a single imperfect piece gets through? I do. You'd think it would be the woman who did the shoddy sewing, wouldn't you, but oh no, it's muggins here that gets stung for it.'

'Back to work, Tewson,' said Adeline.

'Yes, madam.'

'What do you think?' Adeline asked, leading Juliet away.

'She doesn't seem very happy.'

'I didn't mean Clara. I meant what I've shown you. Did you see what they were sewing?'

'It looked like garments.'

'Tailor-mades. It's the latest thing, finished garments to buy in shops.'

'Finished? What about fitting? Who's going to buy something that isn't fitted?'

'Plenty of women. This is the future of dressmaking. You look shocked. You'll never make a businesswoman. No vision.'

'What about all the seamstresses?'

'Those worth their salt will have work. Folk with money will always want to spend it, especially if they think they're getting something special. The Mademoiselle Antoinettes of this world –

or to give her her real name, Elsie Bradshaw – will always have a market. But women further down the pecking order will have greater access to good-quality clothing. I started Tewson's Tailor-mades in the autumn, and orders are climbing. I want my order books full. I've always wanted to see women wearing my garments. I could never have had a salon, not with my background, the widow of a letter carrier, and coming from where I did, but this will do nicely.'

'And you want me to work one of the sewing machines?'

'I said you lacked vision. No, girl, you're my new designer.'

Adeline showed Juliet into a parlour overlooking the back garden. A fire was burning, and on the table was a box like those Adeline had brought to Mrs Maddox's house.

'Here's a list of the garments I want next.' Adeline turned to leave.

'Wait,' said Juliet. What a bizarre way to start a new job. Meeting Adeline's hard gaze, she quelled the impulse to seek instructions. Needing to stand up to her grandmother, she asked, 'How much work will it take to repay you for my time with Mrs Maddox?'

'You make it sound as if you're old enough to strike out on your own. You've no choice but to stay here with me. Be grateful you have a skill to offer. I wouldn't have looked twice at you otherwise.'

The door shut behind her. After a moment Juliet went to test it. Was she locked in? No. She went to the window, recognising elephant's ears in the borders, their large rubbery leaves still winter-red. Hal had told her their proper name, but she couldn't recall it.

Five months. That was how long she had spent at Mrs Maddox's and it was how long she would stay here. She baulked at the thought of living so long with her grandmother. Would Adeline consider the debt repaid by then? What did she owe Adeline, anyway? Adeline hadn't sent her away to help her but to preserve her own reputation. If there had been even a trace of warmth in Adeline's actions, it would be easier for her to be here now, but she didn't want to work for Adeline and she certainly didn't want to live here.

'Well then, do something about it.'

The words, uttered aloud, made her feel stronger. Yes, she would design for Tewson's Tailor-mades, but she must also look to the future – and more than look. She thought of Ingleby's. Judging by the number of designs Miss Lindsay had required while she was away, they were delighted with her. How much was she owed? One guinea per design. She had supplied sixteen, though that didn't mean they had all been accepted, and she had left two guineas in Mr Owen's keeping. Then there were the half-crowns and shillings for the garments that customers had ordered. And presumably Miss Lindsay would want more designs.

Adeline was bound to want to maintain control over her, so she would have to keep any Ingleby's work a secret. She would go there tomorrow after Adeline left for work. She had no money for her fare, so that evening she asked Adeline what she had earned sewing for Mrs Maddox.

'You don't require it at present,' Adeline declared. 'You'll get your dues, but you'll have to wait.'

'For what?'

'For me to decide to give it to you. One: don't be impertinent, and two: the more you clamour for your money, the less inclined I'll be to hand it over.'

She must write to Hal. Juliet's pulse picked up speed and fingertips skimmed across lips that tingled at his remembered kisses, but it was pointless still having feelings for him. Should she tell him she had had her baby? She wrote *Constance Mary Harper, Constance Mary Harper* over and over again until she had filled the page. The name was all she had left of her daughter. Her gaze misted, and the writing blurred.

She placed the sheet in the fire. The flames licked at the precious name until there was nothing left but ashes. She wouldn't mention Constance to Hal. She would tell him there was no secret lover and leave it at that.

Writing Adeline's address at the top of her letter, she allowed herself to wonder if Hal . . . but she wasn't doing this in the hope of a response – was she? Adeline's address was on the letter simply because that was the done thing.

Dear Hal,
I know Mr Nugent has told everyone

No. Even all these miles from Moorside, she was uneasy at speaking out against his lordship's agent – and committing it to paper too. She started again.

Dear Hal,
I know that after I left, a story circulated about another man. I
want to assure you that such a person never existed.

Or was this simply another way of speaking against Mr Nugent, since he had started the story? At least she hadn't named him. She signed the letter and addressed the envelope to *Gardeners' Cottages, Moorside.*

Her resolve faltered. What if Hal waved this letter under Mr Nugent's nose? Surely, he would have more sense. He was good at thinking things through, her Hal.

235

Her Hal?

No, not her Hal. Never again her Hal.

It felt oddly discourteous leaving the house. Being family meant that Juliet could go without explanation, though no doubt the staff would spill the beans to Adeline later. At least she had some money for fares, having remembered the coppers she had earned making buttercups in her early days with Mrs Maddox.

At Ingleby's, she got herself shown to Mr Owen's office by pretending to be expected. He was in the outer office when she entered.

'You!' he exclaimed.

To her consternation, he whirled round and marched into his office. Before the lady clerk could stop her, she hurried after him. He plumped down onto the chair behind his desk and glowered at her.

'I don't know how you have the brass neck to come here.'

'Mr Owen?' The lady clerk appeared in the doorway.

'Fetch Miss Lindsay,' he ordered. Then he made a show of getting on with his work, elaborately ignoring her.

When Miss Lindsay arrived, Mr Owen arranged a chair for her beside his desk and they sat looking at Juliet.

'What have you to say for yourself?' Miss Lindsay demanded.

With a calm she was far from feeling, she said quietly, 'May I sit down?'

'If you must,' Mr Owen conceded ungraciously.

'Where have you been all this time?' Miss Lindsay asked.

'As you know,' she said carefully, 'I've been away and my grandmother has been representing me.'

'I know nothing of the kind,' said Miss Lindsay. 'What I do

236

know is that you vanished without a word and failed to fulfil your commitments. You were supposed to supply designs last autumn.'

'And I did.' *Oh hell.* Juliet snapped her lips together. What a fool she had been.

'Your conduct has caused considerable inconvenience,' said Miss Lindsay. 'Based on the success of your previous designs, I didn't seek out as many new designs as normal in the autumn, because I was relying on your contribution. When that failed to appear, you – you, personally – placed my department in an awkward position. Now you have the gall to show your face without an appointment – not that one would have been granted.'

Juliet stopped herself on the verge of an apology. She wasn't the wrongdoer here. The real wrongdoer would never apologise in a million years. 'I did produce designs for you, but . . .' Much as she felt like dropping Adeline in it, it would be unwise. '. . . but the person who was meant to deliver them apparently didn't.'

'A likely story,' Mr Owen muttered.

'And who is this person?' Miss Lindsay enquired.

'I'd rather not say.'

'Lame, very lame,' murmured Mr Owen.

'What brings you here today?' Miss Lindsay asked.

She couldn't bring herself to mention money. 'I hoped to be asked for more designs.'

'Your nerve takes my breath away,' Miss Lindsay exclaimed, 'considering the way you've let Ingleby's down.'

'I've been let down too.'

'Why didn't you inform me you were going away?' Miss Lindsay asked.

'There wasn't time.'

'And no time, in all these months, to write a letter?' Mr

Owen challenged. 'Or perhaps your mysterious friend failed to post it for you?'

'You have shown yourself to be unreliable and discourteous, both professionally and personally,' said Miss Lindsay.

'Don't forget the aunt was a thief,' Mr Owen added.

Miss Lindsay huffed a sharp sigh. 'I very much want to tell you to leave and never return, but . . .' She frowned through a long pause. 'Your designs were successful last summer.' More frowning. 'I refuse to decide now. Come back next week.'

'Next week—'

'Next week or not at all,' snapped Miss Lindsay.

'Good morning to you,' said Mr Owen. 'Shut the door on your way out.'

Juliet prowled round the house. Angry as she was with Adeline, she was vexed with herself too. She should have asked Mr Owen about her money. *You'll never make a businesswoman*, Adeline had said.

The moment she heard her grandmother return, Juliet bounced into the hall, where Marjorie was taking Adeline's coat. Juliet had expected to follow Adeline into the morning room, but she started up the stairs.

Being ignored made Juliet flare up. 'Wait! I want to speak to you.'

Marjorie gasped. Adeline looked over her shoulder, meeting Juliet's eyes with a stony expression that caused Juliet's stomach to turn somersaults. Adeline continued up the stairs without a word.

Juliet glared after her, then banged into the morning room. When eventually Adeline walked in, Juliet flew to confront her.

'You stole my designs, the work I did at Mrs Maddox's house.'

Adeline walked past her and sat in her usual chair. 'I'm waiting.'

'For what?'

'Your apology. You've made a serious and unfounded accusation.'

'It isn't unfounded.'

'On the contrary, since I've stolen nothing, it must be.'

'You took my designs.'

'They were freely given.'

'Only because you said they were for Miss Lindsay.'

'No.' Adeline's voice hardened. '*You* said they were for Miss Lindsay. I merely instructed you to design.'

'But you let me assume—'

'I don't care what you assumed. All I'm interested in is your work. You should have asked questions, but you were too busy hearing what you wanted to hear. You even made assumptions about me. You told yourself that I – Adeline Tewson – would act as your go-between with Miss Lindsay.'

Her cheeks flamed. Put like that, it did sound preposterous.

'Since you know your designs didn't go to Ingleby's, I deduce you've been in touch with Miss Lindsay. Were you welcomed back with open arms? No? Hardly surprising. No matter. You design for Tewson's Tailor-mades now. I imagine you haven't done any work today, too busy planning this confrontation. Ring the bell.' When Marjorie came, Adeline said, 'I will dine as usual, but take a tray to the back parlour.' She eyed Juliet. 'You have work to do.'

'Very good, madam,' Marjorie said.

'I've a letter to write. It must be posted this evening to ensure it arrives first thing.'

'Yes, madam.'

Adeline waited for Marjorie to go. 'To eliminate the possibility of further accusations, I wish to make it clear that I've set aside your fee for the designs you did while you were away. Ingleby's paid one guinea per design but, whereas Miss Lindsay chose from what you offered, I used all your work, and so you have sixteen guineas.'

'Which you will withhold until . . .'

'Until I see fit. When that will be – or indeed, if the time ever comes – depends on how sensible you are.'

Juliet arranged samples and sketches on the table to make her look occupied while she waited for Adeline to depart. Then she waited for Marjorie to finish upstairs. When the coast was clear, she flew to her room and packed her carpetbag, sneaking it down to the back parlour, then she crept to the hall cupboard for her outdoor things, scuttling back to safety with her arms full. As she was about to make her escape, she heard another door and there was Mrs Harris, the char, lugging her mop and bucket into the hall. Juliet ducked back, cursing. She didn't want to wait for Mrs Harris.

And she wasn't going to. She pushed up the sash window. Dropping her bag out, she clambered through. She tried to pull the sash down behind her. Skulking round the side of the house, she made a dash for the gate and then she was free.

With no cash today for fares, she faced a considerable walk, but so what? She used to tramp for miles over the tops. This was no different. Except that it was. Walking the streets was harder work and the bulky bag, though not heavy, made her arm ache.

At Ingleby's, she made her way to Mr Owen's office. There was no sign of the lady clerk. She knocked on the door, stowing her bag just inside when Mr Owen bade her enter. She didn't get the chance to shut the door before he was on his feet.

'You again! Was it not made clear—?'

'I've come for my money. There should be one guinea per design, plus whatever was earned through customer orders.'

'Make an appointment.'

'I'd like the money now, please.'

'Your impertinence is astounding. I heartily wish Miss Lindsay had never taken you on.'

'I concur with that statement, Mr Owen,' came a voice from the doorway, and in swept Miss Lindsay, brandishing a sheet of paper. Mr Owen hastened to set a chair for her and she sank into it. 'This,' she said. 'This!' She waved the piece of paper. 'We have the truth now, and from an unimpeachable source. I wish I'd never set eyes on you!'

'My dear lady,' Mr Owen exclaimed, 'whatever is it?'

'This girl . . . this person . . . I'm not sure it is fit for a gentleman's ears, Mr Owen. Here, see for yourself.' Miss Lindsay thrust the paper at him, averting her face.

Mr Owen's face turned puce, and he opened and shut his mouth like a goldfish.

'What does it say?' Juliet blurted.

'It explains,' Miss Lindsay replied stiffly, 'where you have been in recent months, and why.'

'Mrs Tewson, whose name is renowned throughout the sewing world, has identified herself as your grandmother,' said Mr Owen. 'She has, very bravely, if I may say so, informed us of the shame you have brought on your family, so that we may take steps to preserve the good name of Ingleby's.'

'If this were to get out,' breathed Miss Lindsay. 'And I was the one who—'

'Who was duped,' Mr Owen broke in robustly. 'Duped, I say.'

'I never intended—' Juliet began.

'Nonsense!' Mr Owen exclaimed. 'When you approached Miss Lindsay, you were aware of your shame, were you not? You have placed this good lady's position in jeopardy. If it should become known she had, however inadvertently, employed a . . . a – fear not, Miss Lindsay, I shall not utter the foul word in front of you.' He glared at Juliet. 'We know now the fraud you have committed.'

'Fraud?' she cried.

'Did you not present yourself as a decent citizen with nothing to be ashamed of?'

She turned to Miss Lindsay. 'I'm sorry if I've placed you in a difficult position, but I never meant—' She stopped, questioning her own honesty. From the beginning of her pregnancy, she had known her days of respectability were numbered, but while she had pictured the anger and outrage she would cause, had she truly never thought about the embarrassment she would leave behind? 'I'm very sorry if I've compromised you,' she told Miss Lindsay sincerely.

'Too late for that,' snapped Mr Owen.

'If you're truly sorry,' said Miss Lindsay, 'leave now and never divulge to anyone that you once worked for me.'

Juliet's heart felt like a dead weight. 'Before I go, please may I have my money?'

'Aside from the question of bringing Ingleby's good name into disrepute,' said Mr Owen, 'there is the matter of the agreement you signed. You agreed to supply more designs upon request – and you subsequently made it impossible for Miss Lindsay to place that request. I'm within my rights to withhold payment. Kindly close the door on your way out.'

Juliet trailed down Market Street in a daze. No money, no prospects, nowhere to live. She found herself on the corner of Rosemount Place. William Turton worked along there. A cold desperation settled on her. It was time he paid his dues.

It was easy to decide, but far from easy to put one foot in front of the other. It seemed a long time before she came to the front steps. The moment she lifted the brass knocker, there would be no turning back. Something hard and fierce bunched inside her throat.

The door opened. She glimpsed a young woman before she turned away, instinctively wanting to conceal herself, but the sound of sniffing and whimpering made her look back, only that seemed nosy and she ducked her face.

'Juliet?' And then again, questioning, hopeful, disbelieving: 'Juliet?'

Her face snapped up in shock. 'Cecily?' And then again, because she couldn't believe her eyes: '*Cecily?*'

Chapter Eighteen

Cecily uttered a great cry, dropped her carpetbag and launched herself at Juliet. Juliet dropped her own carpetbag and promptly tripped over it under the force of Cecily's embrace. They ended up sitting on the pavement, too amazed to get up. Cecily, as well as crying, was now laughing, and something inside Juliet relaxed too. She threw her arms round Cecily, who seemed bigger somehow and it wasn't the bulk of her coat.

Juliet drew back. 'Cecily, you're not . . . ?'

Cecily clamped her lips together hard before she could say 'I am, I am.' She broke down in sobs.

Juliet slipped her arms round Cecily again, her cheek squashing into the brim of Cecily's hat.

'Disgraceful!' A well-dressed gentleman scowled down at them. 'Drunk in the street at this time of day. Be off with the pair of you or I'll call a constable.'

Juliet got to her feet and hauled Cecily up. They looked round for their bags.

'Hurry up,' barked the gentleman.

'We're going,' said Juliet.

'And for your information, we're not drunk,' said Cecily. 'You should get your facts straight, mister, before you go accusing people.'

They hurried away, huddling so close it was difficult not to stumble.

'What are you doing here?' Juliet asked. 'Silly question. You've been to see William Turton.'

'Do you know about him?'

'I know as much as I want to.'

'You mean – my William? The one who came to Moorside?'

'Well, of course him.'

Cecily stopped and faced her. 'Oh, Juliet, you *don't* know. He wasn't the real William Turton. The real William Turton is someone else completely.'

She dissolved into tears again, obliging Juliet to swallow her questions.

'There's a bench round the corner,' she said encouragingly.

Cecily mopped her tears. 'I don't want to sit outside. I'm tired and cold and starving hungry – reet clemmed, as my old nan would say. Oh, Juliet, I'll never see her again. I can't go back, not now. I thought I was going to. Right up until ten minutes ago, I thought I'd go swanning back with a ring on my finger. "Look at this," I were going to say. "I told you I'm not a trollop." I thought I was getting wed. I honestly thought I was getting wed.'

'I know, love, I know, and you're not a trollop. Are you sure you can't go back? Wouldn't your family have you?'

Cecily shook her head. 'Mam would, but not Dad. Let's find a tea shop. I need to sit down before I fall down.'

'I haven't any money.'

'I've a few bob.' Cecily spread her arms and her carpetbag swung and bumped against her. 'Here I stand with all my worldly goods.'

'Likewise.'

'What happened to your secret man? I couldn't believe my ears when I heard you'd jilted Hal.'

She breathed in sharply, the sudden hurt catching her unawares. 'There isn't another man. There never was.'

'But—'

'If you want a cup of tea, I'll keep you company while you have it.'

'Don't be daft. Tea for two and a couple of buns won't break the bank.'

Soon they were ensconced in the corner of a small tea shop. Juliet tried to decline anything to eat.

'Nonsense,' said Cecily. 'You'd pay for me, if it was the other way round. Tea for two, please,' she told the waitress, 'and two lardy cakes.'

'Thanks,' said Juliet. Cecily's presence warmed her. 'Now tell me about William Turton.'

'Or whoever he was,' Cecily said bitterly.

'Start with London.'

'That was an age ago. We were away far longer than I was expecting. I wrote to tell William I was coming back. It was wonderful to see him again.' Cecily glanced at her. 'In fact, I was so thrilled that . . .'

'You let him . . . ?'

'It wasn't a question of letting him. I threw myself at him, that's the truth, and the result is increasingly obvious for all to see.'

'Oh my goodness.' Guilt washed through her. If only she had sent a warning.

'He went away. He said he wouldn't be back for a few weeks

because of work. I was perfectly happy sewing for my bottom drawer. It's all in that carpetbag now. Even when I knew for certain I was' – Cecily glanced at nearby tables, then mouthed 'pregnant' before continuing – 'I wasn't worried because I thought we were engaged. But he didn't come back and didn't come back and . . .'

'Did you try writing?'

'Of course I did, but he couldn't write back to me. I kept waiting for him to come to our meeting place. I wangled it so that I could go there every day, though how I managed it, I'll never know. At first, when he didn't come, I thought, *Fair enough. He's shocked to know he's going to be a dad.*'

'A shock for you too,' Juliet said loyally.

Cecily reddened. 'I planned it. I thought he just needed a push to get him to the altar.'

'Oh, Cecily.' She placed her hand over her friend's.

Cecily took hers away. 'It's my own stupid fault. I trapped him, or tried to. In the end, Mrs Whicker found out and slung me out on my ear. That was horrible, being treated like a slut, but I still thought everything would be fine. I promised Mam I'd be getting wed, so she let me come here. I went to the address William had given me, the one I'd been writing to, and, yes, it was a house where the woman took lodgers, but he'd never been one of them. He'd paid her to let him use her address for me to write to. Five bob he gave her for every letter – five bob! She said he'd turn up now and then to collect them. At this moment, there are three letters sitting there, which means' – Cecily had to draw a breath – 'which means he's never been back since he last saw me. He doesn't know about the baby.' Her eyes filled and she shut them.

'So you went to his office,' Juliet prompted gently.

'What else was I to do? But when I insisted on seeing William Turton, he turned out to be a stranger. I couldn't believe it. I still can't. It means that my William, whoever he was, somehow got hold of the real William Turton's business cards and came to Moorside and kept coming back . . . but why? It makes no sense.'

'It does if you know the other half of the story.'

Love from Rosie. The words still chilled her. Rosie had sent this man to take revenge on her, so he had befriended Cecily, using the law firm story backed up by business cards belonging to the real William Turton. After the attack, he had subsequently returned – at Rosie's behest? – to find out what had become of Juliet, and having learnt of her downfall, he disappeared, but not before taking his pleasure with Cecily.

Quietly, Juliet explained why the supposed William Turton had come to Moorside, her heart swelling as pain filled Cecily's eyes. When she whispered of the attack, Cecily almost choked on an exclamation of anguish and pressed her knuckles to her mouth. Should she admit to her own pregnancy or hug Constance to her as her precious secret? But Cecily had been honest with her and deserved the same in return, especially if, as Juliet hoped, they were going to stick together.

When she brought her story up to date, Cecily blew out a long breath. Touching her stomach, she said, 'Do you realise, this little 'un will be a half-brother or -sister for your Constance?' She laughed tremulously. 'You're going to be an auntie.'

Juliet laughed too, but she wasn't laughing inside. She was consumed by fury and jealousy and a terrific yearning. She would give anything to have her daughter back. Steadying herself, she said, 'I know you've hardly had time to think, but what might you do with your baby?'

'Keep it,' Cecily said immediately. 'I've wanted it all this time and that won't change just because I've been took in by a rotten scoundrel.'

She wanted to say, 'It's not that simple.' She wanted to say, 'You'll have a heck of a time as an unwed mother.'

She said, 'You won't be on your own. I'm going to help you look after my little nephew or niece.'

She meant it too.

'Are you sure we're doing the right thing?' Cecily performed a sudden about-turn, making Juliet, coming up the steps behind, bump into her.

'We haven't a lot to lose.' Juliet made herself sound determined, but really she was as uncertain as Cecily. She reached for the knocker.

'You don't knock,' said Cecily. 'You go straight in. I made an ass of myself earlier by knocking and waiting.'

Walking in was a lot harder than waiting to be ushered. Inside was a wood-panelled hallway with a wide staircase ahead and an open door to one side. The air smelt of beeswax, so the char must be doing a good job. Through the open door came a gentleman in black striped trousers and a dark-grey jacket with cutaway front skirts. His polite expression turned frosty at the sight of them, but instead of feeling intimidated, Juliet felt a spark of annoyance. This was how Mr Owen had looked and she had let him walk all over her, more fool her.

'We'd like to see Mr William Turton, please,' she said.

Before the gentleman could reply, another man popped out of the office, equally smartly dressed, but young and grinning.

'Back again?' he said to Cecily. 'And with reinforcements. My, my, what has Billy Boy been up to?'

He legged it up the stairs, leaving the older gentleman calling 'Mr Stevens!' after him. The front door opened and before she knew it, Juliet found they had been swept into the office and the gentleman was in the hallway, saying, 'Good afternoon, Sir Edward. Mr Winterton is expecting you.'

No sooner had their footsteps faded than someone came hurrying downstairs. Into the office came a young man with strawberry blonde hair and freckles. Looking flustered, he faced Cecily.

'Look, miss, I don't know you and you don't know me. What's going on? Actually, I don't want to know. I just want you to leave.'

'We must speak to you about something the three of us have in common – some*one*, I should say,' Juliet said. 'A young man who has wronged both myself and my friend, Miss . . .' She didn't know Cecily's surname.

'Ramsbottom,' said Cecily.

William Turton's gaze slewed from Cecily's stomach to her own. Juliet squirmed. 'We need your help and then we'll never bother you again.' She nudged Cecily. 'Show him the business card.'

'Where did you get that?' demanded the young man.

'My friend was given it,' said Juliet, 'and I was given one too.'

'This has nothing to do with me.'

'Then I'll knock on Mr Winterton's door and see what he has to say.'

'Now see here—'

She turned to Cecily. 'Perhaps we should ask to see all the young men working here. Maybe one of them helped himself to Mr Turton's cards.'

'They were stolen,' William Turton exclaimed, adding in a mutter, 'I was attacked.'

'Then all three of us have suffered at this brute's hands. Please help us. It'll take an hour of your time, and that includes walking to and from Ingleby's. They owe me money, but Mr Owen won't pay because he says I broke an agreement, and I suppose I did, but it was unknowingly.'

'Ignorance is no defence.'

'In any case, the real reason he won't pay is because . . . I've had a baby out of wedlock.' There, she had said it. 'He thinks that's shameful.'

'He has a point.'

'But is it any reason not to pay me?'

'It depends on the circumstances.'

'The circumstances are these, Mr Turton. If threatening to create a scene in the shop would make Mr Owen pay up, I'd threaten him, but he would merely send for a constable. But if I arrive with legal representation—'

'Hang on a minute—'

'Either you come or I'll wave your card under Mr Owen's nose. If you come, at least you'll have some control over what's said.'

William glowered at her. 'I'll fetch my coat.'

Footsteps suggested the older gentleman was returning.

'We'll wait outside,' said Cecily. 'Goodness!' she exclaimed when they gained the pavement. 'I'd never have believed it of you.'

'I never knew your name was Ramsbottom.'

'Eh, it's a reet good old Lancashire name, that,' Cecily intoned in a heavy accent. She giggled. 'Now you know why I was always so desperate to get wed.'

'Did Miss Phoebe call you Ramsbottom?'

'Did she ever! It was Ramsbottom this and Ramsbottom that, morning, noon and night.'

They were laughing when William appeared.

'I'm glad someone finds this amusing.'

They made their way to Ingleby's, William insisting on carrying both carpetbags. When they arrived, Cecily waited outside with their things while Juliet led the way to Mr Owen's outer office. The lady clerk was at her desk.

'Please inform Mr Owen that Miss Harper is here,' she said.

'I have instructions—'

'Tell him I've brought a legal gentleman.'

The clerk disappeared, shutting Mr Owen's door behind her. Then it opened again and she held it for them.

Juliet knew she must get in the first word. 'Good afternoon, Mr Owen. I'd like to be paid, please.'

'And you have . . . representation?' Mr Owen sounded disbelieving. 'Which firm are you from, sir?'

William looked uneasy, but he had to answer. 'Winterton, Sowerby and Jenks.'

'Does it surprise you that Adeline Tewson's granddaughter has access to legal advice?' Juliet met Mr Owen's eye. 'I know you think I broke our agreement—'

'Think it? I can prove it.'

'—but I designed for Ingleby's in good faith. It was someone else who didn't deliver my work.'

'Really, if you have nothing new to say—'

'That person was Mrs Tewson.'

'I beg your pardon?'

'If you don't pay me, I'll be forced to accuse her publicly of interfering in our business arrangement.'

'You wouldn't dare.'

'I've nothing to lose, but you have Ingleby's reputation to

consider. There's Mrs Tewson's reputation too. Think of the damage.'

'This is outrageous,' Mr Owen spluttered. 'Defame Mrs Tewson? And drag Ingleby's into it?'

William cleared his throat. 'With respect, sir, it's defamation only if it's untrue. Is it untrue?'

Juliet held still.

'I suggest it's in no one's interests to permit this to continue,' William stated quietly. 'And the amount of money can't be much, sir.'

'No – no, it isn't. As a matter of fact, I got out the paperwork after Miss Harper's first unannounced visit.' Mr Owen opened a drawer, removed a sheet of paper and gave it far more attention than it could possibly warrant. 'Naturally I will require an assurance that Miss Harper won't trouble Ingleby's again.'

'Naturally,' William agreed.

'In writing.' Mr Owen regarded William. 'If your firm draws up something, at Miss Harper's expense, of course, I'll look over it in, say, a week's time.'

'I'm sure we could write something suitable now,' William said hurriedly. 'Wouldn't you rather end the matter today, sir?'

'I suppose so.'

When it was drawn up, William turned to Juliet. 'This says you have received monies in full and final payment, even though your agreement was broken through no fault of Ingleby's.'

'That sounds like it was my fault,' she objected.

'It was,' snapped Mr Owen.

'I told you—'

Mr Owen spoke over her. 'It also states that you will do nothing by word or deed to bring the name of Ingleby's into disrepute.'

'There's no need for that,' she said.

Mr Owen sneered and laughed simultaneously, creating an odd snickering sound. 'I disagree. I remember what your aunt did, not to mention your own morals. Sign here.'

'After I've been paid.'

'No sense of honour. Still, that's to be expected.' Mr Owen picked up his accounts sheet and examined it for a long time.

When she couldn't bear it any longer, Juliet burst out, 'How much?'

Mr Owen looked at her, then at the paper, as if he hadn't looked closely enough the first time. 'Two designs at one guinea each. Nineteen full costumes at half a crown each, making two pounds, seven and six. Twenty-nine part costumes at a shilling each. Grand total: five pounds, eighteen shillings and sixpence.'

She had to suck her cheeks to stop herself grinning like an idiot.

'I'll write a cheque,' said Mr Owen.

'Cash – please,' said Juliet.

'Very well.' His heavy tone suggested that only the lowest of the low wanted cash.

The money was counted out, and she signed the agreement and a receipt. Then she and William got up to leave. At the door, she looked back.

'One last thing, Mr Owen. In my grandmother's letter, did she mention she wanted me to design for Tewson's Tailor-mades? No? I thought not. Good afternoon.'

Chapter Nineteen

Outside Ingleby's, William seized a carpetbag in each hand. 'May I walk you to a bus stop?' The poor fellow must have been desperate to get rid of them, and who could blame him?

Juliet cast an anxious glance at Cecily. Her normally bubbly friend had gone quiet, a certain tightness around her eyes proclaiming her exhaustion. Juliet took her hand and looped it through her arm, giving it a squeeze.

'That's kind of you, Mr Turton. We need to get to Platt Fields. We must find lodgings, and that's the only area I'm familiar with.'

A frown tugged at William's brow. 'If you don't mind trying elsewhere, I may be able to assist.'

Cecily sprang to life. 'Why would you help us?'

'The bloke who stole my cards beat me up pretty badly. Anyway, you need somewhere to stay, and my aunt told me about a lady who needs help making ends meet.'

'What about . . . ?' Cecily touched her stomach.

'I assume you'll call yourself Mrs, and as long as you pay the rent and live quietly, Mrs Gillespie will be happy.'

He put them on the bus to Withington, where they asked directions to Heathside Lane. Mrs Gillespie was a kindly widow with deep worry lines. In her sparsely furnished house, shadowy marks on wall and floor spoke of pieces that had been sold. She took in lodgers, for whom she provided meals at additional cost.

'I clean and do washing an' all, if you want,' she said as they stood in her downstairs front, looking round. There wasn't much to see: bed, table, two chairs, hanging cupboard, washstand. 'The Norths and their little boy live up there.' She nodded through the ceiling. 'The Willetts, mother and grown daughter, have the upstairs back and I've two bank clerks in the attic.'

'Where does Mrs Gillespie sleep?' Juliet whispered when she left them.

'Kitchen, I suppose.' Unstrapping her carpetbag, Cecily threw it open. 'Pillowcases, cushion covers, tablecloth, antimacassars,' she declared blithely, but Juliet caught the raw note. 'This isn't what I had in mind for my bottom drawer.'

Juliet opened her own carpetbag, removing Hal's painting of the laburnum walk. 'It's not where I imagined this going on display either, but it will all help make this our home.'

'We must find work.'

'I've an idea about that. Come and sit down.' She took Cecily's hand, and they perched together on the bed. 'We're going to set up as dressmakers – well, not actually dressmakers: that would take too long. My grandmother has gone into tailor-mades. That's what we'll do, using second-hand clothes of good quality, which we'll mend, then refinish to add a dash of style, and if the customer needs alterations, she can pay extra.'

'Do you think we can?'

Recalling the pride of working on Miss Bradley's coat, Juliet said confidently, 'Yes.'

'Mrs Gillespie can tell us where the nearest markets are,' said Cecily, and Juliet blessed her for her support.

The next morning, the gong sounded and Juliet went to the kitchen, joining a lodger from each room to collect breakfast trays of porridge, soft-boiled eggs and soldiers, and a pot of tea.

'This will set us up for a hard day's garment finding,' said Cecily.

At the first market, the second-hand clothes stall was between a cheerful array of bric-a-brac and the sheet music stall. Juliet picked out a grey jacket.

'The lining's come adrift, but it's a good garment with plenty of wear. New buttons and some piping will lift it no end.'

'You are clever,' Cecily said admiringly. 'I'd never have thought of that.'

They bought the grey jacket, a blouse and two skirts.

'Now for the next market,' said Juliet.

'While you do that, I'll find a cleaning job,' said Cecily. 'It'll give us a regular few bob and, let's be honest, I won't be much use visiting markets: I don't know what's suitable without asking you.'

Cecily came home later, having found a job with a theatrical landlady called Mrs Blore.

'Doesn't she mind about the baby?' Juliet asked.

Cecily grinned. 'She says at least I won't be pursued round the house by handsome young actors.'

They worked long into each night on the garments. Cecily might not have an eye for design, but she was a good little needleworker.

'I don't want you overdoing it,' said Juliet.

'No danger of that, love. All of a sudden, I conk out and there's no rousing me.'

Juliet worked on while Cecily slept. Cecily had sent her mum a postcard, saying she was well and not to worry, which had set Juliet wondering if she should write to Hal with her new address. But that would make it look as if she had sent the first letter in the hope of a response, when all she had wanted was to tell him the truth. That should be enough, but in the quiet of the night, it didn't feel enough.

Never mind how it felt. She must concentrate on her sewing.

Finish this seam . . . attach these hooks and eyes . . . add that lace . . .

William turned up on Saturday afternoon. Mrs Gillespie passed their door to answer a knock. Then there was another knock, this time at their door, and William popped his head in.

'I say, I hope you don't mind,' he began, his face bright with self-consciousness.

Cecily exchanged surprised looks with Juliet, but it wasn't surprise alone she felt. The sight of William's good-natured if embarrassed face brought everything thundering back – the desperate eagerness with which she had hovered in that office, dying for her beloved to come downstairs; the sledgehammer shock when a total stranger had walked in; the cold humiliation of having that stranger witness the worst moment of her life.

She could have crowned Juliet for inviting William to sit down. Then Juliet laughed, adding, 'I'm sorry,' because she and Cecily occupied the chairs, and the only other place to sit was the bed, which William glanced at and looked even more embarrassed.

Good. Now he would go.

But Juliet said, 'I'll sit on the bed—'

'Please don't get up. I'll perch on the windowsill.'

'What brings you here?' Juliet asked.

'The office shuts at one on Saturdays, so I thought I'd drop by on my way home.'

'You're not telling me this is on your way home,' Cecily said tartly.

'Well, no, but—'

'So why are you here?' she demanded.

'To see if things are all right. After all, I'm the one who sent you here.'

'We'd never have found such a decent place without your help,' said Juliet.

William looked pleased, but the smile dropped from his face when Cecily gave him the evil eye. He left a few minutes later.

Juliet turned to her. 'You certainly put the mockers on that.'

She shrugged. 'I can't imagine why he bothered coming.'

'I think it was kind of him.'

'I don't suppose he'll come again.'

'No,' Juliet agreed drily, 'not after the reception he got from you.'

But he did. This time, Cecily was on her own. The stupid thing was, she had almost got up to answer the front door herself, but she had left it for Mrs Gillespie, and so missed the opportunity to turn William away on the step. Now here he was in the room. All she could think of was the other William. She had loved him so much and none of it had been real. She had thought herself so clever, when really she had been a gullible idiot.

'Close the door,' she said ungraciously.

William cleared his throat. 'I thought your landlady would want it left open, you know, with you being alone here with me.'

She flattened her lips in irritation. As if she would look twice at this gauche young man! 'There's no need.'

259

William closed the door and waited until she nodded him into the other chair. 'What are you making?'

More irritation. She wasn't about to pretend a welcome by engaging in small talk. 'We told you last time we like being here, so why have you come again?'

'I was hoping we might . . .'

She was too astonished to be outraged. He wanted her to walk out with him.

'. . . be friends.'

Friends? Friends! She felt as though he had made a fool of her, but really she had made a fool of herself. Thank heaven she hadn't done it out loud.

'To be honest, your turning up at the office was jolly exciting.'

'Jolly embarrassing, I'd have thought.'

'At the time, yes, and the other fellows joshed me something awful. But . . . it's the most interesting thing that's happened to me since . . . well, since for ever, actually.'

'And the other chaps now think you're a bit of a card, do they?' Cecily asked tartly.

'Can you blame me? I'm a pretty humdrum sort of fellow. I just hoped . . . well, like I say, that we might be friends.'

How easy it would be to take offence, how easy to tell him never to darken their door again. To her own surprise, Cecily laughed, and the moment for banishing him was lost.

And for some reason she couldn't put her finger on, she didn't mind.

With excitement fluttering inside her, Juliet bought postcards for newsagents' windows. She sat at the table, pen poised.

'You need a name that describes the business,' said William. 'What exactly are you selling?'

'Second-hand garments made good,' said Cecily.

'I want them to sound special,' said Juliet.

'Businesses are often called after the people who start them,' said William.

Cecily waved a finger at her. 'If you write Ramsbottom on that card, I'll bash you one with a saucepan. What was that place where your aunt worked?'

'Mademoiselle Antoinette's.'

'How do you fancy being Mademoiselle Juliana?'

She laughed. 'No, thanks.'

'What's your grandmother's firm called?' asked William.

'Tewson's Textiles, and her tailor-mades are called Tewson's Tailor-mades.'

'Harper's Hand-finisheds,' exclaimed Cecily. 'No— wait . . . Hand-finished by Harper – and we could embroider a tiny harp on each garment.'

'It's a harp*ist*, not a har*per*,' William said, then mumbled an apology as their glares smote him.

'Have you any idea how long that embroidery would take?' Juliet asked Cecily.

'You said you wanted your garments to be special.'

'Like an artist signing a painting,' William added.

She couldn't resist. She spent hours embroidering little harps, then the postcards were written and distributed, but it was Cecily who produced their first customer, a pretty actress called Jessamy De Vere, a name Juliet didn't believe was real for one moment, but who cared so long as she purchased a garment?

'Have you a travelling costume?' Jessamy asked.

Juliet produced the grey jacket with blue buttons and piping, and a smart black skirt that was so free from fault that she had examined

261

it a hundred times, sure she must have missed something. Both garments would need taking in to fit Miss De Vere's petite frame, but she was happy to pay for that, and purchased a blouse too. Juliet pointed out the harps, and Jessamy declared them charming.

Soon they had a couple more customers. Word got round and more came. One morning Juliet was thrilled to be visited by a group of four until she realised they had come merely to gawp, but she remained polite and helpful, and it paid off, because one of them returned for a coat.

'Is it going well?' Mrs Gillespie asked.

'Starting to,' said Juliet.

She had just returned the evening tray, adding the empty plates to the stack awaiting washing-up. Mrs Gillespie sat at the kitchen table, looking tired.

'Do you ever think of moving somewhere smaller?' Juliet asked. 'It'd mean less work.'

'Aye, I think about it, dear, but I doubt I'll ever do it. Fewer rooms might mean less work, but it'd also be less money. It isn't easy. The Willetts have given notice, so I'll need a new 'un.' She smiled wanly. 'There's always summat to worry about, in't there?'

But Mrs Gillespie wasn't so steeped in worry that she failed to think of others, and two or three customers arrived on her recommendation, including a woman from the next road, who wanted them to clothe her daughter's wedding.

'Nowt fancy, mind. She has to be able to wear it afterwards. Same goes for her sister as bridesmaid. And I'd like summat an' all.'

They scoured the markets for possible wedding finery, but it proved hard finding something special for a bride.

'This is the best we've seen.' Juliet displayed a pale-green dress patterned with cream buds and dark-green leaves.

Cecily wouldn't hear of it. 'Married in green, ashamed to be seen.'

'Tell you what, we'll dress Mrs Todd and Noreen from the market, but I'll make Edith's dress. We'll dye it afterwards to the colour of her choice.'

'But – the work!' Cecily exclaimed.

'The goodwill! Think of the friends and neighbours asking where the dress came from.'

'It's a lot of work.'

'I know, and time spent on it will be time other garments don't get done. But every seamstress longs to dress a bride, and I want my first to be perfect.'

She didn't enjoy making the dress the way she had anticipated. Misgivings chewed at her. A rush of customers reduced their stock to almost nothing and there was no time to replace it, even though this was where their real business lay. No stock meant no income, except for Cecily's, which wasn't much. Afterwards they would have to build up their stock and it would be like starting again. Might they have lost potential customers through letting their stock run down so dramatically?

'I hope making Edith's dress isn't a mistake.' She had kept her fears to herself at first, but now they came pouring out, not just to Cecily but also to William. Was this what it was like to have a brother?

'The wedding clothes are certain to drum up business,' said Cecily.

Cecily's loyalty warmed her, but she had to be realistic. 'If we haven't got a good stock, customers won't give us a second chance, and we haven't as much to spend on new things, because of the time Edith's dress is taking.'

'You'll just have to work like stink to make up for it,' said William. 'I'll help. I can cart stuff home from the markets on

Saturday afternoons and if you trust me with a pair of scissors, I'll cut off unwanted buttons.'

That made her laugh and her spirits lifted. There was nothing wrong that darned hard graft wouldn't get them out of.

'It's unfortunate this happened before you had a decent sum put by,' William observed.

Juliet remembered the money Mrs Grove had handed into Mr Nugent's keeping.

'I have money. At least, I think I have. Mr Nugent has my mother's money, including my wages from Mrs Naseby.'

'Ask for it back,' Cecily urged immediately.

'No!' The word burst out. 'I . . . I need to think about it.'

'What is there to think about?'

She felt hunted. 'I don't want Mr Nugent knowing my address. Please – let's talk about something else.'

The others complied, but she saw curiosity and concern in glances that passed between them. She felt edgy. Deep inside, something horrid and cold stirred, and she felt stupid, stupid, stupid.

The wooden gate was open. Just as well. It would fall to pieces if anyone attempted to move it. Adeline walked up the path. Well, walked hardly described it. It was all of three paces. But the doorstep was clean. Not that the chit deserved a clean doorstep after the atrocious way she had behaved.

Before she could knock, the door opened, and a youngish woman with a little lad stopped, then half-stepped forward as though expecting her to stand aside. She dealt them a look and, cowed, they melted against the wall.

She stepped across the threshold, stopping next to the female, her shoulder on a level with the woman's forehead.

'The girl who makes clothes?' she demanded without looking at her.

'That door there,' the woman whispered.

Adeline threw it open, taking in the room at a glance. A few bits of furniture and a rack that, aside from a couple of garments, was gratifyingly empty. The chit stared at her. She was sewing and the fabric – decent quality, Adeline noted – almost slipped through her fingers.

She marched in, like an actress dominating the stage.

'Did you imagine I wouldn't find you? Mr Owen furnished me with the name of the firm you claimed was representing you. Mr Winterton was most surprised when I informed him.'

'William—'

'Your friend has kept his job, though I recommended his dismissal. Mr Winterton did, however, forbid him to come here before close of business this week. I told Mr Winterton I required time to make enquiries. I know about your tawdry business, tarting up cast-off clothes. But that isn't what you're doing now, is it? You're making this from new.'

'It's for a wedding.'

'And you couldn't fob off the bride with your usual crud. Where's your stock?' She suppressed a smile. 'You've run out, haven't you? The wedding dress has taken too much time away from your usual rags. I recall saying you'd never make a businesswoman. Get packed. You're coming with me.'

A gasp. 'I won't.'

'You said that last time, but you obeyed in the end, just as you will this time.'

'Never!'

'Look round. No stock – therefore no money coming in – and

customers who go away disappointed won't come back *and* they'll spread the word. You've failed, girl. And don't forget what you owe me.'

'What about what you owe me?' the chit demanded. 'Things are difficult now, I admit, but if you had the decency to hand over my money, I'd manage.'

'That presupposes I want you to manage.' She looked round as the door opened and another girl walked in. Adeline took one look at her swollen belly and exclaimed, 'Good God, another harlot!' She rounded on the chit. 'Have you learnt nothing?'

'Please leave,' was the stony response. 'I'm not coming with you and I'm sure Mrs Gillespie doesn't want people arguing in her rooms.'

'Mrs Gillespie!' Adeline snorted. 'And she, of course, is a paragon of virtue.'

'What's that supposed to mean?'

'Ask her.' *Oh yes, and see how she cowers at the question.* She drew herself up, towering over the shabby room. 'You'll come back,' she foretold, 'even if I have to get a magistrate to force you.'

The gong sounded, and Juliet fetched their Sunday roast. The kitchen was hot and steamy. Trays occupied every available surface, vying for space with used pans. Plates were piled high with veg to make up for the portions of meat being smaller than was desirable. Gravy boats and jugs of custard balanced precariously on the edges of the trays.

'Roast capon and roly-poly pudding,' Mrs Gillespie told a middle-aged man Juliet hadn't seen before. 'This is Mr Jones, new in the upstairs back. This is Miss Harper, downstairs front.'

'How do? I'd shake hands, only . . .' Mr Jones glanced down at the tray in his beefy hands.

She stood aside to let him pass, then hugged Mrs Gillespie. 'You were worried about being left with an empty room, but you needn't have fretted.'

Cecily had cleared away the sewing things and prepared the table.

'This feels like a celebration,' said Cecily as they tucked in. 'Edith's dress is finished and, in case you weren't listening the first time, it's beautiful and I'm proud of you. Mrs Todd's costume is done and Noreen's only wants hemming, which I can do tomorrow while you, my girl, go down the market. We'll be back to normal in no time.'

After the meal, they sat sewing close to the windows, not simply for the light but also to enjoy the fresh air, which had that sudden special warmth that betokened early spring. A picture sprang into Juliet's mind of Constance in a cradle beside an open sash window, her little fingers reaching to grasp the sunbeams. Pain clutched her heart. She stood up.

'Forget work for once. Let's take a walk.'

They went to the park, strolling arm in arm, as they headed to the bandstand. Holding her hat, Juliet tipped back her head, offering her face to the sun. She had worked so hard recently.

As they neared home, William emerged from the house and hurried towards them, but their smiles were met with an anxious frown.

'I'm sorry,' he began.

'It wasn't your fault,' said Juliet.

'I beg your pardon?'

'Giving my grandmother this address.'

'It's not that. One of the attic chaps let me in and I knocked at your door and went in—' He stopped. 'Prepare yourselves for a shock.'

Juliet loosened herself from Cecily's arm and darted inside. Bursting into their room, she stopped dead. Her lips parted and she expected a loud cry of horror to emerge, but nothing came out. Cecily clattered in behind her and there was a long wail of distress, as though Cecily were crying out for both of them.

The wedding clothes, the new stock, everything – slashed to ribbons.

Chapter Twenty

While Juliet and Cecily, sick at heart, sifted through the ruins of their livelihood, William darted out, returning with a bobby as Mrs Gillespie arrived home from visiting a friend. She started to accompany the constable round the house to ask if the other residents had seen or heard anything, but no sooner had they gone upstairs than Mrs Gillespie came streaming down again, all in a tizzy because Mr Jones had flitted.

'But he's only just moved in,' Juliet said.

'And now he's gone,' exclaimed Mrs Gillespie, and as the tears began to flow, Juliet found herself comforting their landlady just when she most needed comfort herself.

No sooner had she soothed Mrs Gillespie than the Todds swarmed in.

'We've heard such a story.' Mrs Todd was in full flow before she even got inside, with her daughters sobbing in her wake. 'What about our wedding clothes? We're that worried.' Seeing the damage, she pressed a hand to her bosom. 'Oh my. What a thing to happen.' Then she lapsed back into her own concerns. 'What about our

Edith's dress, not to mention mine and Noreen's? The wedding's next Saturday.'

Juliet summoned her calmest manner. 'We won't let you down. Hand-finished by Harper's reputation is at stake.'

'You've not been open for business five minutes. You haven't got a reputation yet.'

'We will have after this, and you'll start it by telling everyone how we rose above this calamity and made beautiful costumes for you.'

When the Todds left, she couldn't hold on any longer. Her hands, which had cleared up so efficiently, became clumsy. Cecily hugged her, and they clung together. She shut her eyes, trying not to cry, but tears squeezed out, burning her cheeks. She let go of Cecily, smearing tears aside with the back of her hand.

'That's enough of that. We have to get on.'

'At least your lovely laburnum painting survived,' said Cecily.

'Which is more than can be said for most of your bottom drawer.'

'The painting is more important.'

As they resumed clearing up, Juliet thought the unthinkable. Was Mr Jones Adeline's spy, sent here to ruin their business? There was no proof, nothing except her own dark imaginings, and if she dared voice them to the police, she would doubtless bring more trouble on herself.

'What will we do about the wedding clothes?' Cecily asked.

'We'll dress Mrs Todd and Noreen from the market, as before, but there won't be time to pick and choose. I'll get more fabric for Edith and begin again.'

'Can we do all that in the time?'

'We have to.'

She set off for the Monday markets directly after breakfast, and she wouldn't have bothered with breakfast had Cecily not insisted. She gave herself until midday to find second-hand garments and just about met her time limit, then she raced into town to buy Edith's material before dashing home.

Aside from stopping briefly to eat, they worked straight through and were still at it when William came that evening.

'However hard this week is,' he said encouragingly, 'next week you can start afresh.'

'We used up the last of our money buying these things,' said Cecily.

'So much for this making our reputation,' said Juliet. 'After this, we'll have a wonderful reputation but no business, because the money's run out.'

William said quietly, 'There's your mother's money.'

She bent her head, fighting so hard not to be stupid, stupid, stupid that her ears buzzed.

'It's your money, love,' said Cecily.

'I realise you don't want to get it yourself,' said William, 'but what if I fetched it for you?'

She looked up. 'Could you?'

'I'd need Mr Winterton's permission. He'd know the correct way to go about it. I'd have to tell him who has the money now.'

'Mr Nugent,' Cecily answered promptly. 'Lord Drysdale's agent.'

Juliet's stomach quivered. The thought of being brought to Mr Nugent's notice, even from a distance, was unsettling.

William returned the next day with news. 'Mr Winterton says your grandmother must confirm your identity. She's your next of kin and she has standing in the community. Mr Lawson, our chief clerk, will make the appointment and accompany you to her home or office, whichever she finds convenient.'

By sewing long into the night, they finished Noreen's dress, which might have felt like a magnificent achievement if they hadn't been drop-dead tired. Rising early with gritty eyes, Juliet mended the costume she had picked for Mrs Todd and unpicked the side seams, tacking in new seams for Cecily to finish. Then she turned to Edith's costume, which had been cut out yesterday. It was depressing to make it a second time. The skirt she had chosen because of all those flaring panels was now a nightmare of seams while the details on the blouse, which she had been so proud of first time round, were horribly fiddly.

They slept three or four hours that night and the next. When Cecily went out cleaning on Friday, Juliet had one embroidered harp to finish. The Todds were due at eleven for the final trying on. Mrs Todd took one look at Edith in her finery, blubbed something about 'my baby getting wed', and before Juliet knew it, all three of them were at it, but they were laughing too, and when they had finished hugging one another, they hugged her.

The room felt very still and quiet when they left.

That was it. It was over – unless she got Mother's money.

She was due to see Adeline later. Mr Lawson, a pixie of a man, arrived to accompany her to the villa in West Didsbury, where Adeline received them with glacial courtesy.

'Thank you for seeing us, madam,' said Mr Lawson. 'We shan't intrude upon your time above a minute. Please will you identify this young person as your granddaughter, Juliet Catherine Harper.'

Adeline looked her up and down before turning her unwavering gaze on Mr Lawson.

'I've never seen this person before in my life.'

When Juliet got home, still dizzy with shock, a letter was waiting. From Hal? Her heart bumped – but he didn't know this address.

'What are you waiting for?' Cecily prompted.

She opened it, and stared in disbelief. She read it twice and even then she didn't believe it.

'I think I've got to go to court.'

'You've *what*?'

William confirmed it later. 'Mr Seton – he's a magistrate – is going to hear your case.'

'What case? I haven't broken the law – have I?'

'I'll see what I can find out. Mr Lawson might pull strings, but not until Monday.'

'This says I'm to present myself on Wednesday morning.'

After the strain of worrying all Saturday and Sunday, they couldn't bear to wait for Monday evening, but went into town and pounced on William the moment he emerged from the building in Rosemount Place. When he saw them, his face went smooth and expressionless, and Juliet clutched her handbag in a tight squeeze. It was something bad.

'It's Mrs Tewson. She wants Mr Seton to put you into her care.'

Adeline took out the letter and reread it. Going behind her back to Ingleby's wasn't the only underhand thing that sly-boots had done. She was clearly angling to worm her way back in with the spurned fiancé.

273

Dear Juliet,

I did not receive your letter until a few days ago and I have given it a lot of thought. I hope you will not mind receiving an answer. I have asked myself many questions since I last saw you and your letter has raised yet more. I thought of showing it to Mr Nugent, but decided against it. This is between you and me.

An awkward letter. A careful letter. One that showed the poor sap hadn't known whether his reply would be welcome. Adeline pressed her lips together. Cunning little minx, she must have worded her own letter cleverly to make him feel like that.

The only thing I am certain of is how much you loved your mother. It was shocking when you did not attend her funeral, but I am sure that only something serious would have prevented you.

That was it. The next sentence – *Won't you please write and explain?* – was shatteringly obvious by its very omission. The poor sap clearly lacked the guts to write it.

The address on the letter was a place up in Cumberland. That was a puzzle, and Adeline disliked puzzles. Then she shrugged. As if it mattered.

She glanced towards the fireplace, but changed her mind. The size of the paper made it suitable for use in the lavatory.

Juliet's stomach had rolled in dread at the thought of standing in the dock, so relief washed through her when she found her case was to be heard in a private office. There was a desk at the front, and Mr Winterton, a tall, bushy-haired gentleman, sat in front of it, as did Adeline, while Juliet was relegated to a seat at the back of the room, as if the matter was nothing to do with her. Cecily and William flanked her.

The magistrate walked in without a glance at anyone and took his seat behind the desk. His chin was bare and prominent between luxuriant side whiskers. His manner was at once slick and bored, as if these proceedings were of little importance.

'Good morning. Are we ready? This should be over and done with in five minutes.'

Juliet gasped, and William nudged her. She snapped her mouth shut. She was under strict instructions not to speak.

'Leave it to Mr Winterton,' had been William's advice. 'You're lucky he's involved, even if it is against his will.'

'Against his will?'

'Be grateful I told him about your mother's money. That's given him an association with this matter, however reluctantly. He wasn't pleased when your grandmother didn't identify you.'

'Mrs Tewson,' said Mr Seton, 'what do you wish to say?'

'The girl ran away after her mother died. The only job she could get was charring. When it was brought to my attention that she had got herself into trouble, I placed her, against her will I may say, in a respectable home for girls of that sort. Since then, I have given her a home and a job, from which she ran away – again. Her pathetic attempt to set up in business failed dismally and she has nothing left. Nevertheless, I am prepared to take her back and provide a stable background.'

'She is indeed fortunate,' said Mr Seton, and for one horrifying moment, Juliet thought he was about to hand her over then and there.

Mr Winterton cleared his throat. 'If I may? Mrs Tewson's information may be factually correct, but it paints a picture of a hoyden. I intend to show that Miss Harper is capable of conducting herself and her affairs in a modest and appropriate manner. I have a character witness waiting outside, who knows her as a decent, hard-working individual.'

He nodded at William, who went to the door and ushered in Mrs Gillespie. William placed a chair for her, and Mrs Gillespie, handbag clutched tightly in her lap, squirmed under the combined stares of the three round the desk.

'This is Mrs Gillespie, Miss Harper's landlady,' said Mr Winterton. 'Mrs Gillespie, please tell us your opinion of Miss Harper.'

'A pleasing young lady, sir. Quiet, civil ways, and the rent up to date. You never saw anyone work harder.'

'You consider yourself a good judge of character?' Adeline cut in.

'I like to think so.'

'Indeed? How good a judge of character were you when you married?'

Mrs Gillespie let loose a cry of distress. Her colour drained away.

Adeline addressed herself to Mr Seton. 'Mr Gillespie is a disgraced railway clerk, in prison for theft. This woman passes herself off as his widow, but for years she lived off his ill-gotten gains.'

'I had no idea . . .' Mrs Gillespie made a choking sound.

At a signal from Mr Winterton, William escorted the drooping figure to the door. Cecily hurried after them, taking poor Mrs Gillespie and sending William back to Juliet. There was a dark look on Mr Winterton's face. Was he about to throw her over?

But he said crisply, 'Mr Seton, are you aware that when Mrs

Tewson was requested to provide formal identification of Miss Harper, she claimed not to know her?'

'It was for her own good,' Adeline retorted. 'She had looked elsewhere for guidance and representation, which she should have received from me.'

'Are you implying,' Mr Winterton enquired grandly, 'that the guidance of Winterton, Sowerby and Jenks is inferior to your own?'

'All I know of Winterton, Sowerby and Jenks,' replied Adeline, 'is that a member of the firm portrayed himself, and therefore your firm, as this girl's legal representative. I recommended his dismissal for that, but I see you didn't heed my advice.' She turned to the magistrate. 'I leave you to draw your own conclusions, Mr Seton.'

'Duly noted.' Mr Seton scratched away with his pen.

'Madam,' said Mr Winterton, 'your remarks—'

'—are the simple truth. Do you deny it?'

Cecily crept back in and slipped across to Juliet. 'I'm taking Mrs Gillespie home,' she whispered.

Adeline addressed Mr Seton. 'I'd also like to point out that this same member of Mr Winterton's firm saw nothing undesirable in the trollop the girl lives with.'

'Mrs Tewson!' Mr Winterton spluttered. 'You surely aren't referring to Mrs Gillespie?'

'I mean this . . . female.' Adeline waved a scornful hand in Cecily's direction. 'Calls herself Mrs and hopes the world will take pity on a young widow, but having looked into the matter, I can assure you the most she's ever had on her finger is a brass curtain ring. She used to be a servant and when serving girls get themselves into trouble, there's no shortage of people to make the man do the decent thing. If that didn't happen in this case, it must be because there were, shall we say, several candidates.'

Cecily uttered a strangled cry and stumbled from the room. Juliet made to follow, but Adeline's hand clamped on her shoulder.

'She's no better than a prostitute,' Adeline steamrollered on. 'Hardly fit company for someone you want to see conducting herself in a – how did you express it, Mr Winterton? – "a modest and appropriate manner"?'

Mr Winterton looked daggers at William. 'When you approached me regarding Miss Harper's difficulty, I had no idea—'

'Well, you have now,' Adeline gloated.

Juliet couldn't bear it. Any minute now Mr Seton would come down on Adeline's side, and Mr Winterton would throw up his hands in relief. She bounced to her feet.

'May I speak?'

It appeared to take Mr Seton a moment to realise where the voice had come from. 'You may not. You are under twenty-one, which is why this matter is up for consideration. Do not disturb these proceedings again.'

William pulled her into her chair. She hissed, 'The money. Ask Mr Winterton to mention my mother's money.'

William got up to murmur in Mr Winterton's ear, and Mr Winterton informed Mr Seton, 'Miss Harper may be in financial straits at present, but her late mother's money is due to her and would provide a certain independence.'

Adeline bristled. 'If that money is retrieved, I'll take care of it.'

Juliet couldn't contain herself. 'The same way you've taken care of the money I earned working for you? Sixteen guineas – and what I earned from Mrs Maddox.' Appealing to Mr Seton, she cried, 'You see, sir, I am capable of earning a living.'

'Be silent or I'll have you ejected,' declared the magistrate.

'That doesn't mean you can run a business or lead a

278

blameless life,' Adeline flung at her. She turned to Mr Seton. 'She needs all aspects of her life closely supervised. The fact that she prefers to sew in the backstreets, when she could be designing for Tewson's Tailor-mades, proves she is incapable of making rational decisions.'

'I agree,' said Mr Seton. 'Her past life is one disgrace after another. Just because she has earned money from Tewson's and Ingleby's doesn't mean she's capable of managing her own affairs. I find in favour of Mrs Tewson.'

Juliet's heart dribbled into her shoes. She couldn't bear to be handed back to her grandmother – wait a moment. She nudged William so hard he had to stamp one foot to keep from overbalancing.

'How does he know about Ingleby's?' she whispered to him, then she leapt up. 'How do you know I worked at Ingleby's?' she challenged.

'Remove this person!' demanded Mr Seton.

'Miss Harper raises an interesting point,' said Mr Winterton. 'You appear to have prior knowledge of this case. Can it be that you aren't impartial? Can you assure me that you and Mrs Tewson didn't decide the matter in advance?'

Mr Seton coughed and muttered something.

Adeline turned on Mr Winterton. 'As right-minded citizens, naturally Mr Seton and I see this matter in a similar light.'

'I'd like to know when this cordial agreement started. Perhaps another magistrate might be prevailed upon to assist us in determining this?'

'There's no need for that,' Mr Seton barked, 'and you will treat me with the respect my position deserves.'

'I'm entirely in favour of treating *impartial* magistrates with the utmost respect. I'm sure you'll display your own impartiality in listening to my proposal for Miss Harper's future. I propose that her late mother's money be placed in a savings bank chosen by Mrs Tewson and myself. Access to the funds will be on Mrs Tewson's and my joint signatures only.'

'Wait a minute!' Juliet exclaimed.

'Miss Harper will receive a modest allowance to keep herself and make her way respectably in the world. Her situation will be reviewed quarterly by Mrs Tewson and myself, together with one of our esteemed impartial magistrates. I propose this arrangement should continue until Miss Harper comes of age.'

'But that's not for years!' Juliet cried. She wasn't quite seventeen yet and there would be another four years – four years! – after that.

Mr Winterton ignored her. 'If my proposal is unacceptable, Mr Seton, I'll formally request the intervention of another magistrate. This will be necessary to show that you're impartial in spite of what appeared to be inappropriate prior knowledge.'

Mr Seton cleared his throat. 'Very well. No need to take matters further. Your proposal seems adequate.'

Adeline leapt in. 'I insist that at the first sign of anything unsatisfactory or unseemly in the girl's personal life or her work, responsibility for her welfare and her money be handed to me.'

'Agreed,' said Mr Winterton.

'The matter is settled.' Mr Seton marched out.

Juliet sprang forward. 'You can't do this.'

'We just have,' said Adeline.

Juliet glared at Mr Winterton. 'I thought you were on my side.'

'It isn't a question of sides. It's a matter of what's best for you.'

'Be careful how you address your elders,' warned Adeline. 'Some might view your outspokenness as *unseemly*.'

'This is to last until I'm twenty-one?' It was unbelievable.

'It won't drag on until then, said Adeline. 'Responsibility will revert to me long before that.' The corners of her mouth moved – on anyone else, it would have been a smile. 'Oh yes, long before that.'

Chapter Twenty-One

Juliet arrived home to find Cecily had been crying over the public humiliation Adeline had dished out, but she wouldn't talk about it, just saying, 'I wonder if I can get more hours at Mrs Blore's. We'll have to stop paying Mrs Gillespie for meals for now and buy ourselves the cheapest things we can.'

'You can't live on bread and dripping,' said Juliet, 'not in your condition.'

'It's only until Mr Winterton recovers your mother's money. Someone's at the front door. I'll go.' Cecily got up, but as she reached their door, it opened and she gasped, backing into the room, white-faced with distress.

Adeline marched in. She didn't touch Cecily, but nonetheless gave the impression of bowling her aside. 'Living here with this trollop is hardly conducive to leading a respectable life. Mr Seton and Mr Winterton were so keen to have the matter settled, they forgot about the harlot you live with, but I haven't forgotten. Mr Winterton's precious agreement is null and void before it even starts. Pack your things.'

'I won't.'

'I think you shall.' Adeline spoke quietly. 'You have no choice. This trollop—'

'Don't call her that!' Juliet flared as Cecily bundled her knuckles in front of her mouth.

'Come willingly or unwillingly. It's all the same to me. I have a man outside who'll . . . escort you, if necessary.'

So, Juliet found herself once more in the back parlour of the villa in West Didsbury. One of those familiar boxes sat unopened on the table and that was how it would jolly well stay. She glanced at the windows.

Adeline's voice was dangerously quiet. 'Set one foot outside this room and I'll inform Mr Winterton you've run away – again.' She went to the door and held it open invitingly. 'On second thoughts, be my guest. Or would you prefer the window, like last time?'

The girl showed pluck, Adeline had to concede that. It was irritating, of course, though preferable to having another spineless ninny to deal with. Adeline's features settled into the well-worn sneer that thoughts of Clara invariably occasioned. Agnes had had more about her than Clara, but in the end she had turned out to be every bit as much of a fool.

Now here was Agnes's brat being obstinate – again. It was a different type of obstinacy, though. Not sulky like Clara's, nor like Agnes's. The girl possessed a quiet determination. Not that resolve would do her any good now that she was up against Adeline Tewson. Adeline had crushed far greater personages than this chit. She couldn't win, and they both knew it. She couldn't leave, because that would be running away. Neither could she ignore the samples indefinitely, because that would make her appear sulky and immature, in need of a guiding hand.

Coming downstairs the next morning, Adeline glanced into the back parlour and nodded crisply upon seeing the box untouched. She went to breakfast with the good appetite that she believed was part and parcel of her relentless drive and inevitable success, helping herself to fresh muffins, which she loaded with fluffy scrambled eggs and crispy bacon.

She didn't look up as the door opened. She sensed the chit's hesitation. Was she wondering whether to refuse breakfast? She would go down in Adeline's estimation if she did. No, she went to the sideboard to investigate the covered dishes.

Adeline left her to it. She went into her morning room. Presently a knock heralded the girl's arrival.

'If you want me to return to the back parlour, I'll go, but I won't do any work for you.'

'You ate at my table readily enough.'

Adeline settled down to read through some papers she had brought home from her office. She wouldn't go to the factory today, but tomorrow she would resume her normal practices as if her life had never suffered any interruption, which would give that girl something to mull over while she sat ignoring the box.

The front door bell jangled, then Marjorie appeared.

'There's a man here, asking for Miss Juliet.'

That young booby of Winterton's, no doubt. How dared he come here?

'He said he knew Miss Juliet when she lived with her mother,' Marjorie added.

'Indeed?' Every sense sharpened. 'Did you inform her he's here?'

'No, madam. I told him to wait outside while I spoke to you. Shall I send him away, madam?'

'Show him in.'

Marjorie returned moments later. 'This way, if you please. Mr Price, madam.'

'Mr . . . Price.' Hesitating before his name was as good a way as any of putting him in his place. She did not offer him a seat.

She took him in at a glance. Better than Agnes's labourer, anyway. She had always imagined him as a thickset clod. This young man was taller than the imaginary Harper and his build was slim, though far from puny. His suit was better than she would have expected from one of his station in life. Either Lord Whatsit paid his gardeners too well or else this fellow had costly tastes.

'I'm sorry to disturb you. I was hoping to see Juliet.'

'And you are?'

'Her . . . friend.'

'Her friend?'

'We used to have an understanding.'

'Are you the cad that got her pregnant?'

'No!' He coloured, but he squared his shoulders. 'I'm sorry, madam, but I'm unsure who you are. I know Juliet has a grandmother.'

'I am Adeline Tewson,' she replied, neither confirming nor denying the relationship.

'Is Juliet here?'

'Why would you imagine that?'

'She wrote to me from this address.'

'That must have been some time ago.'

'Last month. I answered, though not until last week. I hoped for a reply—'

'Spare me the details. You're on a fruitless errand. She was

285

here, but she ran away.' Adeline reached for the bell pull. 'Marjorie will see you out. Good morning, Mr . . . Price.'

This wasn't the battle Juliet had braced herself for. Arguments she could have coped with, but Adeline apparently intended to bore her into submission. She eyed the box of samples with hearty dislike.

The door opened, and Marjorie stood there. 'You're to come.'

To her surprise, Mr Winterton was with Adeline, together with another gentleman.

'You should have consulted me before declaring the agreement terminated, Mrs Tewson,' said Mr Winterton. 'There you are, Miss Harper. This is Mr Davidson, a magistrate who is impartial in this matter.'

'I see no reason for the girl to be present,' said Adeline.

'Whereas I see every reason,' replied Mr Winterton. 'I understand your concerns regarding Miss Ramsbottom, madam, but I've been persuaded to give her the benefit of the doubt.'

'Mrs Ramsbottom, sir,' said Juliet.

'I beg your pardon?'

'She calls herself Mrs.'

'She can call herself the Queen of Sheba,' Adeline snapped, 'but she'd still be a slut.'

'Mrs Tewson, please,' Mr Davidson remonstrated.

'As I was saying,' Mr Winterton continued, 'Miss Ramsbottom—'

'Mrs,' Juliet said, 'unless, of course, you want things to be as hard as possible for her and the baby.'

Mr Winterton resumed, his voice ringing with patience. 'As I said, I'm prepared to give her the benefit of the doubt.'

'On what grounds?' Adeline demanded. 'Come, sir, I'm entitled to know.'

'You may be entitled to know about Miss Harper, but not about *Mrs* Ramsbottom, and certainly not about the other person concerned. Be assured, however, that Mr Davidson was present at the discussion.'

'I am satisfied, for the time being,' Mr Davidson declared.

'One further point, Mrs Tewson, and I think it important to state it in Miss Harper's presence. Any decisions concerning her may be made only by the pair of us jointly, in the presence of a magistrate and with that magistrate's agreement.' Mr Winterton nodded at Juliet. 'Get your things.'

He returned her to Mrs Gillespie's, and not a moment too soon, because Cecily was tearfully packing, unable to meet the rent on her own. Mr Winterton dismissed their thanks.

'Don't thank me. Thank young Turton.'

It was a couple of days before William finally appeared. They drew him in with cries of delight, then exchanged puzzled looks when he cleared his throat and fiddled with his cuffs.

'You've done us the most marvellous favour,' Cecily said. 'Why so glum?'

William went to the window and stood with his back to them. At last he huffed a breath and turned round.

'I've been plucking up the courage to come. When I heard Mrs Tewson had spirited Juliet away, I—well, I told Mr Winterton how Cecily was led on by a plausible fellow, who got her into trouble. I said one reason this man was plausible was because he had my business cards. I told Mr Winterton about being attacked, because I wanted him to believe me about you.'

'Didn't he know you'd been attacked?' Juliet asked.

'Yes, because I was laid up for a fortnight, but he didn't know about the business cards. I didn't realise myself for some time.

And . . . and he didn't know the details of what happened. I never told anyone. I was . . . ashamed.'

'There's nowt shameful in being attacked,' said Cecily.

Yes, there is.

'It happened one dark winter evening after work. I heard footsteps behind me, and then I was being shunted into an alley and having seven bells knocked out of me. I remember being amazed by his strength. I thought, *This is what it's like for a woman being beaten up.* He gave me a good hiding, then slapped me about. I . . . I offered him money to let me alone. I had to spit the blood out of my mouth before I could speak. He laughed, then he took my pocketbook and went through it, then chucked it away. I didn't know he'd taken my cards. Then he . . . he got the loose change from my pockets and stuffed it in my mouth.'

'Oh, William.'

'I tried not to swallow it. My eyes were streaming and my nose was running and I could scarcely breathe, but he kept cramming in more and more. I was terrified. Then he walked away. My mouth was so full, I couldn't get any fingers in to scoop the coins out, and I couldn't spit them out either. By opening my mouth as wide as I could, I managed to shake some free, but then I retched and there was vomit and money and . . . a coin went down the wrong way and I couldn't breathe. I honestly thought I was going to suffocate, covered in blood and snot and vomit, in a stinking alleyway.'

Cecily said gently, 'It sounds horrible. You told Mr Winterton all this?'

'I needed him to know what sort of man had led you up the garden path, so he'd realise it wasn't your fault.'

'Thank you,' said Juliet. 'You know what a difference it's made to us.'

'I wanted you to know as well,' William added. There was a wretched silence before he burst out, 'D'you know what the worst part was? Not the bruises or the cracked ribs. It was the humiliation. That's why I never told anyone. But I decided to tell you now because – because after Mrs Tewson publicly humiliated Cecily, I wanted to come clean. It didn't seem right, my knowing what that man had done to you when you didn't know what he'd done to me.'

Getting up, William turned away and blew his nose, keeping his back to them for a moment – was he mopping his eyes? He turned round with a falsely bright expression.

'Good news. Mr Winterton has written to Lord Drysdale. Your money will be sorted out soon, Juliet, and Hand-finished by Harper will be back in business.'

Chapter Twenty-Two

May 1898

Juliet woke to hear scuffling. She grinned at a stage whisper from Archie, then caught Cecily's soft shushing. The door opened and she shut her eyes, hearing Archie's feet sliding across the floor, then a chinking noise close by her head as something was placed on the bedside cupboard. With an elaborate stretch, she opened her eyes and looked straight into Archie's solemn blue gaze. Her heart did a little flip.

'Good morning, madam,' Archie piped. 'Happy birthday.'

Cecily prompted, 'Tea is . . .'

'Served!' he cried. 'Tea is served. Look, I carried it upstairs all by myself, and Mummy says not to worry, because she'll wipe up the spills.'

'You carried that on your own? Goodness me, how clever. And I bet you never spilt a drop. Mummy's being a meanie.'

'It's your birthday tea.' Archie's face shone with pride.

Sitting up, she reached for the cup and saucer, cocked her little finger and said in a posh voice, 'Modom does so enjoy tea in bed.' She slurped loudly before smacking her lips and expelling a loud sigh of satisfaction, making Archie clap his hands over his mouth in an ecstasy of shock and delight. 'But best of all,' she boomed, putting down her the tea, 'I like eating little boys for breakfast.'

One swoop and she was pulling him into bed with her, not difficult since he always wriggled like mad to get under the covers and then popped up looking surprised at having been captured. Cuddling him close, she peppered him with kisses under cover of pretending to devour him. They surfaced to find Cecily observing them with mock exasperation.

'I don't know which of you is worse. Come on, young man. Leave Auntie Juley to get dressed and we'll make her birthday breakfast.'

Archie scrambled out and scampered away. Juliet smiled after him, a smile that reached deep inside. She treasured Cecily's little boy.

Archie Ramsbottom. 'You can't get much more Lancashire than that,' Cecily had joked when he was hours old.

Juliet had thought of Constance Harper having a brother called Archie Ramsbottom and hadn't known whether to laugh or cry. She had cried a lot – in private – when Archie was small. There was something fierce and angry and despairing inside her, because Cecily had her son with her while her own daughter was goodness knew where. If only she had defied Adeline and never set foot in Mrs Maddox's house. She tried to be glad Constance had a decent, prosperous family. And she was glad. But it could never wipe out her loss.

God, it had been hard – it still was hard – watching Archie grow up, sharing his care with Cecily, telling him bedtime stories, teaching him to count.

'I'm so glad that you . . . well, that you take such an interest in him,' Cecily had said when Archie was still a babe in arms.

'Of course I'm interested,' she had answered brightly. 'I love him. I'm his Auntie Juley.' Then she stopped pretending. 'You must tell me if . . .'

'If what?'

'It's as if my fingertips are hungry for the feel of him.'

'Oh, Juliet.'

'But really . . . really they're hungry for Constance. How could I have given her up?'

'You had no choice, love,' Cecily whispered.

'Didn't I? Or did I tell myself that because it was easier? You were never in any doubt about keeping your baby.'

'It was different with me. For the first few months, I thought I was going to marry my baby's father. When I learnt the truth, it didn't change my feelings towards my child.'

'I thought it wasn't possible to keep a baby. It wasn't until – until I saw her.' The words rasped in her throat. 'I loved her. I still do. I have dreams about her. And I look at Archie and . . .'

'You can't bear it.' Cecily swallowed. 'Do you want us to move out?'

Juliet caught her friend's arm. 'No! Cecily, I adore Archie. You must know that. I couldn't bear not to be with him – or you. You're my family. But . . .'

'But your family isn't complete.'

Juliet lifted her chin. She didn't want Cecily worrying about her. 'I shouldn't have said "but", I should have said "and". And I am privileged to be part of Archie's life since I can't be part of my daughter's.'

Cecily squeezed her shoulder. 'Sweetheart.'

She was Archie's godmother, and William was his adored

godfather. William was dear to both girls, more like a brother than a friend.

She washed her face, and wet her toothbrush before rubbing it in the toothpaste. Their purchase of toothbrushes and a tin of Woods' Cherry Tooth Paste two years ago had been a symbol of the success of Hand-finished by Harper and, goodness, hadn't they felt they had gone up in the world, using real toothpaste instead of salt. This seemed to be a morning for memories.

Well, that was understandable, given what day it was. Twenty-one today. In spite of Adeline's gloating prediction in Mr Seton's office, she had managed to stay out of her grandmother's clutches, though it had been touch and go at times.

No sooner had Mother's money been placed in a savings bank, with Juliet receiving a moderate sum to get by on, than Mrs Gillespie had come bursting into their room in a terrific flap because her landlord had served notice.

'He's heard about Mr Gillespie doing time. He says I'm tainted by it and if I live here, then his house is too-o-o.'

The word elongated into quivering syllables as Mrs Gillespie collapsed in floods of tears. Juliet hugged her while Cecily hurried to put the kettle on.

The following week had passed in a riot of packing and rushing about, as everyone sought new homes before next rent day. Mrs Gillespie wrote to her sister and shed tears of relief when she announced she was going to help her run her boarding house in Southport, so at least that was one person fixed up, which ought to have made Juliet feel less guilty, but it didn't. Was this happening because of her? Could Adeline be behind the spiteful information that had so incensed the landlord?

She had decided on a fresh start elsewhere. Yes, Mrs Todd had sung their praises locally, but that remark of Adeline's about sewing in the backstreets had rankled. She didn't want to rise to the bait, but a spark of ambition had appeared that couldn't be denied.

A letter arrived from Mr Davidson. Unlike the peremptory command from Mr Seton, this was a polite request to see both girls.

'*Please bring your friend, Mrs Ramsbottom.* He even calls you "Mrs".'

'It says Mr Winterton and Mrs Tewson will be there.'

Juliet squeezed Cecily's hand, knowing she was remembering Adeline's public condemnation. 'I don't think you have a choice.'

Mr Davidson made a surprising offer. 'It seems to me that Miss Harper and Mrs Ramsbottom might benefit from moving their business elsewhere.'

'Wait,' Adeline interrupted. 'Your role is to be impartial.'

'In the interests of impartiality, I believe that a move to a new place would start this agreement on the right footing.'

'It so happens we've got to move,' said Juliet. 'Mrs Gillespie's landlord has served notice.' She looked straight at her grandmother, but Adeline didn't blink, never mind blush.

'That puts the matter beyond argument,' said Mr Davidson. 'I know a lady slightly, a Mrs Rosemary Carmichael, who owns property in various parts of Manchester. I have taken the liberty of explaining Miss Harper's situation to her – that is, Miss Harper's whole history – and she is prepared to have Miss Harper and Mrs Ramsbottom in one of her houses.'

'You told her everything?' Juliet said in dismay.

'Indeed, yes, and about Mrs Ramsbottom.'

'And she still wants them?' sneered Adeline. 'That tells us something about Mrs Rosemary Carmichael.'

'Mrs Tewson!' Mr Davidson remonstrated. 'I have here a list of areas where Mrs Carmichael has property.'

'Let me see,' said Mr Winterton.

'No!' said Adeline. 'Start them from scratch, if you must, but it's up to them to decide where.'

'But they don't know Manchester,' Mr Winterton objected.

'So? Let them find out. It's all part of running a business.'

The girls gave the list to William and he suggested Chorlton-cum-Hardy, where the Mersey formed a natural border between Lancashire and Cheshire.

'It's a reasonable area. There's poverty, of course, but you'd find that anywhere, and at the other end, there's the nobs, Lord Egerton and the Kimbers and the Darleys. But what's good from your point of view is the mixture of upper- and lower-middle class.'

'We need two rooms in the best address we can afford,' said Juliet. 'One to live in and one for working.'

By stretching every penny to snapping point, they moved into two rooms in Mrs Livingston's house on Wilton Road, where they had a big upstairs front with a bay window, from where they could see over the hedge surrounding the new recreation ground. This was where they worked, and they also had a smaller room above for living in, which was fine until Archie came along.

'Couldn't we swap the rooms round?' Cecily suggested.

'I know it's hard, love, but it's only while we get ourselves started, I promise. In the meantime, we'll swap the top floor front for the bigger room at the back.'

'Can we afford to?'

Juliet kissed goodbye her plan to put their small profit into more stock. 'We'll manage.'

Then a fresh problem hit them. The second-hand clothes sellers Juliet usually bought from refused to sell to her.

'I've heard you're fancying up my stuff and selling it on at a big profit. I don't like the sound of that.'

'It's ridiculous,' Juliet told Cecily and William in bewilderment. 'What difference does it make to them what I do with what they sell me?'

'You'd think they'd be glad of a regular buyer,' Cecily agreed.

Juliet fell quiet. Could it be Adeline?

'Have you heard of estate sales?' William asked. 'Imagine someone living in the same house for years, then they die and the relatives take what they want, but what are they to do with the rest, especially if the house has to be handed back within the week? There are businesses that will buy everything, including the contents of the wardrobes.'

'How wasteful!' Cecily was scandalised. 'Fancy getting rid like that. Don't the families need the things?'

'They're well-off. They've got their own things.'

'And if they're well-off, the clothes will be of high quality.' Juliet felt excitement stir. She didn't know whether to let it loose or clamp down on it to avoid disappointment, but it wriggled free anyway and she bounced on her toes.

The first time she visited one such warehouse, she thought she had died and gone to heaven. She spent blissful hours sifting through garments, many hanging on racks, others still in their wardrobes. She found an array of vastly complicated skirts from twenty-odd years ago, complete with bustles, and she couldn't tear herself away from a wardrobe of evening dresses. Just to trail her fingers across the velvets, taffetas and shot silks was utter bliss. She even found a crinoline or two, and more pleating, ruching, bows, fringes, flowers, flounces, frills and ruffles than you could shake a stick at.

'And,' she crowed to Cecily, 'there was a whole trunk full of false bosoms.'

'Never! You're making it up.'

They looked at one another, then dissolved into peals of laughter.

She had purchased several skirts and jackets, a three-quarter-length cape with quilted silk lining, and – a gamble, yes, but oh, if it paid off! – an evening dress of royal blue, which might please the eye of a particular customer.

Mrs Plaidy's appointment was the following day, and the blue gown proved irresistible. Juliet set about the alterations with a light heart. Neither did it end there. The jackets and skirts were snapped up, and a bank manager's wife wanted mourning clothes. There had been vast amounts of black at the warehouse, and Juliet was delighted to oblige. This led to a recommendation, and another, and the business steadily grew.

Until the next problem. Unpaid bills. First there was Mrs Cadell, who went away with her purchases and her bill, but didn't pay by the due date. Juliet gave her an extra week before William helped her compose a polite reminder, by which time, Mrs Hickman and Miss Stoneley were also overdue. To Juliet's consternation, Mrs Cadell's reminder was returned, marked *Not known at this address*. Juliet marched straight round there and discovered that Mrs Cadell indeed wasn't known.

Soon there were five customers with fake addresses. Between them, they had ordered fourteen garments, all of which had required alteration. Losing the money was bad enough, but it was the dishonesty that left Juliet and Cecily stunned, on top of which Juliet had to face a quarterly meeting, and there was no chance of hiding what had happened, because the books were always the first things to be examined, with Adeline's eyes flashing from account book to order book and back again, alert for any discrepancy.

And, oh lord, what discrepancies there were this time.

'I don't think we can blame Miss Harper for being taken in by these confidence tricksters,' Mr Winterton said when Adeline had had a jolly good go at doing precisely that.

'Had she been quicker to pursue the Cadell woman for payment, she would have been on the alert. Look at the money she's lost. Really, Mr Winterton, isn't it time to put an end to this pet project of yours? The girl is lurching from one disaster to another.' She swung round on Juliet. 'What precautions have you taken to ensure this never happens again?'

'Come, Mrs Tewson,' Mr Winterton interjected. 'Who can guard against such an eventuality?'

'Precisely,' Adeline snapped.

'Actually,' said Juliet, 'we have taken precautions. If a new customer is unknown to us, we follow her home.'

'You what?' Adeline exclaimed while the men stared in appalled silence. 'You can't do that.'

She shrugged. 'Given the circumstances.'

'Not only is she on the verge of bankruptcy, she's following her customers.' Adeline turned to the magistrate. 'What more proof do you require? Put her under my authority and let that be the end of it.'

Juliet's heartbeats counted the time as Mr Davidson considered.

'It's an exaggeration to talk about the verge of bankruptcy. Let Miss Harper proceed for another quarter. I don't like this idea of following customers, but it's difficult to see what else could be done, and at least she's doing something.'

Following the customers didn't continue for more than a few

weeks, much to Juliet's relief. There were no more Mrs Cadells, and she decided it was safe to go back to normal, which she duly reported at the next meeting. Adeline made a dismissive humphing sound, and Juliet wondered whether her grandmother had been behind the problem women. She gazed at Mr Winterton, willing him to wonder the same thing and challenge Adeline, but he didn't.

At the end of the meeting, Adeline ordered Juliet to bring with her next time all the sketches she had made to show customers how something would look when finished.

'It's important that the quality of her work is overseen,' she told the two men.

Juliet duly produced her sketches, expecting Adeline to look them over on the spot, but she spared them barely a glance. At the end of the meeting, she took them as she got up to leave.

'Wait!' Juliet cried. 'What about my sketches?'

'You'll get them back next time.'

She turned to Mr Winterton. 'She wants my designs for herself.'

An eyebrow climbed up Adeline's brow. 'Perhaps, Mr Winterton, you would care to explain to your protégée the meaning of slander.'

Mr Winterton gave Juliet a look of annoyance. It was one of those moments that popped up every now and again, when she thought he might be about to wash his hands of her.

'There is another possibility, however,' Adeline continued. 'I suggest we test the quality of her work by requiring her to create three designs per quarter. If they're good enough, I'll use them for Tewson's Tailor-mades. If not, it will raise questions concerning her ability in her chosen line of work.'

It was agreed, and the meeting ended. Juliet was too taken aback to absorb it. It was only later that anger set in. She was going to design for Adeline. Twelve designs a year – and they had to be good or her business, her independence, her whole way of life would be at risk.

That was how things had been ever since. To rub it in yet further, Adeline hadn't paid her. When she had dared to raise the question, Adeline pointed out in a voice dripping with condescension, 'The purpose is to determine whether you may keep working or should be shut down. If anyone should be paid, it is I, for providing my judgement.'

Today, however, would see the final meeting. Just some papers to sign, and a visit to the savings bank to put her signature against her savings at long last, and that would be the end of it.

No, not the end. The beginning.

Adeline marched up the steps into the offices of the magistrates' court. This was supposed to be the final meeting. Well, not if she could help it. Mr Davidson and Mr Winterton were waiting in the usual room. They came politely to their feet as she swept in. The chit stood up as well. Adeline had that effect. She had no need to look at the clock to know she was dead on time. The others had arrived early so as not to keep her waiting – she had that effect too.

A table was ready. Adeline and Mr Winterton sat opposite one another like the adversaries they were, one to either side of Mr Davidson at the head of the table, while the chit sat tucked away at the far end, as befitted her status – wait, no, she wasn't in her customary place. Adeline's eyebrows climbed as the girl took a place on Mr Winterton's side of the table. Adeline was about to frame a scathing comment that would send her scuttling back where she belonged, but Mr Winterton spoke first.

'I've invited Miss Harper to sit beside me, as this is somewhat of a special occasion, being the day of her coming of age.'

'Here we are for the final time,' said Mr Davidson.

'Designs,' said Adeline.

'I haven't brought any,' the chit said quietly.

'What?' Anger was followed so swiftly by delight that Adeline felt as though firecrackers were exploding inside her. 'There we are, then. The agreement has been broken.'

'One moment,' said Mr Davidson. 'Why haven't you provided designs, Miss Harper? You know you're required to.'

'Not today, surely? The designs were done so my grandmother could report back as to their success or otherwise, but as this is the last meeting, there can be no need for her to report back in the future.'

Adeline snorted. 'The purpose of the designs was to prove her ability. Whether this is the final meeting is irrelevant.'

'Mrs Tewson,' Mr Davidson said, 'have Miss Harper's designs been of good quality?'

'And have you used them at Tewson's Tailor-mades?' Mr Winterton added.

There were times when Adeline wished she could breathe fire. 'Yes, I have.'

'So, nothing to worry about in terms of Miss Harper's ability,' said Mr Davidson.

'The point is that she should have provided designs today. Are you going to be taken in by that poppycock about my reporting back? For her not to bring designs shows her slapdash attitude. She lacks the steady character necessary to run a business.'

'I'm inclined,' said Mr Davidson, 'to overlook the matter of new designs. I believe Miss Harper has proved herself more than capable in that area.'

'Hear, hear,' Mr Winterton added.

The meeting moved on. The chit produced her accounts. Adeline pored over them, but they were immaculate. The meeting moved inevitably to a close. Well, although it didn't appear on the agenda, there was one matter left, if anyone remembered, and Adeline certainly wasn't going to offer a reminder.

'That brings this meeting to an end,' Mr Davidson said, 'unless there is any other business . . . ?' He was already tidying his papers.

'Actually, there is something else.' The chit had the gall to meet Adeline's gaze. 'My money. I'm still owed payment from when I worked for you in the belief I was designing for Ingleby's, and there's also what I earned sewing for Mrs Maddox.'

'I don't carry that kind of money on my person,' Adeline stated grandly. 'There will have to be a further meeting next quarter.'

Today was moving day. Garden Cottage was a sturdy house opposite Chorlton Green, with a door in the centre, window either side, two windows above. 'Like a child's picture,' Cecily had exclaimed delightedly when they saw it for the first time. 'When Archie draws that picture, he'll be drawing a real place.'

It was a busy morning. Helped by Mrs Livingston and a couple of neighbours, not to mention Archie, Cecily moved their things. She wanted to get their new home shipshape before Juliet returned from her meeting.

'I can't get over how lucky we are,' Cecily told Mrs Livingston for the umpteenth time.

Everything had happened so smoothly that she felt it was meant to be. They had decided ages ago to leave Mrs Livingston's once Juliet turned twenty-one. Mrs Livingston was the sort of landlady lodgers dreamt of, and she loved Archie almost as much as they did. A competent needlewoman, she even sewed for them. But her house felt inseparable from the agreement, and the girls longed to leave that behind.

Mrs Tewson didn't know they were moving, neither did Mr Winterton.

'It won't put you in an awkward position, will it?' Juliet had asked William.

He grinned. 'You don't imagine old Winterton passes the time of day with plebs like me, do you? And if he did, he wouldn't discuss a client's business.'

'Is Juliet a client?' Cecily asked, impressed.

'Sort of.'

Out of gratitude to Mrs Livingston, they gave her heaps more notice than necessary, and had spent many a happy hour poring over advertisements for rented property and visiting various places, anxious to see what they could afford. Then Mr Kenyon, the rent man, popped in to see them, having heard of their plans from Mrs Livingston, and offered to show them another of Mrs Carmichael's properties, Garden Cottage, which was due to fall vacant at the right time.

For Cecily, it was love at first sight.

'One of the front rooms will be the sewing room,' said Juliet, 'though it's smaller than the sewing room we've got at the moment.'

'Oh, but the garden is so pretty,' Cecily cried, leaping to the cottage's defence. 'Imagine our ladies seeing that when they come. We can have our own parlour, and a bedroom each. Even the rent is perfect.'

'I'm sure it should be higher. We must make sure there hasn't been a mistake.'

But Mr Kenyon assured them that the moderate rent was indeed correct.

'Then we'll take it,' Cecily had cried at once, and the next moment she and Juliet were hugging one another.

By the time Juliet came home from the meeting, all their things had been moved. Not that they possessed much. They hadn't owned any furniture until the last few days, when they had purchased a few essentials second-hand. Mrs Livingston had pressed a couple of pieces on them as well.

By that evening, they had got everything straight.

'Shall we hang the laburnum picture in the parlour?' asked Cecily.

This will have pride of place on our parlour wall one day. Juliet made herself smile. 'Yes. That would be just right.'

Archie suddenly collapsed in a heap, and remained dead to the world while they undressed him and put him to bed. They sat downstairs, lingering over a light supper of cheese and pickle.

'Not exactly a birthday feast,' said Cecily.

'Trust me. This is the best birthday I've ever had.'

'How did the meeting go? There hasn't been a moment to ask.'

'Who cares? It was the last one and that's what matters.'

'How was Mrs Tewson?'

'Simmering, as you can imagine.'

'Better than exploding.'

'She did that a couple of times.' Juliet described what had happened.

'There's going to be another meeting?'

'No. You should have seen Mr Winterton's face. I think he'd have throttled Mr Davidson if he'd agreed. But both of them were as desperate as I was for it all to be over, you could tell.'

'What about the money?'

'My grandmother is going to send it to Mr Winterton, and I'll collect it.'

'Did you mention moving?'

'No fear. Mr Winterton will know soon enough when I write to thank him for everything he's done, but if the old battle-axe gets to hear of it, it won't be from me.'

Cecily laughed. 'We'll hear bloodhounds baying at the moon and we'll know she's found us.'

There were no baying hounds, but there was a moment's warning. Alone in the cottage, Juliet was at work on a new blouse for herself, with a stand-up collar and a generous V in the front that ran from shoulders to waist, which she intended to infill with lace. This was to be her working blouse, something pretty and stylish that showed her ability with the needle. Glancing up, she spied Adeline at the gate. She dashed to the front door and shot the bolt, a childish gesture, but when the handle turned as Adeline attempted to march straight in, she was glad of it. The knocker banged. She waited before she answered it.

The instant the door started to open, Adeline barged in and through the first door she saw, which took her into the sewing room. Juliet had barely entered the room before Adeline rounded on her.

'Did you imagine I wouldn't find you? I found you easily enough the last time you ran away. Evidently you lack the intellect to have learnt from that experience.'

'We didn't run away. As soon as I reached twenty-one, without falling flat on my face in spite of all the difficulties that came my way, Cecily and I were free to do as we liked.'

'Ah yes, that slut you call a friend. Why Mr Winterton persisted in viewing her as an appropriate companion and colleague is beyond me. But I see now that she has her uses. Tell me: is it the landlord she's dropping her drawers for, or the rent man? It must be one or the other, or how else could you afford this house?'

She forced herself to rise above the monstrous slur. 'We can afford it because the business is doing well.'

'Not that well, it isn't. I've seen the books, don't forget. Well, if it isn't the slut, it must be you. Please don't waste my time with a pretence of outrage. I haven't forgotten having to pluck you from the gutter.'

She fought to take control. 'If you've said everything you came to say, please leave.'

'Don't imagine you'll get away with this.'

'Why not? We coped with everything else you tried to do to us.'

'I don't know what you mean,' Adeline said grandly and swept out, leaving the door wide open.

'Be grateful you didn't have a customer with you,' said Cecily. It was easy for her to shrug it off because Juliet hadn't repeated Adeline's offensive remarks. She was determined not to dwell on it. She loved their new home, was thrilled and proud that they could afford such a pretty cottage. It was excellent for the business too. Their customers commented favourably, and new ladies arrived, attracted by the newspaper advertisement they had laboured over. Such was demand that they often called upon Mrs Livingston's services, and her presence at Garden Cottage became a regular feature.

Best of all, Juliet began to visit a higher class of lady at home. Mrs Arnold, the bank manager's wife, made appointments at Garden Cottage, but Mrs Palmer, whose husband was something high up in the same establishment, was waited on at home. 'The snob trade', Cecily called it, but Juliet loved it. It made her picture Mother sewing for Lady Margaret. Not that any of Juliet's at-home ladies were on a par with her ladyship, but Hand-finished by Harper was going up in the world.

'It's a good job your mum taught you to speak properly,' Cecily observed.

'That's because she had elocution lessons when she was young. My grandmother knew she'd have to speak nicely if she was going to have her own salon.'

'And now here you are rubbing shoulders with the nobs. I know I call them the snob trade, but I am proud of you. You've turned your business into a success.'

'*Our* business,' Juliet corrected her.

'Not deep down. If I was mown down by a runaway horse, would the business continue? Yes, it would. But if you were mown down . . . See?'

'Oh, Cecily, you don't feel—'

'Jolly lucky is how I feel. I wouldn't be bringing up my son in a place like this without Hand-finished by Harper. This has given me the chance to be respectable. Every morning when I wake up, I think how lucky we are to have Garden Cottage.'

Discussing Garden Cottage's many merits was one of Cecily's favourite conversations.

'And you could spit from here to the school,' said Juliet on one occasion.

Cecily groaned. 'Don't say that. I don't want him to be old enough for school.'

Juliet didn't reply. All of a sudden she couldn't. Her feeling for Constance had subsided to a quiet ache, but there were moments when it swelled to an anguish so intense she couldn't breathe. All she could think was that Constance, five months Archie's senior, would start school when he did, and Juliet hadn't seen her since she was newborn. She couldn't imagine what she looked like now. Or at least, she could imagine, because didn't she gaze at little girls all the time to help her keep pace with her daughter's development? But it wasn't the same as knowing. And she couldn't let go of that painfully precious memory of the tiny baby that would for ever be the only real image in her hungry heart.

Chapter Twenty-Three

The rumour came as a huge shock. The first Juliet knew of it was when two or three of her ladies cancelled appointments. She didn't think anything of it, but then others did the same. No reasons were given, and she was left bemused and anxious.

It was Mrs Palmer who spoke out.

'I shan't require your services after all,' she said in a chilly voice when Juliet went to her grand house off Palatine Road to measure her for a coat. 'I've heard that that young woman who works with you is no better than she should be.'

'Where did you hear that?' Juliet exclaimed.

'From Mrs Baker-Johnson.'

'But didn't she recommend me to you?'

'Indeed, and now she is trying to undo the recommendation.'

'By spreading rumours,' Juliet stated flatly.

'I'm not interested in rumours. I'm interested in the truth. If what I've heard is true, I require you to quit my house immediately. Furthermore, I'll inform other ladies of my acquaintance. So – is it true?'

'No, madam,' Juliet said with quiet dignity.

'Then you'd better set about proving it,' advised Mrs Palmer. 'Otherwise your business will be ruined. When you've proved it, you may return. Until then I don't want to see you – and neither will any lady of quality.'

'But how can we prove it?' Especially since the rumour was true.

'There's a little boy, isn't there? Rumour has it that it says *Father unknown* on the birth certificate.'

She didn't allow so much as a flicker to cross her face. 'Thank you for telling me. Business has dropped off recently, but we'd no idea why.'

Mrs Palmer sniffed. 'Good day, Miss Harper. I shan't see you again unless this unfortunate matter is dealt with to the satisfaction of the ladies who are currently feeling let down and bamboozled by you and your . . . associate.'

'Do you suppose my grandmother is behind it?' Juliet wondered. 'We blamed her for everything else, though we never had a shred of proof. But what could she gain from it? The agreement's over. She can't make me go back.'

'Maybe she thinks you'll end up begging her for a job,' Cecily suggested.

'Never!' said Juliet. 'I'm going to see her.'

On the doorstep in West Didsbury, her heart almost misgave her. She hadn't been here since Adeline had removed her from Mrs Gillespie's. She had an odd, cold feeling that if she crossed the threshold, she might not come out again, but that was plain barmy, so she pulled the bell and tried to quell her suddenly rapid heartbeats.

When she was admitted to her presence, she made a point of

surging in and having the first word, which she was sure would have been Adeline's own tactics.

'There's a rumour that's damaging my business. I think you started it.'

'Good afternoon to you too,' replied Adeline. 'Marching in here, raising your voice. They didn't teach you much about courtesy at that lord's place, did they?'

'Answer the question.'

'You haven't asked one.'

She pressed her lips together. 'Did you start the rumour?'

'A rumour? How intriguing. What's being said? It's difficult to see how it could be worse than the truth.'

'Someone is spreading a rumour that Archie is illegitimate.'

'Archie?'

'You know perfectly well who he is.'

'The slut's brat. Well now, that's an interesting point. Are you correct in calling it a rumour when it's actually true?'

'Did you start it? That's all I want to know. I'm sure you did.'

'If you're sure, why are you asking?'

'I'm sure you've done other things too – those women with false addresses, Mrs Gillespie getting kicked out of her house. You did all that – and more.'

'Did I?' Adeline's eyes gleamed. 'This is becoming more intriguing by the minute. You're dismissing the truth as rumour, and you're making serious accusations with no proof. Your grip on reality leaves something to be desired.'

She fumed. She had come here all het up, ready for a battle royal, and Adeline was making mincemeat of her simply by being her usual patronising self. It was unendurable.

'It so happens my solicitor is in the drawing room,' Adeline continued. 'Would you care to repeat your slander in front of him? It would make things so much more straightforward, should I wish to take you to court.'

Juliet turned on her heel.

'Leaving already? But I'm sure you haven't said half what you came to say. One moment, girl. When your business dries up, and it will, your room will be waiting. I'll give Marjorie instructions.'

Two weeks later, with more cancellations behind them and no work in front of them, Juliet and Cecily were in despair. It looked like the end. It was hard to bear after everything they had been through to get this far.

Mrs Palmer sent a postcard, requesting Juliet to call on her.

'What does she want?' Cecily asked, the gloom in her voice edged with fear.

'She doesn't say. She'll probably ask for Archie's birth certificate.'

Cecily winced and the little vertical frown lines that had gouged their way between her brows in recent weeks deepened, but she held her head up. 'What will you say?'

'I'll say it's beneath our dignity to cave in to the rumour-mongers.'

'I've been thinking. If I were to leave, you could start again.'

'You don't imagine I'd let you take my nephew away, do you? Whatever we do, we'll do it together.'

But Mrs Palmer astonished her by saying, 'Your reputation has been saved, thanks to Mrs Carmichael. She personally visited Mrs Baker-Johnson to set her mind at rest. Shall I stand up to be measured?'

Juliet was so surprised that it took her a moment to twig what Mrs Palmer was saying. 'I haven't brought my work basket.'

'Why else would I send for you? Never mind. I expect one of my staff can produce a tape measure. Ring the bell.'

When she got home with her news, Cecily was as baffled as she was. They couldn't wait till rent day so they could ask Mr Kenyon.

'Mrs Livingston told me, and I told Mrs Carmichael, and she made it her business to look into the matter, her being your landlady. I'll be sure to pass on your appreciation.'

'Please do, Mr Kenyon.'

When he had gone, they looked at one another.

'Well!' said Cecily. 'What an extraordinary person she is.'

'She's obviously decided to take us under her wing. She knows the truth, remember, because Mr Davidson told her.'

'Perhaps something bad happened to her years ago and she knows from personal experience how hard it can be when your reputation is in tatters,' Cecily speculated, 'so now she helps girls like us because she understands.'

Juliet groaned, and chucked a cushion at her. 'Honestly! You sound like a story out of *Vera's Voice*.'

Christmas wasn't long away, and Mrs Palmer required a new gown. There wasn't much time, but Juliet was determined to fulfil the order. Their old customers were sticking their heads over the parapet and they had resolved not to let down a single one, even if they didn't sleep a wink between now and Christmas Eve.

As well as a gown for herself, Mrs Palmer had decided to treat her two married daughters, Mrs Thomas and Mrs Furnivall.

'My husband has met Sir Henry Darley, who recently came into the baronetcy,' Mrs Palmer informed Juliet at the first fitting. 'We'll be among a select few whom he is having to dine at Darley Court in the middle of December, so I'll need this gown for that. Then we're entertaining on Boxing Day, and I hope Sir Henry can be persuaded to join us.'

'That would be a tremendous feather in your cap, Mama,' declared Sally-Ann Thomas with a broad wink at Juliet, which Juliet affected not to notice. Honestly, the familiarity with which some ladies treated their seamstress! And these same ladies would be outraged if the seamstress took the liberty of responding in kind. 'It's a good job Emily and I are married or you'd be lining us up for Sir Henry's inspection.'

'And where would be the harm in that? It would be most agreeable to have a title in the family.'

Sally-Ann shuddered ostentatiously. 'In that case, I'm glad I'm unavailable. That's one family I wouldn't care to marry into. The Darleys are cursed.'

'Cursed?' Liberty or no, Juliet had to ask.

'Yes,' beamed Sally-Ann.

'No,' said Mrs Palmer repressively.

'Only think of it, Mama,' Sally-Ann burbled. 'The last four baronets have all died tragically.'

'No, they haven't. Sir Clement and the boy, I grant you, but not Sir John. You can't call it a tragedy when a soldier dies, and certainly not old Sir Michael. He was ninety if he was a day, and he slipped away in his sleep.'

'Ah, but his tragedy happened long ago, losing his wife and son in childbirth.' Sally-Ann turned to Juliet. 'After Sir Michael, the title went to a nephew or cousin or something, and that was Sir Clement. He died in a motor accident, which was ironic because he was on his way to – or was it from? – a motor show, of all things, down south.'

'Ridiculous,' muttered Mrs Palmer. 'We never had any need in my day for landau shows.'

'So then his young son inherited, only that didn't last five minutes because he was carried off by the scarlet, and after that it was Sir John, who'd been in the army, man and boy, all his life. He was abroad and never once saw Darley Court in all the time he was baronet, poor fellow.'

'You make it sound as though he was baronet for decades,' her mother said drily. 'There can't have been more than three of four years between Sir Clement's death and his.'

'Sir John died at Omdurman two or three months ago,' Sally-Ann finished. Her eyes were sparkling so much that you'd never guess she'd been relating one death after another.

'There.' Juliet stood back. 'Is that comfortable, madam? Then, if you'll kindly hold still a few minutes more, I'll just . . .' She let her words trail away. Her ladies enjoyed being fussed over, but they hadn't the smallest interest in the details.

'Will you invite Flora McKenzie for Boxing Day, Mama?' Sally-Ann asked.

'Certainly not.'

'Oh, but Mama, she's a dear soul and she's having a frightful time.'

'And whose fault is that?'

'Not hers. She's not the one who lost all the money.'

'Lost? Squandered, you mean. Your father said to me time and again that Robert McKenzie was too fond of taking risks, which is all very well for a bachelor with no one to ruin but himself, but not at all the thing for a man with responsibilities. And then,' and here Mrs Palmer's voice dropped, 'to abdicate his responsibilities in such a way.'

'You'd invite Flora if she were a rich widow,' Sally-Ann said accusingly. 'Of course, if she were a *rich* widow, she wouldn't be a widow at all, because if there'd still been money, Robert wouldn't have blown his brains out.'

'That's quite enough, thank you,' Mrs Palmer reprimanded her. 'Flora is a dear girl, and I'll invite her to tea, but I no longer regard her as dinner company. There, Miss Harper, have you finished?'

'Yes, thank you. If we could make an appointment for the final fitting . . . ?'

Juliet headed for home, with Mrs Palmer's gown folded into a vast leather bag she had found at one of the warehouses. Its original use had been to accommodate a gentleman's evening attire when he was away overnight, and it did just as well for her purposes. She also carried her work basket – her very own, the one Mother had given her all those years ago. It had been returned to her, along with her clothes and other bits and pieces, when Mr Winterton had arranged for her to have Mother's money. This was the work basket she took with her to her at-home ladies, while Mother's was used in the sewing room.

In spite of the bulky carrier and work basket, Juliet stopped off at a jeweller's, a little Aladdin's cave containing mostly second-hand stock, where the owner, an elderly man with a quavery voice, had promised to clean a cameo brooch before she purchased it as a Christmas gift for Cecily. The brooch was duly presented for her inspection before it was boxed and wrapped by the old man's middle-aged daughter.

She had been looking for something special to give Cecily. Without her friend's companionship and support, she wouldn't have been half so brave in recent years. Besides, with Cecily happy to be responsible for the domestic side of their lives, she was free to concentrate on the work she loved.

At home, wanting Archie to share the fun, she took him aside while Cecily was getting their tea ready, whispering her plan to him and loving the way he wriggled with excitement at taking part in a secret, but when, with much shushing and giggling, they crept upstairs and she stowed her little parcel in the back of a drawer, Archie was scathing.

'That's not a good hidey-place. I know a good one. I know the best one ever.'

'Show me.'

Archie trotted into his little bedroom, dropped to the floor and started scrambling his way under the bed.

'I'm not hiding it in the chamber pot,' said Juliet.

Archie laughed so hard that she ended up laughing too.

'Shush,' she admonished. 'Mummy will hear. Now where's this hiding place?'

He disappeared beneath the bed. After a moment, she joined him, careful not to bang her head. Archie's little fingers worked away at a piece of skirting board under the head of the bed and it came away.

'There,' Archie said proudly. 'There's a hole.'

'However did you find it?'

'I was exploring.'

'Under the bed?'

'Yes.' He made it sound perfectly reasonable. 'Who put it there?'

'Someone who used to live here, I suppose, someone who liked hiding presents.'

'Will you tell me a story about them?'

'Best wait till after Christmas. We don't want Mummy getting wind of what we've done.'

She gave Archie the important job of putting the little parcel into the hole. Then he clicked the skirting board back into place, and they wriggled out backwards.

'Remember – not a word,' she warned, brushing him down.

They hurried downstairs to find Cecily laying the table.

Archie swaggered in. 'Don't ask me, because I'm not going to tell you.'

'Oh, aren't you?' cried Cecily and pretended to try to tickle it out of him.

'Honestly,' Juliet remarked later, 'I'm surprised we've never had the police round, the way that boy shrieks sometimes. It sounds like blue murder.'

'He's got a good pair of lungs on him,' Cecily said fondly. 'Tell me about today.'

'Sally-Ann Thomas was there.'

'What gossip did she pour forth this time?'

After hamming up the curse of the Darleys, Juliet described Flora McKenzie's difficult situation.

'The husband lost their money and then shot himself?' Cecily repeated. 'Men are such beasts.'

Winter gave way to spring. The front garden provided a pretty pastel display of anemones and primroses, garnering many an approving glance from Juliet's customers. It was a different matter round the back, where they had a big vegetable patch, with shallots and early potatoes already in, the rest of the garden being Archie's playground, complete with a swing hung inexpertly but determinedly by Juliet and Cecily, who had resolved to do the job themselves sooner than ask a man, an attitude that had flummoxed William.

Mrs Palmer summoned Juliet, wanting a new gown for daytime.

'I have just the fabric,' said Juliet, sifting through her samples to produce a damask in blue and gold. 'I suggest a matching bolero jacket, leg-o'-mutton above the elbow and fitted below.' She drew a sketch, but when Mrs Palmer sighed, she said, 'If this isn't to your taste . . .'

'Don't mind me. I shall never be happy with my wardrobe until they bring the bustle back. This is perfect. While I remember, a lady of my acquaintance, a friend of my two girls, wishes to make an appointment with you.'

'I'll be happy to wait on her.'

'No need. She'll come to you. Her name is Mrs Flora McKenzie.'

Oh yes, the lady who was widowed last year in such appalling circumstances.

Mrs McKenzie duly wrote, suggesting two or three dates. That was polite of her. Usually ladies offered a single date and expected Juliet to make herself available. She replied by postcard, and Mrs McKenzie and her maid arrived at the appointed time.

Juliet was sitting at the front window, on the lookout but sewing at the same time so as not to be obvious. A figure appeared at the gate, and she was glancing away politely when her head swung back double-quick and the sewing fell from her fingers.

The sleeve lady.

Flora McKenzie was the sleeve lady from outside Mademoiselle Antoinette's.

Which meant she might possibly . . . she might possibly be Constance's mother.

Chapter Twenty-Four

'I wish to go into half-mourning.' Flora McKenzie was dark and slender with a natural gravity that added to her beauty. She plucked at the band of black crepe round her cuff. 'Horrid stuff.'

'It's not very flattering,' Juliet murmured. The Queen had a lot to answer for. 'I have some lavender.'

'No. Lavender is a happy colour in our family. I won't have it used for . . . this.'

'Mauve, then. I'll use the deepest I have, so it's as far from lavender as possible.'

'Thank you.' Flora indicated the bag her maid had carried. 'I have a gown with me.'

Juliet performed a mental juggling act in which Flora's mourning took priority. 'It'll be ready on Thursday. I'll deliver it.'

'My maid can collect it.'

'It's part of the service. Shall we say two o'clock?'

Nothing was going to stop her getting inside Flora McKenzie's home.

On Wednesday night she lay awake, her mind so active it felt as if an ant colony had taken up residence in her head. She plunged unexpectedly into a deep sleep in which she dreamt she was racing round Mrs Maddox's house, searching for Constance.

The visit to Flora was a colossal let-down, but that was her own fault, because what had she expected? That was an easy question to answer: Constance. She had expected – well, hoped for, longed for – Constance.

'What was the house like?' Cecily asked that evening. Juliet had made no secret of going there, though she hadn't shared her real reason. She had never said a word about what she had seen – or dreamt – at Mrs Maddox's, and the possible connection between Flora and Constance. That was her private piece of madness.

'They have the upstairs of a big house in Fallowfield.'

'I thought they lost all their money?'

'They can't have lost everything.'

'If I lost so-called everything but ended up in a big house, I'd be as happy as a pig in muck. Mr McKenzie must have been soft in the head to do himself in.'

Juliet had come home in a cab with the rest of the mourning, having promised to return it next Tuesday, asking if she could call at half past four, hoping that, so near teatime, the children might be in evidence. The ants were back inside her brain, and not even the news that Mrs Treadgold, one of her at-home ladies, had been burgled could dislodge them.

But Tuesday came and went with no sign of the young McKenzies, not even a half-finished jigsaw on a table providing an excuse to murmur, 'You have children?' Just as well, really. No – it wasn't just as well. Such an impertinence would have been neither here nor there, because she was never going to see Flora McKenzie again. The sewing was finished, and the only way she would see

Flora again was if Flora didn't cough up and she had to march round and demand payment for services rendered.

'And while you're counting the money, Mrs McKenzie, could you please tell me if your youngest is a little girl born in February '94 and adopted through a Mrs Maddox of Freshfield?'

As if. As flaming if.

Juliet continued as normal, but underneath she felt dazed. She could almost wish she had never met Flora – and that was a barefaced lie if ever there was one. In June, she went to measure Sally-Ann Thomas for a tennis costume. She was admitted by Winnie, the parlourmaid, who led her upstairs.

'Madam's got her friend Mrs McKenzie visiting, so you'll need to wait a while.'

Mrs McKenzie! The moment Winnie disappeared, Juliet slipped back down to the hall, lurking by a potted palm, hanky at the ready. A door opened, and Sally-Ann and Flora emerged.

She bent down. 'I dropped my . . .'

Another door opened and a horde of girls came streaming out, different sizes, different ages. Winnie appeared too, with jackets and hats. Juliet seized a straw boater, whereupon an older girl presented herself. She was thirteen or fourteen, her light-brown ponytail tied with green ribbon. Hazel eyes met Juliet's as she smiled and said thank you in a way that suggested no airs and graces.

Flora McKenzie put her hands on the girl's shoulders from behind. 'This is Lily, my eldest.'

'We call her Lily-Lavender,' chimed in another voice, and Juliet regarded a younger girl, ten or so, jamming a coral-pink felt hat onto reddish-brown curls. Her jacket and skirt were coral-pink too and had to be hand-me-downs, for surely no one would put

322

that colour fabric with that colour hair on purpose. 'Lavender's her favourite flower and her favourite colour and her favourite scent and her favourite anything else you can think of.'

'And this little monkey is Frances,' said Flora. 'Don't let the big blue eyes fool you. Come along, girls.'

In the middle of the hall, four girls, who must be Sally-Ann's for the simple reason that they weren't putting hats on, were clustered together, bending over what must be a small child, getting her ready. The blood drained from Juliet's flesh. In a few seconds the bigger girls would step away and she would see – she would see—

Please God, don't let me faint. Every moment of her life since Mrs Maddox had taken her baby had been leading to this. She braced herself for the sledgehammer blow of love.

Sally-Ann's girls scattered, and Juliet felt . . . astonished. That wasn't what she was meant to feel. She was meant to feel . . . recognition – wasn't she? She had assumed her daughter would have her blue eyes and fair hair, yet this child's eyes were brown, and the hair beneath the ribbon-bedecked boater was dark and thick with a wave running through it. And Juliet had always been slender, while this child was a sturdy little thing. Mind you, that box-pleated frock didn't do her any favours. It would turn the most petite tot into a cube.

It wasn't love that shook her to the core, but doubt. Flora's presence at Mrs Maddox's might have been a dream. Even if it wasn't, two babies had been adopted that day. This could be the other.

Except that it couldn't. Not for any sensible reason, but because she had told herself all these years that the sleeve lady had taken Constance. She had thought it so much she had made it real.

Then the child looked straight at her. Brown eyes and a little button nose and a sweet mouth. Her bones turned to wax. She leant against the newel post to stop herself sinking to the floor.

The little girl trotted across. For one insane moment, Juliet thought she must have recognised her real, true mother and was running to her instinctively. She stood straighter, poised to sweep her daughter into her arms.

But the child slipped her hand into her big sister's.

'Time to go home, Izzie,' said Lily.

Izzie? Juliet turned the name over, with a feeling not far from disgust. Isobel? Isabella? Or had she misheard? Was it Lizzie? *Don't you know her name is Constance?* She clamped her mouth tight shut.

The McKenzies were leaving. She had to stop them. She needed more time. She wanted to take Izzie-Lizzie-Constance aside and feast her eyes, and touch her cheek and her hair, and . . . and be her mother.

She went upstairs and measured Sally-Ann for her tennis costume.

'Cecily will be sorry she missed you,' Juliet told William, 'and Archie too, of course.'

William smiled indulgently. 'He's a grand little chap.'

'Not so little any more. He's five next week.'

And Constance – Izzie or Lizzie – would be five years, five months. A month had dragged by since that episode in Sally-Ann's hall, a month during which she had woken every morning, got out of bed, done her work, and gone back to bed at the end of the day and somehow not died of anguish.

She drew a breath, shut her eyes, opened them and smiled. It was the only way.

'Are you coming to the party?' she asked. 'Can you bear the company of six small, overexcited boys?'

'Wouldn't miss it. After Cecily's stuffed them full of paste sandwiches, I'll take them in the back garden and chase them in ever-decreasing circles, then they can go home in time to be copiously sick. I've got it all planned.'

Juliet laughed. 'Archie's lucky to have you.'

'I'd like a couple of lads of my own one day. Now I've been promoted, I can think about settling down.'

'William! How exciting. Do you have a girl in mind?'

'No, but you could help by lining up candidates from among your customers.'

'Speaking of which, Miss Taylor is due in five minutes.'

'Good-o. Is she pretty and likely to be sensible with the housekeeping?'

'Miss Taylor is old enough to be your mother, but I'm sure she'll be glad to know you considered her. Now get gone before she arrives.'

Miss Taylor was accompanied by a dark-haired young woman in her twenties.

'This is my niece, Verity Forbes. She's going to help me choose between the green and the blue you showed me. Verity works, which is why this appointment had to be on a Saturday afternoon.'

'What do you do?' Juliet asked Verity.

'I'm a clerk at Perkins and Watson, the building company on Wilbraham Road.'

'Don't be modest, Verity.' Miss Taylor turned to Juliet. 'She isn't *a* clerk, she's *the* clerk.'

Verity's eyes twinkled. 'Clerk and tea lady.' She was pretty when she smiled. Her sensible brown jacket and skirt, and ivory blouse were suitable for her station, but the hat, with feathers sticking out, added a note of dash.

The blue was duly chosen, and Juliet set about measuring Miss Taylor.

'You get *Vera's Voice*,' Verity observed.

Juliet glanced round, embarrassed that the magazine had been left in the sewing room.

'I get *Story Weekly*,' Verity added. 'Don't pull that face, Auntie Phil. The wind might change.'

'Romantic tripe,' said Miss Taylor.

'If you keep old copies of romantic tripe,' Verity said to Juliet, 'would you like to swap? I could bring mine round next Saturday afternoon.'

Juliet readily agreed. She and Cecily would enjoy having a new friend.

Archie's party was a wild success – 'wild' being the operative word, Cecily thought with an indulgent smile. They had had the usual party games before tea, and now she and Juliet stood at the back door, laughing as William rushed about with the boys, pirates one minute, bears the next, but whatever the game, it inevitably involved a great deal of chasing and catching and swinging about. William had long since shed his jacket. Now he pulled off his tie, shrugged off his waistcoat and unfastened his cufflinks, pushing up his sleeves to reveal unexpectedly strong forearms. Cecily's heart picked up speed. William thrust his waistcoat and tie at Juliet.

'What's wrong?' Juliet mocked. 'Is the pace too much for you?'

William's reply was a grin that transformed his serious face, showing the boyish fun-lover underneath. His hair was mussed. Cecily had an odd desire to muss it some more.

'He's in his element with children, isn't he?' Juliet observed as William dashed back into the fray with a roar that sent little boys squealing in all directions. 'Lucky girl who gets him. He'll make a wonderful dad.'

A good husband too. Kind, generous, good-natured, a good provider. The sort of man who would cherish his family. Why had she never noticed how attractive he was? Cecily's heart skittered sideways. Archie had filled her life to overflowing from the moment he was born. It felt strange to have room suddenly for this new feeling. Exciting, too. She gazed across the garden, her heart yearning towards William. If she caught his eye, would he realise just as she had done? Would his heart start doing funny things, the same as hers?

'Here you are. I hope you don't mind my coming round the side. I knocked but you didn't hear.'

'Welcome to the bear garden,' said Juliet. 'Cecily, this is Miss Taylor's niece, Verity Forbes.'

'Any chance of more lemonade?' William came over, one side of his wing collar askew. A child dangled from under each arm.

Cecily gazed at him, willing him to understand the new consciousness in her smile.

Juliet introduced Verity. 'And this is William Turton, the birthday boy's godfather.'

William dropped the boys, and they scampered away. He stepped forward, then stopped, endeavouring to straighten his appearance.

Verity laughed. 'Don't trouble on my account.'

Cecily willed them to shake hands and get it over with, so she could claim William's attention. But when their hands fell away from one another's, instead of glancing round, William's eyes stayed fixed on Verity's face.

* * *

Soon Verity and William were walking out together. Juliet was pleased for them, but as the weeks went by and an Indian summer gave way to a chilly autumn, Cecily became surprisingly grumpy about it.

'We don't see as much of him. It's to be expected, I suppose. That old saying "A son's a son till he takes a wife" obviously applies to male friends too.'

'You surely don't begrudge him the chance of happiness?' Juliet asked.

'It isn't fair on Archie. William used to come round at least once a week and now – well, when was the last time?'

As Christmas approached, William appeared, seeking advice on a gift for Verity.

'I wondered about a piece of jewellery. Perhaps like the brooch Juliet gave you last Christmas, Cecily.'

'You can't give her jewellery,' said Cecily. 'Not unless – unless you're engaged.'

William flushed. 'We aren't.'

There was a prickly moment, broken when Archie looked up from where he was playing on the rug to announce, 'If you want, Uncle William, I can hide your present in my hidey-place. What are you getting me?'

'Was I horrible?' Cecily asked later.

'You were, a bit. We might see less of him, but he'd never drop Archie.'

'I know.' Cecily groaned. 'I've been a bitch, haven't I?'

'Well . . . you sound jealous of him.'

Cecily looked at her. 'It's not William I'm jealous of. It's Verity.'

'Verity?'

'For pity's sake! Do I have to spell it out?' Cecily fixed her with a look.

She caught her breath. 'Oh, Cecily, you mean . . . ?'

'Yes, I do mean, for all the good it's done me. I've liked him since Archie's birthday party.'

'But that's where they met.'

'Exactly.'

'I had no idea.'

'Good,' Cecily said tartly. 'I don't want him realising. Look, I know I've been crabby. Let's invite them to tea, and I promise to be on my best behaviour.'

Juliet's heart went out to her friend. William had handed himself into Verity's keeping, lock, stock and honourable intentions.

'I never thought there'd be anyone else.' The crispness vanished as Cecily opened her heart. 'I've had eyes for no one but Archie for so long, which was just as well, with me being a pretend widow and him illegitimate. But that's just another thing that makes William perfect. He knows the truth and he's never held it against me. I feel guilty about having feelings for him.'

'Sweetheart.' Juliet reached for her hand. 'Why?'

'Because all his life until now, Archie has been everything to me, and now . . . now he isn't any more.'

'You mustn't blame yourself for that.'

'Can't help it.' Cecily sniffed, giving her shoulders a shake. 'What about you? It's a long time since Hal.'

Responding to Cecily's honesty, Juliet opened up. Painful though it was, it was a relief to speak of it. 'There'll never be anyone else, if that's what you mean. I still have feelings for Hal. I wrote to him, you know, when I was at my grandmother's, but he didn't write back.'

'But you wanted him to.'

'Oh yes, so much. I thought he'd want to come rushing to the rescue, but he didn't, so that's that.'

* * *

William was so obviously delighted when Juliet invited him and Verity to tea that she was heartily relieved she had thought to issue the invitation when Cecily wasn't present, but William came back a day or two later, rather shamefaced, with a refusal.

'Verity would rather not, if you don't mind. She doesn't want us looking official.'

'But you're walking out,' said Juliet.

'Verity thinks once you start visiting folk as a couple, it raises expectations. She doesn't want to feel she's being rushed into anything.'

'That's a fine carry-on!' Cecily exploded the minute William left. 'She has the chance of this thoroughly decent man and she doesn't want to be rushed. Stupid creature! Why is she walking out with him if she doesn't have her eye on getting wed? That's flighty.' She had the grace to look abashed. 'Hark at me sounding all prim and respectable.'

'Pure as the driven slush, eh?' Juliet hugged her. 'That's my girl. Help me get ready for Mrs Baker-Johnson tomorrow.'

Mrs Baker-Johnson wanted a gown for what she grandly called the winter season, including Mrs Palmer's Boxing Day do. Hope immediately leapt inside Juliet – surely Mrs Palmer or one of her daughters . . . But none of them sent for her, so there was no hope of news of Flora McKenzie.

Mrs Baker-Johnson, whose taste ran towards garish colours, was tactfully persuaded into a handsome cream satin to which Juliet added crimson velvet at the neckline, cuffs and hem. She also provided a short matching cape trimmed with sable from a moth-eaten coat that had cost next to nothing, but which contained sufficient good strips to entice the Mrs Baker-Johnsons of this world to splash out on an exotic piece of trim. She imagined the discreet murmurs of, 'Yes, dear, sable, so exquisitely soft to the touch,' as if Mrs Baker-Johnson possessed a whole wardrobe stuffed with fur. It added to Juliet's professional standing to be able to offer these special pieces.

On her way home from her final visit to Mrs Baker-Johnson, she spotted Verity Forbes across the road. Should she? Yes, she crossed over to say how do.

Verity looked embarrassed, then said straight out, 'I hope you didn't mind my refusing your invitation.'

'William explained.'

'No offence intended.'

'None taken,' she lied with a smile.

'It's just that William's so keen—'

Juliet stopped her right there. 'I don't want to discuss him behind his back.'

'Of course not.' Verity eyed the work basket. 'Been out sewing?'

'Delivering. The basket comes in case of last minute alterations.'

'I hope your customer was pleased.'

'She was, thank you, and believe me, Mrs Baker-Johnson would be the first to say if she wasn't.'

'Baker-Johnson? York Road? What a coincidence. A couple of our chaps were there yesterday, doing a repair.'

'I was forgetting you work for a builder.'

'Nasty business. They had burglars.'

'How horrible. I didn't know.'

Going home, she was glad she had made the effort. She felt sorry too, because it had reminded her of her immediate liking for Verity the first time they met, but she couldn't see anything coming of it, not with the way Cecily felt about William.

* * *

Christmas came. Archie was almost hysterical with excitement. With much giggling and shushing, Juliet, Cecily and William dragged a tree inside while Archie was in bed, and decorated it with glass baubles and clip-on candles. Next morning, leaving the curtains closed, the girls lit the candles and watched breathlessly as Archie walked in and stood transfixed, mouth and eyes perfect circles of wonderment.

Juliet thought of Izzie-Lizzie-Constance, and her heart swelled. Izzie-Lizzie-Constance: she had trained herself to call her that, preparing herself for her daughter's different name. Preparing herself. That was a joke. She hadn't heard of the McKenzies in months. January would bring not just a new year but a new century. Was it time to make a fresh start? To put Izzie-Lizzie-Constance behind her?

Oh yes, and how was she supposed to do that? Even supposing she wanted to, which she emphatically didn't. How could she ever turn her back on her child, however hard the circumstances?

Because Hand-finished by Harper formed her one link with Flora and her children, the lack of contact left Juliet with the unsettling feeling that the business wasn't flourishing, which was downright silly when the fruits of success were all around her. They had a woman three mornings a week to do the rough. They had bought a carpet sweeper, though Cecily hadn't trusted it to start with, because it took so much less effort than a beater. They had a canteen of cutlery, and a marble clock that pinged the hour – both second-hand, of course, but in good nick. They had even invested in a shiny brass coal scuttle. It was the first time in their lives – coal scuttles at Moorside didn't count – either of them had ever had a real coal scuttle instead of a bucket. They took turns to polish it, buffing it up with plenty of elbow grease, and graciously accepted compliments from Mrs Livingston on how they were going up in the world.

At long last, the spring brought the summons Juliet had yearned for. Sally-Ann Thomas wanted a costume for bathing.

'And the girls, too, of course. We're taking them to Llandudno at Whitsun,' she said, happy as always to spill information all over the place. 'We're staying at the Imperial. The girls can't wait, and neither can I. My husband says I'm the biggest child in the house.' She gave a gurgle of laughter. 'Mama is outraged that I'm intending to bathe. Well, it's not so much the actual bathing as the wearing of the costume.'

Juliet was going to make the costume, and had selected a pattern with a skirted tunic and a choice of knee- or ankle-length trousers. With a daring twinkle, Sally-Ann chose knee-length. Juliet recommended a simple waist sash, and white braid and lace for trimming, together with a white cap.

'Lots of lace,' Sally-Ann decreed. 'You can never have too much lace.'

Juliet jumped in. 'I remember thinking Mrs McKenzie would suit lace.' She held her breath.

'She isn't Mrs McKenzie any more,' Sally-Ann said. 'She's Lady Darley.'

'Lady Darley? You mean – Sir Henry Darley?'

'The very same, and a pretty one in the eye for my mother that was, I can tell you. Refusing to have poor Flora to dine, because she wasn't quite the thing any more – did you ever hear the like?'

'When was the wedding?'

'Last autumn. They met late summer and married two months later.'

'That was quick – I mean, romantic.'

'Helped along by the real world, I'm afraid. After the burglary, Sir Henry refused to wait a moment longer and had the banns called that same week.'

'He was burgled?'

'No, Flora was, poor love. They took a sapphire ring that belonged to her late mother. She was distraught. Sir Henry, dear man, couldn't whisk her up the aisle fast enough. The two older girls were bridesmaids, and little Izzie carried a basket of flowers.'

Izzie. Not Lizzie. Definitely Izzie. It was like being forbidden to call her Constance ever again.

'She looked adorable,' Sally-Ann went on. 'Well, they all did, such pretty girls, and all so different.'

Three girls, all different – because they had different parents? If Izzie was adopted, why not the other two? If the girls were adopted, might Sally-Ann be aware of it? Was there a tactful way . . . ?

But it was too late.

'Not like my girls, peas in a pod . . .' And Sally-Ann burbled on about them for the rest of the session. Deborah's piano lessons were pure torture for everyone; and Grace was coming up sixteen now, imagine that, and they had got her a gold locket for her birthday, which was a kind of tradition, because her parents had given her and Emily gold lockets on their sixteenth birthdays; and Laurel had won the school prize for handwriting, which must mean she had inherited her handwriting from her papa, because Sally-Ann's was appalling; and Maudie . . .

Juliet made the bathing costumes in double-quick time, adding lashings of lace. She spent every waking moment devising subtle ways of bringing Flora and her daughters into the conversation, but when she went to deliver the costumes, she didn't get over the threshold.

'If Mrs Thomas is indisposed . . .'

'Not unless sobbing yourself into a frenzy counts.' Winnie dropped her voice and whispered dramatically, 'We've had burglars. Some of Madam's jewellery got took: her pearls and a gold locket and, such a shame, a matching locket that was for Miss Grace's birthday.'

'I'm sorry to hear it. I'll make another appointment when things have died down.'

'No need.' Winnie twitched the parcel from her hands. 'She can send for you if owt wants doing.'

And that was that. No more hope of access to Izzie.

Chapter Twenty-Five

A fortnight later, the miracle happened. That was how it felt – a miracle. Lady Darley, Flora McKenzie-as-was, sent a postcard, requesting Juliet come to Darley Court.

'Just like your mum,' Cecily declared, 'dressing a real lady.'

On the day, she sent Juliet on her way with a goodbye hug.

Juliet walked past Hardy Farm, which was as far as she had come in this direction before, and came to the walls of the Darley grounds, like the walls round the parkland at Moorside, only these walls were brick and his lordship's had been stone. That wasn't the only difference. You couldn't see Moorside from his lordship's front gates, but you could see Darley Court. It was nothing like as massive as Moorside, but it did have something Moorside didn't. She didn't know the right word, something French, but it was like a huge covered porch for a carriage to drive under so the ladies and gentlemen didn't get rained on when they descended from the vehicle.

Her daughter lived here. Constance Mary Harper of Darley Court. It was too much to hope that the girls would be present, though that hadn't stopped her hoping every step of the way. She was shown into what she supposed from her skimpy knowledge of Lady Margaret was the morning room, a pleasant room with pale-green walls and that fancy plaster stuff that rich folk had round the tops of their walls. The chimney piece was white marble, and the soft furnishings were green and fawn and dusty pinks, so that even though the furniture was mostly of dark wood, the overall impression was of lightness.

And there was Lady Darley, looking every inch like Flora McKenzie, except for being better dressed. In that moment, Juliet knew she wasn't here to make something for her ladyship. Lady Darley would patronise a smart salon in town, possibly even Mademoiselle Antoinette's. Flora McKenzie had been smart enough in the remnants of her former finery, but Lady Darley, in her morning gown of soft blue with its crossover bodice, was the last word in elegance.

'Miss Harper, how good of you to come.'

Her manner was elegant too. Flora had been civil – more than civil, Juliet thought, remembering the loving laughter with which she had introduced her daughters. But it was appropriate that a baronet's lady should exercise more restraint, especially when dealing with the lower orders.

'I'd like you to make a couple of dresses for my eldest daughter.'

'Lily,' said Juliet. To Flora, she might have chanced saying, 'Lily-Lavender,' but not to Lady Darley.

'You remember,' Lady Darley said, smiling. 'I'd like her to have some new things, but she isn't old enough to be taken to a salon.' A pause, then she said delicately, 'I want her to have new clothes, you understand. I know most of your work involves making over existing garments, and I deplore waste as much as anyone, but I want Lily to have something brand new and special. I hope . . . I hope it might cheer her up.'

'I can easily sketch a few ideas for you. Perhaps if I could measure Miss Lily . . . ?'

'She's supposed to be here.'

Lady Darley tugged the bell, said Miss Lily was to go to her room to be measured, then led Juliet up a grand staircase. Lily's room was formally furnished but with pretty touches, as befitted a privileged young lady: an embroidered silk coverlet on the bed, a basketwork chair with a chintz-covered cushion, white muslin drapes hanging from the half-tester and caught up by bows of lavender satin.

While they waited, Lady Darley looked from the window. 'My husband is having redesigning work done on the grounds.'

Juliet joined her. She couldn't see anything wrong with the gardens. More money than sense, some folk.

'He's having renovation work done too. Over that way – you can't see it from the house – is the old folly, a circular building, and you can go upstairs and step outside and walk all round. When you leave, I'll have you shown out of a side door. Follow that path – see? – and once you get past the laurel ledge, the folly will be in sight. Beyond it is a gate you can use. Much quicker for you than walking down the drive.'

'Thank you. The folly sounds interesting.'

'Not really. There's a ditch all round that needs draining and filling in, with a ramshackle little footbridge that needs replacing. And when you're up on the terrace, the parapet is way too low. I've told my daughters they're not permitted anywhere near the folly until the parapet is made bigger – where's Lily?'

She rang the bell and gave orders for Miss Lily to come

immediately. When Lily came, which wasn't as immediately as all that, she slouched in, head down, not meeting eyes. Where was the pretty, smiling girl from last year?

Lily submitted to being measured, but barely looked at Juliet's swift sketches. Eventually her mother excused her.

'I apologise for my daughter. I don't know what's got into her.' Suddenly Lady Darley was swept away by the power of Flora's anxiety. 'She used to be such a sweet, happy girl, but in recent months she's become . . . sullen, that's the only word for it. When my husband is present, she behaves better, though she's quiet. But when it's just her and me – well, you see the kind of behaviour I'm treated to.' She blinked over-bright eyes. 'I worry that . . . that she feels I've remarried too soon.'

'What does Sir Henry say?'

'I haven't told him.' A sigh. 'I can't bear to spoil things. He's been so good.'

Juliet put her heart and soul into Lily's dresses. She visited Darley Court three times more, to show fabric samples, to perform the first fitting, then to deliver the dresses.

In her room, Lily tried them on, then escaped.

'As you can see, things haven't improved,' Lady Darley said. 'Thank heaven my other two are still the children they were.' She smiled. 'I feel I ought to show them to you so you can see.'

Please do! Eager to prolong her visit, she remarked, 'Miss Lily said thank you this time without being prompted.'

'Unlike last time. I do so hope she'll grow out of it. Sir Henry would be deeply upset if he knew. Why, only yesterday he gave her the most thoughtful, personal gift. He thinks the world of her – of all three of them. I'm so fortunate.'

'What was it, if I might ask?'

'Do you remember Frances saying how Lily's favourite—what is it, Banks?'

'Sir Henry has come home, m'lady. You wished to be told.'

'Thank you.' She turned to Juliet. 'I must go. Banks will see you out.'

Juliet got ready to leave, then followed the lady's maid along the corridor, but as they turned the corner onto the main landing, Banks stopped, and Juliet realised there were voices below. Lady Darley had run downstairs to greet her husband. Juliet couldn't resist craning her neck to peep. Cecily would never forgive her if she went home without the baronet's description.

Her mouth slackened and heat filled her face. It was a struggle to breathe. She needed him to stand there, so she could look and look.

Lady Darley disappeared arm in arm with Mr Nugent.

Juliet trailed home, feeling she was part of a distant dream. Mr Nugent – here. It had been common knowledge back at Moorside that he was from a titled family and if enough people died, he would be a lord or a sir or something. Well, those people had died, but not for one moment, as she had lapped up Sally-Ann's eager ramblings, had she imagined . . .

As she trudged alongside the churchyard wall, with Chorlton Green coming into view, she pulled herself together. She had never breathed a word of how Mr Nugent had interfered with her and now, for Cecily's benefit, she had to make his step up in the world sound like a delicious piece of gossip. She felt sick.

As she rounded the corner, neighbours were clustered outside Garden Cottage. A constable stood at the gate. She raced across.

'Now then, miss,' said the bobby.

'I live here.'

'Are you Miss Harper? You'd best go in.'

The door opened before she reached it, and Cecily ran into her arms.

'The police are searching the house. They've even been down the garden and searched the privy. They won't say what they're looking for.'

Panic surged. 'Where's Archie?'

'Mrs Livingston took him home with her.'

'Miss Juliet Harper?' A man appeared on the step. He was wearing a coat and hat, not a uniform.

'I'll come indoors,' she said.

'No need. I'm Inspector Crawley and I'd rather you accompanied me to the police station.'

An odd noise blurted from her mouth as all her questions tried to burst forth simultaneously. She managed to ask, 'What's happening?'

'I think you know the answer to that, miss. Now, if you don't mind . . .'

She was ushered from the garden. The neighbours fell back to let her by, her skin prickling under their collective gaze. At the further end of the Green, Inspector Crawley steered her onto Beech Road and headed for the police station, where she was taken into a cramped room, bare except for a table with a chair on each side.

'Sit down, Miss Harper. Now then . . .'

She was asked to confirm her name and address, which seemed stupid when he knew them. Then he asked questions about her work. They were easy to answer, but it was unsettling and confusing not knowing the reason behind the questions. Inspector Crawley made her explain the difference between the Garden Cottage customers and her at-home ladies.

'Who are they, these ladies whose houses you visit?'

She rattled off a list, at the end of which Inspector Crawley left a long silence. She fought not to fidget.

'You missed out Mrs Baker-Johnson.'

'Oh – I forgot.'

'Most convenient. Also Mrs Treadgold.'

'I haven't seen her in ages. I went to her house just the once.'

'Just once? You said you visit these ladies several times. You discuss their requirements and – ahem – measure them, then there's trying on and—'

'I meant, I made only one garment for her, but that involved the usual visits. Inspector, please tell me what this is about. I'm sure I could be of far more help if—'

'What do you know about a locket belonging to Mrs Thomas?'

'Her parents gave it to her for her sixteenth birthday. Pure gold.' He gazed at her expectantly, which somehow forced her to add, 'She had a gold locket ready for her daughter's sixteenth birthday, only . . .'

'Only it was stolen, along with Mrs Thomas's. Then there's Mrs McKenzie, Lady Darley as she is now.'

'The sapphire ring.'

'The sapphire ring. It's worth a mint.' He leant forward. His skin was pockmarked. 'Why don't you save us all a lot of time by telling me where it is. It'll go against you if my men find it first.'

Cold washed through her. 'You mean – you think . . . ?'

'When my men find your horde, I'll have all the proof I need. The only thing we don't know is whether you committed the thefts yourself or if you had an accomplice.'

'But I didn't—'

'You've been clever, I'll grant you that, changing from one

342

method to another. You didn't steal from Mrs Treadgold or Mrs McKenzie until long after you worked for them, but you stole from Mrs Thomas and Mrs Baker-Johnson in the middle of making their clothes. And you bided your time between thefts. But in the end, you were the only thing that linked all four ladies. It was Mrs Thomas who made me realise. Normally, I deal only with the head of the household, but Mrs Thomas would have her say, and a jolly long say it was. It was when she said "Just like dear Flora" that things fell into place.'

She found the strength to fight back. 'I was with Lady Darley not three hours since—'

'Lady Darley is unaware of today's developments. I'll call on Sir Henry later, after you've been formally charged. Where were you on the following dates?'

Dates and times were barked at her until her head span. She was ready to weep when the door opened, and a copper looked in. Inspector Crawley got up reluctantly. There was a murmured exchange, followed by a dark silence.

Inspector Crawley came back. 'You're free to go – for now. My men didn't find anything at your address.'

'That's because there was nothing to find.'

'This doesn't mean you're off the hook. I'll have you in the end.'

Juliet stumbled home, so exhausted her vision was blurred. No, not from exhaustion, a mist of tears. She tried to mop up before she arrived, but it was no use. She ended up sobbing in Cecily's arms, even though Archie was hovering close by.

With an effort, she stemmed the flow and disengaged herself from Cecily. 'Silly Auntie Juley. It's nothing to worry about, Archie. I'm upset because people I know have lost some precious things and not even the police can find them.'

'Precious things? You mean . . . jewels?' Archie's face lit up. 'They're not lost. They're in my hidey-place.'

Cecily was so fraught after the day's upsets that it was all she could do not to smother Archie in hugs while he explained about playing marbles in Auntie Juley's bedroom when a marble rolled beneath the hanging cupboard. Attempting to fish it out with a stick, he had flicked out a little bag, which proved to contain jewellery, which he had taken great delight in hiding.

'Thank goodness he did,' Juliet breathed, 'or I'd now be locked in a cell.'

They stayed up talking in whispers long into the night. What else was there to do but return the stolen jewels to Archie's hidey-place? But it went sorely against the grain with Cecily.

'I don't like thinking he knows where they are.' Worry squirmed inside her.

'I agree, but it's the safest place.'

'We could take them onto the meadows and chuck 'em into the Mersey.'

But Juliet shook her head. 'We ought to return the jewellery to its owners.'

'And how will we do that?'

'I don't know.'

They talked in circles about how the jewellery could have got into Garden Cottage.

'The Thomas burglary was back in March,' Juliet remembered. 'Who's been here since then?'

Their customers were easily eliminated, because none had been left on her own.

'That leaves Mrs Livingston,' said Cecily. They looked at one another and shook their heads.

'Who would want to make me appear a thief?' said Juliet.

'And how did they get into the cottage?'

'A break-in,' Juliet suggested.

'Without leaving a trace?'

'Forget *how*,' said Juliet. 'Let's concentrate on *who*. The only person who's ever—'

'Mrs Tewson,' Cecily finished. 'But there was never any proof.'

'Even so—'

'Why would she? She wants you to work for her, not go to prison.'

'Maybe to punish me because I haven't given in. But it's difficult to believe she'd go that far.'

The question whirled around in Cecily's head, adding to her worries. Because if Mrs Tewson wasn't responsible, who was?

Juliet was still awake as the dawn chorus began. When her head wasn't full of Adeline's possible involvement, she was wondering if Inspector Crawley had called at Darley Court. That reminded her she hadn't mentioned the new baronet's identity to Cecily. She must tell her at breakfast.

Cecily's eyebrows shot up in surprise, but to Juliet's profound relief, her friend had too much on her mind to dwell on it for long.

Sunday, the day she could be sure of finding Adeline at home, saw Juliet in West Didsbury, where Marjorie left her standing on the step, eventually returning to report, 'Madam is not at home.'

The lid popped off her annoyance and she barged in. Marjorie tried to overtake, but she got to the morning room first – and there was Adeline. Surprise, surprise.

'I need you to answer a question,' said Juliet. 'Are you responsible for making me appear a thief?'

'This has a depressingly familiar ring. Didn't you throw accusations around last time you were here? The difference is that on that occasion, you at least waited to be invited in. Blood will out, I suppose. You are, after all, a labourer's daughter.'

'Insults won't distract me.'

'How noble.'

'If my name isn't cleared, I'll tell the police you bear me a grudge.'

'Nonsense. It's well known how I've helped you. I cleaned up the mess when you got into trouble. I gave you a job and a home, and even after you ran away, I took it upon myself to guide you, along with those highly respectable gentlemen, Mr Winterton and Mr Davidson.'

'You've done everything you can to make my business collapse.'

'There you go again, making unfounded accusations.'

'You won't be satisfied until I'm designing for you.'

'Your modest success making over old clothes for the middle classes has gone to your head. It may be true that I was once prepared to nurture your talent, but no longer. I am satisfied with my new designer – well, she's hardly new these days. I took her on shortly after your last visit. I expect you've heard of her. She was employed for a number of years by Mademoiselle Antoinette.'

'Miss Alexandrina?' Juliet's voice was a squeak of surprise.

'Or Dora Holroyd, as I prefer to call her.' Adeline smiled unpleasantly. 'Clara is livid.'

'I can't get over the thought of my grandmother employing someone from Mademoiselle Antoinette's,' Juliet said to Cecily. 'What a feather in her cap.'

'What made Miss Alexandrina change allegiance?' Cecily asked.

'Money? Surely she couldn't have been fed up of designing beautiful, expensive gowns.'

'Perhaps it was something as mundane as convenience,' Cecily said drily. 'Miss Alexandrina might sound as though she lives next door but one to Buckingham Palace, but Dora Holroyd could easily live within spitting distance of Tewson's Textiles.'

If Adeline truly had given up on her, that was something to be glad of, but Juliet didn't feel glad. She felt more worried than ever. Could she have an unknown enemy? It was a frightening thought.

They were discussing it when there was a knock at the door, and there was Verity Forbes with some magazines rolled under her arm.

'I wondered if you'd like to do another swap?'

'Cecily,' Juliet called over her shoulder, 'it's Verity Forbes.' To Verity, she said, 'Come in.'

After some small talk, Verity said, evidently delivering a rehearsed speech, 'I know there's been awkwardness because of William and me, but I'd like us to be friends.'

'We invited you to tea,' Cecily pointed out.

'The pair of us, yes, but I don't want to be seen simply as William's other half.'

Cecily muttered something and hurried out.

'Is she all right?' Verity asked.

'She's got something in the oven.'

'Suppose William hadn't been here that day I came round last summer,' said Verity. 'We'd have been friends, wouldn't we? I think we'd have been good friends.'

Honesty compelled Juliet to nod.

'Can't we be friends even though I'm seeing him? What difference does it make?'

'It isn't because you're seeing him. It's because . . .'

'Because I haven't thrown myself at him the way he'd like me to? Not to mention the way my mother wants me to. I love my job – you of all people must understand that. I like my independence; I like having my own money, even if it isn't much. I don't want to settle down and be a housewife yet.' She smiled ruefully. 'You'd understand better if you weren't so fond of him, but you're old friends, so you want him to have what he wants.'

'We worry that you're keeping him dangling.'

'And I worry about being persuaded into something I'm not ready for.' Verity sighed. 'I'd best go.' At the door, she stopped. 'I admire what you've achieved here.'

'Thank you.'

'I wonder how easy you'd find it if you had to give it up.'

Cecily came creeping out. 'Has she gone?'

'Did you hear?'

'Every word.'

'Are you all right?'

'No, but I will be.' Cecily released a long breath. 'You'd think you'd get used to it, wouldn't you? You'd think it wouldn't hurt so much, but it does.'

Who should turn up but William, so full of concern that he pulled Juliet to him in a huge hug and kissed the top of her head. She felt hideously uncomfortable. Poor Cecily, how wretched for her to have to witness William spontaneously holding someone else. She gently freed herself, not wanting to hurt William's feelings either.

'I've just heard about the search,' William said. 'Mr Winterton is friends with a local superintendent, name of Grant. Grant knows Juliet used to be a sort of protégée of Mr Winterton, so he told him

348

about the suspicions against you. This was at a dinner last night. Mr Winterton sent for me today to find out what I knew. You could have knocked me down with a feather.'

Cecily described the arrival of the police and how they had gone all over the cottage, poking about in every cupboard and drawer. 'They even rummaged about up the chimney.' She shuddered. 'The place hasn't felt the same since.'

Juliet related what had happened at the police station, surprised to find her hands trembling. William knelt in front of her, taking one of them and thrusting his handkerchief into the other.

'Have a good cry if you need to. I'd be bawling my eyes out if it was me.'

Using the pretence of dabbing her eyes, she moved away.

'Can you do anything?' Cecily asked.

'I wish I could.' William raked fingers through his hair. 'This Crawley fellow must have felt pretty sure of himself to haul Juliet off to the police station like that.' He took out his pocketbook. 'Here, take one of my cards. You too, Cecily. If anything else happens – anything – insist that I'm sent for. I'll see you get proper representation.'

Bless him, he was offering the best support he could, but the principal effect was to make Juliet feel churned up all over again. She spent another sleepless night, tormented by worry. If not Adeline, then who was responsible?

Someone had hidden jewellery inside Garden Cottage – but how? How do you enter a locked house without leaving a trace? She sat bolt upright. You use a key. Who had keys? She and Cecily, no one else. Wait – Mrs Carmichael, the owner. Someone must have stolen her key. Juliet frowned. This someone had gone to a frightening amount of trouble.

Tomorrow was rent day. Juliet decided to write a letter and ask Mr Kenyon to deliver it. No – it would be agony waiting for a reply. Better to see Mrs Carmichael immediately. But if she asked Mr Kenyon to arrange an appointment, how long would that take? There was only one thing for it. She would follow him.

Mr Kenyon called at Garden Cottage early the following afternoon, as usual. Juliet was already loitering across the Green. She spent the next two hours following at a discreet distance. When he boarded an omnibus, she leapt aboard at the last moment, praying he was delivering the rents to Mrs Carmichael personally and not to an office.

He alighted near Alexandra Park, and presently she found herself at the foot of half a dozen steps leading to a front door. Mounting the steps, she raised the gleaming knocker.

'Good afternoon. May I see Mrs Carmichael, please? My name is Juliet Harper and I'm one of her tenants.'

After a delay, she was ushered into a room. Mrs Carmichael was on her feet, facing the door.

Mrs Carmichael. Mrs Rosemary Carmichael.

Older, thinner in the face, but instantly recognisable.

Juliet whispered, 'Rosie . . .'

Oh, dear God, Rosie.

Chapter Twenty-Six

'You're cleverer than you used to be, finding me like this. The po-faced bitch I remember wouldn't have had the brains, let alone the guts.' Rosie's smile fused contempt with amusement. 'Look at your face. I can hear Mrs Whicker saying, "Don't gawp, girl". It's not often you see a full-blown gawp like that. By,' and she put on a broad Lancashire accent, 'I'd say thee were reet short o' nous, lass. Do you understand or should I translate? You and your mother always fancied yourselves a cut above.'

'Rosie—'

'Wait a moment. You didn't know, did you? You came here not knowing you were going to find me. So, actually, you're as dim as ever you were. Still, you're here now. I suppose I should ask how and why.'

'I came for help.' Unbelievable as it seemed now.

'Help you? That's rich.'

'You helped before. I mean, Mrs Carmichael helped.'

Rosie's satisfied expression took Juliet back years. She was a young girl again, frightened of the beautiful bully. It was extraordinary how it rushed back.

'Such a good, generous person, Mrs Carmichael,' Rosie remarked.

'She – you gave us somewhere to live. You knew who we were, didn't you? You knew all along.'

'Thanks to good old Roly Davidson. That's Mr Davidson to you.'

'Mr Davidson! He called you a slight acquaintance.'

'How discreet, but we've been more than that in our time.' Rosie tossed her head, just like she used to. Her hair was as dark and luxuriant as ever. Scooped away from her face and worn high, it boasted a fullness of shape that most women achieved only by using pads. 'He told me how he'd been dragged into a confounded arrangement to oversee a foolish girl's attempts to be independent. Just think – if he hadn't been vexed – if he hadn't mentioned your name . . . but he did. I couldn't believe my ears – or my luck.'

'You gave us a home to keep watch on us. Were you the one who put all those difficulties in our way? The market traders who stopped dealing with me, the women who didn't pay . . .'

'Stop whining. You coped, didn't you?'

'So it was you.'

'Don't be stupid. It was Mrs Tewson who tried to destroy you, but each obstacle merely made you more determined, which suited my purposes. I stepped in only when that whispering campaign looked like getting out of hand.'

How grateful they had been. 'You wanted me to succeed?'

'There's no point in bringing someone down if they haven't climbed up.' Rosie looked at her, sly and assessing. Waiting.

Then she understood. 'You organised it. You made me look like a thief. You arranged for the jewellery to be hidden for the police to find.' Her thoughts leapt ahead, slotting things into place, while her feelings stumbled behind, trying to take it all in and accept it. 'You organised the burglaries too. You made me look like a thief.'

'Except I didn't, did I? The police should have found the jewellery. What have you done with it?'

'You don't imagine I'm going to tell you?'

'How prudish, positively virginal. But then you always were a prig, weren't you?'

'Well, I was certainly a virgin.' The air snapped with tension, with injury and old hatreds, never forgotten. She stood straighter. '. . . until you sent that man to attack me.'

'My brother. He did a good job, didn't he? And you deserved it. I was attacked by a bloke with a grudge against my brother, and you helped him do it—'

'I did no such thing—'

'So I made sure the same happened to you.'

Dear heaven. Rosie's brother had angered another man to the point where the man took his brutal revenge on Rosie, and Rosie then engineered the same fate for Juliet, who had made an honest, if calamitous, mistake. What kind of family did Rosie come from?

'Bring her down: those were the instructions I gave my brother. Bring the bitch down. I was angry with him for cosying up to Cecily, but it meant he could go back later to ask what had become of you. Good old man-mad Cecily.' Rosie's eyes gleamed. 'I know Gideon foisted a brat on you, but is he a daddy twice over? That boy of Cecily's – is he the father?'

'No.'

'Shame. The timing's right.' Rosie smiled. Amused? Disbelieving? Playing games?

Don't get drawn in. 'And to think I came here for help.'

'Yes, let's think about that, shall we?' Rosie's eyes flashed immediately. 'You got me into the worst situation of my life. Then it turned out I was up the stick and it was only a matter of time before I got slung out. Does it please you to know that my insides are so messed up I can never have another child?'

'I'm truly sorry to hear that.'

'And the Home for Orphaned Daughters wouldn't keep our Hannah once they were informed of my disgrace, so she was sent to the workhouse. I tried getting her out, but they said I was a bad example. They said that for the good of her morals, they were putting her to work in their laundry instead of making her available for positions that came up on the outside. You know what that meant, don't you? Once you have a job in the workhouse, you can never leave unless someone respectable claims you. From that moment, that was what I wanted. It was my fault she was in there. I should have run away the moment I knew I was pregnant and taken her with me, but I didn't do anything. I could hardly string two thoughts together. I've regretted that ever since. My brother gave me a good hiding for it, too, when I came to Manchester to find him.'

'Your brother . . .' Juliet swallowed.

'The one and only.'

'Didn't he have a job? Couldn't he have got Hannah released?' Released? That made her sound like a prisoner, but then, you were, really, once the workhouse had you.

'Haven't you been listening? The workhouse wanted someone respectable, a pillar of the community, and Gideon was never that. He lives by his wits, and yes, that's a polite way of saying he makes money, or takes it, any way that suits. But I wanted property.

354

Property is respectable – and it had to be my property, not Gideon's. Property means staying in one place, and he'd never do that. So I needed money and I earned it by going with men. Are you shocked? Or do you think that, after what happened in the shrubbery, it couldn't make any difference? I tell you this,' and Rosie dropped her voice to a hiss, 'it made it a hundred times harder. I had one rule: I wouldn't do it flat on my back. I had to be on top – don't look away. Don't you dare turn away from me. If I want you to hear these things, you'll bloody well listen, do you understand?'

Part of Juliet wanted to march out of the house and slam the door, show Rosie she couldn't be bossed, but Rosie's tale had her hooked.

'Gideon was in with a gambling circle, which included professional gentlemen, and he made the necessary introductions. As soon as I could, I bought a tumbledown place on the edge of a slum. Gideon booted out the tenants – immigrant scum, weeks behind with the rent – and I had the place deloused and distempered, filled it with factory families, and put every penny of rent towards buying the next place. And that was how it started.'

'What about your brother?' The question drained all moisture from her mouth. 'Where is he now?'

Rosie shrugged. 'Gone his own sweet way. As I began to gain my place in the world, he didn't like playing second fiddle.'

'Did you rescue Hannah?'

'Don't you have any idea how long it took? It was two years before I got that first house, and another year before I got the next, but Hannah had got a good position, so I knew she'd be all right. Eventually I started buying better properties, and that was when Mrs Carmichael was born. I'm a respectable businesswoman now. I rub shoulders with important people, and I've rubbed more than that with some of them in the past. You'd do well to remember that.'

The door opened. 'Mummy! Mummy!' A little girl, about the same age as Archie, ran in. At the sight of Juliet, she stopped and clapped her hand over her mouth. The gesture was so comical that Juliet couldn't help smiling. She was a dear little thing, all ringlets and ribbons and jammy smears.

'Not now, Abby.' Rosie's voice contained not one shred of sharpness. Juliet had never heard Rosie sound kind before. 'We'll have a story presently.'

The child nodded, and ringlets bounced. She skipped away, bursting into song the moment she was through the door.

'She's adorable,' said Juliet. 'Abby? Short for Abigail?'

'Leave my daughter out of this.' Rosie's voice had hardened again, her brown eyes so dark they were practically black.

'If you wanted to keep her safe, you should have thought of that before you organised those thefts and tried to blame them on me. I'm going to the police.'

'Feel free. Accusing your highly respectable landlady will give them a good laugh.'

'You won't get away with this.'

'Now then, don't let's descend into melodrama.'

'You put me under suspicion of theft.'

'You got off lightly. You were supposed to rot in prison. You still could, if the police return and find the jewellery. I'll await developments with interest. Now get out of my house.'

Juliet hated to feel beaten. She turned to go, but as she reached the door, Rosie spoke again.

'It all started with you wanting a maiding position.'

'I didn't—'

'You were so determined to get what was Hannah's by rights. But she won in the end. That post she was allowed to leave the workhouse for? Remember the job you got at Mr Nugent's, the one you never went to? Hannah got it, and quite right too.'

'Where have you been? I've kept your meal warm,' Cecily fussed as Juliet opened the front door. 'William's here. He came straight from work. He brought a wooden train for Archie.'

'How kind.'

'He's a kind person. You had a card by the teatime post. It's on the mantelshelf.'

William rose as Juliet entered. 'Cecily says nothing more has happened. That's good.'

'Mrs McLoughlin cried off her appointment this morning,' said Cecily.

'I meant, nothing more with the police. It's rotten about the customer, but you said she lives near the Green, so it's inevitable she knows about the search. It'd be more damaging if she lived a couple of miles away and she'd heard.'

'Read the postcard,' said Cecily. 'Lady Darley wants you. Isn't it wonderful? I rather think the larder and pantry are running low, so I'll do the rounds of the shops tomorrow, including the greengrocer's where Mrs McLoughlin's daughter works, and you know what a gossip I am: I just won't be able to keep my mouth shut about all we've done for Lady Darley and how she personally writes you postcards when she wants you. If Mrs McLoughlin doesn't come crawling back, I'll eat my hat. In fact, I'll stop her in the street and eat *her* hat.'

William laughed. 'That I'd like to see. I'll be off now, but I'll drop in tomorrow. I don't want you facing this alone.'

'Come and eat with us,' Cecily insisted. As the door shut behind him, she sighed. 'Don't worry – I'm not getting ideas.'

'I believe you. Thousands wouldn't.'

Later, when Archie was asleep, Juliet told Cecily about following Mr Kenyon. 'And you'll never guess who Mrs Carmichael is: Rosie.'

'Rosie?' It took a moment. '*Rosie*? *Our* Rosie? Rosie from Moorside?'

'I threatened her with the police, but I'm sure there's nothing to connect her with the burglaries, and she probably has a dozen lackeys who'll swear blind her Garden Cottage key never moved from its place.'

'We must get rid of the jewellery.'

'No. That really would make us criminals.'

'What will she do next?' Cecily asked.

'Hard to say. Possibly nothing. It didn't sound like she tipped off the police to come here. In fact, Inspector Crawley told me he was the one to put two and two together.'

'It might have taken months for the police to make the link to you, and Rosie was just going to sit and wait.'

Juliet felt shivery. 'Let's give notice and find somewhere else to live.'

'Not with what's hidden upstairs. Besides, a new landlord would make enquiries and hear about the police coming after us.'

'So we're stuck here.'

That in itself was a victory for Rosie.

Juliet slipped through the gate behind the run-down old folly, glad she had permission to use this shortcut.

What would be required of her today? More dresses for the ungrateful Lily? But it was costumes for bathing.

'Normally, I order my garments from a salon in town,' her ladyship explained, 'but not something like this.'

'It so happens I made some costumes recently.'

'For Mrs Thomas and her girls. That's why I sent for you. We're taking our holiday together. It turns out that Whitsun is a bad time for Mr Thomas to be away from the office, so Mrs Thomas suggested she and I take our girls and go together.' She dropped her voice. 'I'm hoping it might perk Lily up, poor love. A change of air, you know.'

Juliet would dearly have loved to encourage more details, but what if her ladyship regretted speaking freely and never employed her again?

'I'll sketch the costume, shall I?' It took just a few pencil strokes. 'There's a choice of length, knee or ankle.'

'Ankle, definitely, and the same for the girls.'

She had to clear her throat before she could ask, 'Are the young ladies available for measuring today?'

Five minutes later, she was upstairs with Frances and Izzie. Her heart drummed in her chest. Izzie!

'Me first, if Lily's not here,' Frances announced. 'It's troublesome being the middle one. You never go first and you don't get fussed over.'

'Life is hard,' Lady Darley said drily, but Juliet caught the underlining note of indulgence.

It was difficult to concentrate on Frances's measurements with Izzie so near. 'Your turn now, missy.' She tried to hide her feelings beneath a false joviality. She was touching her daughter, actually touching her. This was what she felt like, warm and firm. She smelt of soap and honey. She should never have let her go. Trying to drag her composure into position, she said, 'I'll need Miss Lily too.'

'She said you've got her measurements,' Frances replied.

'I need to measure her for trousers.'

'Trousers!' Frances crowed. 'We're having trousers! Does Lily know, Mummy? I'll fetch her.'

Izzie kept looking down to see what Juliet was doing.

'Stand up straight, chick. There's a good girl.'

She gently lifted the child's chin. The touch of Izzie's face left a tingle in her fingers. She went back to work with the tape measure, only to find Izzie peering down again, craning her neck in an effort not to bend her back.

Juliet laughed. 'Standing up straight means not looking down.' She heard the indulgence in her voice. What a terrible mother she would have made. She would have spoilt her rotten.

Frances bounced in, towing Lily.

'There you are.' Lady Darley smiled encouragingly.

'We're having *trousers*, Lily-Lavender,' Frances announced.

'I've told you before,' Lily snapped. 'That's not my name.'

'Yes, it is,' Izzie piped up. 'You're Lily-Lavender because lavender's your favourite.'

'Not any more,' Lily declared, 'so stop saying it.'

And Juliet knew.

She knew what the thoughtful, personal present was that Sir Henry Darley had given his eldest stepdaughter the day before her previous appointment here.

She just knew.

Juliet slipped across the gardens, slowing as she left the house behind, or maybe it was shock that was making her drag her feet. She couldn't bear to think of the lavender candle Sir Henry had given Lily, the thoughtful, personal present that had so delighted poor unsuspecting Flora. She couldn't bear it. She was a young girl again, worried sick about her mother, having to be grateful, hating to be grateful, vulnerable and disgusted and scared and desperate and stupid, stupid, stupid.

And now it was happening to Lily. Dear, sweet Lily – because she was a sweet girl, Juliet was sure of that, remembering the pleasant, smiling girl she had seen in Sally-Ann's hall. 'Lavender is a happy colour in our family,' Flora had said. But not any more. Sir Henry Darley and Lily. Mr Nugent and Lily. Old feelings swarmed all over her, so well-remembered it was as if they had never gone away. She was frightened and frozen and humiliated and stupid, stupid, stupid. No wonder Lily's behaviour had altered. She was like Juliet, unable to tell anyone, unable to speak out, but unlike Juliet, she had a mother who was fit and healthy, and she must ache for her mother to know, to realise, to ask the right questions. Lily might be sullen on the outside, but on the inside she was pleading for mercy and release.

Juliet felt sick and trembly. She needed to stop, get a hold of herself. The folly was ahead. No one would know if she slipped inside. She walked across the rickety footbridge and mounted the steps to push the door. It looked big and heavy, but it gave easily. She found herself in a circular chamber, unfurnished and dim and damp, in which was a spiral staircase.

Going up, she emerged into a small round room. A door opened onto the terrace with its low parapet – its too-low parapet. She saw what Lady Darley meant. The folly was only one storey tall, but that low parapet made her stomach swoosh, as if she were much higher off the ground.

Standing there, arms wrapped round her middle, she hugged herself, not seeing anything. A man's voice exclaimed, 'It *is* you!' There was a wild scramble inside her head, a moment of pure panic at being found by Mr Nugent, even though it wasn't his voice, followed by a gush of relief at seeing a young man instead – then anger at being disturbed when her thoughts were so important – then she was clobbered, that was how it felt, clobbered by shock when she saw who it was.

As Cecily left the greengrocer's, she saw Verity Forbes. Instinctively, she stepped back, then wished she hadn't. Talk about obvious. Pinning on a smile, she stepped outside again, looking Verity in the eye as she drew close.

'I thought I'd left my purse behind, but I hadn't. Silly me.' Did her laugh make her sound as guilty as she felt?

'How are you?' Verity asked. 'You and Juliet. William told me about your troubles. He's most concerned.'

Cecily wanted to swat her aside. How dared this girl presume to tell her about William's feelings? Vexation was followed by misery. Verity had a perfect right. 'We're fine, thank you. Aren't you at work today?'

Verity held up a bundle of letters. 'I'm posting these.'

'I won't keep you. I'm sure you need to get back to the office.'

As Verity continued on her way, Cecily watched. She felt all bothersome, as her nan would have said. She hated herself for being rude, but how else was she supposed to behave? Verity Forbes was the last person she wanted to cosy up to. She felt a surge of resentment and protectiveness on William's behalf. There was Verity, with the chance of an adoring husband and a comfortable family life, and she was buggering about clinging to her independence. The word rang with a distinct sneering sound in Cecily's head.

Then something inside her crumpled. She was bad-hearted. An urgent feeling of despair ballooned inside her as she tasted again the jealousy that had tormented her each time one of her sisters had acquired a fellow. Now she was jealous of Verity Forbes. Yet she knew that Juliet would have welcomed Verity as a friend had it not been for the William situation, and so would she.

Archie had been the sun, moon and stars to her before she fell in love with William. She had to recapture that.

Except she couldn't, because you couldn't recapture something that had never been lost. Archie was still all the world to her, but somehow her treacherous heart had made room for William too.

Juliet stared as Hal darted through the door – and stopped dead. Had he run up the stairs to pull her into his arms, then thought better of it? She was dazed with shock, but beneath that, a great yearning took hold. He was . . . older. Stupid thought. Of course he was older. He was closer to thirty now than twenty. He had filled out, though his frame was still slim and strong. There were fine lines around his eyes that hadn't been there before. Her fingertips tingled with the need to touch this new part of him she didn't know. She remembered the cheerful young man with the kind eyes, leaning on his spade to chat, sleeves rolled up. He used to push back his cap on his head. With a jolt of remembered desire, she recalled preferring him like that to togged up in his Sunday best. He still wore a cap, but otherwise was in a tweed suit. He looked prosperous. Not rolling-in-it prosperous, but capable, able to earn a decent living.

Able to support a wife and family.

Had he got over her and met someone else?

'Juliet,' he said. 'It really is you.' He smiled. Goodness, she remembered that smile.

'What are you doing here?' Stupid question. He was here. That was all that mattered. After years apart, here he was, here they were, together. How could it matter why? She wanted to check her hat, smooth her hair, make herself look perfect.

His arms fell to his sides. 'I could ask you the same question. I noticed someone up here and came to say it's not safe, especially after that shower earlier. It gets slippery. Or if you meant the question in a wider sense . . .' He glanced away from her towards the view. 'I'm here to extend the gardens.'

'So you've achieved your ambition. Congratulations.'

'It's been a hard slog, but, yes, things are going well for me. What about you? What brings you here?'

'Dressmaking.' Her heart was thumping so hard she could barely speak.

'Sewing for Lady Darley? Your mother would be proud.'

'What about your parents? How are they?' As though she and Hal were casual acquaintances who bumped into one another occasionally and observed the usual courtesies.

'Fine, thank you.'

'Is your dad the head gardener now?'

'Has been for the past five years.'

Five years. And she and Hal had been apart longer than that. She would be twenty-three shortly. Twenty-three, and the mother of a six-year-old. Isadora. Where had that sprung from? She might not be Isobel or Isabella. She could be Isadora.

And Lily was being interfered with by Mr Nugent.

'This is ridiculous,' Hal exclaimed. 'We're talking as if there had never been anything between us.'

'I wrote to you, but you never wrote back.'

'Ma took against you after you disappeared. When you wrote, she hid the letter instead of posting it on, and I might never have found out about it, but when I visited, Dad asked me what you'd

364

said in your letter, so Ma had to admit what she'd done.'

'You wrote back?' Hope clutched at her chest.

'When I didn't hear from you again, I went to the address on the letter.'

Her flesh prickled. 'You went to my grandmother's house?'

'She said you'd run away.' Hal lifted his shoulders in a gesture of helplessness. 'I had nowhere else to look. I hoped you'd write again, but you never did.'

'You wanted me to?' she whispered.

'Of course I did. I wanted to know that you were well and safe. I wanted to know what had happened. You left so many questions behind. You missed your mother's funeral, for pity's sake – her *funeral*.'

'All right, don't rub it in.'

'But – to miss her funeral, Juliet.'

Suddenly she was trembling with anger. 'Don't you dare use that shocked voice with me. You have no idea . . . no idea.'

'When you vanished, Mr Nugent – Sir Henry – hell, I don't know what to call him, talking about the past like this. He said you'd run off with another man, that you were having his child. I didn't know what to think. Well, I did – I knew there couldn't possibly be anyone else – but then why had you run away? You planned it, didn't you? Ma wrote letters about the things you'd taken with you, which proved it was planned.'

He scrubbed his face with his hands. He didn't wear gloves. No, Hal wouldn't. He might have risen in the world, but he would never stop working with his hands, and would never wear gloves at work unless he was doing something that required his hands to be protected. Oh, there was a lot to be said for having bare hands at work. Hadn't her own hands touched her daughter? When she had drawn her gloves on afterwards, it was like pushing the feel of Izzie inside her gloves to snuggle close to her skin.

For all the good it would do her.

'I went home for your mother's funeral. There was just time to get to the church, though I wanted to go to the cottage, to see you, to hold you and say how sorry I was not to have been with you when she passed away. If I'd had time, if I'd gone to the cottage . . . what would I have seen? What happened that day? And then Mr Nugent sent for me and accused me of being the father of your child. He said there was no doubt about your condition, because you were suffering from morning sickness. He said if it wasn't mine, you must have had another chap on the side and you'd run off with him. I couldn't believe it – and yet what else was I to think? I had to go back to London. After that, Mr Nugent got his lordship to sponsor me as apprentice to the garden designer. He gave me a real leg-up, Mr Nugent did.'

'And got rid of the one person who knew there was no secret lover,' Juliet said sharply, then gasped. Her cheeks burnt with shame. 'I'm so sorry. That sounded as if I don't believe in your talent, and I do. I always did. You know I did.' She willed him to believe her.

'I know,' Hal said softly. He shook his head on a frown. 'But if there wasn't another man, why would Mr Nugent believe you were expecting a child? What happened that day, Juliet?'

What happened that day? *What happened that day?* The words spilt out in a frantic rush in her head. *I'll tell you what happened, I'll tell you what happened* – and it swooped back once more to consume her. It was painfully near the surface, because of Lily, and now it stormed out with unprecedented vigour – the shame, the guilt, the disgust and despair, the fear, the gratitude, stupid, stupid, stupid.

Her eyes burnt with angry tears, but she refused to let them fall. It was her secret shame, her secret guilt.

Lily's secret shame, too, now.

She couldn't tell Hal about Mr Nugent, about having to be grateful. Fear and loathing uncoiled inside her. Stupid, stupid, stupid. But it wasn't just because she had nursed her secret for so long that she couldn't speak now. It was because of Lily. She had to help Lily. It was Lily's only chance. She had to save Lily.

And afterwards, maybe she could – could she? – whisper the truth to Hal. But not until afterwards. She forced her torment back into the dark box where she kept it.

When she didn't speak, Hal finally said, with an edge of desperation in his voice, 'I can't tell you what it means to see you again.'

Hope jolted through her. 'Really?'

'I've dreamt of this for so long. There's never been anyone else for me. But I have to ask. I have to know. Was there a baby? Your grandmother asked if I was the father. Was there really a child?'

Anger flared – no, not anger, nothing so tame as mere anger. Rage such as she had never known in her life burst forth and there was no stopping it. Rage at the way they had been kept apart all this time. Years! Bloody years. Rage against Rosie and her brother, against Mr Nugent, against Adeline, against herself for being so young and in need of support, for giving up her beloved baby. Cecily had never considered giving up her baby.

'Was there a child? Was there? She's up yonder in that posh house. She's bright-eyed and rosy, and so fetching you could eat her for breakfast. Her name is Constance – except that it isn't

367

Constance – it's Izzie, Izzie McKenzie, when she should have been Constance Mary Harper. My daughter, my baby. She's in there and I'm out here, and all I have is the hope that her mother will send for me to make a dress. Does that answer your question?'

Chapter Twenty-Seven

Juliet crept into Garden Cottage. She felt punch-drunk. Hal. Izzie. Lily. Mr Nugent. Hal – *Hal*. Her heart had remembered. She was weak and shaky from when she had exploded. And, as if that wasn't bad enough, she had turned tail and run for it.

She badly needed to be alone, but William was laying the table – a man laying the table! – and making mistakes with the cutlery, much to Archie's vociferous indignation. She felt her heart fold up and sink. Here was William yet again inadvertently displaying himself as ideal husband and father material, which meant she was due for another evening of heartache from Cecily. Pleading a headache, she escaped upstairs, though for all the good it did her, she might as well have stayed to play happy families, because she couldn't gather her thoughts sufficiently to gain control of them. Hal was there, in her mind, claiming his place. She had blurted out the truth about Izzie to him. Everything felt so horribly complicated.

She must concentrate on Lily.

She rose with the dawn to make a start on the bathing costumes, cutting them out and tacking them together for Mrs

369

Livingston to finish. They were ready for fitting by teatime. By sewing other garments into the evening, she made time to take them to Darley Court tomorrow, a day earlier than expected, so she dropped a postcard in the pillar box that evening, politely suggesting the change.

When she arrived, Lady Darley appeared agitated.

'I'm sorry, but I shan't require your services in future. It's my husband's decision. He says – no offence – but he says you're not high class enough for a baronet's lady and his daughters.'

'I see.' She did see. She saw that Hal had mentioned her name to Sir Henry. What must Sir Henry have thought, knowing that the girl from long ago was living in the vicinity of Darley Court and, worse, had been coming into his home?

But no more. Not unless today's fittings went horribly wrong and the costumes needed redoing, which they wouldn't, because she was too good at her job for that. She stopped halfway up the stairs and had to force frozen limbs to move again. This could be the final time. After her husband's decree, Lady Darley might see no need for her to be present when the finished garments were tried on, so this could be the end of her contact with Izzie. *Constance Mary Harper, Constance Mary Harper*, she chanted in her head, like a prayer. Somewhere on the periphery of her mind, she was aware she needed to get Lily on her own. She should concentrate on that, but it was hard when her impending loss was smothering her.

'Izzie McKenzie!' Lady Darley exclaimed in a mock telling-off voice. 'What's that down the front of your pinafore?'

'Marmalade,' Frances chirped at once.

Juliet looked. There was her darling girl smeared with jam. No, not jam – marmalade. It was another child who had been smeared with jam. Abigail Carmichael. She shook her head as if to dislodge Abigail, but for some reason the child wouldn't be turfed out. Two little girls in smeary pinafores.

'I'm not putting it on here,' Lily said hotly. 'I'm going to my room.' Snatching up the garment, she was gone.

'Careful,' Juliet called after her. 'It's only tacked.' Too late, she realised she had missed the chance to see Lily alone. 'Perhaps I—'

'Leave her,' said Lady Darley, her voice low with emotion.

Izzie in her costume was the most gorgeous sight Juliet had ever beheld. She stared, trying to imprint this moment on her heart, terrified that the image would shatter and vanish when she left, as it surely would. *Constance Mary Harper, Constance Mary Harper.* Her daughter's name was a plea for strength.

Then, just when she most needed to apply her attention to Izzie, she realised what was wrong about Abigail Carmichael. Two little girls in smeary pinafores. Abigail was the same size and age as Izzie and Archie, but the child from Rosie's attack should be a little older, a little bigger, a bit more mature. And Rosie had said she couldn't have more children. So Abigail wasn't hers, couldn't be. Hannah. Abigail was Hannah's. But where was Hannah? And if Abigail was hers . . . Oh, dear heaven. If Abigail was of a similar age to Izzie and Archie, and Hannah had gone to the job at Mr Nugent's that Juliet had run away from . . .

It was over. The fittings were done, and the costumes were fine.

'We're leaving for our holiday tomorrow,' said Lady Darley.

'But I thought you were going—'

'We were, but my husband can take us tomorrow and return the day after. Please deliver the costumes here for the housekeeper to send on.'

Dazed, she walked home. Marching into Garden Cottage,

she removed the sewing from Mrs Livingston's hands and calmly instructed her to take Archie for a walk.

'What is it?' Cecily demanded, but Juliet, hanging on by a thread, wouldn't utter another word until they were alone.

She was shaking deep inside. Soon she would be shaking on the outside too. 'There's something I never told you about Lady Darley.' And out it came, about the sleeve lady, and seeing her, or possibly dreaming it, at Mrs Maddox's, and the identity of Izzie McKenzie.

'It might have been a dream,' Cecily whispered.

She pressed her fingers to Cecily's mouth. 'Don't say it. Don't make light of my situation.'

'I'm not. I swear I'm not.'

'She's my daughter,' Juliet breathed. 'That's how it feels.'

'Why did you never tell me? I'd have understood.'

'Don't!' It came out on a spurt of tears. 'Don't blame me for not saying. Don't you think it's bad enough without that?'

'Sweetheart, I never meant . . . Come here, come here.'

She was wrapped in Cecily's arms, being rocked like a child, Cecily's cheek pressed against her scalp. The tears came then, hot and fierce, bursting through the tangle of anguish, while Cecily cuddled and murmured and rained little kisses into her hair.

At last, Juliet drew back, exhausted.

'Are you all right?' Cecily whispered.

'No,' she said, 'but I will be. I have to be.'

At Rosie's house, the moment Juliet said her name on the doorstep, something glittered in the footman's eyes, and he was already closing the door as he said, 'Mrs Carmichael is not at home.'

She stood transfixed for a moment before going down the steps.

If Rosie wouldn't let her in, she would wait for her to come out. If necessary, she would come back tomorrow and the next day and every day.

Eventually, a carriage came clopping along the street, halting outside Rosie's house. The front door opened, and Rosie emerged, clad in a three-quarter-length coat of red fur with wide sleeves and deep, turned-back cuffs. Behind her came a smart gentleman with a cane, the sort used for show, not for leaning on.

Juliet darted across the road and clutched Rosie's arm. 'I have to see you.'

The gentleman with the cane and the servant holding the carriage door both stepped forward.

Juliet hissed, 'It's about Abigail, and if you won't see me, I'll bellow it from the rooftops.'

Rosie pulled her arm free, then she said, addressing the men, 'There's something I must attend to.' With a dazzling smile, she turned to the gentleman with the cane. 'The properties will have to wait, Hugo. Don't let anyone else have them. My carriage is at your disposal.'

Rosie swept indoors, Juliet on her heels. Rosie barely stopped for the maid to receive her outdoor things before heading for the same room as last time. She turned in a challenging swirl of turquoise silk to face Juliet.

'What's this about?'

'What happened to your child?'

'You met her the last time you came uninvited.'

'Abigail isn't yours. She can't be – not if you're being honest about getting your insides messed up. She isn't old enough.'

'She's mine,' Rosie said in a low voice, 'in every way that counts.'

Juliet nodded. She could understand that. 'What became of your own?'

'I couldn't get rid fast enough.'

'Adoption or knitting needles?'

Rosie's eyebrows shot up. 'My, you have developed claws, haven't you?'

'I want the truth.'

'Who the hell d'you think you are, coming here, making demands? What has any of it to do with you?'

'More than you think.'

'Spare me your riddles.'

She pulled in a breath. 'Abigail is Hannah's daughter.'

'So?'

'Where's Hannah?'

'I've heard enough.' Rosie reached for the bell.

'She's dead, isn't she?' Juliet said quickly, and Rosie's hand froze in mid-air. 'Why else would you have adopted Abigail?'

Rosie threw her a dangerous look. 'If you imagine this information is going to be of any use to you—'

'I'm not here to blackmail you. I just want the truth.'

Rosie laughed, a mirthless sound. 'I think you've already worked it out. Congratulations. Now leave.'

'Who is Abigail's father?'

'So that's it. You're here to see if you can besmirch Hannah's good name posthumously. You're hoping she was unwed.'

'I'll tell you what I hope. I hope I'm wrong. For Hannah's sake, I hope I'm wrong.'

Until now, Rosie had been her adversary. Now, a sudden sharp stillness as she focused her attention showed she was intrigued.

Pushing home what she hoped was a momentary advantage, Juliet said softly, 'Please tell me. You said you had to leave her in the workhouse, but then she got that job.'

Rosie's face changed as a battle took place and distrust was set aside – for now.

'It was such a relief to me, her being offered that post. I was allowed to see her before she left the workhouse, and we talked about how those women in Mr Nugent's household were no spring chickens and Hannah could end up in a senior position if she worked hard. We said goodbye. We didn't expect to see one another again. I was still earning money servicing the needs of gentlemen who didn't get enough of it at home, or who didn't get the right sort at home, and even though the money was building up and I was as determined as ever that one day I'd have enough decent property to call myself respectable, that day seemed a long way off. Hannah was better off without me. There was a chance of her one day being housekeeper to a gentleman. Imagine that! Our Hannah – a housekeeper! I thought I'd burst with pride.'

'Did you write to her at Mr Nugent's?'

'What, and me no better than I should be? No, I wasn't going to queer things for her. But I told her an address she could use to find me and made her learn it by heart.'

'What happened?'

'The following June, she arrived on the doorstep. Literally. She got as far as the steps and collapsed. She didn't have the strength left to scratch at the door, let alone knock. She'd walked all the way from Birkfield. I don't know how long it took, but the weather had been rotten for two or three weeks. She was ill with pneumonia and thin as a stick, apart from her belly. She went into labour the next day. It had to be a forceps delivery, and afterwards . . . her heart gave out.'

'Leaving you with Abigail.'

'She was so tiny. She was early, though I don't know by how much. Everything I've done since then has been for her.'

'Did Hannah name the father?'

'No, she bloody well didn't! She wasn't capable of talking. She rambled a bit, but I was more interested in keeping her warm and conserving her strength – what there was of it. All I wanted was for her to pull through.' Rosie's voice had risen. She made an effort and dropped it again. 'I don't know who the father is. I've wondered about it – tortured myself with it. Hannah wasn't stupid. She'd already suffered because of my pregnancy; she wouldn't have jeopardised everything for some fleeting pleasure. Yet the alternative is that she was forced.' Suddenly her voice was a husky whisper. 'I can't bear that thought.'

'You're imagining a groom or a footman, and Hannah being thrown out for being no better than she should be.'

'Why, yes—'

'I think it was Mr Nugent.'

'Mr Nugent?' There was disbelief as well as shock in Rosie's voice. 'Rubbish! He never had that kind of reputation.'

'Why do you think he wanted me under his roof? He likes 'em young. Not little-girl-young, but ripe-young, ready for picking. Why d'you think I ran away?'

'He used to bed you?'

'He was going to. He was . . . "breaking me in", he called it.'

Rosie's face went white. Shock and sympathy on Juliet's behalf? No. 'And I let Hannah go in your place.' She looked round, but her eyes were glazed. 'Hannah getting a good job, and not just that but your job, that was the cherry on the cake for me. I never for one moment—'

'I'm sorry. I don't know for certain. If Hannah never said, then no one knows. I only know what happened to me.'

Rosie flared up so suddenly that Juliet took a step backwards.

'Trying to take it back? You come here, do your damage, then say it might all be a big mistake?'

'No. Now I've heard about Hannah, I'm sure I'm right.'

'Why did you come here, spreading this filth?'

'It's the truth.'

'That makes it worse. Came to rub my nose in it, did you? Want to make me think bad thoughts every time I look at my daughter?'

'I came because he's doing it again. Do you remember how folk used to say he was from a titled family? Well, he was – he is. And the title is his now. He is Sir Henry Darley of Darley Court in Chorlton.'

'Sir Henry Darley? There was a piece about him in the paper a while back, about the work he's planning to have done on the grounds. There was a photograph of a battered-looking old folly that needs to be made safe. And that's Mr Nugent from Moorside? Sir Henry Darley?'

'The very same.' Juliet leant forward. 'And he's breaking in one of his stepdaughters.'

'You think I care?'

'You should!' Juliet cried. 'You bloody well should! How d'you think her mother would feel? How would you feel? How are you feeling right now?'

After a bad night, Juliet was up early, creeping about so as not to disturb Archie, who would be out of bed like a shot if he heard her. She was coming downstairs when she noticed the envelope. She picked it up, noting its quality. Her name was written on it in a neat hand. Opening it, she unfolded the letter and instinctively glanced round, as if someone might be watching.

Darley Folly, this evening, 7 o'clock.

Hal. No, he would write a proper letter, and sign it too.

Mr Nugent. Sir Henry Darley. It must be. What did he want? To threaten her? To make it clear that no evidence existed to prove what had occurred all those years ago? He couldn't possibly know she had guessed about him and Lily. Could he? Irrelevant. She was going to tell Lady Darley as soon as she came home from North Wales, regardless of how difficult it was to gain access to her.

What about this appointment? The old fear rose up. But this wasn't just about her, it was about Lily. Lily was safe at present, but suppose Sir Henry decided to join his family in Wales? Could she prevent that? Only if she met him. She would tell him that if he left home before the others returned, she would write to Lady Darley at the Imperial Hotel, and surely Lily then would break down and say her piece.

Juliet felt strong and determined, brave even, then her skin crawled beneath his remembered touch. She had to clench every muscle she possessed to stop herself trembling. She was going to face this, for Lily's sake.

But perhaps she needn't do it alone. She needed a witness. Cecily? Or – yes, William. The presence of an educated, professional man would surely give Mr Nugent pause.

William was coming for tea, as was now usual.

'Will he come early?' Archie mithered. 'He doesn't work Saturday af'noon.'

'Maybe,' said Cecily, 'if you're very lucky.' She glanced at Juliet, a guilty look, and Juliet knew she was thinking of her own luck.

William wasn't early. In fact, he was late, which was most unlike him.

Juliet dragged him aside. 'I need to ask you a favour.'

'I want to speak to you too.'

And, damn her faint heart, she seized the chance to postpone. 'You first.'

William flushed. 'The reason I'm late is I've spent the afternoon with Verity. We talked about the future and . . .'

'She turned you down. Oh, William.'

'No. I didn't ask her. I know I was gone on her for a long time, and I wouldn't want you to think I was trifling with her, but this business with the police suspecting you shook me up badly. It's made me realise things . . . like who's important to me. I'm so used to thinking of you and Cecily as friends, almost as sisters, that I never realised before—'

Her lungs couldn't fill properly. 'William, please don't—'

'What? Not you, love: Cecily. I've come to realise what she means to me. I know I'm just good old Uncle William, who makes an ass of himself playing with Archie, but do you think Cecily could ever . . . well . . . do you?'

A cold calm descended on Juliet as she climbed the spiral stairs. A mistake to come alone? But she couldn't have asked William to accompany her, not after he had confided his hopes about Cecily. When Archie was put to bed, she had announced she was going for a walk and hurried out.

Reaching the top of the steps, she opened the door, a flash of nerves twisting in her stomach at the sight of that too-low parapet. She stepped outside, only to have a cry wrenched out of her as her heel skidded and she nearly flew over backwards.

A hand grasped her arm and jerked her upright.

'Careful,' Mr Nugent said. 'It's slippery.'

Heart banging, she scuttled away before turning to look at him.

379

Older, thicker-set, better dressed, though he hadn't been badly dressed before.

'Though why it should be slippery, I don't know,' he added in a bland, conversational tone. 'We haven't had rain. Well, Juliet – or is it Miss Harper now you're grown up? You'll always be Juliet to me. Not that you're as appealing as you once were.'

'Too old now, am I?'

'Bitterness doesn't become you. I prefer to remember your . . . gratitude. Do you remember how grateful you were?'

'I remember being interfered with, and not being able to stop it in case you threw us out of our cottage. I remember not being able to tell anyone, because I didn't know how to say it and, anyroad, everyone was beholden to his lordship, which meant we were beholden to you, because you were the one who did everything. His lordship never lifted a finger.'

'As he was entitled not to. Not that I'm following his example. I like to be occupied. My tenants have reason to be glad of me. Hence also my interest in improving the grounds. I gather you met Price. A happy reunion, was it? Dear me, what a vexed look. The old Juliet, or should I say the young Juliet, the grateful girl I used to know, would never have looked at me in that way.'

'I was never grateful,' she cried, appalled to find the years slipping away, leaving her stupid, stupid, stupid.

'Oh, but you were,' came the reply in that calm, smooth voice from the past, the voice she had never been able to say no to. 'What would have become of your mother, your poor, sick, dying mother, but for your gratitude?' He moved away, standing at the parapet, broad-shouldered, head up, master of all he surveyed. 'Is that why we're here?' he enquired scornfully. 'To reminisce on your gratitude?'

'I don't know. You tell me. Do you intend making threats?'

'Threats?' The word was a bark of contempt. 'What need have I to threaten you? You have an inflated idea of your own importance if you imagine yourself worthy of my notice. In fact, the more I think of it, the further your gratitude slips from my mind until I can't imagine what you're referring to.'

'How convenient! I wish I could forget it. Are you going to forget the others' gratitude too?'

'What others?'

'Don't pretend I was alone. I refuse to believe that.'

'Why?' he mocked. 'Don't you want to feel special?'

'Was Hannah grateful?'

'Hannah?'

'She came as a maid into your household after I ran away.'

'Ah yes . . . Hannah.' The way he said it left her in no doubt. 'With Hannah, it was fear. The workhouse does that. She was scared witless of being sent back. She had nowhere else to go, you see, unless she wanted to join her sister in a life of prostitution.'

Something crackled in the air. Juliet glanced round, but they were alone. It was just her imagination.

She wanted to be strong, needed to show she had fight in her. 'Don't tell me. Your memory of her is fading too.'

'I have my position to consider. A title, property, money. I didn't have to petition for club membership: the secretaries of the best clubs sought me out. I am welcome in the smartest drawing rooms in South Lancashire and North Cheshire. My wife is an excellent creature, a credit to me socially and domestically, as well as being adept at visiting the sick and the provision of food baskets. She is the perfect lady of the manor in all respects.'

'Including providing you with a ready-made family of three

young daughters. I know what's going on with Lily. Is it fear with her as well? I can't imagine it's gratitude.'

'Fear?' His face twisted in distaste. 'Certainly not. Fear is so unpleasant. No, for Lily, it's protectiveness. She believes she's protecting Frances from a fate worth than death.' With a sigh, as of regret, he turned away. 'She doesn't realise Frances is too young. But she won't always be. And then there's little Isolde.'

Isolde. Her name is Isolde.

You will never ever lay one finger on my child.

She stepped forward, careful even in that moment of the slippery surface. She thrust her hands full onto Mr Nugent's back and heaved with all her might. It took him a long time to topple. His feet scrambled, but couldn't find any purchase; his arms flailed and grabbed, but his hands caught nothing. Juliet fell too, landed hard on her knees. Her chest banged against the low parapet. There was a terrific stabbing pain, and she couldn't breathe.

And then he was gone.

Before she could look down, hands grabbed her from behind. 'Not you as well, you fool.'

Juliet turned. Stared. She would have said, 'Rosie,' except that she hadn't yet started breathing again.

Chapter Twenty-Eight

Cecily kept Archie up as long as she could. Normally, she was strict about bedtimes, but if she despatched Archie, William might take it as his cue to leave, and she wanted to hang onto him as long as possible. But when William glanced at the clock and raised his eyebrows in Archie's direction, she knew she had to give in.

'I'll wait here while you put him to bed, if you don't mind,' said William. 'I need to tell you something about Verity and me.'

Disappointment clenched in her stomach, but she smiled and made a show of chasing Archie up the stairs.

'Can Uncle William come and tell me a story?' Archie asked when he had said his prayers and she had tucked him in.

'Not tonight, chick. Settle down. You've stayed up later than you should.'

'That shows I'm a big boy.'

'Yes, it does. Night-night.'

She kissed him, and he wriggled down in the bed. Her heart turned over. Not so long ago, he had been the only occupant of her heart, but now there was someone else in there as well, and that someone was about to tell her that he was engaged to Verity flaming Forbes.

Downstairs, William stood at the window, gazing out. He turned to look at her. He pulled at his collar. What did he have to feel uncomfortable about? She was the one who was in a sticky situation. She was going to have to act the part for all she was worth. She wasn't having William telling Verity later, 'I rather fear Cecily *likes* me, if you know what I mean,' and Verity thinking back and identifying lots of little clues, and feeling triumphant because William had been hers all along.

She sat up straight.

'I'm glad to get you on your own at last,' said William.

No point in letting this drag on. Better to get it over with. 'You said something about you and Verity. I take it congratulations are in order?'

'What? No! Far from it. We – well, we shan't be seeing one another any more.'

Concern for his distress swamped all other feelings. She leant forward sympathetically. 'William, I'm so sorry. Did she turn you down?'

He blinked. 'That's what Juliet said too. Is that what you both expected? If you must know, I was the one who broke it off, but that's between you and me – and Juliet. If Verity wants to tell other people it was her decision, obviously I'll go along with that. Not that there are many people to tell,' he added ruefully. 'Our walking out together wasn't exactly something she proclaimed from the rooftops.'

'I'm sorry you've been let down.' And she was too. Should she be celebrating his disappointment? Looking for her own chance? Offering comfort and pushing that comfort in a certain direction?

She didn't feel like doing any of that. She wanted to give him a shoulder to cry on if he needed it. 'Verity never made a secret of not wanting to be tied down.'

'That isn't why I ended it. I mean, obviously, I always knew she had different ideas to mine about what happens when a couple gets together, and that was difficult. I wanted so much for her to want what I wanted.' He raked a hand through his hair. 'I'm not doing this at all well. I shouldn't be talking about Verity – only I have to, to start with, because I need you to know I haven't played fast and loose with her.'

'Of course you haven't. You're the most honourable person I know.'

'I say, do you mean that?' He smiled and his laughter lines appeared, then he looked sombre. 'Honourable?'

'That's a good thing.'

'I know, but . . . Cecily, I've done this all wrong. I've done everything all wrong. I thought Verity was the girl for me, but she wasn't. When the police started investigating Juliet, I was so worried I couldn't stop thinking about it, and I realised it was because . . . well, because it was more than worry, it was . . . love. I – well, I . . .'

She shut her eyes. No wonder he had spoken in Juliet's absence. He was in love with Juliet and wanted to know if she thought he stood a chance. Pain ripped across her heart. It had been bad enough when he had been involved with Verity, but if he now loved Juliet . . .

'. . . I love you, Cecily. I love you. Do you think you might see me differently, as something more than your friend? As a suitor? I know I'm springing this on you, but I couldn't wait any longer. And it goes for Archie too, naturally. You and he are one and the same, as far as I'm concerned. Do you think you could give me a chance?'

Her eyes sprang open and she gazed at him, her fingers covering her mouth.

'I'm sorry. I've taken too much on myself. Perhaps I'd better leave. I've done this all wrong. I apologise.'

She went to him and caught his hands. 'No, you oaf, you've done it all right. Just say it again so I know it's real.'

'Do you mean it?' His fingers squeezed hers.

'This is what I've wanted for so long and I thought it couldn't ever happen. I hated Verity Forbes for coming along just when I realised how I felt about you.'

'We're not supposed to be talking about Verity.'

'Verity Forbes is an idiot,' said Cecily. 'She could have had you, but she's an idiot, and I'm grateful for it, because now I've got you instead.'

'You and Archie have got me.'

'Me and Archie. Oh, he loves you so much.'

William took a step back from her, a look of certainty and resolve on his face. 'I haven't made the best fist of telling you, but I'm going to do the next bit properly.'

Her heart expanded as he went down on one knee. She caught her breath and tried to sniff discreetly to keep tears at bay.

'Cecily Ramsbottom—'

'Don't! Don't spoil the most romantic moment of my life by using that awful name.'

'Cecily, will you do me the honour of becoming my wife and allowing me to be your son's father?'

Oh, how perfect. If she had ever wondered how much she loved him, she knew it in that moment, when he included her beloved Archie in his proposal.

'Yes,' she breathed. 'Yes, as long as . . .'

386

'Anything.'

'As long as Archie can be Archie Turton. I want him to have the same name as I have.'

'Of course. He'll be my son.' He smiled. 'My lad Archie.'

Rising to his feet, he enfolded her in his arms and kissed her. Cecily melted into the embrace, feeling warm and excited and safe.

'Let's wake Archie and tell him,' said William. 'We're going to be a family, so he ought to know.'

Hand in hand, they went upstairs. Cecily sat on the bed and roused her son, soon to be William's son as well. Archie was drowsy, and she thought maybe he hadn't twigged what he was being told, then he snapped awake.

'Did Uncle William go down on one knee?'

She laughed in surprise. 'How do you know about men going down on one knee?'

'Silly Mummy. Everyone knows that.'

'Yes, I did,' said William. 'You have to do these things properly.'

'Do it again.'

'What?'

'Do it again,' Archie insisted. 'I want to see. Say what you said, and Mummy must say what she said too.'

William sank down on his knee. In Archie's presence, the second proposal was even better than the first.

'Well,' said Rosie, 'I didn't see that coming. More to the point, neither did he. I'd never have believed you capable.'

Juliet pulled herself closer to the parapet. Rosie had hauled her to her feet, but she had promptly sunk down again. Now she realised it was a good thing she had, because peering over the edge made her head swim. Or perhaps that was shock. She looked down, aware of Rosie beside her. Mr Nugent was below, head first in the ditch, limbs spread, unmoving.

She asked, 'Is he dead?'

'If he isn't, he soon will be. His face is in the water.'

'Ought we . . . ?'

'Ought we what? Don't spoil a perfectly good murder by rushing to the rescue.'

'Murder? But I . . .'

But she what? Hadn't meant it? But she had. She hadn't planned it, but in that moment, she had meant it. For the sake of her beloved child, she had meant it.

She sank back from the edge.

'You saved me a job,' said Rosie.

Juliet looked at her. 'You were going to . . . ?'

'Damn right I was, after what you told me about Hannah.'

Juliet tried to think. She had to force her mind to focus. 'How did you know to come here?'

'I sent notes to you both. I knew you'd each think the other had written, and I could think of only one possible topic of conversation, and I was right. I was sure you'd bring Hannah into it.'

'You wanted to know for definite.'

'I was all set to shove him over the edge, but you saved me the bother.' Rosie glanced over the parapet, then back again. 'Bring me the jewellery. I'll have it taken to a bent pawnbroker I know of in Chester. I'll ensure the police find the things in his shop. It'll take time, but your name will be cleared.'

'Won't the pawnbroker . . . ?'

'Find himself in hot water? I damn well hope so. He cheated an acquaintance of mine and, as you know, it never pays to get on the wrong side of me.'

'You're helping me?'

'You killed the fiend who dishonoured my sister. On your feet. We need to get away.' Rosie hauled her up. 'Watch yourself. It's slippery. Poor Sir Henry, taking an evening stroll, deciding to have a look at what needs doing to his folly, and goes head first over the parapet. Still, accidents happen.'

They went downstairs. Juliet opened the door, averting her face from where the body lay, then realised Rosie wasn't behind her. After a moment, Rosie emerged from the gloomy interior.

'Here.' She thrust a bucket into Juliet's hands. 'Get rid of this.'

'What?'

'You're the murderer. Get rid of the evidence. Well, why did you think it was so slippery up there?'

Rosie walked away.

Arriving home, Juliet was so exhausted she could barely drag one foot in front of the other. The front door opened before she reached the garden gate. Cecily and William came spilling out to draw her in. Cecily's face was bright with happiness, but she exclaimed in concern at the sight of Juliet.

'What's happened? You look dreadful. All your colour's gone.'

'Nothing. Just a fall.'

'Come in, and let me look after you. Sit down while I put the kettle on, and then . . .' Cecily reached for William's hand. They beamed at one another and then at Juliet. 'Then we've got something to tell you.'

She smiled through the shock and fatigue. She was so grateful to be home. 'I think I know what it is.'

'We're engaged. Isn't it wonderful? William went down on one knee and asked me properly.'

'I hope you said yes.'

'Of course I did, silly. Then we woke Archie and told him. He's thrilled to pieces. He made William go down on one knee and do it all over again, so he could watch.'

'I hope you're not going to leave me out. I want to see it too.'

'Actually, you're looking a bit green,' said William. 'Maybe you need—'

'Maybe I need to see you going down on one knee. I promise you, there isn't anything that could make me feel any better than that.'

William obliged.

Chapter Twenty-Nine

'It's exactly as I said, Mama,' Sally-Ann insisted. 'The Darleys are cursed.'

When Mrs Palmer didn't deign to reply, Sally-Ann fixed Juliet with gossip-laden eyes. Juliet longed to encourage her. Had Mrs Palmer not been present, she would have done so, and professional etiquette be hanged. As it was, she simply crammed pins between her lips and bent over Mrs Palmer's hem.

'A black gown, if you please,' Mrs Palmer had decreed. 'It's not every day one goes into mourning for a baronet with whom one has been on dining terms.'

And here she was, standing on a small stool while Juliet crawled in a circle, putting up the hem. She had a wardrobe full of black at Garden Cottage. There was a steady demand.

'Poor Flora, what a blow,' Sally-Ann prattled. 'They've barely been married five minutes – and then for her to be away when it happened. She's pulled herself together now – one has to – but I assure you, for the whole of that first day, she was *distraught*. At least an accident is easier to come to terms with than what happened the other time. Easier to explain to the children, and of course he wasn't their father.'

Juliet discreetly spat pins into her hand. 'If I may ask, how are the children?'

'Izzie's a bit young to take it in. It's hit Lily hardest, poor lamb. Being that bit older, she understands more. She went dead white when we told her, and I thought she'd faint clean away, then she sobbed and sobbed. Young Frances, who, between you, me and the gatepost, is a bit of a madam, seems more bothered about what will become of them next. She soon realised Darley Court belongs to someone else now.'

Impossible to delay longer. Juliet said, 'If you'd like to step down,' and Mrs Palmer descended and paced to the mirror. Juliet and Sally-Ann flanked her, standing slightly behind, and all three regarded her reflection.

'Are you positive full black is quite the thing, Mama?' Sally-Ann ventured. 'He may be a baronet, but he's not family.'

'One should always accord rank its proper respect,' Mrs Palmer replied.

'I'm not going into full black, and I'm Flora's friend.'

'I hope you'll be correctly attired for the funeral.'

'I promise I'll be swathed. It was everyday garb I was thinking of – which is why I'm here. I haven't come to see you, Mama. I'm here to beg Miss Harper to sort out my half-mourning.'

'You may wish me to provide something for your daughters as well. I know they're friends with the McKenzie girls.'

Sally-Ann sighed. No gossip now, just sorrow. 'Those poor children, losing two fathers. It doesn't bear thinking about.'

How strange it felt, carrying on as normal, but she had to. She needed to. When news had spread of Sir Henry's accident, Juliet hadn't found it hard to react appropriately. If anything, it was a relief to release some of the shock that had held her frozen.

'It's all anyone can talk about,' Cecily reported, coming in with the shopping. 'I keep remembering how we knew him years ago.'

'Did you tell anyone?' Juliet asked, dread hollowing her voice.

'No.' Cecily pulled a face, eyes thoughtful. 'It wouldn't be right somehow, spreading it about that he was a land agent. I know it's not exactly speaking ill of the dead, but let folk remember him as grand and important, eh? It's politer.'

'I took the jewellery back to Rosie today. She's going to arrange for it to be found elsewhere.'

'I just can't understand why she's doing that for us.'

'She says I've been punished enough.' And perhaps that wasn't so very far from the truth.

'I should think so too!' Breathing shakily, Cecily cupped her hands over her mouth. 'What a relief. It's only when something's sorted that you realise how worried you were.'

Aside from that, it was business as usual at Garden Cottage – well, perhaps not entirely as usual, what with Cecily singing round the house, and Archie bouncing with glee as the time approached for William's daily visit, bouncing that commenced earlier with each day that passed.

'I'm having a new daddy,' he informed anyone who would listen. 'So far he's just been my uncle, but now he's going to be my daddy.'

'I think it's sweet,' Juliet told Cecily.

'So did I until this morning. We were in the baker's and an elderly couple smiled at him, which was all the encouragement he needed to tell them about his uncle being his new daddy. I happened to look round, and you should have seen the look these two women were giving one another. Honestly, he might as well have announced his daddy had finally decided to make an honest woman of me.'

Juliet couldn't help laughing, even though she could see how miffed Cecily was. Oh, but it felt good to laugh again.

As Juliet walked into the office of Perkins and Watson, Verity Forbes looked up, her professional smile freezing when she saw who it was. Juliet hovered in the doorway. She had come here prompted by kindness and concern, and awareness of the friendship that never was, but now she questioned the wisdom of it.

'I'll go away, if you'd rather.'

'No – stay. I'm stopping for dinner in a minute. There's a place I go to along the road, just to treat myself, you know, if I feel I could do with a bit of a lift.' Fetching her coat and hat from the stand, she checked her appearance in a small mirror on the wall. 'I've been treating myself quite a bit lately.'

Soon they were sitting, awaiting the arrival of pork cutlets. The table linen was worn but clean, which seemed to sum up everything about the modest establishment, including the tired-eyed old biddy waiting on them.

'How is William?' Verity asked in a bright voice.

'He's fine.'

'I'm glad to hear it. He deserves to be happy.'

'Yes,' Juliet said, 'he does.'

There was a flutter, and Verity pressed the back of her hand against her mouth. A sharp blink, a quick sniff, and she was in control again. 'The thing is, I was rather expecting him to be happy with me.'

'I didn't realise . . . I mean . . .'

'Go on,' challenged Verity. 'Spit it out.'

'I'm not saying you didn't seem fond of him, but . . .'

'Just because I wasn't in a mad rush to get engaged and dig Granny's veil out of mothballs doesn't mean I didn't care. I cared very much.' Verity spoke the words almost gingerly, as though they might shatter if she didn't take pains with them. 'Unfortunately, I didn't appreciate how much until too late. Feel free to say "I told you so." You won't be the first.'

'I wouldn't dream of it.'

'I'm thinking of having it engraved on my mother's headstone when the time comes.'

'William never set out to hurt you. You know that.'

Verity smiled sadly. 'Yes, I do know. Not that it makes it any easier. I should have snapped him up when I had the chance.'

'You had your reasons,' Juliet reminded her.

On a note that smacked of desperation, Verity said, 'All I wanted was time. Time to enjoy walking out together.'

'You said you valued your independence.'

'And I did. I do. I love working. When William came along, it was wonderful. I had my job, my independence and now a lovely fellow. I wanted to enjoy things the way they were, but I felt I was being pushed into getting engaged and I didn't want that. Not yet, anyway.'

'But you would have in the end?'

'How was I to know he'd go off and meet someone else?'

'It wasn't like that, and you know it. It just . . . happened. Circumstances.'

'You don't have to leap to his defence. I know what a decent man he is. Believe me, I know better than most, when I think how patient he was with me. But in the words of my dear mother:

"You kept him hanging on too long, Verity, and he went off the boil."' Verity fetched a deep sigh. 'As you say: circumstances.'

Juliet answered the door, and there was Inspector Crawley. She smiled, certain he was here to tell her she was no longer under suspicion.

'We're here to conduct a further search of the premises,' he announced, and the next thing she knew, half a dozen coppers came pouring through the door.

She pulled herself together. 'Cecily!' she called. 'Take Archie to play on the Green.'

'If you wouldn't mind accompanying me to the station, Miss Harper?' said Inspector Crawley.

'Auntie Juley! Auntie Juley!' Archie came tumbling towards her, arms outstretched.

She scooped him up, cuddling him close. 'Be a good boy and look after Mummy. I won't be long.'

She handed Archie into Cecily's arms, and they exchanged full looks. Thank heaven the jewels were no longer here. But that didn't stop this being a frightening experience.

At the police station, she was dragged through the same old questions, with the inspector pouncing on any answer that deviated in the smallest detail from before. With her heart pounding and anxiety tying knots in her stomach, she fought to keep a clear head.

At last she was permitted to leave.

'You haven't seen the last of me,' was Inspector Crawley's parting shot.

Back at Garden Cottage, Juliet and Cecily sat huddled together, outraged and vulnerable, while Mrs Livingston, who had heard on the grapevine and come hurrying round at once, bustled about, making tea and keeping Archie busy.

When William arrived, he was horrified. 'You should have sent for me.'

'That was a mistake, not sending for William,' Cecily whispered to Juliet later, when he had reluctantly left.

'It's because we know my name is going to be cleared. We must be careful how we act in future,' said Juliet. 'We mustn't give the game away.'

But, oh, how long was it going to take?

Mrs Baker-Johnson conceived a fancy for something flower-sprigged with lots of ruching, and Juliet hoped she could satisfy her long-standing customer without making Hand-finished by Harper a laughing stock, but when she arrived to take Mrs Baker-Johnson's measurements, the lady of the house wasn't available. That was surprising. Mrs Baker-Johnson might have lamentable taste in clothes but there was nothing amiss with her manners.

'Not available?' she asked the maid.

'Not in, miss.' Sylvie's eyes danced. 'She's down the cop shop. It's ever so thrilling. The police have found her rings as was burgled, and Mr Baker-Johnson had to go and identify them, even though he swore blind he wouldn't know them from a jar of curtain rings, but the police insisted, so off he went, only they ended up having to send for madam to do the identification, and that's where she is now. She'll be that relieved to get her jewellery back. So will them others as had theirs took an' all.'

Juliet listened in increasing delight.

Surely it wouldn't be a breach of professional etiquette to visit the Thomas household to express her pleasure at the return of Sally-Ann's possessions? She went there straight from the Baker-Johnson household.

'Grace's locket too,' Sally-Ann said. 'A bit late for her birthday, but never mind.'

'Was Lady Darley's ring returned?'

'Yes. She was overwhelmed, you know, something good happening after everything else. Which reminds me. She needs the girls' summer coats to be done over for mourning, and I suggested you. She'll never find anyone better than you and she knows it.'

While Juliet waited in hope to hear from Lady Darley, she also waited for Inspector Crawley to tell her she was no longer under suspicion. And waited.

In the end, she marched to the police station and asked to see him, suffering agonies at the last minute in case Rosie's plan hadn't worked properly and her name was now associated with that of the bent pawnbroker.

'You're no longer a person of interest in this enquiry,' the inspector informed her, and that was that. He couldn't have been more ungracious, and she felt narked, then she shrugged it off. As she walked home, a weight slid off her.

But the best was yet to come. As she walked into Garden Cottage, Cecily waved a postcard at her.

'Lady Darley wants you back – oh, what's wrong? I thought you'd be pleased.'

'I am, you dope,' she managed to say before she dissolved into tears and walked into Cecily's outstretched arms.

Chapter Thirty

A great many people attended the funeral, a lot of them grand ladies and gentlemen arriving by carriage. Juliet, there by virtue of having been employed as seamstress, took her place among the lower orders, from where she saw Lord Drysdale and Lady Margaret walk up the aisle. Whatever seamstress it was who had put Lady Margaret in that cape with the ruched black lace wanted her bumps feeling. A few folk around her wondered aloud who the distinguished strangers could be, but she didn't enlighten them.

Outside, when it was over, she was threading her way through the quiet crowd when a conversation made her prick up her ears.

'Who was that who walked in alongside Lady Darley? Her sister? Quite a lot older, if so.'

'My dear, haven't you heard? That was the heir – the heiress, I should say. Sir Henry was the last of the line. No more men, so the title dies with him.'

'And that dumpy, middle-aged creature has inherited?'

'Everything but the title. She's plain Miss Brown, and having seen her, I shouldn't think they come much plainer.'

'What of Lady Darley? Will she stay on at Darley Court?'

'My dear, we're all waiting with bated breath. Would you want to keep your beautiful, titled predecessor? Of course, she might prefer to leave. I imagine there'll be an annuity.'

Another voice chimed in. 'I heard they're knocking down the folly.'

'Juliet,' said a quiet voice. Hal, looking extraordinarily handsome in black. She almost pressed a hand to her heart, but restrained herself. 'Do you have a few minutes?' he asked.

She nodded, and he indicated that she should lead the way through the group of mourners.

Once they were clear, she asked, 'Will the gardens be redesigned now Sir Henry's gone?'

'Yes, though not to the same extent.'

'Miss Brown's already decided? Even before the funeral?'

'She got down to business right away. I thought it as well to be in the staff line-up when she arrived, and I can tell you, she may have gone upstairs a weary traveller, but she came back down very much mistress of the estate. Shall we go for a walk on the meadows? We need to talk, and I'm not going to let you dash off like you did last time. You mean far too much to me to let that happen.'

Little was said as they walked onto the meadows, where the torn-looking rosy petals of ragged robin wafted in the breeze above ground dotted with golden buttercups and early harebells. There was white clover, too, thick with bees.

She felt a wave of nostalgia. 'Ella Dancy used to say the best honey came from clover. Did you know her?'

'I can put a face to the name.'

'Such a lovely face, too. It used to grieve me that someone so beautiful couldn't get married, because of her domestic responsibilities.'

'What of your responsibilities?'

'I have more than enough to think about with my work, and Cecily and Archie are my family now. That's Cecily's little lad. He's nearly six.'

'And there's your daughter. You had her adopted by Lady Darley.'

'It was none of my doing!' she exclaimed. 'My grandmother sent me to a place where these matters are sorted out. I was never meant to know who . . .' A throb raged in her throat, forcing her into silence.

'She's had the best possible start in life,' Hal ventured.

'Better than being the illegitimate child of a penniless girl, you mean? For your information, her so-called wonderful start included a father who blew his brains out and . . . and—' And a stepfather who was looking forward to enjoying her in his vile way in years to come. She flung Hal a sidelong glance. 'You've clearly decided adoption was the best thing.'

He stopped walking and turned to her. She could have touched him had she reached out. She clenched her hands into fists and buried them in the seams of her skirt.

'I'm trying,' Hal said, looking into her eyes and making it impossible for her to look away, 'to give you my support. I'm trying to show you that, whatever happened to you, I would have stood by you, if I'd been there. I'm trying to show you respect and compassion.'

'But you don't know what happened.'

'No, I don't. I hope you'll tell me. You've told me you bore a child. I never truly believed that until you said it, and it came as a colossal shock. But here I am. I haven't walked away. I haven't turned my back on you. I want to understand. Even after a separation of some years, I hope you still feel able to trust me.'

She did, oh, she did.

Could she speak of it? That other time, back at the folly, she had told herself she couldn't – yet. She had vowed to concentrate all her effort and thought and determination on rescuing Lily. She had feared being weakened by an outpouring of old memories just when she most needed to be strong for the sake of another suffering girl.

Or had that been an excuse? Was she going to hug her shameful secrets to herself for ever? Fear, shame, loathing, the desperation to do right by Mother as she faced a lingering death. Her skin tightened all over her body. Inside her sleeves, the muscles in her arms went rigid. Dirty girl, grateful girl, stupid, stupid, stupid. The horrors of the past shoved the present aside, threatening to send her crumpling to the ground.

'Juliet?' Soft as Hal's voice was, it penetrated the heartache that swirled around her, the same voice that had steadied her years ago when she wriggled through that tiny gap to rescue little Sophie. *You'll need to take a step into thin air before I can reach your other wrist . . . Do you trust me?* He was her safe place, then and now. Always.

'You want to know what happened to make me run off? Well, I'll tell you. Mr Nugent did. My mother was so proud that I was going to be his sewing girl, but actually he wanted me as his bit on the side.'

'His what?'

'His trollop, his slut. He had a taste for girls about that age.'

'But that's . . . I can't—'

'Can't believe it? Like you could never bring yourself to believe that I had really had a child? Lucky you. Unfortunately, I don't have that luxury.'

'Was Mr Nugent the father?'

'No. He never . . . he never went the whole way.'

'Then what did he do? How can you be sure of his . . . intentions?'

402

'How d'you think? Because he'd already made a start. Why do you imagine my mother received special treatment in her final days? Because I paid for it by submitting to his touching and his stroking and . . . licking.' A dark sigh shuddered out of her. Sourness invaded her mouth. 'On the day I ran away, he was going to rape me. That's why I disappeared. In any case, I was going to run away before I had to move into Arley House, but because he went for me, I had to leave immediately. He made me miss my mother's funeral. There! You were so shocked that day at the folly, because I skipped the funeral. Well, now you know. It was the last thing I could do for my mother, and he robbed me of it.'

A cluster of golden cowslips caught her eye, and over there, near a shallow pond, was a pale-pink haze of delicate lady's smock. It was easier to concentrate on those than to realise she had finally shared her horrible secret. What must Hal think of her now?

'When did this start?' His voice was raw. 'Was it . . . after I left for London?'

She hung her head. Then she lifted it, and looked straight at him. 'Before that.'

His jaw slackened, but he didn't look away. 'Why did you never say anything?'

'I was too ashamed, too frightened.'

Removing his cap, he pushed fingers through his hair in a gesture that made her yearn for the young couple they had once been.

'I had no idea . . .'

'No one did. He was clever. Everyone admired his generosity towards my mother. I felt . . . isolated.' She gave her feet a tiny wriggle, making sure they were planted firmly on the ground. 'And . . . I wasn't the only one. He was doing the same to Lily McKenzie, Lady Darley's oldest daughter.'

'His own stepdaughter? Are you sure?'

'Positive. I confronted him, and he admitted as much.'

'The poor girl. And she's so young.'

'She's about the same age I was.'

He made a move towards her, but she danced away, eyes smarting with tears.

'You haven't asked about my daughter's father.'

'Can you face talking about it, after what you've just told me?'

That nearly undid her. Such consideration was more than she deserved. No. She mustn't think like that. She wasn't at fault; she had never been at fault. She filled her lungs with the pure air of the meadows. It wasn't the same as the air on the moors. It was kinder, less brisk. Hal was her safe place.

'Do you remember Rosie?'

He blew out a breath. 'I remember being summoned into Mr Nugent's presence to be accused of being the father of her baby.'

She experienced a strange sensation, as if her insides were dropping. Quietly, she related what had happened: how she had assumed a stranger was Hal and how Rosie had later taken her terrible revenge, how she had gone to Mrs Maddox's and later recognised the lady who was now Lady Darley.

'You poor love. I wish I could have helped you through it. You know I'd have done that, don't you?'

'I've managed. I've had to.'

'And you've built a successful business.'

She smiled. 'Years ago, you said I should, while you were busy climbing your own ladder.'

'I did, didn't I?'

'So, what now?' She was ready to ask. The shadows of the past had thinned. They were still there; they would always be there, but perhaps they wouldn't clog her heart any more. What next? She was ready to . . .

'What now?' he said. 'I think you need to talk to Lily McKenzie.'

'What?'

'You said Mr Nugent made you feel isolated. You bore your burden alone. Don't you think it would help Lily to know she's not the only one?'

She opened her mouth to say – she didn't know what she was going to say. She braced herself for the sinking feeling of defeat, or to feel conflicted, at the very least. Instead she felt alert and determined, filled with a powerful sense of resolve. Talking to Lily was the right thing to do.

'And afterwards,' she said, 'we'll talk about the future.'

Juliet left it a few days. She could hardly do something like this immediately after Sir Henry's funeral. Emotions would be too raw. But she mustn't leave it too long. Lily deserved to be supported. Besides, with Darley Court now in the hands of Miss Brown, and with her ladyship and her daughters possibly not remaining, who knew what might be happening in the household? She presented herself at the kitchen door and asked for Miss Banks.

After a while, her ladyship's maid appeared. 'Good morning, Miss Harper. What can I do for you?'

'Please could I see Miss Lily? I need to check some measurements.'

'It isn't like you to have to come back and check. But Miss Lily happens to be in her room at the moment, so you'd best come this way.'

Miss Banks led her up the backstairs, emerging onto the landing where Lily's room was. Miss Banks knocked and opened the door.

'Excuse me, Miss Lily, but Miss Harper wishes to have a

minute of your time to check the measurements she took.'

Juliet inserted herself into the room before Lily could say yes or no. 'Thank you,' she said to Miss Banks. 'I'll find my own way down the backstairs.'

The lady's maid went on her way, and Juliet shut the door. Lily looked pale and thin; her black dress did her colouring no favours. Did her young heart rebel against wearing mourning for the man who had molested her?

Lily stood still, her arms slightly away from her slender frame. 'Measure away, Miss Harper.'

And she almost did. Rather than saying what she had come here to say, she almost postponed it for a few minutes. She felt light-headed, but she maintained eye contact as she walked across the pretty bedroom and stood before the unsuspecting girl.

'Lily,' she said, and saw the girl's eyes widen at being called by just her name. 'It's hard for me to say this, but I know what Sir Henry did to you.'

Lily's hand flew to her mouth as a strangled gasp struggled to be heard. Then she swung away. 'I don't know what you mean.'

'Yes, you do, sweetheart. I know because he told me, and he told me because . . . he did the same to me when I was about your age.'

Lily fixed her gaze on Juliet's face.

'He gave you a candle, didn't he? He gave me one too, but mine was a rose candle. No wonder you ended up hating lavender.' Her heart beat heavy and slow. 'He used to come to me at night. He touched me and—'

'No!' shrieked Lily. 'Leave me alone.'

Juliet grasped her arms and wouldn't let go when she wriggled. 'It wasn't your fault, Lily. You wanted to protect your sisters. With me, it was protecting my sick mother. He made me feel dirty and wretched. Is that how you felt? Please, even if you can't bear to talk about it, just listen to me, so that you know you're not alone. He made me feel I was the only person in the world he had ever or would ever do it to, and that was part of his power. It wasn't just the two of us, either. I know for certain of one more girl, and who knows whether there were others?'

Lily sagged, and Juliet caught her as she started to sob. Odd words and jumbled sentences mingled with moans of distress as she started to unburden her soul. Taking her to the window seat, Juliet held her close, murmuring comfort and understanding. At last Lily quietened.

She gently shifted Lily so that she sat up straight. 'There's one more thing. You have to tell your mother.'

'No.' Lily's eyes were huge.

'I'll come with you. We'll do it together. But she has to know. You can't carry this secret for the rest of your life. Believe me, I know. I kept my secret for years, and every so often it has risen up and devoured me. If you tell your mother, she'll be horrified, but she'll know it was his fault. I'll tell her for you, if you like, but she has to be told.'

The door opened, and Lady Darley looked in. 'Miss Harper, I didn't know you were here. Lily! What's the matter? You've been crying.' In an instant, she was at her daughter's side.

'You may well never want to see me again after this, Your Ladyship,' said Juliet, 'but Lily and I have something to tell you about Sir Henry.'

Juliet stood outside an empty shop on Wilbraham Road with Clara. Her aunt, in spite of her obvious curiosity, was stiff-backed and unyielding, but that didn't stop Juliet bubbling with high spirits.

'Look at the situation: a smart antiques shop next door and just across the road from the Lloyd's Hotel, which has a cabbies' shelter outside, so there's usually a cab or two about – very handy for my more well-off customers. I shan't visit ladies at home any more – well, apart from Lady Darley.' It would be easy to single her out as a special case because of her title, and no one would ever guess the real reason – assuming, of course, that Lady Darley still wished to know her. 'Come inside.' She produced the key – her very own key, to her very own shop – and they went in. 'This is where the customers will be waited on. I'll have gowns, fabrics and accessories on display. Through here are various rooms. The building goes back further than you might expect, and there's upstairs as well.' She opened doors. 'Workroom . . . office . . . a retiring room for the staff.'

'You're having staff, are you?'

Juliet stilled. Clara's mouth thinned, then it twisted as she huffed a sigh.

'I was about to say something mealy-mouthed. I had the words ready in my head. But I'm not going to say them because . . . that isn't how I feel. No one was ever proud of me, and I know how much I longed for it. I don't flatter myself that it means anything to you, but I look at what you've achieved and I feel . . . proud.'

'Oh, Auntie Clara.'

'Like I say, there's no reason for you to care.'

'There is. We're family. You're my only family. I don't count Grandmother, any more than I imagine she counts me. I didn't bring you here to show off. I brought you because . . . Auntie Clara, I hope you'll want to work here with me.'

Clara flushed and looked away. 'I don't know what game you're playing.'

'I'm serious. I know how hard things have been for you. Grandmother has bullied you for years.'

Clara gripped her elbows. 'I was never good enough. I never got my own salon, and that was all she cared about.'

'So what? You worked for Mademoiselle Antoinette and she employs only the best. It would give my dressmaking business a huge boost if I could say that you worked here.' She waited until Clara met her eyes. 'This isn't going to be a fancy salon. But I have more customers than I can cope with and I'm taking on staff, including an apprentice. I'll do the designing, and you'll be senior seamstress, in charge of the other women.'

'Senior seamstress?'

'Senior seamstress, chief seamstress – I don't care what you call yourself as long as you join me. How would you like to be Miss Clara? Miss Clara, our senior seamstress,' she announced, as if addressing a customer. 'I want to develop my dressmaking service into something bigger and higher class. That's what I want to be known for. You can be known for it too. There's a flat over the shop, complete with kitchen and bathroom. It's yours if you want it. I'll need one of the rooms as a fitting room for clients, but that would still leave you with a sitting room, a bedroom and the box room.'

'You're offering me a home?'

'The moment I saw it, I imagined it full of your embroidery and cushion covers and patchwork. You'll turn it into a little palace.'

'What about the name over the door? Are you going to be Mademoiselle Juliette?' Clara pronounced the name with a flourishing French accent.

'Actually, I thought I'd be Miss Constance.'

'Constance? Who's she when she's at home?'

'It reminds me of someone. Actually, what I would really like to have over the door is *Constance and Clara.*'

'And Clara?' Clara stared. 'You'd do that?'

She burst into tears.

Saturday dinner promised to be a riotous affair, not just because Hal was coming, but because that morning a letter had arrived from Lady Darley – not a postcard, mind, but an actual letter – giving Juliet her new address, thanking her in the warmest terms for her kindness to Lily and assuring her that her services would shortly be called upon.

'And not just for the girls but for herself,' said Cecily, reading over Juliet's shoulder. 'That's wonderful.'

'Yes,' Juliet said firmly, 'it is. I'll be able to watch Izzie grow up. I'll be the seamstress her mother relies on, the seamstress her oldest sister has a special affection for. If Lady Darley and Lily are both true to me, Izzie will be too. And one day . . . one day I might even make her wedding dress.'

Cecily hugged her from behind. 'You're going to be famous for your wedding dresses, Juliet Harper. Mine is going to be beautiful. Even seeing the design made me cry. I shall probably blub all the way through the ceremony. Are you sure I can't help to make it?'

'Positive. It's my wedding gift to you, though Mrs Livingston has begged to be allowed to do some of the fancy-work. I'm doing the harps, though.' A scattering of tiny harps, ivory on ivory.

The girls prepared the cottage pie early, and Cecily grated the cheddar to go on top. It could go in the oven later. Feeling festive, Cecily suggested Canterbury pudding to follow. Juliet chucked an extra glass of sherry into it, and then another.

'Steady on,' said Cecily. 'It's meant to be one glass.'

'Well, you did say you were feeling festive.'

'We'll be feeling a lot more than festive after that.'

William arrived and took Archie for a walk. This was their new routine, a father and son walk each Saturday morning.

'Can we go and see our new house?' asked Archie.

'We can stand on the pavement and look over the garden wall,' promised William, 'but only if you promise not to pull faces. We mustn't scare the people who still live there.'

Juliet squeezed Cecily's hand, enjoying the look of pure happiness on her friend's face. The house that Cecily and William would move into after their wedding wasn't part of Rosie's empire. That was important. Juliet and Cecily had given notice on Garden Cottage. Juliet might share the flat with Clara for a while . . . or she might not need to.

She glanced at their marble clock. Hal would be here soon. She moved about the cottage, tidying what was already tidy, too excited to be still. She hadn't been excited like this since . . . since she was a girl of fifteen, falling in love for the first time.

When Hal arrived, Cecily dragged him straight into the parlour. 'Look!'

'My painting. You've still got it.' His face was bright with pleasure.

'Of course I have,' said Juliet. *This will have pride of place on our parlour wall one day.* She dipped her chin to hide what she feared was a blush.

Thank goodness William and Archie arrived home. She performed the introductions.

'William, I want you to meet my dear friend, Hal Price. Hal, this is Cecily's fiancé, William Turton.'

'He's my uncle,' announced Archie, 'and he's going to be my new daddy.'

'And this rascal is Cecily's son, Archie.'

'How do you do, Archie?' said Hal.

'We've just been to see our new house for when Uncle William marries Mummy. Then we went to see Auntie Juley's new shop. It's a new home for Hand-finished by Harper.'

'The name has changed, Archie.' Warmth expanded inside Juliet's chest. 'I didn't want to say anything until I was certain, but I saw Auntie Clara yesterday and she's agreed to join the business. It's going to be called . . .' Her chest tightened. What if they didn't like it? '. . . Constance and Clara.'

'Who's Constance?' asked Archie.

'Constance is a very special person,' Hal told him, 'and one day when you're older, we'll tell you about her.'

'When Uncle William marries us and starts being my daddy, I won't have an uncle any more. Are you—?'

'That's enough of that, young man,' cried Juliet, not knowing whether to laugh or blush.

'I think young Archie has a good point,' said Hal. He addressed Cecily and William. 'Do you mind if I spirit Juliet away for a while?'

'Be my guest.' Cecily gave Juliet an indiscreet nudge.

With happiness radiating through her body and her thoughts scattering to the four winds, Juliet put on her hat and accompanied Hal over the road onto Chorlton Green, where they sat on a bench.

'The last time I saw you, you said you wanted to talk about the future,' said Hal. 'Are you ready to do that now?'

'Yes. Opening up to Lily and her mother, and helping Lily to open up in her turn, was a healing process for myself as much as it was for Lily. I feel as if I have shed a weight from my heart.'

'A weight has been shed from my heart as well. All this time, I've worried and wondered about you and what really happened.

I've achieved a great deal professionally and I have a busy life ahead, but it's not enough. Without you, it's not enough. There's never been another girl, no matter how lonely I felt – and there were times when I was desperate with loneliness. But you were the only one I wanted. I went to your grandmother's house with such hopes, and when she told me you had vanished, it felt as if the world had tilted sideways, and I thought I would have to spend the rest of my days clinging on for dear life.' He took her hand. 'Will you put my world to rights for me, Juliet?'

It was a moment before she could speak. 'I'm falling in love with you for the first time all over again. That's how it feels. Now and always.'

'I'm not asking you to give up your work. My own work is important to me and I would never make light of your commitment to yours. I warn you, I might not be the ideal husband, because there will be times when I have to be away for weeks on end. But if you'll have me, I swear I'll love you until the day I die and I'll be the best of fathers to our children.'

She had the warm, comforting and blissfully exciting feeling of everything slipping into place.

'If you're serious,' she said, 'you'll have to go down on one knee.'

'Making me do it properly, are you? I'll take that as a good sign.'

'It's not for my benefit,' said Juliet, 'but I think you'll find Archie will expect it.'

Acknowledgements

I should like to express my gratitude to the following people:

Kirsten Hesketh, whose monthly guest blogs on my website, as well as being enormously enjoyable to read, also took the pressure off me at various crucial moments.

Deborah Smith, for her friendship and support. Thanks, Debs.

The members of Deborah's online reading group, especially Chris Bartholomew, Vera Jevons Wordsworth, Joy Hanley Quale, Celine Fairbrother and Aileen Searle, who were among my first readers.

Marina Byrom, for her kindness and encouragement.

All the team at Allison & Busby, in particular Kelly Smith, Ailsa Floyd and Jenn Goodheart-Smithe for working their magic behind the scenes.

And Jen Gilroy, for always being there.

SUSANNA BAVIN has variously been a librarian, an infant school teacher, a carer and a cook. She lives in Llandudno in North Wales with her husband and two rescue cats, but her writing is inspired by her Mancunian roots.

susannabavin.co.uk
@SusannaBavin